P9-DCN-452

Dear Reader,

When I began my writing career twenty-five years ago, I wrote genre romances under several pseudonyms: Dorothy Phillips, Dorothy Glenn, and Johanna Phillips. These novels told variations of the classic story of a man and a woman who meet, fall in love, and marry after overcoming obstacles in their relationship.

The books are being reissued at the request of you, the reader. They have been out of print for fifteen years.

When I first started writing, my husband and I went on many road trips. During one of them we traveled through the lumber area of Montana where I got the idea for *Hidden Dreams*. We stayed in a small, quaint motel—a far cry from the novel's setting, which is the rugged and often dangerous world of a logging camp. The second novel in this book is *She Wanted Red Velvet*, and it came to life in my mind as my husband and I continued our journey.

I enjoyed writing the shorter romances, and I hope they're as entertaining to you as my more recent stories.

Sincerely,

Dorothy Garlock

Books by Dorothy Garlock

DOROTHY GARLOCK

Wishmakers

WARNER BOOKS

NEW YORK   BOSTON

This book is a work of historical fiction. In order to give a sense of the times, some names or real people or places have been included in the book. However, the events depicted in this book are imaginary, and the names of nonhistorical persons or events are the product of the author's imagination or are used fictitiously. Any resemblance of such nonhistorical persons or events to actual ones is purely coincidental.

If you purchase this book without a cover you should be aware that this book may have been stolen property and reported as "unsold and destroyed" to the publisher. In such case neither the author nor the publisher has received any payment for this "stripped book."

Compilation copyright © 2006 by Dorothy Garlock
Hidden Dreams copyright © 1983 by Johanna Phillips
She Wanted Red Velvet copyright © 1986 by Dorothy Phillips
Excerpt from *On Tall Pine Lake* copyright © 2006 by Dorothy Garlock
All rights reserved. No part of this book may be reproduced in any form or by any electronic or mechanical means, including information storage and retrieval systems, without permission in writing from the publisher, except by a reviewer who may quote brief passages in a review.

Photo illustration by Stanislaw Fernandes
Photo of dandelion by Angelo Cavalli / Getty Images

Warner Books
1271 Avenue of the Americas
New York, NY 10020

Printed in the United States of America

First Mass Market Paperback Printing: August 2006

10 9 8 7 6 5 4 3 2 1

ATTENTION CORPORATIONS AND ORGANIZATIONS:
Most WARNER books are available at quantity discounts with bulk purchase for educational, business, or sales promotional use. For information, please call or write:
Special Markets Department, Warner Books, Inc.
1271 Avenue of the Americas, New York, NY 10020
Telephone: 1-800-222-6747 Fax: 1-800-477-5925.

Table of Contents

Wishmakers

BOOK ONE

HIDDEN DREAMS

To Marcia Volk and Betty Secory
for their constant friendship

CHAPTER ONE

WEARING A PLAIN black dress, dark stockings, and high-heeled pumps, Margaret Anthony stood at the door and bid good-bye to each of the somber guests as they filed past.

"Thank you for coming, Senator . . . It was a comfort to have you here, Mr. Westmoreland . . . Good-bye, Mrs. Engleman . . . No, I won't forget to send something to the bazaar . . . Thank you . . . Dad would have been pleased you were able to come, Professor Downing."

"Good-bye, my dear," one society matron gushed. "My, my, you've been such a brave girl through all of this. I know you'll miss your papa. Do let us know if there's anything we can do. This is an awfully big house for one small girl, but then of course the servants have been here for years . . ." The woman speaking glanced down her long nose at the quiet figure dressed in dark green silk standing well back in the shadows of the stairway, then sniffed and made her departure.

Margaret closed the door and leaned wearily against it. Her eyes sought those of the woman by the stairs.

"It's over, Rachel." Her tone clearly implied it had been an ordeal.

"Yes, it's over," Rachel Riley quietly replied. The older woman's face was pale and her expression conveyed warmth and concern for the girl who everyone had said looked so young and fragile and tired.

Margaret, however, was neither as young as she looked, nor as fragile. Her looks belied the toughness within, a legacy from her father. There was steel in her, and Rachel had often reminded her of it. Without that inner strength—and the older woman's support—Margaret wouldn't have been able to survive the loneliness of being the only child of an industrialist who had lived with the constant fear that his daughter might be kidnapped or harmed because of his great wealth.

Margaret took the pins out of her dark hair and let it fall over her shoulders like an ebony stream, then breathed deeply and unbuttoned the collar of her dress.

"I'm glad they're gone. I'm not sure Daddy would have wanted them here, although he *was* a stickler for doing the respectable thing." Her gaze shifted around the marble-floored entryway. "Funerals are so ghoulish. That's what I was thinking while everyone was milling around, talking about Daddy in hushed tones. It's all so deceitful!" she continued bitterly. "Why didn't they make an effort to see him while he was living?" She slipped out of the pumps and, with one shoe dangling from each hand, she padded across the room.

"You and I were the only two people here who truly loved him, Rachel. Some of them didn't even like him, some feared him, and most were jealous of him because he had all the material things they wanted. Most of them came because it was the thing to do—and because they wanted to be seen by the others who came because it was the thing to do." She gazed at Rachel's drawn expression. "This has been especially hard for you, hasn't it?"

"Only because I knew it was difficult for you, dear. I said my good-bye to Edward weeks ago."

"Oh, how I wanted to kick that snooty Mrs. Engleman, sniffling so prettily over Daddy. She hadn't seen him for five years! I was almost tempted to giggle when she choked back a sob as she passed the casket. I know if he could have, Daddy would have sat up and said *boo!*"

Rachel's lips turned up at the corners slightly. She was half a head taller than Margaret, and age had lined her face, but she was still slim and graceful, Margaret noted fondly as the two women climbed the circular stairway together. Both of them looked at the closed door at the top of the stairs and then walked to the end of the hall and into a small sitting room.

Margaret picked up the house phone. "Edna, would you send us up some coffee, please?"

"Is everybody done gone, Miss Margaret?"

"All except Mr. Whittier. He's still in the study. If he rings, tell him Rachel and I are resting."

"Yes, Miss Margaret. I'm bringin' you some food, too, and don't you be arguin' about it. That bunch what was here ate up six trays of them little sandwiches you had brought in, *and* the cakes and coffee. I think they come to *eat*—"

"You'll probably get all kinds of offers now, Edna," Margaret gently interrupted. "Everyone will want Edward Anthony's cook. We'll lose you to—"

"Why, I never! You hush up, now! Ain't nobody goin'

to get me out of this here house as long's there's an Anthony in it," she sputtered. "I'll be comin' up there myself. Why, I never heard the like!"

Margaret smiled at the dogged loyalty, hung up the phone, and let her shoes drop to the floor. "Edna will be up with a tray." She sank down onto a velvet-covered couch. "The buffet looked lovely, Rachel. I kept thinking how pleased Daddy would be that at least everything proceeded in a correct manner."

Rachel turned from the window. "Yes. Edward was always so emphatic about protocol."

"For the first time in my life I feel at loose ends." Margaret sighed resignedly. "I feel as if I've been unmoored from something. Can you understand that?" she studied Rachel for her reaction.

"I think so," Rachel said hesitantly. "Your father had a very strong personality."

"I won't say Daddy was domineering, but he made me do things, not because I wanted to, but because it was what he wanted. That is, I did nothing, because he wanted me to do nothing."

"He loved you very much."

"And he bound me to him with that love," Margaret said firmly, feeling for the first time since the funeral as if she would cry. "Don't think I'm ungrateful for that love, Rachel. I loved him, too. And because his heart was so bad these last few years I was obedient to his wishes and left my own life in limbo. You don't know how I longed to have a job, get an apartment, have friends my own age. Once I talked to him about it, and he brought up that kidnap attempt again. But that was ancient history."

Rachel sat down on the couch beside her. "He was obsessed with the fear that you might be taken and held for ransom."

Margaret grabbed Rachel's hand. "Great wealth isn't the blessing some people think, is it? Many times I wished Daddy was poor. I'm afraid the few men I did date had their eye on Daddy's money, or on a position higher up the social ladder—except for Justin, of course. I haven't had an opportunity to meet anyone else these last few years. At least I got to go with Justin occasionally—even if two security men did tag along each time." She grimaced and fell silent.

After a long pause, Rachel said, "I want to talk to you about Justin. I hadn't planned to do it quite yet, but this seems to be the right time." She hesitated again.

Justin Whittier, the man who was soon to be her husband, Margaret mused. He'd been a bulwark of quiet strength over the past several months—and Margaret's sole connection with the outside world. The only times her father had seemed happy to see her go out she'd been on Justin's arm. What could Rachel possibly have to say about Justin that could be causing her such obvious distress?

"What is it, Rachel? Is something wrong?"

"Do you love him, Margaret?" Rachel asked bluntly.

Margaret turned wide eyes toward the woman who had been like a mother to her for as long as she could remember. Why was Rachel asking that? Of course she loved Justin; she'd agreed to marry him. He was strong, solid, gentlemanly—almost too gentlemanly, she thought wryly. But what could be wrong with that? She managed an uncertain smile. "He's comfortable to be with, and I like him very much."

"I know he's pressing you to set the date, but I don't want you to drift into a marriage unless you're sure you love him. He's a good, reliable man, devoted to the Anthony interests, but he's almost as old as your father was when you were born. Now there's nothing wrong with loving an older man, but . . ." Rachel's voice trailed away.

"But what?" Margaret prodded, growing more anxious by the second.

Rachel looked at her searchingly, as if fighting some inner battle. Then, with the look of one rushing in where angels feared to tread, she blurted out, "It isn't enough just to be comfortable with him! You deserve more than that. Does he make your pulse race when he's near you? Do you feel all warm and glowing when he touches you?" Margaret's face must have betrayed her turmoil, and Rachel hurried on. "If he doesn't, you mustn't give up your youth for him—not unless you truly love him."

Margaret laughed nervously. "Well, he doesn't do any of those things yet, Rachel," she admitted honestly, "but he says he loves me. And Daddy wanted us to marry; it was all decided."

"Edward thought he'd leave Justin in charge of us, and that our lives would go on just the same as before," the older woman said ruefully.

"And you don't want them to?" Margaret watched her with concern.

"It's all right for me. I'm sixty-five years old. But you're twenty-five." Tears appeared in Rachel's soft blue eyes. "I don't want life to pass you by without your tasting the joys of being young, daring, falling in love with a man who sets your heart racing . . ." She looked away, as if regretting what she was about to say next. "Edward was wrong not to set you free." Then, as if to soften the words, she added, "But he was afraid for you."

"And you're not?"

"Yes, I'm afraid for you, too. But the world is full of risks. You either take them and live to the fullest, or you hide behind these stone walls and closed gates and merely exist."

"Oh, Rachel. When I was a little girl I always wished that you were my mother. I used to dream that you would marry Daddy and I'd call you Mom. I want you to know that I've thought of you as my mother all these years."

The tears broke free and rolled down Rachel's cheeks. "Thank you for saying that, darling. I've always thought of you as my daughter."

"Daddy was born years and years too late, Rachel. He believed that women were put here to be taken care of, and he amassed a fortune to take care of his."

"Yes, he did. He worked terribly hard," Rachel responded pensively.

"It's a shame you and Daddy never married," Margaret continued wistfully.

"We were . . . very good friends."

"I know that. I don't know how he would have managed without you. You devoted your life to us. It doesn't seem fair, somehow."

"I've had a very rich life. Edward depended on me, and I had you, dear. Even when you were away at boarding school I knew you'd be returning for vacations. And your father and I had a special kind of understanding. I've not regretted a moment of the time I've spent in his . . . employ. You, Edward, and the church have been my life. Now I have you and the church."

Margaret walked down the hall, her footsteps a mere whisper on the thick Persian carpet. Out of habit she looked at the closed door where her father had spent the last few months of his life, then continued down the circular stairway, through the formal living room with its silk-covered couches, Aubusson rug, Louis XV tables and chairs, silver ornaments, and priceless paintings hung at just the proper vantage points.

At the end of the room she pulled aside the heavy damask drapes and pushed open the French doors, stepping out onto the long terrace. During the past summer she'd often stood here at this hour, breathing deeply, looking out over Lake Michigan. This morning the sun was so bright she squinted as she paused at the terrace wall. It was a perfect day. Perfect for picnicking, for sailing, or for a wandering down the beach. But the very idea was ridiculous . . . for her.

Margaret suddenly realized she had made the transition from child to woman without really being aware of it. Her mother had died in childbirth, and she remained nothing more to Margaret than the face with large dark eyes and a small, pointed chin. There was nothing of that woman in her as far as Margaret could tell, and not much of Edward Anthony either. More than likely his hair had been black when he was a young man, and his eyes brighter, greener. But Margaret's first memories of him were of a slightly stooped man with sparse gray hair and eyes that peered out from behind thick lenses. Myopia obviously ran in the family, she thought regretfully. Still, he'd been her hero, her best friend, her companion. She knew he'd loved her with every ounce of his being. She also knew of his fear that she would somehow be taken from him. She knew hers was not a life to be pitied, and yet, she'd had her disappointments . . . and her hidden dreams.

Her mind flashed back to the time she'd come home from school to find her father with a house guest. That had happened occasionally when he was feeling poorly and needed to confer with one of his business associates.

Margaret had seen the man only briefly, but his image was forever burned into her memory. She had stood at the top of the stairs and watched him in the foyer below. His tall, angular frame was in sharp contrast to her father's hunched figure. His face was deeply tanned, and he had soft brown hair and clear blue eyes. He wore heavy boots, a corduroy jacket, and jeans. He stood, his hands deep in the pockets of his jeans, his head tilted attentively as he listened to what her father was saying. Then he looked up. His eyes caught and held hers while a quiver of apprehension raced through her body.

That evening she took special care dressing for dinner, but her father didn't bring their guest to the dining room. Disappointed, she deliberately went to the study when she discovered the two men would be having dinner there, and her father was forced to introduce her. Duncan Thorn was a business associate from northern Montana. His bright blue eyes had flicked over her, then away as if he were impatient with the interruption. That look made it clear he considered her worse than useless. His disregard had rankled. It rankled even more as years went by, and she realized he'd been more right than wrong.

The next day Thorn was gone, and when she asked her father about him, he shrugged and dismissed the man as he did anyone he considered unsuitable for his only child. At different times during the years Duncan Thorn's face had come to Margaret's mind, and she'd wondered about him. Now she had to push aside the uncomfortable feeling that thinking about him was somehow being disloyal to Justin.

Margaret leaned her elbows on the terrace wall and watched a freighter glide slowly behind the peninsula that jutted out into the lake. This could be a turning point in her life, she realized, remembering Rachel's words. She could marry Justin, and he'd move into the house, assuming his position as monarch, protector, decision-maker. Or she could postpone the marriage, try her wings, as Rachel had suggested, take her chances and exert some control over her life. The seed Rachel had planted in her mind had grown to such proportions that she could scarcely think of anything else. The idea of an immediate marriage to Justin was suddenly less reassuring than it had once been. She tried to push the niggling doubts aside. But it was true, she had never experienced any of the sensations she read about in romance novels— except maybe that one time when the tall Montana woodsman had looked up at her from the foyer below.

A blue and yellow sail appeared on the lake, then a green and orange one. The small boats skimmed recklessly across the water. They were having a race. What fun, Margaret thought. Suddenly she felt young and daring, and she knew what she had to do. She would account to no one for a while, no one but herself.

Rachel—and Justin, she guiltily reminded herself—would understand.

Margaret and Rachel looked at each other as the lawyer's voice droned on and on. There were no surprises in the will. The family home was left to the two of them, Rachel being described as "dear friend and faithful companion." Margaret was left the bulk of the estate, with ample provisions made for Rachel and the family retainers. The vast conglomerate Edward Anthony had built during his lifetime would remain under the direction of the board of trustees, with the exception of the Anthony/Thorn Lumber Company. Margaret's ears pricked up, and she looked over at Justin's stalwart figure as she tried to correct her vagrant thoughts.

"Out of respect for my late partner, August Thorn, I place control of the business in the hands of his son, Duncan Thorn. I bequeath my shares in the company to my daughter, Margaret, and further state she cannot sell them without first offering them to Duncan Thorn at a reasonable market price."

It took the lawyer almost an hour to read the rest of the will. His voice droned on about royalties, commodities, real estate, and investments—all very dull stuff to Margaret, who listened with interest only to the part about the Anthony/Thorn Lumber Company. She was a business partner with Duncan Thorn, who had regarded her so contemptuously when she was a shy teenager. Would he even remember the girl whose heart had pounded so furiously when she looked down at him from the balcony?

She knew that those glancing occasionally at the heir to the Anthony millions—including Justin—would have been surprised to read her thoughts: *Never again, as long as I live, will I be regarded as a useless little rich girl. I'll not be coddled and protected as if I were a child. I'm going to experience life outside these stone walls—and make that life count for something beyond keeping the Anthony fortune intact!*

The scene with Justin, when she handed back the diamond, was explosive—so much so that she wondered why she'd never noticed his short temper before.

She walked into the study the morning after the will was read, placed the ring on the desk in front of him, and nervously waited for him to look up and acknowledge her presence.

"What's this, Margaret?"

"It's the engagement ring you gave me, Justin." Seeing his puzzled expression, she explained, "I need time to gather my thoughts, to find the direction my life will take now that Daddy is gone." She paused. "I realize it's not fair to keep you dangling while I try to find myself." There, she'd said it. She was surprised to hear herself speaking so calmly; she had fretted over this confrontation for hours last night.

Justin got slowly to his feet, his face turning a dull red, perspiration popping out on his high forehead. Alarmed at his obvious dismay and trying to make things easier for both of them, she blurted, "It isn't as if we've ever declared undying love for each other." She would have liked to withdraw the last words; they were rather cruel. After all, she was fond of Justin, and up until a few days ago she'd thought he'd soon be her husband.

"What do you mean? You know how much I care for you."

"I know that we like each other very much, but I also know that that's not enough of a reason for us to consider marriage right now." She was trying to be sensible, trying to spare them both more pain. "I'm sorry if it will cause you embarrassment, but I really need time to think, to do things on my own. Surely you can understand that, can't you, Justin?" she pleaded.

"You're not going to marry me?" He spoke slowly, his tone intimidating. "What nonsense is this? Put that ring back on your finger! You *will* marry me! It's what your father wanted!" He was almost shouting.

Stunned and horrified by his reaction, Margaret was silent for a moment as her reeling mind flashed back to other times when her father had stood behind the desk telling her that she would not leave the estate without a bodyguard, she would not go to camp, she would not be allowed to drive the car . . .

"It might have been what my father wanted," she finally said with quiet dignity, "but it isn't what *I* want. I'm not sure I love you, Justin. And right now I don't even like your behavior. You're trying to turn yourself into a replica of Edward Anthony. And when I marry, I want a husband, not a second father!"

"Why you ungrateful little—" He cut himself off, then continued more calmly: "I've handled everything for you. I've given my life to this company, and—"

"You've been paid for it," Rachel's quiet voice pronounced from the doorway. "Now that Edward isn't here for you to confer with, I think it would be better if you conducted business from the office in the city."

Margaret walked slowly to the door, smiling gratefully at Rachel as she passed. Painful as it was, she had taken the first step in controlling her own destiny. Now she had some emotional sorting out to do.

Justin came to the house several times during the next few weeks. He apologized profusely for his outburst, but for Margaret the shock of his behavior was still too fresh. He tried to court her, bringing her flowers and asking her out to dinner and the theater. Her resolve to live life firsthand growing, she accepted his apologies but refused his invitations. Evidently realizing that she'd made up her mind to postpone the marriage, he finally stopped pressing his suit. Recognizing the return of the sensitive man she had known, Margaret was grateful for his understanding.

She called him one morning and asked for a dossier on the Anthony/Thorn Lumber Company. He seemed reluctant to send it, as if he thought her request a personal threat to his position, but the file arrived by messenger and she spent a day going over the information before returning it.

Rachel expressed surprise when Margaret announced she was making a trip to Montana to look over the operation she now partnered with Duncan Thorn.

"Why? Why do you want to go there?" Rachel's hands visibly trembled as she poured from the silver coffee service. "I thought you'd prefer to go on a skiing vacation, or take a cruise."

"I want a *reason* to do something. I want to be involved, Rachel. I may want to buy Mr. Thorn's shares."

"Buy a lumber company? Darling, you've got to walk before you can run! That's a whole new world up there!"

"Anywhere will be a whole new world for me," Margaret reasoned.

Rachel was quiet for a long while, but then she conceded, "Maybe you're right. At least you'll be safe up there. Duncan Thorn may give you a rough time, but he's August Thorn's son, and he'll see that no harm comes to you. Yes, I think for your maiden venture into the world, that's as good a place as any."

At the airport Margaret kissed Rachel good-bye. Justin had offered to accompany her to O'Hare, but she had declined. She'd never taken a trip alone before, never handled her own tickets or traveler's checks, and she wasn't sure she wanted Justin to see her so rattled.

The plane was boarding, and she had only a moment to hold tightly to Rachel's hand and whisper, "I love you . . . I'll miss you . . . I'll call often . . . Take care of yourself."

"I love you, too. Have a wonderful time, and don't forget: you look very beautiful, like a well-groomed, smart sophisticate who's able to take care of herself."

"You're sure no one's trailing me?"

"I'm sure. I told Justin if anyone did I'd see that he was fired!" Rachel smiled. "That put the fear of God into him! 'Bye, darling." Rachel hugged Margaret once more and pushed her toward the gate.

Margaret boarded the plane, outwardly composed, but inwardly she felt rather frightened and lonely. But she was also determined, she reminded herself. She watched a young girl in jeans and extremely high heels shoulder her bag and walk down the aisle. I must be at least ten years older than she, Margaret thought resentfully as she settled in for the flight, and she acts as if she hadn't a care in the world.

The airport at Kalispell, Montana, was small. A portable stairway was wheeled out to the plane, and there was but a short walk across the windswept runway. Margaret's eyes skimmed the small waiting crowd, looking for broad shoulders and brown hair. Duncan Thorn had called the house to leave a terse message: "I will comply with Miss Anthony's wish to arrive incognito and be met in Kalispell."

A man wearing khaki pants and a red mackinaw—and a battered hat atop iron-gray hair—leaned against a wall. He was holding up a scribbled sign that read: "Miss Anderson." As Margaret walked slowly toward him, he grinned, crumpled up the paper, and stuffed it into his pocket.

"I figured you was the one," he said. "I'm Tom Mac-Madden. I was sent to fetch you."

CHAPTER TWO

MARGARET'S EYES FEASTED on the panorama stretching out before her: forest-covered slopes giving way to a winding river with a small cluster of buildings along its eastern bank. In the distance the sky was edged with snowcapped mountains. There was a soft quality to the afternoon light as it filtered through the clouds, evidence of the autumn sun's waning strength. This was Montana, the northwestern corner of Montana, and it seemed a million miles away from Chicago, where she had boarded the plane that morning.

The battered station wagon bumped along, then rolled to a slow crawl as it rounded a blind curve of the dirt road. The driver jerked his head toward the view they had just passed.

"That's Aaronville down there. It ain't much of a place compared to Kalispell, or even Columbia Falls, but it must have four hundred folks, countin' kids. Most of 'em work for Anthony/Thorn one way or t'other. The sawmill's on north a ways."

As they approached it, Margaret could see that the

town of Aaronville was even smaller than it had looked from above. There was one long street that ran parallel to the river; others branched off at intervals, only to go a short way and stop. There was quite a selection of stores, some faced in stone or brick and some wooden ones that needed paint. A white church was set back on one of the dead-end streets, its cupola stark against a background of trees whose leaves were various autumn colors of faded green, muted rust, and brilliant gold.

"So, you goin' to be stayin' long, Miss *Anthony?*"

Margaret had sensed that Mr. MacMadden's curiosity had been eating at him ever since he'd met her at Glacier International in Kalispell. Now she knew why. Despite her surprise, Margaret registered that his tone revealed his doubt that she would extend her visit.

"I haven't decided," she said with such confidence Rachel would have been proud of her. "It depends on a number of things. I may decide to buy Mr. Thorn's shares in the company."

He gave her a sidelong glance and whistled through his teeth. "You don't say? Chip ain't said nothin' 'bout that. There's been Thorns in lumberin' here as far back as I remember."

"Chip? You must mean Mr. Thorn?"

"Everybody 'round here calls him Chip. He sent me down to fetch you 'cause he wanted to rout out some campers that's been a mite careless with their fire." He took advantage of a fairly smooth section of road to glance at her again. "He sure was surprised when he got word you was comin'."

Margaret looked out the window, seeing nothing of her surroundings. All she saw was a mop of gleaming brown hair and a pair of bright blue eyes staring up at her from the foyer below. I'll bet he was surprised, she thought. I'll just bet he was!

The station wagon now cruised easily over blacktop. The people on the sidewalks, mostly women and children, cast curious glances at the car. Evidently strangers were of a rarity to elicit comment. The driver lifted a hand in greeting once or twice and drove on through what seemed to be the entire town.

"I didn't see a hotel, Mr. MacMadden," Margaret finally commented.

"Ain't none. Call me Tom."

"But where will I stay?" she questioned, her newfound confidence faltering ever so slightly.

"Chip said to bring you out to the house. All there is in town is a roomin' house, of sorts." He grinned. "I ain't thinkin' you want to stay there."

"I knew the company owned a house, but I thought Mr. Thorn and his family used it."

"It's a big house. Must have five or six rooms."

"Five or six . . . rooms?" She hoped she sounded suitably impressed.

"Yeah." Tom grinned proudly. "Real fine house."

"Mr. MacMadden—ah—Tom, Mr. Thorn knew of my wishes to arrive as a guest, an employee, or simply as an observer without revealing my identity. I fail to understand why he took you into his confidence."

"He done it 'cause I've known him since he was a tad and 'cause I knew your pa and 'cause I know a hell of a lot more about this company and how it started than anybody else 'round here. I saw your picture once, and I'd a known who you was the minute I clapped eyes on you.

That's why he told me and sent me to fetch you. Far as anybody else knows, you're Maggie Anderson come to help out for a while."

"Margaret Anderson," she corrected. As the station wagon once again jostled them over deep ruts, Margaret commented, "The road's very rough."

"It gets smoothed out once in a while. Gets hard use. Wait 'til you're on it after the whistle blows. Can't see for the dust the young hellions raise goin' to town to get a beer."

Margaret swiveled to look at the brick-red dust swirling behind them as they headed along the rough trail. There was a fine film of it over everything in the car, including herself. She could even feel it grit between her teeth when she brought them together. She was certainly going to need a bath before she met her . . . partner.

"We've come quite a way from town. Is it much farther?"

"Not much."

"Do you live out here, too?"

"I got a little place down the road a ways."

"But, you do work for the company?"

"I don't work for nobody but me, Tom MacMadden."

"Oh. Then I'll certainly owe you something for picking me up."

He swung his head around, started to say something, then clamped his mouth shut and looked back to the road. Presently he said, "No trouble. I was glad to do it for Chip."

Suddenly Margaret was as nervous as if she were approaching the guillotine. She fervently wished for the confidence she'd felt while she was planning the trip.

What would she say to this man? She would be crowded into a house of five or six rooms with him and his family! Would his wife resent her? Maybe she should have stayed at the rooming house! She was on the verge of telling Tom to turn the car around and head back to town when signs of habitation again appeared.

A house was set in a clearing some distance from the main road. What sloped from the back of the house to the river below couldn't really be called a lawn, but it was devoid of trees and brush. The structure was a simple uncluttered design of plain lumber that had apparently been stained brown but that was now faded and weathered. It had a long, wide porch facing the road and a big square chimney on the side. There were no shrubs, and the grass in front of the house had a very trampled look. The drive continued past the house toward a long, low garage that housed several vehicles. A path led to the river and a wooden jetty where an outboard motorboat was moored. Two other small houses to the north completed the "estate."

Tom pulled up to the side of the house and stopped. "This is it," he announced.

"Where's the mill?" Somehow Margaret had visualized a mill with a brick and glass office building attached and the owner's house set off to the side and surrounded by a white picket fence.

"The mill's on down the road a ways. It's so damn noisy when it's runnin' you can't hear yourself think. Don't look like Chip's got back yet. Leastways I don't see his Jeep. Guess you might as well get out and make yourself at home."

Without another word he got out of the car, took her

bags from the rear, carried them to the porch, and set them down. Margaret followed on trembly legs. This certainly wasn't what she'd expected.

"Is there no one at home?" she asked, struggling to keep the poise she'd been wearing like a borrowed coat since boarding the plane.

"I doubt it, if Chip or Penny ain't here. Dolly's still in the hospital down at Kalispell," he said casually, as if she should know what he was talking about.

"Who lives over there?" She inclined her head toward the other two houses.

"Curtis and Keith, foremen. The womenfolk are home; the car's there. Kids'll be coming on the school bus soon. Well, I'd better get along. You'll be okay. Chip will come aroarin' in soon. If not, Penny'll be gettin' off the bus— unless she's stayin' in town with Miss Rogers, that is."

He turned to leave, and Margaret felt acute panic. "Mr. MacMadden—Tom." She held out her hand. "Thank you. I didn't realize it was so far from Kalispell to the mill."

"Ain't no distance at all in this country." From his expression, Margaret gathered that shaking hands with a woman was a novelty for him. "Hope you find out what you come for, ma'am." He walked purposefully to the car and got back in. "Door ain't locked. Nobody much locks up around here."

"Thank you again for bringing me out."

With his hand to the brim of his hat he saluted and then drove away. Margaret watched him, feeling as misplaced as an elephant in a tree. Try my wings and see the world, she thought. Ha! Nonplussed, she looked across the clearing to the other house and saw a curtain quickly fall into place. Knowing she was being watched, she shouldered her bag, draped her red jacket over her arm, and walked into the house as nonchalantly as the teenaged girl she'd seen on the plane.

Margaret hesitated inside the door and looked around. The room was half the width of the house and paneled with warm pine. The fireplace was huge, the furnishings plain and uncompromisingly masculine. Chairs and sofa were covered in a soft brown leather, and the floor was carpeted in light tan, along with several braided scatter rugs. A bookcase ran the length of one wall and was filled to overflowing with hardcovers, paperbacks, magazines, and newspapers. At least this is a reading family, Margaret thought as she took it all in at a glance.

There was another door straight across from where she stood. She walked over, tentatively opened it, and found herself in a short hall with more doors. One gave way into a kitchen the size of the living room. It was bright and cheery, with an oak table standing before a window that commanded a view of the river. Margaret's gaze skimmed over a large cooking range and white counters, and came to rest on a pile of dirty dishes stacked in the stainless-steel sink. She shuddered in distaste, took another look around the room, then peeked into a white tiled bathroom at the end of the hall. To the side of that was another open door. The room beyond had a double dresser and a wardrobe with the doors standing ajar. The bed was unmade, and piles of masculine garments were heaped in the middle of it as if ready for the laundry. Feeling braver, she opened the door across the hall. If it was a bedroom, austerity was the key word for it. With its iron bedstead, four-drawer chest, and looped rug on the bare floor beside the bed, it reminded Margaret of the rooms at the convent where they had put the hard-to-handle girls. She closed the door and looked into the next room. It was larger than the other two. There was a large double bed and a small youth bed covered with stuffed animals. Small scuffed shoes were set beside shiny black patent leather pumps. A ruffled blouse was draped across a chair.

Margaret gave a sigh of relief. Duncan Thorn was married and had a child. At least now she could exorcise those broad shoulders, blue eyes, and glistening brown hair from her mind. Perhaps that would provide the impetus to send her back to down-to-earth Justin. Had Tom said Thorn's wife was in the hospital? She wished she had questioned him further, but there was something standoffish about the man.

She returned to the living room, placed her jacket across the back of a deep reclining chair, and deposited her shoulder bag next to it. She could at least carry her bags into the house. She couldn't believe that they planned for her to use the small bare room at the back, but there seemed to be no other. And the bathroom—there was only one! She'd never shared a bathroom with anyone in her life. Oh, why hadn't she stayed in Kalispell, rented a car, and driven out here the next morning?

She carried in her small cosmetics bag, opened it, and took a wet cloth from a plastic wrap to wipe her face. It felt good to remove the road grime. Feeling somewhat refreshed, she returned to the porch to get the rest of her luggage.

A dust-covered Jeep came careening off the road into the drive, followed closely by a pickup truck with several men standing in the back. They waved and whistled at the stream of cars that moved on toward town in a cloud of dust. The mill must have closed down for the day.

Margaret suddenly felt as if all the air had been squeezed out of her. What was she to do? She couldn't turn and run into the house, much as she wanted to. She was Edward Anthony's daughter, co-owner of the Anthony/Thorn Lumber Company. The thought stiffened her spine. She stood quietly, hands clasped in front of her, and waited for the Jeep to stop beside the house.

The driver sat for a minute and looked at her. The pickup pulled up behind him, and the men spilled out. The door of the Jeep jerked open. Duncan Thorn was big without being bulky, his shoulders broad beneath an open mackinaw. He had the same brown hair, the same blue eyes, and the same tanned face, but a mustache had been added. She would have known him in a crowd of a million people. She fleetingly wondered if she'd be able to say the same about Justin if she had seen him only once years ago.

Thorn bounded up onto the porch. "Hi, sweetheart. I see you made it!" Strong hands snatched her to him, and he placed a hard kiss on her lips. "C'mon boys, meet my girl, Maggie Anderson. What's the matter, honey? So glad to see me you're speechless?"

Speechless wasn't the word. Stunned, dumbfounded, shocked beyond all understanding was more in keeping with Margaret's feelings. She tried to push herself away from him, but his arms bound her tightly.

"Let me go," she hissed, glaring up into amused blue eyes.

"Play the game . . . darling," he hissed back before

kissing her again quickly and whirling her around to meet the grinning men lined up at the edge of the porch. "Here she is. Didn't I tell you she was a beaut?" With an arm clasped tightly about her, he drew her forward. "Maggie, this is Jase, Pete, Harry, Whistler, Pegleg, Keith, and Curtis."

In a daze Margaret offered her hand to each man, trying to smile through their bone-crushing grips. "How do you do. I'm very happy to meet you."

The chorus of male responses was immediately forthcoming. "I'm doin' just fine, darlin', and so's old Chip now you're here." . . . "Wheeeee, she's a looker, Chip!" . . . "You ain't got no sister, have ya, honey?"

"Okay, you guys. Clear out. See you tomorrow."

Margaret stood trembling in the curve of Duncan Thorn's arm and watched the men pile back into the truck and head toward the two small houses to the north.

Duncan dropped his arm from around her and picked up her cases. "Open the door," he said without looking at her.

Shaking more from nerves than from the chill of the evening, she followed him into the house. He set her bags down at the entrance to the hall and flipped the light switch, but nothing happened. He muttered a curse, then jerked the screen from in front of the hearth, knelt down, and put a match to the fire already laid in the grate. The fine kindling burst into flame. He stood for a minute and watched it, then replaced the screen.

"I'll turn on the generator. I forgot I shut it off this morning." He glanced at her standing beside the door. "Make yourself at home." He strode into the back of the house, and soon she heard a door slam.

Margaret went to the large chair and leaned against it, thankful for these few minutes to pull herself together. Had there been sarcasm in his words, or was it her imagination? Everything he had said, done, was beyond the realm of her imaginings! Nothing was as she'd thought it would be! What had he meant—my girl? She had to get out of here. He was married and had a child, who would be getting off the school bus any time now, according to Tom. She picked up her red jacket and put it on.

"Going somewhere?" He came through the doorway, reached over, flicked the light switch, and the room was flooded with light.

"Explain your asinine behavior!" She was so angry her voice trembled.

He laughed, and she felt her face turn a dark red. "I didn't think it asinine at all. I thought it was kind of fun. You would've, too, if you'd seen that surprised look on your face."

Her features froze into a glare. No one had ever dared speak to her like that! "It was inexcusable for you to demean me in front of those men," she said icily.

"Demean? Come down off your high horse. You're no *princess* around here." The laughter had left his eyes. "You wanted to be incognito, and the big wheels at Anthony's wanted you safe. So I gave it a lot of thought, and decided there was no way you'd be safer than as the fiancée of Chip Thorn. Not many young single women come to this area. The men would've been after you like bears after honey. Is that what you wanted, *Miss Anthony?*"

There was no doubt in Margaret's mind that the last words, so softly spoken, were meant as an insult. Anger flared anew, but she quickly controlled it. She had promised herself she would handle whatever came up as the result of this impulsive trip.

"Let's get a few things straight, Mr. Thorn. That little show you put on out there"—she jerked her head toward the porch—"placed me in a position where it will be impossible for me to stay on here. I'm going back to Kalispell, and when I return it will be as Margaret Anthony, co-owner of this operation."

"Like MacArthur, you'll return."

"I don't appreciate your humor."

"I didn't think you would. I doubt if you even laugh at the funny papers," he said drily. "Why in the hell did you come here, anyway? If you're worried about your interest in the mill, you can read the financial statement prepared by the accountants."

"I wanted to learn about the business firsthand."

"Why this business? You must have a hundred others you could play around with." He seemed to make a conscious effort to wipe all traces of mockery from his expression. "Have you come to offer me your shares?"

The question caught her off guard, but she hurriedly rallied her thoughts. "Maybe. Are you interested?"

"Sure, for the right price." His dark brows drew together sharply. "Sit down and we'll talk about it."

"I'd prefer to leave. We can talk about it another time."

"Scared you off already, have I? Well, I didn't figure you'd last long. But I did think it would be longer than"—he looked at the gold watch strapped to his wrist—"twenty-two minutes."

"That was your intention, was it not? By introducing me as the *other* woman in your life, you knew it would be impossible for me to stay," she said, hoping her sweet smile was masking her cold anger.

"What do you mean by that? I haven't had any woman in my life for a good many years—permanent, that is."

She made herself look him directly in the eyes. "Tom said your wife was in the hospital and your child would be getting off the school bus." She felt color rise while she spoke.

"My wife?" He laughed, and Margaret suppressed the impulse to hit him. "I doubt if Tom said my *wife*. He probably said Dolly was in the hospital, and Penny would be getting off the bus. So that's what's bugging you!"

"I'm not exactly *bugged*, Mr. Thorn," she flared, "but you'll have to admit this was all rather confusing, particularly in view of your *greeting*."

"Dolly is my housekeeper. Penny is her granddaughter," he explained tersely. "They've been with me for about five years. I have no children. Kids belong in a marriage, not out of it. I'll have mine when the time is right." The banter had vanished from his voice, and there was unmistakable intolerance in the set of his mouth.

"Admirable of you," she murmured.

"Sit down. I'm not taking you to town tonight." He lifted a tool from the assortment hanging beside the fireplace and poked at the glowing coals on the grate, then lifted a small, neatly cut log onto them.

Margaret could feel the warmth from the fire seeping into her, and she wanted to move closer to it. Instead, she crossed to the window. Darkness had settled quickly; it was that time of year.

He followed her to the window, and she saw his dark reflection mirrored in the glass. It was slightly blurred, but she could see that he was big, powerful—that image was perfectly clear. She didn't turn around. She didn't want to look at him because that same breathless feeling she'd had when she first saw him almost eight years ago was descending upon her again.

She said the first thing that came into her mind. "I'd planned on staying at a hotel."

"There's no hotel in Aaronville."

"There is in Kalispell."

"That's fifty miles from here."

"I could get a helicopter to transport me."

"Oh, hell!" he said with disgust. "I forgot you had Fort Knox to draw on. Well, go ahead, if you want to blow your cover."

"Well, I can't stay here!"

"Why not? The damn house is half yours."

He moved away from her, and she turned to see him standing with his back to the hearth. She shut off a powerful physical memory of his lips against hers.

"Do you want me to draw a chalk line down the middle of it?" he asked.

"That will hardly be necessary." She was determined not to let him get to her again.

"It really blew your cool when I kissed you, didn't it?" He placed a hand on his chest. "Forgive me. It was an impulsive action, for which I beg your pardon."

A word came to her mind that she dare not use. *Smart-ass!*

"It wasn't that," she snapped with a lift to her shoulders. "I've certainly been kissed before."

"How come you've never married? Couldn't Ed find anyone good enough for his *princess?*"

"I was engaged to be married, and I . . . postponed it, not that it's any business of yours."

"Before or after Ed died?"

She had never heard her father referred to as Ed before. "After," she admitted without thinking.

"Did you sleep with him?"

"No!" She caught herself up, conscious that she had allowed him to antagonize her again.

He laughed, his eyes almost half shut as he looked at her. "Justin Whittier is too old for you, anyway. What was Ed trying to do? Put a watchdog on his little *princess* to keep her safe in her ivory tower?"

"Stop calling me that!" Her poise completely abandoned her, and she heard herself nearly shouting. He was exasperating! He knew all about her, so why the questions?

"Now we're getting down to the real Margaret Anthony. Just a spoiled brat!"

Margaret drew in a deep breath. "Hardly a brat, Mr. Thorn."

"I know how old you are, but you're a brat nevertheless. I also know about old Justin. I make a yearly trip to Chicago to confer with the powers that be. The last time I was there Ed told me that, although you would own his shares in Anthony/Thorn, I was to be the trustee. And you would have to offer them to me before you sold them elsewhere. He wasn't doing me a favor, mind you. He simply had a perverted sense of loyalty. He did it because he and my father had known each other when they were both poor, and he'd bailed my father out when he was having trouble with this mill. Does it surprise you to know that Edward Anthony was once poor?"

"No," she responded equably. "My father worked hard for everything he had."

"Not everything. Some things just fell into his lap after it was lined with gold."

"Are you an inverted snob, Mr. Thorn?" she asked softly, gratified to see that she had, at last, touched a raw spot.

"Hardly that, princess." His voice was low and impassioned. "But enough of this sparring. Are you going to stand around all evening in those ridiculous shoes and that hundred-dollar dress?"

Margaret opened her mouth to say, "Hundred-dollar shoes and five-hundred-dollar dress," but she choked back the retort and asked instead, "Shouldn't the little girl be here by now?"

"Penny stayed in town. Tomorrow is Saturday, and a friend of mine is taking her to see Dolly." He picked up the suitcases and carried them to the small, austere room, where he set them down with a thump. She had no choice but to follow him. "All yours," he said, switching on the light beside the bed. "Penny moved into Dolly's room for the duration, and I found this bed in the attic. This is the bathroom." He reached around the corner and switched on a light. "We may have to share the same towel, since the wash is piling up." His grin was devilish, and she didn't know if she should take him seriously or not. "Stick around, Maggie, and you'll see how the other half lives."

She started to protest again. She despised the nickname Maggie. But even that was better than *princess!*

"Thank you, Mr. Thorn. I'm sure I can manage just fine."

"I think you'd better forget about the Mr. Thorn business, Maggie. Call me Chip, unless we're with someone—then you can call me darling . . . or sweetheart." He was smiling wickedly.

"Don't count on it . . . Chip," she said haughtily, concentrating on keeping her own lips from curving upward.

"You'd better be careful, or you just may smile, princess. I know you can: you smiled at me one time, long ago, when you were a teenager." He laughed aloud. "It didn't take Ed long to hustle me out and away from you."

Rankled again, she snapped, "I wouldn't know. I don't remember ever seeing you before."

He moved past her into the hall, and she faintly heard him murmur, "Liar."

In the tiny bedroom she slammed the door shut, drew the shade against the night, and kicked off her shoes. The bare floor was cold. She stood on the looped rug beside the bed, opened one of her cases, and dug around until she found a pair of blue silk slippers. They weren't very warm, but they were better than nothing.

The closet was barely large enough to hold her clothes, and it was equipped with flimsy wire hangers. She grimaced when she hung her slacks and the wire sagged. Then she giggled. So this was freedom, seeing the world, trying one's wings, et cetera, et cetera.

Margaret put her things away carefully, removed her dress, hung it in the closet, and, preparing to freshen up, slipped into a long blue silk robe. With her cosmetics case in hand she opened the door a few inches and looked out. The bathroom door was closed. Did that mean *he* was in there? She listened carefully, and could faintly hear water running. He was in the bathroom. She'd have to wait. The room was cold, so she wrapped a blanket from the end of the bed about her shoulders and sat down to wait. This is ridiculous, she thought. I can't believe this is really me in this bare room. It's almost as if I were back at the convent school being punished for something or other.

An impish grin curled her lips, although she was still shivering from the cold. The first time she had been banished to such a room she had been twelve years old. Wishing desperately to be accepted by the group a year her senior, she had accepted a dare to put a rubber squawker under the cushion on the teacher's chair. When the teacher sat down it made a loud, rude sound, and the sister's face turned crimson. Life had certainly been less complicated in those days.

She sat on the bed, one leg crossed over the other, swinging her foot idly, thinking about the events in her life that had brought her to this moment. There was a loud thump on the door, and then it swung open.

"It's all yours, Maggie." Chip stood in the doorway, his chest bare, a towel around his neck.

CHAPTER THREE

MARGARET FELT A flickering of panic at the sight of his bare chest, sprinkled with golden-brown hair, and his flat muscled stomach. His feet were bare, and the white edge of his underwear was visible at the top of his low-slung jeans. He certainly was virile! She hid her confusion with arrogance. "Do you practice being rude, or does it come naturally to you?"

His laughter filled the room. "Ouch! I felt those icicles! Was I being rude? I knocked."

"Then barged right in." She hid the shock of having him walk into her room quite well, she felt. At least he wouldn't know that a thousand tiny nails were clawing at her stomach.

"Why were you wrapped in that blanket? Are you cold? Well, for Pete's sake! Didn't you bring anything warmer than that thing you're wearing?"

"How was I to know I'd be staying in a barn without heat?"

"We have central heating. I just haven't turned it on."

He grinned ruefully and flipped the towel from around his neck to around hers, gently drawing her toward him.

"What are you doing?" Alarm made her hands grab at the towel, but they found his wrists instead. She quickly released them and laid her palms flat against his chest to act as a barrier between them. Her eyes widened with fear. "Don't!" Her voice was shaking. He watched her with narrowed eyes, his head bent toward her.

"I still don't know why you came, Maggie. But I'm damn glad you did."

She pushed against him, her palms in the curly hair of his chest. "I told you, Mr. Thorn."

"Chip."

"Mr. Thorn," she said stubbornly.

"Chip," he said so softly that a shiver touched her spine. Then he continued in the same soft voice, "Have you ever made love, Maggie? Real love? Vital, hungry, gut-crushing love?"

"Why are you talking to me like this?" The warmth of his body, the minty smell of his breath, the charm of his smile, was invading every corner of her mind.

"I don't know. I think I like to tease you. You're awfully pretty, Maggie Anderson." He left the towel hanging around her neck and released her, turning to open the small wardrobe. "Is this all you brought?" He looked at each garment and pushed it down the rack. "Where in the hell were you going to wear these?" He brought out a blue silk suit and a white ruffled blouse. "Didn't anyone tell you this is rough, cold country? Pack it all up. Tomorrow we'll buy you some jeans and flannel shirts. Anyone could look in that closet and tell there's five hundred dollars' worth of clothes there and that you're no ordinary working girl."

"More like five thousand," Margaret said waspishly, angrier at herself for standing meekly and allowing him to go through her things than at him for doing it.

"My God!" He shook his head gently, chidingly. "And you expected to lose yourself in this country dressed in those?" He jerked his head toward the closet. "You'd stand out like an outhouse on a moonlit night!"

"A *what?*" she squeaked.

He seemed to have difficulty swallowing, and for a moment Margaret thought he was going to choke. Then he flung back his head and roared with laughter. It was the last straw, the very last straw. She charged for the door, giving him a hard jab in the stomach with her elbow on the way by, which caused him to sit down on the bed so hard that the frame gave way. Mattress, springs, and all hit the floor.

Margaret threw a look over her shoulder and saw only his legs and bare feet protruding from the bedclothes. His head was covered, and he was blindly trying to grab the bed rails. Wild, hysterical laughter bubbled up from inside her and echoed through the room. She scrambled for the bathroom, slammed the door, and frantically shot the bolt into place. She leaned against the door and laughed until her sides hurt and tears ran down her cheeks.

The knob rattled. She jumped away from the door.

"You little devil! You'll have to come out of there sometime."

"You asked for it! I don't particularly appreciate being compared to a latrine." She tried desperately to sound angry, but it was impossible to keep the grudging amusement out of her voice.

"Hurry up and get out of there. You'll have to help me set the bed up again."

"I don't have my case."

"Soap and towels are in there. What more do you need?"

There was a brief silence, and then a door slammed. Margaret waited a moment, before easing the bolt back and opening the door. She scurried across the hall and into her room. Arms clamped around her from behind. "Gotcha!" he whispered.

"That's not fair! You tricked me!" The laughter continued to escape her lips as she struggled in the arms that held her.

"This is just so you'll know who's boss around here, my girl." He swatted her on the behind with familiar ease. "Wash up and put on some work clothes. Do you want to eat before or after we tackle that mountain of dishes in the sink?"

"I don't have any work clothes, and besides, I'm a guest." She was trying to get past him to the door. Her eyes were dancing, and she couldn't keep the grin off her face.

"There're no guests around here, princess. No work, no eat!" His voice was stern, but his face wore a warm smile.

By this time Margaret had reached the bathroom and shut the door. She stood before the mirror over the wash basin. The woman who looked back at her had healthy pink cheeks and sparkling eyes. Oh, dear, she thought wildly. This is the most fun I've had in my entire life.

Thank you, dear Rachel, for jarring me out of my humdrum existence.

When she returned to her bedroom, a worn gray sweatshirt lay across a chair. Margaret slipped into the tailored slacks of her Jourdan suit, then pulled on the sweatshirt. It came to mid-thigh, and the sleeves were about a foot too long. There wasn't a mirror in the bedroom, so she couldn't see herself, but she knew she must look ridiculous. What would Justin say if he could see her in this getup? At that moment, her life in the dark mansion on Riverside Drive seemed a million light years away. *You're awfully pretty, Maggie Anderson.* Why did the words keep coming back again and again, and why the devil was she feeling so happy?

Margaret came into the hall at the same time Chip was passing through with his arms full to overflowing with dirty clothes. He went into the kitchen, opened a door, and threw them down the stairway into the basement.

"Gotta do the wash. This is my last pair of clean jeans." He looked her up and down. "Warmer now?" He reached for her arms and began to roll up the sleeves of the sweatshirt. "We'll go into town tomorrow and buy you some decent clothes. How long are you staying, anyway?"

The question caught her by surprise as she watched his strong hands rolling up her sleeves.

"I have no definite plans. I want to stay long enough to make up my mind whether I want to keep my shares or not." It sounded like a lame excuse even to her own ears, and she glanced at him quickly. He frowned slightly, then lifted his head and looked full into her eyes.

"Good. I hate timetables unless they're absolutely necessary. I meant it when I said to pack up all that stuff in there. Dolly will be back the first of the week, and she's no dummy. She'd spot those expensive clothes right away, and she might figure out who you are." He had finished with the sleeves and turned back to his room. She followed and stood in the kitchen doorway. "Everyone would feel awkward and uncomfortable if they knew you were Ed's girl, half owner of the mill that's been their bread and butter all these years." His arms were loaded with clothing again, and he tossed them down the stairs after the first load.

"I don't understand why they'd be any more uncomfortable with me than they are with you." The statement was unreasonable—she knew it the moment she said it—but she had to defend her right to be here.

"They've known me all my life. I'm one of *them*." He put his hands on his hips and eyed her narrowly. She wished he would put on a shirt. "Dolly and the rest of the women would watch every word and count to ten before they spoke to you, afraid you'd take offense and their husbands' jobs would be in jeopardy. Or else—"

"That's not true. I wouldn't—" she began.

"Let me finish." His voice, harder now, stopped her in mid-sentence. "Now that I've met you, I don't think it'd be something you'd do consciously. But people used to having as much money as you just naturally throw their weight around. Oh, I don't mean in any obvious way, but it's there all the same—the air of knowing who you are, the important Miss Margaret Anthony. If they think of you as Maggie Anderson, they'll be natural with you."

"Who do you mean by *they?*" Her voice came out sounding very taut.

He raised his eyebrows. She stood very still, waiting. "The women, the people in town, the men who work their tails off so this company will show a profit and their jobs will remain secure. Me. I'm trying damn hard to forget who you are."

"Why? I'm no threat to you. Daddy took care of that in his will. You're the man in charge. You don't have to sell your shares or buy mine if you don't want to."

He gave her a dry smile. "That only goes to show how naïve you are. I wasn't talking about business, Maggie." His eyes glinted as if he were angry. "This was something that had to be said. Now let's get on with what has to be done. Do you want to do the wash or the dishes?"

Margaret took a deep breath, her pulses thudding like a jackhammer in her head. Her eyes went to the dark stairway leading to the basement, and she felt panic building. She'd never started a washing machine in her life!

"I'll do the dishes," she said quietly. "That is, unless you think your precious Dolly will resent her kitchen being tidied up by a snob like Margaret Anthony." Hurt pride thickened her voice.

Chip's hard hands grabbed her arms and turned her toward him. Her eyes, faintly misted, met his.

"Little fool! I told you this for your own good. Believe it or not, I want your visit here to be pleasant. You'll need a tougher skin than what you've got if you're going out into the real world. You've been cushioned against the nastiness of life, and you're not used to being told how things really are. I've spoken the truth, whether you like it or not."

Margaret had never seen eyes like his on any man.

There was strength and stubbornness there, just as there was in the rest of his face—and in his hard muscled body, for that matter. But it was mostly in his eyes, so soft a blue, yet so deep, seeming to contain a knowledge that was strangely disconcerting. It was as if he knew everything about her—everything, from her sheltered life, which was common knowledge since the kidnap attempt, to the fact that this was her first sojourn into the world without backup assistance from the Anthony conglomerate. He even knew about Justin!

"You're tougher than you look," he said at last. "You'll make out." His voice softened, and Margaret realized she had been staring. Her eyes turned cool. She tried to restore a calm facade, angrily thinking that he expected her to fold under his criticism. She'd be damned if she would!

"Have you anything more to say? Any more expert opinions?" She hoped she'd manage to inject an I-don't-give-a-damn-what-you-think note into her words.

"No. Sure you don't mind getting dishpan hands?" He was baiting her now, and his wide grin proved it. "You can do the wash and I'll do the dishes, if you prefer."

"I'll get on with it if you ever turn loose of me."

"Okay. Hop to it, and I'll be back to help. Then we'll have to rustle up some grub. I don't know what's here, but we'll find something." He disappeared down the basement stairs, and Margaret looked despairingly at the stack of dishes in the sink.

A line from one of her favorite movies leapt to her mind. *You can do it, Bronco Billy.* She pushed the rolled-up sleeves of the sweatshirt past her elbows and began to stack the dishes in some semblance of order on the counter as she had seen Edna do before putting them in the dishwasher. The next step was to stop up the sink and fill it with water, but the water drained out as fast as it ran in. She was sure it had something to do with the small metal basket in the bottom of the sink, but she wasn't sure what. She lifted it out, looked at it, and set it back. The water still drained. Damn!

An arm reached around her, and a hand gave the basket a twirl. It settled deeply into the hole. "Try that."

She filled the sink and generously added the detergent she found beneath it. The suds bubbled up. She slid a plate from the stack on the counter into the suds and began scrubbing vigorously.

Again an arm encircled her, and this time a large hand lifted hers from the suds and unfastened her diamond-studded wristwatch. Chip wiped it on a towel and held it to his ear.

"You can't wear this thing around here. Where shall I put it?"

"In my cosmetics case," she said without looking at him. She continued to wash the plates, placing them carefully in the other side of the sink.

Chip returned and began drying the dishes. They worked silently. Margaret found it soothing and satisfying to see the pile of soiled dishes gradually becoming smaller. She wondered what he'd think if he knew this was the first time she'd washed dishes since her last year in high school when the sisters gave her clean-up duty for sneaking a copy of *Peyton Place* into the dormitory.

"Why are you smiling?" Chip suddenly asked.

"You wouldn't understand," she said.

"Try me," he replied, apparently not a bit abashed. "It must have been something funny to make your lips curl like that."

"It wasn't anything, really. I was just thinking about my years at the convent school."

"I can't think there'd be anything about *that* to make you smile." He walked to the end of the counter and put the clean, dry dishes on a shelf.

"It had its moments."

"Is that where you'd been that time you came home from school and I was there with Ed?"

"Yes. The furnace needed repair, and they sent us home for a few days." *Damn!* She'd just admitted remembering his visit! Mercifully, he didn't seem to feel like teasing her this time.

"Did you like the school?"

"I don't know. I never had anything else to compare it with. But from programs I saw on television, other schools looked like more fun. Of course, Daddy wouldn't hear of it."

"Didn't you ever rebel against the tight rein he kept you on?"

"Oh, a few times. Then Thomas, our chauffeur, died saving me from being kidnapped. He was an old man, and he didn't have a chance, but he drew attention and the kidnappers ran. For a long time after that I was afraid to go out."

They worked silently for a while, Margaret almost disbelieving she was really in this house in the north woods washing dishes with the man who had drifted in and out of her thoughts for so many years.

Chip had put on a white T-shirt, socks, and canvas shoes. The shirt only emphasized his maleness, and Margaret found her gaze wandering to him again and again.

"I'm rather surprised you didn't have someone come in while your housekeeper was away," she finally said as she was letting the sudsy water drain from the sink.

"Penny and I were doing fine. I was going to ask Curtis's wife to come over and get the place all spiffed up before Dolly came home. Dolly's a spit-and-polish housekeeper. Likes everything bright and shining. 'Course now that you're here, it'd look strange if I had someone come in to do the work."

"I'll be glad to lend a hand," she said quickly. "It's only fair to tell you that there are some things I haven't done before, but I'll give them a try if you point me in the right direction."

"I can do that, all right. I'm good at pointing people in the right direction." His grin was so charming she had to turn away from it. "How about some homemade stew for supper? There're cartons of it in the freezer. I'll thaw it out," he said, suiting action to his words.

Margaret leaned against the counter and turned to watch him, marveling at his efficient grace as he pulled open drawers and swiftly set two places at the table.

"If you dig around in the freezer for some rolls, I'll pop them into the oven and we'll be sitting down to a meal before you know it," he offered.

Margaret hadn't eaten since the noon meal on the plane, and the aroma of the warming stew was certainly appetizing. Soon she was accepting Chip's invitation to sit across from him and start eating. The fragrance wasn't the only good thing about the stew; it was excellent, thick with meat and vegetables. She caught Chip's eye and said earnestly, "This is delicious."

"Sure it isn't just because you're hungry?" he teased.

"Maybe that, too," she admitted.

He offered her some cheese, and then she watched him deftly hack off a sizable piece for himself. The hairs on the backs of his hands and wrists seemed to glisten in the light as he placed a heated roll on his plate and one on hers.

"Why did you tell Tom MacMadden who I was when you think it's so important for the others not to know?"

He held her gaze for a long moment. "I knew I could trust him. I also knew he'd be the first one to figure out who you really were, so it seemed best to have him in on the secret right from the beginning."

"He's nice, but he seemed somewhat standoffish."

"That's because of who you are. People are inclined to be a little awed by someone like you. You're almost a celebrity, you know."

"That's silly!"

"No it isn't. Wouldn't you be a little awed by Queen Elizabeth?"

"Yes, but that's different."

"No it isn't." He laughed.

"It doesn't seem to affect you." She could have bitten her tongue for saying the words.

"How do you know?" He raised his brows, and mocking eyes wandered over her face. "I may just be a damned good actor."

Margaret swallowed on the sudden aching tightness in her throat. "Ready for coffee?"

"Sure. You'll find some mugs in the cupboard."

Grateful for an excuse to move out from under his gaze, she walked over to the counter to pour from the electric percolator. She was brought up short by his next words.

"Would you have married old Justin if Ed hadn't died?"

Margaret carefully set a mug down in front of him and took her place opposite. "I haven't asked you about your private affairs. Why should you inquire into mine?"

"Ask away. My life's an open book." His grin did nothing to put her at ease. She wished desperately she could be as relaxed as he was. He disturbed her in more ways than she cared to acknowledge. She'd never met anyone quite so aggressively masculine in her life.

"Why haven't *you* married? I imagine you're the most eligible man in the county."

His grin widened. "The woman I marry will have to want no other life but this. I haven't met her yet."

"You mean you haven't fallen in love yet? Or don't you consider that a requisite for marriage?"

"You evidently didn't or you wouldn't have let yourself get engaged to old Justin," he countered.

She could find no answer adequate to express her thoughts at that precise moment. She bit her lip, aware of the sardonic twist to his. He'd never understand her reasons for the engagement. She wasn't even sure she did anymore.

"I thought we were talking about you, not me," she said in sudden exasperation.

"So we are. Now what was the question? Oh, yes. Do I consider love a prerequisite for marriage? Yes. Yes, I do.

I don't think I could stand a woman day in and day out unless I loved her desperately. Out here a man needs a woman he can rely on. I'd want a couple of kids, and I'd have to put up with my wife's bitching because they'd ruined her figure. That would take patience as well as love. There's more to being a wife than providing a man with a housekeeper and a sleeping partner."

"There is?" Her own tone dripped mockery. "Then you wouldn't want a woman who had an eye on a career outside the home?"

"Absolutely not, sweetheart! I'd be all the career she could handle."

The gleam in his eye was the spur that caused her to snap. "Well, you'd better find one young enough to idolize your kind of machismo!"

"Idolization isn't what I want."

Margaret was too incensed to notice how much he seemed to enjoy baiting her. He had stopped eating, and his eyes were alive with amusement.

"No? You merely want subservience?"

"No . . ." He seemed to be considering. "It wouldn't be a one-way street. She'd have her compensations."

"I can imagine what!"

He roared with laughter, and she felt her face turn crimson. "Didn't old Justin ever even *try* to get you into bed?"

"No!" Her heart was thudding against her ribs, and she answered without thinking.

Chip got up from the table and stood looking down at her. "He was a fool," he said softly. There was a slight rasp in his voice that caused her whole body to tense.

"He was a *gentleman*," she defended, striving to keep her tone level.

He laughed again, and she wanted to kick him. "Oh, God! It's like you've just arrived out of the Victorian age. Sweetheart, if the desire's there, a man forgets all about being a gentleman! Old Justin had his eye on your papa's money, not his mind on getting you into bed! You're damn lucky you escaped him."

Ablaze with rage at his presumption, Margaret jumped to her feet. "Who do you think you are to stand there and analyze my life? You know nothing about it! You don't know what it's like to be caged up on an estate and not allowed to go to the drugstore by yourself, or to shop, or to choose your own friends. Just shut up about my life! And . . . wash your own damn dishes!" She stalked into her bedroom and slammed the door.

Margaret couldn't remember a time when she'd really let herself go and shouted. It felt good, she was stunned to realize. If Chip Thorn thought she was going to knuckle under and fall on her face before him, he was badly mistaken. She'd done her stint of being subservient to a man's wishes. The thought drew her up short. Never before had she thought of her relationship with her father in quite those terms. She had wanted to please him because he was old, he hadn't long to live, and he loved her. Chains of love were strong. But Chip wouldn't understand that.

The door opened behind her, and she whirled around.

"Sorry, I forgot to knock." He studied her for a moment, his features uncertain. "I'll help you set up the bed."

"Thanks."

Afterward Margaret went to the kitchen and washed the few dishes they had used. Chip was in the basement. She could hear him whistling through his teeth over the hum of the dryer. He'd been quiet since her outburst. She kept seeing him in her mind's eye as she'd seen him that first time. He hadn't changed much during those years, though he was more self-assured now, older. She wondered how he saw her. He had called her naïve, right out of the Victorian age. Did she really project that image?

"Maggie! Come on down and I'll show you how to run the washer. Dolly may not be able to get down the steps for a while."

Chip was patient with his instructions, and he seemed to think nothing of it when he handed her a pile of his underwear to fold. They were still warm from the dryer. She folded the white shorts carefully and placed them in a pile, then folded and stacked the T-shirts. They carried them upstairs and she followed him to the door of his bedroom. It was neater now.

"Come in, come in. The underwear goes into that drawer." He rapped on the bureau drawer with his knuckles. "The socks in the one above." He hung his shirts and jeans in the closet, which she now saw was arranged neatly. "Do you have anything warm to sleep in? The house gets cold at night when the fire in the fireplace dies down. I'll have a load of fuel oil trucked in, and we'll start that monster in the basement." He tossed her a pair of blue and white striped flannel pajamas. "You'll probably only need the tops." He grinned devilishly.

"Thanks. I'll buy some things tomorrow if you'll drive

me to town." She was determined not to let him get her rattled again.

"I'm planning on it. Better get to bed. You look tired. The day's not only been long for you, it's been quite a change, going from one world to another."

She looked at him sharply and realized he hadn't meant the words to be critical or sarcastic.

"Yes. It has been a tiring day. Good night."

She left for the bathroom, quickly washed her face and brushed her teeth, and made it back across the hall to her bedroom with a sense of relief. There was a key hanging on a nail above the door. It gave her some feeling of security to turn it in the lock before stripping off her clothes and sliding into the top of Chip's pajamas.

She was in bed with the light already out when she heard him pad across the hall and into the bathroom. He came out, stood a moment outside her door, then tried the handle.

"Get this damn door unlocked," he called brusquely.

Margaret lay quietly, her breathing coming in ragged gasps. There was a pause, then a hard thumping. She sat up.

"Open the door, Margaret."

Margaret? She jumped out of bed and turned the key, resisting the impulse to cower away from the muscular figure clad only in a pair of jeans who towered above her when the door was flung open. He reached around and took the key from the door.

"If you were trying to lock me out, forget it! If I wanted a woman badly enough, I wouldn't let a locked door stand in my way. We don't lock doors up here for a damn good reason—safety. If you'd ever been in or near a forest fire you'd understand and not want to be locked into a room fumbling for a key. Now get into bed and quit letting your imagination run away with you. See you in the morning." He turned on his heel and left her standing barefoot and shivering.

CHAPTER FOUR

MARGARET WOKE TO the smell of bacon frying, and she lay with her eyes closed, listening to the clatter of pans. Chip must be in the kitchen cooking breakfast. She opened her eyes a crack and squinted at the window. The shade was still drawn, but a dim slit of light told her it was not yet sunup. She groaned and snuggled farther down into the warm bed.

It seemed only minutes since she had crawled back into bed thinking she would never go to sleep in this house with Duncan Thorn sleeping in the next room. But exhaustion had overcome the desire to lie quietly and think about the day's events, and she had slept deeply, untroubled by dreams. The strangeness of it all hit her now. Here she was, feeling as safe as if she were behind the stone walls of the Chicago estate—and she had never slept outside a security-protected house in her life!

She reached for the glasses she'd left on the table beside the bed and swung her feet to the floor. She shivered as her toes touched the cold bare planking. Opening her bedroom door a crack, she saw that there was a light on in the kitchen but the hallway was empty. Minutes later she had showered and was in the bathroom pulling on her slacks and a soft cashmere sweater. Chip's sweatshirt went on over the outfit, and the chill finally began to leave her body. With her glasses still perched on her nose she went back to the bedroom, found the container with her contact lenses, and slipped it into her pocket. She then made the impulsive decision to show Chip Thorn a makeup-free face adorned with dark-rimmed glasses. She sneaked a quick look in the mirror from her cosmetics case.

"Will the real Margaret Anthony please stand up!" she whispered to the face that stared back at her.

The kitchen, when she reached it, was empty. She felt strangely disappointed, but she hastily brushed the sensation away. It took her less than a minute to ascertain that Chip was not in the house. She went to the back door and out onto a small porch. There was a wonderful, needle-sharp scent in the air: fir and spruce, and other smells, too, that she couldn't identify. The breeze coming off the river was cold, yet exhilarating in a way city air never was. She noticed that the boat was gone from its mooring and the river was empty of life. It was as smooth as a mirror, its far banks edged with lush green forest.

She turned back to the house, moved into the kitchen, and stood absolutely still, realizing that this was the first time in her life she had ever been alone, really alone, in a house! She wondered why the thought didn't fill her with terror. She whirled around the room like a young child, and she saw the note propped up against the electric percolator.

"Fix yourself some breakfast. I'll be back about nine o'clock. The clock over the mantel tells the correct time in case that worthless doodad you call a watch stopped when you dunked it in the dishwater. Chip."

She hurried into the living room and glanced at the large clock. While she stood there it began to strike the hour, its soft tones oddly comforting in the quiet house. Seven o'clock. She had two hours to get used to the idea of being alone.

Breakfast was, of necessity, first. She plunked a couple of slices of bread into the toaster and set out butter and jam. It was exciting to be alone, doing for herself. She opened cabinet doors until she found a box of cornflakes. Humming softly to herself she set out a bowl, went to the refrigerator for milk, pulled a stool up to the counter, and poured herself a mug of coffee. She had always eaten a good breakfast, but this morning she ate as if she were starved.

Over her second cup of coffee she realized that this would be a good time to tidy up the house—while there was no one there to witness her fumbling attempts. She left her mug beside the coffee pot and washed up the rest of the breakfast dishes.

When there was nothing else she could do in the kitchen she went to the basement and reviewed what Chip had told her the night before about starting the washing machine. Easy. Nothing to it. There were still four pairs of jeans on the sorting table. She lifted the lid and stuffed them into the washer, turned the dial to warm water/cold rinse, added a cup of detergent, and filled the little tub on the side with bleach as she had seen Chip do the night before. She pushed in the knob and the tub began to fill. Enormously pleased with herself, she skipped back up the stairs.

An hour later she had made her bed, run the vacuum cleaner over the living room rug, and made an effort to clean the bathroom. For the first time she acknowledged the value of the homemaking class at the convent school.

The door to Chip's room was closed. Margaret hesitated for a long moment before she opened it and looked into the room. She was high on the excitement of her accomplishments, and the desire to have everything just right when he returned was the impetus she needed to enter his room. But there was nothing there that needed to be done. The bed was neatly made, the bureau that had been littered the day before was cleared off, the double doors of the wardrobe were closed. Margaret felt a strong desire to linger, to sit down on the edge of the bed and let the smell of his aftershave and the woodsy odor of his clothing surround her.

The slam of a car door caused her to jump guiltily. She backed out of the room and closed the door. Chip had come back sooner than she expected! She hurried to the kitchen, poured herself a cup of coffee, and perched on the stool. The front door opened and closed. Margaret waited, her eyes on the kitchen door. There was silence. Not even the sound of footsteps reached the kitchen. The silence lengthened, and Margaret felt her throat close with fear.

"Chip?" She waited expectantly. There was no answering call. Panic began to build as the silence became unbearable. "Chip?" She shouted his name. There was no sound. Nothing. Terror put wings to her feet, and she bolted for the kitchen door and jerked it open. She glanced over her shoulder, expecting to see someone lunging for her.

"What're you hollerin' for?" A young girl stood in the doorway. She wore jeans, a red and blue checked mackinaw, and heavy boots. Her hair, shoulder length, was drawn back and hooked over her ears.

"Who are you?" Margaret gasped, her heart pounding from fright.

"Who're you? I heard Chip had a woman here. What're you so scared for?"

"Why didn't you answer when I called out? You scared me half silly," Margaret said crossly, closing the kitchen door with a bang.

"Why should I? You wasn't callin' me." The girl, who looked to be in her mid-teens, moved to the cabinet, took down a mug, and poured herself a cup of coffee.

Make yourself at home, Margaret thought resentfully.

"Where's Chip? He's not at the mill." The girl went to the refrigerator and diluted her coffee with milk from the half-gallon plastic jug. She was evidently familiar with her surroundings.

"I don't know where he is," Margaret said brusquely, returning to her perch on the stool. "But he'll be back soon if you care to wait."

The lithe figure leaned casually against the counter, her calf-length boots with the jeans tucked into the tops crossed nonchalantly. The girl's gaze remained on Margaret's face as if searching for some plausible alternative to the obvious.

"Everybody said Chip had a woman here. I wanted to see what she looked like."

"Now you know," Margaret said drily.

"Did ya sleep with him?"

"Did I . . . ?" The girl's frankness had rendered her speechless.

"You heard me! You ain't dumb. Ain't very pretty, neither."

"Thanks a lot!" Margaret looked down to hide a faint smile.

"I heard he's goin' to marry you. I never thought he'd take up with no city girl."

"Why not? City girls aren't all that bad."

"I only know what he said, is all. A lot of city girls have been after him. He always said they didn't know their backside from a hole in the ground." Irritation infiltrated the girl's tone. "Where're you from, anyhow?"

"Chicago. That is, a small town near Chicago," she improvised quickly.

"I suppose he met you when he went there to meet with that old man who owns part of the mill. I heard the old man died, so I guess he won't be going there no more unless it's to see you." The girl sank down into a chair. "What's your name?"

"Maggie." Margaret was surprised at how quickly the name came to her lips. "What's yours?"

"Elizabeth, but I'm called Beth. We live on the other side of the mill. My pop is foreman of one of the logging camps," she said proudly. Curiosity was patent in the girl's wide eyes. "How long are you gonna stay? There's not much to do up here—not like what you're used to."

"I haven't decided how long I'll stay. I just came to see if I'd like it here."

"So there's nothing . . . settled?" Eagerness had crept into the girl's voice, and Margaret felt a rush of sympathy for her, because she was sure, now, that Beth had a crush on Chip.

"Oh, no. Nothing's settled."

"That's good. I sure hope he don't get you pregnant."

Margaret's mouth dropped open, but she couldn't think of anything to say. The girl's bluntness stunned her. She got off the stool, looked around for something to do, then remembered the clothes in the washing machine.

"Excuse me. I've got to take some clothes out of the washer." Somehow she liked the sound of the words. It was crazy, but they made her feel a little important.

"I can help. I'm used to doin' 'round here. I told Chip I'd come and clean while Dolly's gone, but he didn't want me to. Guess he thought folks'd talk."

"No. Sit still. I'll just put them in the dryer."

Margaret went down the basement steps and lifted the lid on the washer. The wet clothes clung to the sides of the tub. She lifted them out to put them into the dryer, and her heart leapt into her throat. Big white splotches everywhere—all over the jeans! With trembling hands she looked at each pair, holding them at the waist and letting the long, slim legs hang down. The splotches were on the legs of some, on the front and back of others. What in the world had happened? What had she done wrong? More important than that, what was she going to do now?

"Maggie?" Beth called from the doorway at the top of the stairs. "Chip's back. He's tying up the boat."

Margaret opened the dryer and shoved the jeans inside. She turned the dial as Chip had told her to do, and the drum began to turn, the zippers from the blasted jeans making small clicking sounds as they whirled. She'd have to decide later what to do about the jeans. She only knew that she didn't want that child upstairs to see the mess she'd made.

Margaret took big gulps of air into her lungs to calm herself, then straightened her glasses, smoothed her hair, and calmly mounted the steps.

Chip came in the back door as she reached the kitchen. Their eyes met and held. He smiled, a half-smile at first, beginning with his mouth, lifting it wide, then crinkling his eyes.

"Morning, sweetheart."

"Morning." It was the oddest feeling. She felt as if she were coming alive. She knew the endearment was for Beth's benefit, but it caused a warm feeling of belonging to course through her.

"Hi, Chip."

"Hi, Beth." He strode across the room and wrapped an arm around Margaret. A finger approached the tip of her nose and slid upward until it reached the crosspiece of her glasses and firmly pushed them into place. "Hi," he said, just to her, his voice low, with a caress in its tone. The smiling blue eyes moved from her eyes to her lips, which were curved in a nervous smile.

She felt the soft brush of his mustache on her cheek, then his lips, firm and warm, against her mouth. It was a slow, unhurried kiss, and when he raised his head his eyes glinted into hers with devilish amusement. She was trembling, shaken to her roots, and she stared at him almost angrily.

"How're you doing, Beth?" he said to the girl who stood beside the door with a stricken look on her face.

"Fine. You?"

"Fine. What are you doing out and around so early? I thought schoolgirls liked to sleep in on Saturday mornings."

"Well . . . I had to go to town. Thought I'd stop by and see . . . when Dolly's comin' home."

Margaret noticed how Beth kept her gaze on the floor, and she could see herself when she first met Chip years ago in her father's study. Inner conflict was tearing the girl apart. Margaret rushed to say something to fill the silence.

"Beth and I had a nice visit. I'm glad she stopped by. Another time I'd like to go to town with you, Beth."

"That'll be okay, I guess. I've only got that old pickup, but it gets me there." Now she was looking from one to the other of them, her gaze watchful. "Guess I'd better get goin'." She moved toward the kitchen door to go back out through the front of the house. Then turned, her eyes anxious. "Are you really goin' to *marry* her?"

"If I can talk her into it, I am. Don't you think I've made a good choice?" Chip's tone was even, his face serious. He tightened his arm to keep Margaret beside him.

"But you said the woman you married would want to spend her life here in Flathead. You said city girls don't know nothin' but primpin' and dressin' up like that old man's girl. You said she was useless as tits on a boar. You said—"

"I was wrong, Beth," Chip interrupted. His voice was stern, but there was an undertone of gentleness. "City girls are like any other girls. If they want to adjust to this life, they can."

"But—"

"Run along, Beth. Are you keeping your grades up like you promised?"

"And if I don't, I suppose you'll take the old pickup back!" Resentment flared on the young face.

"You're damn right I will! A bargain's a bargain."

Margaret watched the emotions flicker across the girl's face, and she forcefully moved out from the circle of Chip's arm. "Like I said, Beth. Nothing has been decided." She wanted to say, *He's lying! I'm the useless one he told you about.*

"Don't you love him?" Beth asked hopefully, her eyes dark with hurt.

"Of course she does. She told me so last night." Chip shrugged out of his jacket and hung it over the back of a chair. His glance at Margaret dared her to contradict him.

Beth's face tightened angrily. "You get her pregnant before she decides and I'll never speak to you again!" She shot Margaret a stricken look and bolted out of the room. The front door slammed as she left the house.

"Why did you tell her that? It was . . . unkind," Margaret finished weakly.

"Unkind? You think it's better to let her hope?" His voice was brusque. "It's time she stopped hanging around here and got a boyfriend her own age."

"You didn't have to be so brutal. You didn't have to lie about being . . . about me."

"I had two reasons for saying what I did. She'll spread it up and down Flathead Range that you're here as my fiancée, and she'll get over her silly romantic notions about me."

"You had no right to involve me. You should've talked to her father."

He looked at her with irony in the twist of his lips. "She doesn't have one. Well, I guess she does have one ... somewhere. The bastard left them about six weeks ago."

The words were slow to sink in. When they did, Margaret was puzzled. "But she said her father was a foreman at one of the logging camps."

Chip shrugged. "Beth makes things up. She'll never admit that he pulled out and left them. She always has a reason why he's away. He's in the hospital, or he joined the service and is in Germany, or some other lie."

"Oh, the poor girl!" She frowned up at him. "All the more reason to show a little compassion."

He took a deep breath, as if making some inner decision. "Don't tell me how to run my affairs, Maggie. You know nothing at all about the situation."

"Maybe not. But I learned a little more about you— and your opinion of the *old man's girl!* I'm surprised you'd want someone so useless to even pretend to be your fiancée!" His smile only increased her irritation.

"I knew you'd pick up on that." His grin deepened, and he reminded her of a tiger that had just been thrown a piece of raw meat.

She felt a hot wave wash over her body as he blatantly surveyed her slender figure. His eyes slowly lifted to her face. She might be technically inexperienced, but she interpreted his look to mean she wasn't entirely useless.

The sexual assessment in those blue eyes left her chilled but angry.

"Your jeans are in the dryer, you chauvinist . . . creep! I hope you enjoy wearing them!" She jerked her head toward the basement door, and her glasses slid down her nose. Chip reached out with a forefinger and pushed them up before she could jerk her head away.

"You look kind of cute in those glasses. Why do you wear the contacts?"

"Because I want to!" she snapped defiantly.

"Good enough reason, princess. Now, run along and get a jacket so we can go to town and buy you some decent clothes."

She instantly hated him for speaking to her as if she were no older than Beth, and she retorted sharply. "My clothes are *decent*. They may not be suitable for this country, but they are *decent*."

"Of course they are, honey," he said placatingly. "Now run along. And, princess," he drawled, "you'd better put your contacts in; I don't want to be pushing your glasses up all day."

She had wanted to anger him. Instead she had amused him, and that annoyed her. She ground her teeth and went to her room, closing the door softly because she wanted so badly to slam it. The sweatshirt came off over her head and the glasses with it. She grabbed up her cosmetics case and went to the bathroom, shooting the bolt into place, defying him to tell her she couldn't lock the bathroom door. Forest fires be damned! She had finished putting in her contact lenses and was carefully applying makeup when she heard the bellow from the kitchen.

"Maggie! What the hell did you do to my jeans?"

Instead of feeling frightened, as she had when she'd discovered the splotched jeans, she was almost pleased. Revenge was sweet!

"I only did what you told me to do," she called innocently through the door.

"Damn it! You've ruined four pairs of my best jeans. They'd been washed just enough to be comfortable."

"Sorreee! I'll call Fort Knox and get the money to buy you a truckload." She held her hand over her mouth to keep from laughing.

"I told you to bleach the *white* things, damn it," he yelled from the door to his room.

"Oh, is that what I did wrong? Well, I'm so *useless*, I can't remember things overnight." She deliberately made her voice sound young and helpless.

The firm closing of a door was his response, and Margaret claimed a small victory. She fastened tiny diamond clips to her ears and slipped her diamond-studded watch onto her wrist. Back in her room she looped the jacket from her Jourdan suit over her arm, picked up her bag, and went out to the living room.

Chip stood with his back to the hearth, although there wasn't a fire burning. The blue eyes studied her, and she could tell her defiance had hit target. He wanted to present her as a dowdy girlfriend, and she was having no part of it. She kept her head erect, meeting his eyes unsmiling. A faint frown pleated his brow, but he remained silent until he shrugged into his mackinaw.

"The minute they find out who you are, you're leaving on the next plane." He made the statement softly, but he might as well have shouted the words that accompanied his cool, cool look.

"I have as much right to be here as you do," she answered, her voice sharp.

"No, you don't. I'm the trustee, remember? Even more than that, all I'd have to do is leak it to the papers that you're here, and the Anthony corporation would see to it you didn't leave the house without a couple of bodyguards. Is that what you want?"

"You know it isn't!" she protested.

"Then why the hell don't you behave yourself?" He couldn't keep the exasperation out of his voice. "Oh, hell! C'mon." He opened the door and waited for her to pass through. "Wait here," he said when they reached the porch. "I'll bring up the other car. I doubt if you'd care to ride to town in the Jeep."

Margaret climbed into the dusty car and idly wondered if comfortable cars had been banned in this area. At least it was enclosed, which was an improvement over the one he'd driven yesterday, she thought ruefully.

She glanced at Chip's set profile as they drove on in silence. After ten minutes or so, Chip finally said, "Most of the timber you see off to the left is on land leased by Anthony/Thorn."

She made a pretense of looking in the direction he indicated. Somehow her sense of defiance had vanished in the face of his silence. It still rankled that he thought her useless and had announced that opinion to his friends. Suddenly she saw, as if in a scene unfolding, the complete emptiness, the barren waste, of her life. She had done nothing, worked at nothing, was responsible for nothing except speaking softly and seeing that she didn't upset her father. There had been Rachel to run the house, Edna to manage the meals, and Justin to see that the bills were paid. There had always been someone to see that life ran smoothly and comfortably. Chip hadn't been too far wrong about her, not that she'd ever admit it to him.

"How did you get the name Chip?" She longed to be friends with him again. It was too wearing to be at loggerheads. She smiled when the word came to mind; it was very appropriate.

He glanced at her. "Why are you smiling? It's logical a lumberman would nickname his son Chip. You know the old saying 'a chip off the old block'? I used to follow my dad around the logging camps; the name came naturally."

"I wasn't smiling because of your name. I'd about figured that out for myself. I was thinking it's much nicer to be friends than to be at loggerheads. I don't know where I got that word from unless I heard my father use it."

"As you might have guessed, the term is a common one here for describing a disagreement. But it's also used in marine biology. A loggerhead is a very large carnivorous turtle."

"Are you interested in marine biology?"

"Only mildly. I'm too wrapped up in the lumber business and a few other projects I have going to branch out with another interest."

"It must be a very satisfying life," she said quietly.

"It has its moments—and its drawbacks—just like everything else." The road was steep and winding, and Chip concentrated on driving and didn't speak until it straightened out again. "What do you plan to do when you return to Chicago?"

"I haven't decided. I'm trying my wings, you know."

She hadn't meant the sad note to creep into her voice, but it had.

"Yes, I know. Just be careful and don't get your wings scorched, little butterfly." His grin was so charming she could do nothing but smile back at him.

As they approached Aaronville she slipped the diamond-studded watch and the earrings into her handbag. There had been an imperceptible change in her thinking since she'd met this man.

CHAPTER FIVE

THE DUST-COVERED ROAD to Aaronville seemed infinitely shorter than it had the previous day when she'd driven over it with Tom MacMadden. Still, it was full of hills and curves, and Margaret was relieved when it finally began to flatten out into the valley and she could see the town stretched ahead. Houses were scattered at intervals on both sides of the road, each with its own neat garden displaying orange pumpkins amid the drying vines, huge stacks of firewood, and wood smoke curling from cobblestone chimneys.

Chip turned the car down a side street before they reached the business district, traveled down what appeared to be a little-used road, and swung into an alley behind a store. He parked the car in an area reserved for loading and cut the motor.

"We can go in the back door and get you fixed up with some clothes that won't make you look quite so conspicuous." He looked at her as if expecting an argument, and his expression told her he was ready to overrule any protest she might make.

She acquiesced. "Okay. This is your territory, so we'll play it your way."

"Good girl. C'mon." He smiled with his eyes as well as his mouth. There was charm in his face again, and Margaret felt herself responding to it.

The back of the building was dark and piled from floor to ceiling with cardboard boxes. Chip reached for Margaret's hand and led her through the stack of merchandise. As they came in out of the direct sunlight the room seemed incredibly dark to Margaret, and she followed closely along behind Chip. She hooked her toe on a box and stumbled. His grip on her hand tightened.

"Hold it! Am I going too fast?" He turned and slipped his hand through her arm, gripping her waist.

"I'm as blind as a bat in the dark," Margaret murmured.

"I'll have to remember that." His soft laughter made her laugh back, although she wasn't quite sure what he'd meant.

Chip pushed open a swinging door, and they entered a store unlike anything Margaret had ever seen before. The counters and tables were piled high with work clothes of all kinds. The aisles were narrow, and Chip had to release her arm so they could walk single file to the front of the store.

"Hi, Roy."

"Hi, Chip. How ya doin'?"

"Fine. Dottie around?"

"Sure I am. I'm hiding behind this stack of coveralls." A small, plump woman with short curly hair and a bright smile emerged from behind a center table.

"Hello, Dottie. I want you to meet Maggie." Was that

pride in his voice? He put his arm around Margaret. "Darling, these are a couple of my best friends, Dottie and Roy Lemon."

Margaret held out her hand. "It's nice to meet you," she murmured.

"Same here. We were wondering when this devil was going to bring you in to meet us." Dottie looked up at Chip fondly.

"Maggie needs some clothes, Dottie. She brought all the wrong things because I forgot to tell her to bring outdoor clothing. Fix her up with some jeans and shirts, boots, socks, and a warm mackinaw." He still had his arm tightly about Margaret, as if he were reluctant to let her leave his side.

"Sure thing. Come on, Maggie. There's nothing I like better than to run up a bill on Chip."

"Oh, no! I'll pay for my things."

Chip took her purse from her hand. "They don't take credit cards here, sweetheart."

"Yes, they do. The sign beside the cash register says so."

"Not yours," Chip said firmly. "Run along with Dottie. Or would you rather I helped you?" He grinned down at her, but his eyes were not smiling.

When Margaret came out of the cubbyhole of a dressing room she found Chip waiting with Dottie. She paused, uncertain, while he eyed her critically. The jeans were a little big at the waist, but otherwise they fit perfectly. The soft cotton shirt with the snap fasteners was tucked smoothly into the waistband.

"Now that's more like it." Chip reached for her hand and fastened the cuffs of the shirt, then inserted his finger into the waistband of the jeans. "You need a belt. How do they feel?"

Margaret looked up at him. He seemed taller than ever because she had left her shoes in the dressing room, but his eyes were warm. "They're a little stiff," she admitted; "I'm sure they'll be okay after they're washed a few times." She tossed him a teasing glance.

He was standing very close, and he bent toward her and murmured in her ear, "Sure. I'll wash them for you like you did mine."

It was the kind of patter that passed between people who had known each other a long time, Margaret reflected. She tilted her face up to his and felt more alive than she ever had before. This sweet, comfortable familiarity was like heady wine.

"I want a shirt like yours." She ran her fingertips over the soft flannel. "And some boots like Beth had on this morning."

"She's running up the bill on me, Dottie. Oh, well, I'm a sucker for a pretty face."

When they left the store Margaret was wearing jeans, a green cotton shirt Chip had insisted she buy, and comfortable rubber-soled running shoes, and she was carrying a red and black checked mackinaw similar to Chip's. The Jourdan suit was stuffed into a brown paper sack.

Chip tossed the bundle containing her new wardrobe into the backseat of the car. They had bought sweatshirts, calf-high boots, more jeans and shirts, and at the last minute Chip had added a long flannel nightgown and fleece-lined slippers to the pile.

"Okay. Now let's get something to eat."

Margaret dug into her purse for a comb. "I look a mess

after trying on those clothes." She combed through the soft waves brushing her cheeks, then smoothed her bangs.

Chip grinned at her. "Some mess. Look at yourself." He tilted the rearview mirror so she could see.

"I don't have on any lipstick, and I forgot to bring it," she moaned.

"Good. You don't need any."

They drove slowly down the main street until they found a place to park, and Chip angled the car in facing the curb.

"Saturday is a big shopping day here," he explained. "Friday is payday at the mill."

"I thought the mill ran on Saturdays during the busy season."

"We've shut it down to just Saturday mornings now. By this afternoon the town, especially the bars, will be full. C'mon. This place is known for its homemade pie."

They met on the sidewalk in front of the car, and Chip tucked her hand in his. By now it was a familiar gesture, and Margaret's fingers found spaces between his. Several people gave Chip a friendly greeting and eyed Margaret with interest.

The diner they entered was small, with a row of booths down one side and a counter with low barstools down the other. The window was full of green plants, and a vine growing in a large pot reached the ceiling by way of a small lattice. The woman behind the counter was blond, middle-aged, and pleasant. She greeted Chip with easy familiarity, extending a friendly acknowledgment in Margaret's direction.

Chip led Margaret to a booth. "This place will be loaded in another half hour."

"What'll you have, Chip?" The blond woman set two cups and a thermos pitcher of coffee onto the table. Her eyes darted from Chip to Margaret.

"This is Maggie, Donna. She's here to visit for a while. I'm showing her the sights."

"That won't take long," Donna said, rolling her eyes heavenward. "If you bat your eyes when you go through this town you'll miss it altogether."

Margaret was uncertain whether she should offer her hand. She hadn't expected to be introduced to a waitress. Chip, for all his status as the man who supplied most of the jobs in the area, was certainly on familiar terms with the people who lived here.

"Give us a couple of tenderloin sandwiches and a slice of your famous apple pie, Donna." He reached across and covered Margaret's hand with his. "Okay with you, sweetheart?"

Margaret nodded while butterflies of happiness danced in her stomach. She saw the woman raise her brows. Chip was clearly announcing that she was more than a casual friend here for a visit. Even if it was just a subterfuge to protect her identity, this sense of belonging to Chip was the most sensuous, lovely feeling she'd ever experienced. She immediately felt a moment's remorse as Justin's face flashed before her eyes.

"Like that, is it? Well, it's about time, Chip Thorn. You've driven all the unattached females between fifteen and forty wild for too many years now. It's time you picked one and put the others out of their misery."

"If that's the case, how come you haven't been giving

me the come-on?" That irresistible charm spread over his face again, and Margaret's eyes couldn't leave it.

"Honey, if I weren't more than five years on the top side of forty, you'd not've had a chance. I'd have been after you like a coon dog on a hot trail." She flounced away, giving Margaret a wink over her shoulder.

"I can't get over the fact that everyone knows you so well." Margaret had allowed her hand to rest beneath his while the waitress was at the table. Now that there was no longer an excuse, she slid it into her lap.

"You mean you're surprised because everybody calls me Chip instead of Mr. Thorn and no one stands at attention when I walk by?"

"No, I didn't mean that. From what I've learned, the company is the principal employer in this area, and these people look to you for their jobs." She knew she was on shaky ground, and she wished she hadn't brought up the subject.

"That's true. If Anthony/Thorn folded, this place would be a ghost town in a couple of years. I don't intend for that to happen, and the people know it." He studied her for a moment. "Are you wanting to sell your shares and wash your hands of this puny operation?"

"No!" The denial came without hesitation, and something inside her contracted with hurt. She didn't want to talk about the mill today. There would be time enough for that next week when she visited it.

"When is Dolly coming home?" Donna slid a basket containing a giant sandwich in front of each of them.

"Monday or Tuesday. Arlene Rogers took Penny over to Kalispell today. We'll know for sure when she brings her back tomorrow."

"Arlene Rogers? Humph!"

Margaret looked quickly at Chip to see his reaction to Donna's grunt of disgust, but he was spreading mustard on his sandwich, his face expressionless.

"Before you go, I'm going to sell you some tickets to the dance tonight," Donna announced when she returned with the catsup bottle. "The V.F.W. is having a benefit for the Secorys, who were burned out last week. Betty and the kids have moved in with her sister, and Larry is out at the place trying to clear a spot to put up another house. How many tickets do you want?"

"A hundred," Chip replied calmly.

"I thought you would," Donna remarked just as matter-of-factly. "Ought to take your girl to the dance. If she can survive that, she's tough enough to winter with."

"Want to go, honey?" Chip's eyes twinkled at her, and Margaret carefully placed the large bun in the basket to hide her confusion.

"I didn't bring anything to wear to a dance."

"Oh, you don't dress up at *our* dances," Donna said quickly. "It's a square dance. Most everyone wears cotton skirts, some wear jeans—the ones that have the little behinds and look cute in them," she said with a forlorn shake of her head.

"We'll buy a skirt if you want to go." Blue eyes met hers with a definite challenge in their depths.

"I always get me a dance with this gorgeous hunk. You'd not cheat me out of that, would you?" The woman placed her hand on Chip's shoulder, but her smiling eyes were on Margaret.

"I certainly wouldn't want to do that. I suppose I'll have to stand in line to get a dance with this gorgeous hunk myself," Margaret teased, and she was delighted to see Chip squirm a little in his seat.

"That settles it. I'll get your pie."

The pie was an enormously thick wedge of crispy pastry oozing fruit and topped with vanilla ice cream. Margaret agreed it was delicious, but after the sandwich she was able to take only a few bites. Chip finished his and reached for hers.

The diner was filling rapidly by the time they were ready to leave. Chip answered greetings as they waited beside the cash register to pay the bill. Margaret was conscious of the speculation in the looks she was receiving and she was acutely aware of the fact that Chip's proprietary attitude toward her was creating the impression that they were far more than friends.

"Let's go over to the office," Chip suggested when they reached the sidewalk. "It's only a few blocks; we can walk." Again he took her hand, dwarfing it in his palm, and they strolled down the street past shops, bars, eating places, and a brand new bank. They took their time, looking into store windows. The sign in one said: YOU'LL NEVER GET A LEMON AT LEMON'S.

Margaret tugged on Chip's hand to stop him. "This is where we bought my clothes. It looks different from the front. Do they sell skirts here?"

"Maybe. We'll take a look after we've been to the office." He squeezed her fingers. She looked up and lost herself in his smiling blue eyes.

The square brick building sat at the end of the street. It was unadorned except for a small bronze plaque that read: ANTHONY/THORN. Chip unlocked the door, and they walked into a tastefully furnished reception area. He led her through a hallway and into his private office.

"Sit down if you like, or look around. I've got a few things to do."

"Is this where you work?" She looked at the large desk, the leather swivel chair, and the framed map on the wall studded with different colored flag pins.

"Part of the time. We have a very capable office staff, so I spend most of my time out in the field. The blue shaded area on the map is the area we're working this year. The green is next year's, and the orange the year after that. The flags with the *C* are logging camps, the *E* flags are equipment stations, and so on. Next week I'll take you out to one of the camps. You might as well see the whole show while you're here."

"I'd like that," she murmured.

While Chip sat at the desk and thumbed through some documents, Margaret wandered out into the hall and looked into the other offices. The telephone on one of the desks reminded her that she should call Rachel. She sat down and dialed the number. After a few rings Rachel was on the phone.

"Margaret? Are you all right?"

"Of course I am! I wanted to let you know that I arrived safely. Mr. Thorn is showing me around this morning. We're in the company office in Aaronville."

"Aaronville? Oh dear! Well . . ." she said hesitantly, "the country must be lovely there this time of year. Where are you staying, dear? How can I get in touch with you without going through the office?"

"I'm staying out near the mill. The company owns a house there. Don't call me at the office, Rachel. It would be awkward. I still don't want anyone here to know who I am. They're very curious about strangers as it is. Chip . . . Mr. Thorn . . . has introduced me as . . . a friend."

"Are you feeling a bit more confident about being on your own?"

"It's strange, but I do. Mr. Thorn inspires confidence. Sometimes I find it hard to believe I'm really here. I should have done this five or six years ago."

"Yes, and I feel bad that I couldn't convince Edward to let you live your own life."

"I'll never regret those years, Rachel. It gave Daddy peace of mind having me there, and . . . I knew I was loved. Oh, by the way, there's a man here who knows who I am. Mr. Thorn had an emergency and couldn't meet the plane, so he sent a man named Tom MacMadden. Mr. Thorn said he'd figure out who I was anyway, so he might as well be in on the secret from the beginning. If you need to reach me and all else fails, you can contact him." There was silence on the other end of the line. "Rachel? Are you there?"

"Yes, dear. I heard you. What did you think of Mr. MacMadden?"

"He's nice. A real earthy, independent type of man. He seemed put out when I asked if he worked for the mill."

"Well, I doubt if I'll need to contact him. Give me the number at the house where you're staying, and I'll call there if I need you. Of course, you could call me every few days."

"I'll do that anyway. Hold on for a minute and I'll get the number from Chip." Margaret punched the button to put the phone on hold and went into Chip's office.

The big chair at the desk was empty. A quick glance told her he wasn't in the room. She stood beside the door and looked down the hall. The building was quiet. Was he in the men's room? She waited a minute, then walked quickly toward the front foyer, a nervous flutter in her stomach.

Margaret stepped into the room and felt her heart jump into her throat. A man, a big man with a black beard, was coming toward the door. He was less than a couple of yards away, and he stopped short when he saw her. She stood riveted to the floor, her hand raised in horror to her mouth, and watched the man reach for her. Then, terror-stricken, she turned blindly and ran.

"Chip! Chip!" she shrieked.

Miraculously he was there at the end of the hall, a haven—safety! Desperate, Margaret stumbled toward him and threw herself into his embrace. She wrapped her arms about his waist and buried her face against his chest. His arms enfolded her.

"What the hell? Maggie?"

Margaret glanced over her shoulder to see the big man standing at the end of the hall, his palms raised and a look of puzzlement on his face. She burst into tears.

"Did Boomy frighten you? I'll admit he looks like a bear, but he's harmless. He works here on our electronic equipment."

Margaret barely heard the words over her racking sobs. Humiliation replaced fright. Once again she'd made a fool of herself, and of course Chip had to witness it.

"I'm sorry." The tears were pouring down her face, and she was desperately trying to control her voice. "I couldn't find you and . . . then he was there."

"You were talking on the phone, so I went back to the storage room. Now don't cry." His hands moved up and down her back, and he held her protectively close.

"I was talking to Rachel Riley. She wanted the number at the house so she could call me." She choked back her hysteria, knowing she was going to have to lift her face and look at him.

"Is she still on the phone?" he asked patiently.

"Yes. I put it on hold." She drew away from him and glanced down the hall. It was empty. "She'll wonder what's happened."

"C'mon. I'll talk to her." He frowned, then smiled. "I'll have to ask Boomy to come around more often."

They went back into his office, and Margaret plucked a couple of tissues from a packet on the shelf and wiped her eyes. Chip picked up the phone.

"Miss Riley, this is Chip Thorn." His voice was abrupt, businesslike. "No, there's nothing wrong. Margaret couldn't find me. I'd gone to the storage room." He listened for a moment. "I don't think it would be wise for you to call her there. The phone is on a seven-party line. If you feel you must get in touch with her, you can call me here at the office. I'll know the call is really for her, and I'll have her call you back." He swiveled in the chair, and Margaret couldn't see his face, but his voice held a note of impatience. She was feeling too wretched to wonder why.

Chip put his hand over the mouthpiece. "Do you want to speak to her again?" He looked at her intently. She nodded, and he handed her the phone.

"I'm back, Rachel," she said in her brightest tone. "I'll call again soon." She glanced at Chip, whose eyes had iced over like a winter frost. "I love you, too. 'Bye." She replaced the phone carefully, not wanting to look at Chip, who was still watching her very closely.

"You think I'm paranoid, don't you." She looked away from him to some distant spot behind his head, but she could still see his face. Instinctively she knew she would always see his face; it would be forever etched in her mind.

The softness of his voice brought her eyes back to his. "Are you?"

"Yes." The whispered word was an admission she hadn't even made to herself before.

Chip got up from the chair and moved around the desk. His hands found her shoulders, and his thumbs made little circling movements in the hollows beside her collarbone.

"The first step in solving a problem is admitting you've got one," he said reassuringly to the top of her head.

Her eyes fastened on a spot at the base of his throat. She found herself tongue-tied. Her mind went blank, and she couldn't think of anything to say. It seemed quite natural to rest her forehead against the spot she had looked at so intently. They stood silently until they heard a door closing in another part of the building. Chip moved away from her, but he slid a hand down her arm to clasp hers.

"Come and meet Boomy."

The large, black-bearded man insisted on taking the blame for frightening her.

"I'm sure sorry I scared you. I didn't see Chip's car, and my first thought was that someone had broken into the office. You were as much of a surprise to me as I was to you."

"I panicked. My only excuse is that in the city we keep three locks on every door." Margaret decided she liked Boomy. He was big and woolly, but soft and gentle, like a teddy bear.

"I know about that. I lived in Washington, D.C., for several years. This is the best place to live and raise kids. I suppose even this place will fill up eventually, and we'll all put three locks on the doors, but for now my wife and I are enjoying it. I'd like you to meet her sometime."

"I'd like that." Her fingers curled tightly around Chip's. She welcomed his confidence, his self-assurance.

"We'll be at the benefit dance tonight. Maybe we'll see you there." Chip's fingers spread against Margaret's rib cage and urged her to the door. "C'mon, sweetheart, let's see if we can find you a party dress."

Her heart brightened and she looked up at him with merry devilment. "Does that mean I can run up the bill?"

The warm blue eyes were amused, the whisper a husky caress. "Sure. But you'll have to suffer the consequences."

CHAPTER SIX

FEELING SOMEWHAT LIKE a sixteen-year-old getting ready for her first date, Margaret dressed for the evening out with Chip. She had chosen a full, dark cotton skirt from a rack in the store. It had a deep ruffle edged with eyelet lace on the bottom, and Chip had insisted she buy a simple, emerald-green blouse to go with it. She carefully applied her makeup, turned her hair under with the electric curling iron, and stared at herself in the mirror over the bathroom sink. Was that young-looking person really she? Wrinkling her nose, she gave herself a big smile. "Calm down, Margaret Anthony," she said to the starry-eyed reflection. "You're acting like a kid on Christmas morning!"

But there was no way she could heed her own advice when she pivoted for Chip's inspection. "Will I do?" Her voice quivered a little in spite of her attempt at control.

"You'll more than do!"

"You don't look so bad yourself," she flirted. Her eyes moved over his polished boots, pressed jeans, snap-fastened shirt, and the kerchief tied about his throat. "You had more jeans?" she asked innocently.

"Later we're going to have a talk about that," he said threateningly, and without further comment he ushered her to the door.

Margaret's high spirits had given way to nervousness by the time Chip parked the car—a heavy sedan this time with soft leather seats. They walked the block to the V.F.W. hall which was brightly lit and resounding with music.

The man at the door took their tickets and greeted them warmly. "Hi, Chip. We've got a good crowd already."

They went inside, and Margaret looked around with amazement. It was a scene from the musical *Oklahoma!* A caller was in full swing, naming the steps to the music played by a band rigged out in true country-western fashion: fringed, sequined shirts and cowboy hats sporting a variety of feathers. Three groups of dancers were on the floor, foot-tapping and sashaying vigorously. Wooden folding chairs were spaced along the walls, and at the far end, under the American flag, a long table groaned with the weight of the food spread over its surface.

They stood just inside the door while Margaret scanned the room. She stayed close to Chip, both hands clutching his arm while he exchanged greetings with people who called out to him.

"Well, what do you think?"

Margaret raised her gaze to see Chip watching her with a quirk of a smile that spread to an indulgent grin. His eyes, full of unmistakable admiration, caught and held hers. She felt a warm glow of happiness start in her knees and work its way up. At that moment they were the only two people in the world as far as she was concerned. She stared, her lips slightly parted. Someone jostled her, and she looked away and let her hands fall to her sides.

"I didn't realize I was holding on to you so tightly."

"Who's complaining?" He caught her hand, drew it into the crook of his arm, and covered it with his. She looked up, unable to keep her eyes from his, and she lost her heart in the blue depths while her insides melted like a snowball on the Fourth of July.

"What do you think?" he repeated.

"I never imagined anything like this. Everyone seems to be having such a good time."

Chip laughed down at her. "They'll have a better time as the evening wears on."

The three groups of dancers dissolved into couples when a violin player stepped to the microphone and began playing a waltz. The lights were lowered, and a revolving spotlight cast beams of colored light across the ceiling.

Chip didn't ask her to dance; he simply drew her into his arms and moved out onto the floor. Despite his height, he was lithe and graceful, moving slowly, allowing her time to adjust to his lead. Margaret had always loved to dance, but she'd found precious few opportunities to do so—except for the stuffy social affairs she'd attended with Justin. She idly wondered if he had enjoyed those galas and benefits any more than she had.

She relaxed against Chip, and he responded by drawing her closer still. His steady heartbeat against hers and the warmth of his utterly masculine body was a powerful stimulant to her already heightened senses. Here on the dance floor they fit together perfectly. Heedless of the consequences, she pressed herself to him, her eyes half closed. Her lips parted with pleasure as she felt him nuzzling her hair.

"I was waltzing with my darling, to the Tenn-e-ssee waltz . . . ," he sang softly into her ear. His hand moved lower on her back, and his arm tightened.

Margaret was throbbingly aware of his hand, his lips, his warm breath, his soft crooning voice, and the scent of his soap-clean skin enveloping her. She felt as if her body had merged with his, and when he embraced her with both arms, she let hers slide around him and rested her face in the curve of his neck. When the music stopped, the lights came on and she looked up in surprise, blinking into the blue eyes that smiled down at her. Chip perceptibly tightened his arms before he slackened them to let her move away.

"You're nice to hold, Maggie Anderson." His hands moved down her arms to clasp hers.

"You too," she murmured, not really caring that she was looking at him with glazed, desire-filled eyes.

"Hi, Chip. Hi, Maggie." They had stopped near the buffet table, where Donna, the waitress from the diner, was slicing a huge chocolate cake.

"Where did all this food come from?" Margaret asked.

"Everybody contributes something," Donna explained. "I baked this cake."

Margaret looked quickly at Chip. "Shouldn't we have brought something?"

"Sakes alive—no!" Donna sputtered. "With Chip's help the fund's gone over two thousand. That and the insurance will give the Secorys a good start again. You just have yourself a great time. But hold on to your man. There's at least a dozen women out there just waitin' for you to turn loose of him."

Margaret's eyes went wide with innocence. "Really? I didn't think anyone would have him but me. And that's only because I'm a stranger and don't know anyone else."

Donna let go with a peal of laughter, and Chip's fingers found their way to Margaret's rib cage and pinched her.

"She's hard enough to handle without any help from you, Donna." He looked into Margaret's laughter-filled eyes. "If you're not careful, I just might leave you to walk home, my girl." He must have seen the quick look of apprehension cross her face, for he quickly added, "But on second thought, I may need someone to help me push the car out of a mud hole if it rains."

Not waiting for a response, he spun her toward the dance floor as the caller announced the next number. "This is a simple one, Maggie. Let's join in."

"I don't think I can do it," she protested with mild alarm. Unheeding, he drew her along.

"Sure you can. I'll help you, and so will the others." He swung her out onto the floor and in among the nearest group, placing her in the center, with one hand holding hers, the other at her waist. The steps were simple enough, and repetitive. After she got over her fear the first time his hand left hers and she was on her own, she began to enjoy herself. The others in the set gave friendly assistance, and she responded with smiles of pure pleasure.

"I never thought I'd find myself actually square dancing," she exclaimed with enthusiasm when the music ended.

"And very well, too." Chip raised his brows questioningly when the music started again. "Want to try another?"

The smile that had been continually curving her lips spread. "Why not?"

As Chip had predicted, the dancers became more rowdy as the evening progressed. By the time the buffet was served, the hall was full and overflowing into the bar next door where the drinks were available.

Once Margaret was whisked away by a bearded lumberjack who thought it an accomplishment to have stolen the boss's girl for a dance. Her eyes clung to Chip as she was propelled about the room by the young giant. When the dance was over, he was there, and she reached for him like a lifeline in a storm.

"Shall we go?" he murmured, his lips close to her ear. "From now on it'll only get more and more boisterous."

She nodded eagerly, and they made their way through the jostling crowd to the door of the room where Chip had left his coat and the woolen shawl he'd borrowed from Dolly's room for Margaret to wear.

On the way to the car they didn't talk. The air was crisp and cool, the moon clear and bright. Margaret knew she had acted young and naïve and was afraid to guess what Chip must be thinking. Instead she simply allowed herself to feel his arm about her, guiding her along the dark street.

"Hungry?" he asked when they were inside the car.

"Not really. Are you?"

"No. Shall we go home then?"

She nodded, watching him in the flashing lights of a passing car. His face was turned toward her as he inserted the key to start the car. It was incredible that a twenty-four hour period could have affected her life so drastically.

"What are you thinking while those great, green eyes are looking holes through me?" His voice came softly out of the darkness over the soft purr of the engine.

"What were *you* thinking?" she asked, unwilling to answer his question.

"I was thinking that you have the most beautiful eyes I've ever seen." With one hand he reached out and pulled a strand of hair from under the shawl.

"Thank you." She was suddenly flustered at this turn in the conversation, but absurdly pleased by the compliment. Her gaze swept the shadowed outline of his face and saw his eyes gleaming at her through the darkness.

"Move over." His hand was on her knee. "Closer," he commanded softly after she moved a few inches toward him. She moved again, and he adjusted his own position until their shoulders were touching and her hip and thigh fit snugly along the length of his. "That's better." He shifted the gears and put the car into motion.

After they had driven only a few blocks, the lights of the town were left behind. Margaret looked straight ahead at the tree-lined road, glancing covertly from time to time at Chip's hands, strong and brown on the wheel. He flipped on the radio, and they drove with only the sound of soft classical music filling the moonlit silence of the night.

Margaret willed herself to remember that she had only known this man since yesterday. No, she reasoned, she had known him since that long-ago day he had looked up at her from the foyer below. He placed his hand in her lap, interrupting her thoughts. Without hesitation she pressed her palm against his, and his fingers entwined with hers.

"I like holding your hand, Maggie Anderson."

Margaret felt a small stab of disappointment. *Maggie Anderson.* He didn't want to think of her as Margaret Anthony. He wouldn't want to hold Margaret Anthony's hand. She pushed the negative thought aside, wanting nothing to spoil this ethereal moment. For the rest of the drive she hovered against his masculine strength in a dreamlike state. He briefly released her hand to adjust the heater, then blindly sought it again. She clasped it and laced her fingers through his.

At the house he drove straight to the garage, parked, and turned off the lights. The darkness was absolute. Margaret closed her eyes briefly, and when she opened them there was no difference. He was still tightly holding her hand. She loosened her fingers, and as his palm slid from hers she leaned away from his shoulder. He shifted sideways as his arm arched over her head.

"Is your heart beating as fast as mine?" His hand was on her shoulder, his voice low and full.

"I don't know." The uneven rhythm of her breathing was making speech difficult.

He found her hand and brought it inside his jacket, holding it over his heart. The steady pounding against her palm vibrated up her arm and into her chest, where her own heart picked up speed.

"Doesn't it always beat like that?" she whispered.

He touched a light kiss to her eyelids, and the soft

brush of his mustache was both sensuous and distracting. "Only when I've run five miles . . . and when I'm aching to kiss a pretty girl." His hand on her shoulder was gently insistent, his lips skimming her cheek. "I want to kiss Maggie Anderson." His voice was a low, husky murmur. "I'm afraid when I take you into the house you'll be Margaret Anthony again."

"You wouldn't want to kiss Margaret Anthony?" The magic was slowly fading.

"I don't know Margaret Anthony, but I know Maggie. She's sweet, wholesome, unpretentious—"

"Don't forget naïve, vulnerable and . . . paranoid," she interrupted.

"Okay. Naïve and vulnerable, but refreshing and fun to be with."

He moved his lips from her cheek, and she knew they were coming to meet hers even before she felt their touch. Slowly, deliberately, his mouth covered hers, pressing gently at first while he guided her arms up and around his neck and then wrapped her in his. His kiss deepened, and she leaned into it, floating in a sea of sensuality where everything was softly given and softly received. His lips were seeking, and she automatically parted hers in invitation. The touch of his tongue at the corner of her mouth was persuasive rather than demanding, and she gave herself up to the waves of emotion crashing over her.

The soft utterance that came from his throat might almost have been a purr of pure pleasure when, at her unwitting insistence, he expanded the kiss with a pressure that sought deeper satisfaction. The fervor of his passion excited her, and she met it with unrestrained response.

She felt her mind whirl and her nerves become acutely sensitized with the almost overwhelming need to melt into him and ease the ache of her aroused body. Caught in the throes of desire, she pressed herself against him, her arms winding around him with surprising strength.

Resisting the pressure about his neck, Chip lifted his head as if to look at her. His breath came quickly and was cool on her lips made wet by his kiss.

"I've a feeling I shouldn't have done that," he confessed in a raspy whisper. His hand had moved up to the nape of her neck, and his fingers threaded into the hair that tumbled there.

"I didn't ask you to," she protested, trying to collect her scattered senses.

"I know that, sweetheart." His voice was slurred with an obvious effort to control his breathing. "It's the damnedest situation I've ever been in. I should be avoiding you like the plague; and here I am, holding you, kissing you. I must be out of my mind!"

Tears spurted into Margaret's eyes—the result of nerves strung taut by his onslaught on her senses, and her disappointment over his obvious regret at having shared himself with her for that brief moment.

"Why did you kiss me if you feel so guilty about it now?"

"I wanted to kiss you while I was still thinking about you as Maggie," he said candidly.

"Maggie, but not Margaret Anthony," she confirmed tightly. "Is Margaret so terrible?"

"Not terrible, just remote. She's a princess in an ivory tower, who's condescended to visit her subjects. With the stroke of her pen she can buy an ocean liner or an island in the Pacific. She can amuse herself in a small community such as this until she gets bored and flits away to find new and amusing things to do."

"If that's what you think of me, why didn't you just tell me to get lost when I first arrived? Why have you bothered with me?" She despised the tears that flowed onto her cheeks.

"You know the answer to that. Even if I am the trustee, you have a powerful lot of stock. With a good set of lawyers, whom you already employ, you could make things very difficult for us here." He had pulled away slightly, yet his arm was still around her, his hand on her shoulder. He was speaking smoothly, reasonably, with no censure in his voice.

"It was decent of you to go beyond the realm of duty and take me to the dance, but you didn't have to go so far as to act as if you enjoyed it." Hurt was making her voice sharp.

"I didn't have to act—I did enjoy it."

"Then how different are you from Margaret Anthony? You were bored, and you amused yourself with a naïve, stupid woman who has never been out from under the watchful eyes of a paid staff, who has never had lunch in a public diner, who has never gone to a dance that only got more boisterous as the night wore on, who has never been kissed in a dark car after a date . . ." Her traitorous voice betrayed her on the last word. She sat shuddering.

"Maggie, I'm sorry." He tightened his arm, but she remained stiff, her head turned away from him.

"What for? You've a right to your own feelings, just as I've a right to mine."

"I'm still sorry."

"For me? You needn't feel sorry for me until I lose my pen. Then I'll be in real trouble!" She had to sniff. She tried hard to make it a small one, but he heard anyway.

"Damn it, don't cry! It was just something I had to say." His fingers tried to turn her face toward him, and when she held it firmly away, they stroked her cheeks to wipe away the tears.

"Don't!" she exclaimed sharply. "You . . . you . . ."

"I said I was sorry, Maggie. I was only—"

"You . . . popped out my contact!" Her hand grabbed at his wrist.

"You're kidding!"

"No, I'm not. Don't move. It's probably on your hand."

"Holy hell! What'll we do? We'll never find it in the dark."

"Do you have a flashlight?"

"In the glove compartment. Can you reach it? Do you think the damn thing is still on my hand?"

Margaret managed to reach the flashlight and put it into the hand of the arm that was around her. Chip fumbled with the switch and flashed the beam onto his hand. The light played over the long tanned fingers with the clean, well-shaped nails, and the wrist with the fine dark hair that came down to the back of his hand.

"See anything?"

"No, but then I've only got one eye. I'm not seeing too well out of it."

"I think it's gone, princess."

"Don't call me that!" She pushed at his arms. "Let me out of this car. I don't care if we find it or not."

"Hold still!" The light flashed up onto her face when

she moved his arm. "Hold still! It's there on your face, beside your ear." He carefully took the tiny, clear disc between his thumb and forefinger. "What'll I do with it?"

"Give it to me. I'll keep it in my mouth until I get into the house."

"Aren't they more trouble than they're worth?" he queried.

"You're the one who told me to wear them," she said crossly. She plucked the contact from her fingers with her tongue.

"Careful. You might swallow it, and then you'd really be in trouble."

They left the car and walked silently to the house. Chip switched on the light and stepped aside to let her enter ahead of him. She knew he was watching her, but she refused to meet his eyes as she walked past him and through the house to the small, barren bedroom.

"I'll build up the fire. We'll have something hot to drink," he called after her.

CHAPTER SEVEN

"MARGARET ANTHONY, YOU'RE a real loser! What's more, you're an idiot for standing here talking to yourself."

She grimaced at her reflection in the mirror of the medicine cabinet and washed the tear-streaked makeup from her face. She wasn't looking forward to going into the other room, but it was either that or go to bed and lie there wide-eyed and miserable for hours. The house was cold, damned cold. The only warm place was beside the fire.

Margaret slipped her contacts into the soaking solution and reached for her dark-rimmed glasses. For a moment she contemplated telling Chip to arrange her way back to Chicago, but then she remembered his taunts about the princess in the ivory tower. That was what he expected her to do—run. Damned if she would!

The big room was empty but warm. A cheery fire crackled in the hearth. She had braced herself to meet Chip's appraisal and was relieved to have a short reprieve. She grabbed some magazines and curled up on the end of the couch, not caring that her random selection had been *Field and Stream, Woodsman of the North*, and *The American Rifleman.*

She was flipping pages with shaking hands when Chip came into the room carrying two steaming mugs. He set one of them on the table beside the couch.

"Here's something to warm you up—a lumberjack toddy."

"Thank you," she murmured. She turned a page and stared at the colored picture of a flock of birds in flight and a highly polished rifle.

"Do you plan to load your own shells this year?"

"Uh . . . what?" She glanced up at him and automatically pushed her glasses farther back on her nose. "I couldn't shoot an animal if I were starving to death!"

He reached down and took the magazine from her hand. "Then this isn't the reading material for you." He gave her a dry smile. "Have you ever been fishing?"

"Once, in Acapulco. We went out on a boat and Daddy caught a big swordfish. I felt sorry for it and wanted to let it go, but they said it would die anyway because it had been hooked so deeply. We had our picture taken with it, and Daddy had it mounted on a board." She shivered, remembering.

Chip sat down on the couch and stretched his long legs out in front of him, then drew them up and removed first one boot and then the other. He was wearing ragg-wool socks. No wonder he doesn't feel the cold, Margaret thought resentfully.

Glancing at him in a secret, sidelong inspection, she concluded that Chip Thorn was almost unbearably attractive in his snap-fastened plaid shirt and tight jeans. That type of clothing suited him. She wondered vaguely what he'd look like in a business suit. Handsome, she grudgingly decided. He was like a chameleon; he would adapt to any environment or situation. As if becoming aware of her gaze, he slipped an oblique look at her and she turned away. He was something far beyond her comprehension: a man a woman would love or hate but never be indifferent to. It was a shred of comfort to know he had enjoyed kissing her. The blood in her veins raced crazily as memory flashed back to those moments in his arms. She picked up the warm mug and gulped, immediately coughing and groping blindly for a spot on which to set the cup down. It was taken from her hands.

"Easy. That's a pretty strong drink." His hand patted her gently on the back.

"What . . . is . . . it?" she gasped.

"Whiskey, sugar, ginger, and hot water. Sip it slowly and it'll warm you clear to your toes."

"I wanted to be warm, not on fire!" She felt her heated blood begin to gather in her cheeks.

His hand made circles on her back. "You okay? You really are a babe, aren't you, Maggie?"

"If you know so damn much, you tell me!" She was in no mood to be teased.

He smiled into her eyes and pushed her glasses up on her nose. "Smile for me, Maggie. You've got a beautiful smile. Why are you so stingy with it?"

She gave him an overbright smile, showing all her teeth, and she saw the laughter twinkling in his eyes. Before she knew what he was doing, he had lifted her legs up and across his lap and was removing her shoes.

"Hey—what—?" she choked in surprise.

"It's easier to relax with your shoes off. Didn't anyone

ever tell you that?" He slipped the pumps off her feet and gently dropped them to the floor. One hand rested on her ankle, the other on the bottom of her foot. "They're cold!" he said with surprise, and he began to rub her feet and ankles vigorously.

"Of course they're cold. Nylons and open-toed shoes weren't designed for warmth," she snapped, wishing desperately for the strength of mind to blot out the sensuous tingle of his stroking fingers. She swallowed hard and, without thinking, asked, "Why do you live in this barn of a house? It seems to me you'd want to live closer to the office."

It hadn't come out exactly as she'd wanted it to, and he answered defensively.

"What's wrong with it? It may not be what you're used to, but I doubt if there's a house in the state that is." His grip on her feet tightened. The charm had left his face, and his lips twisted sardonically. "In case you haven't noticed, this house is far more comfortable than that of any of our employees."

"How would I have noticed? I've not been in another house. I only know that this one is damned cold." Their eyes met in a piercing glance. She picked up the mug and sipped at the warm drink. It was surprisingly good when taken in small doses.

"You think this is cold? You should be here in January when the temperature gets down to twenty-five below." She looked away from him and tried to swing her feet off his lap, but he held them and continued his massage.

After a few minutes he lifted her legs from his lap, saying, "Why don't I make us another drink?"

A sharp feeling of apprehension struck Margaret as

she watched him leave the room. His very presence was beginning to mean everything to her.

Neither said anything for a long while after he returned with the hot mugs. He put more wood onto the fire, replaced the screen, and sat back in the recliner.

Margaret was feeling more relaxed now. The drink was warming her, as Chip had promised. The soft glow of the lamp behind the couch, the dancing flames in the hearth, and the music coming from the stereo Chip had turned on all added to the feeling of time suspended. She let the music wash over her. It was the score from a romantic movie. She would have guessed he'd prefer country-western. They sat in companionable silence and sipped their toddies. When her cup was empty he took it from her hand, placed it on the table, and sat down beside her on the couch.

"Talk to me, Maggie." His eyes gleamed through half-closed lids, and Margaret felt her heart jump as his appreciative gaze wandered over her face. "You have lovely eyes," he murmured.

"Not as lovely as yours," she said, obeying a totally reckless impulse.

"I can hardly believe you're real," he said huskily, his voice promptly making her heart turn flip-flops. "How could you have come out of that place as sweet as you are?"

"What do you mean?" It seemed to her she was always asking him that.

"Sweet. That's the only word to describe you."

"Are you sure you don't mean—"

He quickly put his fingers over her lips. "I mean sweet. May I have this dance?"

"I'll have to check my dance card," she quipped.

He reached for her glasses and placed them on the table beside her mug. "You won't need these. I like to look into those shining green pools and try to figure out what's going on in that mind of yours."

"I can't see six inches past my nose," she protested.

"I won't be any farther away than that." He smiled at her, a warm, almost loving, smile and pulled her to her feet. She melted into his arms without a trace of nervousness. They moved slowly to the romantic music. He rested his cheek on the top of her head. Margaret was so enchanted by the magic of it all that she was afraid to speak lest the spell be broken. She relaxed against him, oblivious to everything but the feel of his arms encircling her, the hard strength of his hands that lay flat on the taut swell of her hips, pressing her to him with urgent force.

"I don't really like this feeling I have for you," he whispered into her hair, and she wasn't quite sure she'd heard correctly.

"You don't want to like me?" she asked, her heart hammering crazily against his chest.

"No," he whispered huskily. "I was all prepared to dislike old Ed's spoiled darling."

"And now?"

"Not spoiled, but still a darling."

She was slowly losing the ability to think rationally. Her arms encircled his body, glorying in the feel of his hard warmth. "Do you think I may be a little drunk from the whiskey? I should be saying something like 'Unhand me, you cad.'"

"You haven't had enough whiskey to be drunk. So why aren't you kicking and fighting and calling me a seducer of innocent maidens?" His lips were nuzzling her ear, and they felt so good she pressed against them.

"I don't know." She tilted her head back so she could look at him. "Did you ply me with drink so you could seduce me?"

"Uh huh. Are you going to resist me?" There was a teasing glint in his eye.

"I haven't decided," she readily admitted.

He held her tightly in his arms, scarcely moving to the music. "I want to kiss you with your arms about my neck, feel your breasts against me, and hold your hips in my hands. Okay? Then you can decide if you're going to that cold little room or staying with me." He brought his hands around to clasp hers and guide them upward. When they were moving on their own accord he wrapped his arms all the way around her so that his hands rested on the sides of her breasts. "You're a delicious armful, Maggie. Maggie, Maggie, puddin' n' pie, kissed the boys and made them cry."

"That was Georgie Porgie, silly." She laughed softly and, in complete disregard of the common sense that told her she was acting wanton, unrestrained, and foolish, she placed soft little kisses on his neck.

"It's no wonder they cried!"

His fingers lifted her chin, and a sweet, wild enchantment rippled through her veins as his mouth moved over hers with warm urgency. The desire to push her fingers through his hair was irresistible. It was so thick and so soft, like the mustache that had swept across her cheek and was now pressed tightly beneath her nose. Her head was spinning helplessly from the torrent of churning desires racking her body. The intensity of these feelings was strange to her, and she was powerless to control them. The sensations were heightened when his tongue caressed her lips, sought entrance, and found welcome. The male hardness pressed against her was an erotic stimulant, arousing her, taking her over, and making her want the physical gratification of uniting with him in the most intimate way.

"Maggie . . . sweetheart . . . we shouldn't have started this." His crossed arms moved down, and his hands cupped her buttocks, hard.

Caught in a spinning whirlwind of sensuous desire, Margaret was nonetheless aware that his pulse was racing as wildly as hers. She was causing this! His virile, vitally strong body was reacting to hers!

"Why not?" she whispered recklessly.

He stood very still for several seconds as if absorbing her words. Then his lips moved hotly down her cheek in search of hers, found them, and molded them to his in a devastating kiss. Her senses responded with a deep, churning hunger for his touch, and she rose on tiptoe, arching to meet his height, her fingers clinging to his shoulders. Stirred by her incredible arousal, she met his passion with intimate sensuousness and parted her lips to glide the tip of her tongue across the edge of his teeth.

"God! Sweetheart . . . help me stop this while I still can!"

Finding what her body had craved for so long, Margaret ignored the danger signals flashing in her brain and allowed the warmth of his tenderness to wash over her. The world could be ending the next minute and her only concern would be to stay with him, relieve them both of the trembling hunger bedeviling them.

"Don't stop." She moved her hips against him in instinctive invitation.

"Don't tease me!" he whispered harshly. "I'm not a man to be teased!" His lips raked her face from cheek to chin.

"I'm not teasing!" she moaned desperately, afraid that he was going to move away from her.

"I'll not be satisfied with just playing. It's everything or nothing!" he whispered raggedly.

She burrowed her face against the warmth of his neck. "I know," she whispered back. "Love me, Chip."

Her hushed request seemed to act as a potent aphrodisiac, and his body responded with violent trembling. He pulled her roughly against his hard arousal, as if to leave her no doubt that he was desperate for relief. "You're sure?"

"Please!"

"Oh, sweetheart . . ."

It was only a couple of steps to the couch. Chip's arms left her to lift the seat, take a blanket from the storage space, and flip the back of the couch down to make a small bed. Margaret stood with her back to him, worried by her lack of sexual experience and racked with the violence of her own need for him to make love to her. Her eyes were wide open, staring at nothing, when she heard the click of the lamp switch and realized the room was now lighted only by the fire.

Arms encircled her from behind, and warm lips and a soft mustache nuzzled the sensitive spot below her ear. His hands moved to cup her breasts, squeezing them gently.

"You're the most utterly feminine woman I've ever

met." She closed her eyes and let the soft purr of his voice and the feel of his hands consume her. "I think you've be-witched me. I seem to have lost control where you're concerned. My head says stay away from you, but my hands want to know every soft curve of your body. Mag-gie . . . Maggie . . . come quench this thirst I have for you." One hand moved down to pull her tightly back against him.

His persuasive whisper, the touch of his hands, called out to something deeply feminine in her, and the explo-sion of sensation choked off her voice. His fingers worked at the waistband of her full skirt, then the zipper, and he moved back so that the fabric could fall to the floor. He lifted the loose blouse up and over her head and turned her in his arms. Lace bra, briefs, and pantyhose were all that covered her. She kept her eyes closed, rev-eling in the glory of his touch.

"You're beautiful, sweet Maggie. Small, perfect, and beautiful." He blew gently into her ear, kissed her temple, and stroked her back with hard palms. "I get the feeling you haven't done this before . . . and yet you couldn't have reached the age of twenty-five and not have," he murmured hoarsely.

"No," she breathed. "I couldn't have."

"Who was it? No, don't tell me. I don't want to know!"

She lifted her face, and their eyes locked for a long moment before he reached out and unfastened her bra. He swept the straps from her shoulders and moved a fraction away from her. The lacy cups remained curved about her upthrust breasts. Slowly he peeled them away and looked at the white skin tipped with dusky rose. In the flickering firelight he shaped his hands to cup her breasts, and she looked down to see sun-browned fingers moving seductively over her sensitive nipples. A tremor pulsated across her nerve endings, and she pressed her breasts into his hands. Her breath came in small gasps, and her eyes sought his.

He stepped back for a moment, and her body felt bereft without his touch. It seemed to take an eternity for him to strip to his shorts, and crazily she found herself wondering if they were the same ones she had folded so carefully from the dryer. His hands reached for her again and pulled her to him.

His shoulders were wide and powerful, his chest smooth except for a sprinkling of dark hairs in the center. It felt pleasantly rough against her breasts. His waist was narrow, and there was not an ounce of extra flesh on his flat stomach. Free of shame and embarrassment, she ran her palms over his body, from the hollow beneath his armpits to the elastic at the top of his shorts, around and over his back. He stood still, his head tilted down toward hers. She pulled away and smiled up at him, her lips parted with the pleasure of touching him. She saw his nostrils flare with a quick intake of breath when her fingertips moved lightly down to his navel. Her eyes followed her fingers, and instead of being frightened by the obvious arousal they encountered, she exulted in her power to excite this man of her hidden dreams. She raised her eyes to his and saw the smoldering desire he was holding tightly in check.

"I want to know all of you," she whispered.

He hooked his two index fingers into the top of her pantyhose and began to work them down over her hips.

Forgotten was the coldness of the room as the smoky look in his eyes and the intimate touch of his fingers heated her blood. She watched his face, her chin tilted almost fearlessly, as joyous thoughts whirled and flitted through her mind. This is the most precious moment of my life . . . I'll have this much of him to remember forever . . . for this small space in time I'm all he wants . . . me, Margaret Anthony. Oh, God, help me to make him want me with him always!

She felt a lightness, a sweetness, and a rightness when he lowered her to the couch and pulled the blanket up over them. She gave a shiver of pure pleasure.

"Are you cold?" he asked solicitously. His arm moved beneath her head and he gathered her to him, holding her naked length against his.

"No. But . . ." She clutched him tightly, her hands biting into the warm, solid flesh of his back.

"But what? You can't have doubts now," he moaned hoarsely against her cheek. "It would kill me to stop." He pulled her even closer to him.

"Not that, darling!" Her hand moved to his face, and she pressed her palm to his cheek. "It's just that . . . this has been amazingly easy for you, hasn't it?"

A low protest came from his throat. "Don't think of that! I want, you want . . . I've never wanted a woman as much as I want you!" His broad hand moved down her spine, found her taut buttocks, and pressed hard. The evidence of his need was captured against her.

The feel of his body, the stroking of his hands, the warm moistness of his breath, the love filling and spilling from her heart, erased the last shred of her inhibitions, and with a soft cry she gave herself up to the sweet abandonment he was urging upon her, telling herself that no matter what happened in the morning, she would have this night to remember always.

Their mouths met and were no longer gentle. They kissed deeply, hungrily. His hand found her breast, cupped and lifted it. And then his lips were on her nipple, setting off small explosions deep within her. Each stroke of his tongue and brush of his mustache caused her to melt with mindless pleasure. Her own fingers curled feverishly into the solid muscle of his back, and her lips made forays against his neck.

His hand moved down over her stomach, and his fingers toyed with the soft curls. She welcomed the gentle fingers with parted thighs and an urgency that incited him to lift his mouth to hers in a kiss that stripped away everything but the need to assuage the ache building to unbearable heights within her.

"Now? Darling . . . now?" He slid smoothly over her body, seeking entrance while she waited in rapt and aching anguish. Everything he did felt so good and right that she was caught up in overpowering desire and the need for physical release. She pressed herself to him, her arms winding tightly around his neck.

His hips made a sudden jerking motion, paused, and then lifted from her. His trembling body lay heavily upon hers, and he gulped air frantically.

"Lord! Maggie, why didn't you tell me?" His chest heaved as he attempted to control his breathing. "This is your first time!" he said accusingly.

"I can't help that! Don't stop!" she pleaded, her need for him overcoming all the other emotions that ran the gamut from embarrassment to pride.

"I thought . . . I thought . . ."

"I chose you! I want it to be you!" Her hands feverishly clung to him, holding him tightly while she rained fervent kisses on his cheek and throat.

Chip raised his head, his eyes searching her passion-clouded ones, and then with a muttered whisper he closed his arms about her in fierce demand.

There was no room for fear or regret as he entered her, reverently guiding her to accept the gently rhythmic sliding. The pain-pleasure of their joining would be forever imprinted in her memory. She was part of this man. He was the universe, vibrating with all the love in the world, and he was lifting her to undreamed of sensual heights. She no longer wanted him to be gentle as her need rose to meet his. They reached the top of the mountain together in cataclysm of pleasure that left her trembling in his arms as they exchanged soft, moaning kisses and their bodies melted together in the aftermath of heated sensation.

Chip's damp skin tasted salty against her tongue, and the woodsy odor of him tantalized her nostrils as her fingers clutched the blanket to bring it up and over his shoulders. She cradled him in her arms, and with the soothing motions of her hands up and down the length of his spine she tried to communicate the happiness she'd felt making love with him. She wanted him to know that it had been more than just a sexual experience.

Chip rolled over on his side, taking her with him. They lay face to face on the pillow, noses an inch apart, legs still intimately entwined, hands and arms clinging. The fire had burned low, the light dim, but they stared into each other's eyes. As their breaths mingled, he moved his face a fraction and placed a light kiss on her lips.

"Why? How?" His voice was a mere whisper against her lips.

"Why? Because I wanted my first time to be with you." He was looking into her eyes and there was something in his face she had dreamed of but never hoped to see. Was it a little like . . . loving? No, she was simply seeing what she wanted to see. "What was the other question?" Her words melted away on her lips as he kissed them lightly again.

"How did you manage to stay so innocent?"

"It just happened. There wasn't much of an opportunity. Not that I would have been promiscuous," she added hastily. He smiled. "I wasn't allowed to go on unchaperoned dates when I was younger. Later . . . well, later there was Justin."

"And?" he prompted.

She hesitated, then began honestly, "I was fond of him, and he told me he loved me. I don't think I ever knew there could be . . . so much more . . . until tonight," she stammered. "Oh, I'd dreamed of it, but . . . I don't want to talk about this!" she blurted with a breathless catch in her voice.

"Then don't." Chip possessively gripped her thigh.

A chill slid down Margaret's spine at the thought of lying naked in another man's arms. And she had almost married another. Her hand moved convulsively over Chip's back and pulled him tightly against her.

Tenderly he caressed her and kissed her lips time and again. "I'm glad," he finally whispered. "I'm glad there was no other man before me. I'm glad no other man has ever held you naked in his arms like this!"

She could feel a stirring between them, and she smiled against his throat. Her hand found his hard, flat belly, slid upward over his ribs and chest caressingly, and lay palm down over his thudding heart.

"Was it . . . did I do . . . all right?"

He rolled her onto her back and raised his head so he could look at her. "Why the hell do you think I've got this silly grin on my face?" He deposited quick, darting kisses on her parted lips. "I feel like a kid on Christmas morning."

"Did Santa bring you everything you wanted?"

"You bet! And more." He kissed her forehead gently. "Were you disappointed with your first experience? I wanted it to be good for you." His voice was deep and husky, his expression one of great tenderness.

Her arms tightened about him. "It was wonderful. Thank you, Chip," she whispered, her voice full of joyous tears.

"Sweetheart . . ."

CHAPTER EIGHT

MARGARET TURNED HER face and let her lips drift along the smooth skin of Chip's collarbone, finding the hollow of his throat, where she planted a tender kiss. They lay pressed close together in Chip's bed. He had fallen into a deep sleep after their tumultuous lovemaking, and she had lain satiated, cozy, and content in his arms. She had responded vigorously to his instruction in the elementary pleasures of loving, and now she cherished the knowledge that he was her first and only lover.

She had been embarrassed when he urged her to the bathroom after their first lovemaking; embarrassed, too, that it was he who insisted they use something to protect her against pregnancy during the rest of the long, delicious night spent in his bedroom. Now, warm and nude, cozily stretched against his very male body, she felt a sickening thud in the pit of her stomach when she thought of how readily he'd produced the precautionary device. But he was a man in his mid-thirties, she told herself. No one could doubt his fundamental virility—it radiated from every pore in his aggressively masculine body.

Frantically she pushed the thought of his being with someone else out of her mind. What she really wanted to do was bury her face in his shoulder and whisper to him that he was hers now. She would give him all the loving he'd ever need. But of course she couldn't say that. He'd simply taken what she had freely given. He cared no more for her than he had earlier in the evening when he'd called her "old Ed's spoiled darling." Tears of regret slid from her eyes. He would never see her as a woman capable of living beside him as his life's companion. Her heart ached at the thought of leaving this place, leaving him. She shut her eyes tightly to hold back the tears. Don't spoil it, she cautioned. Hold him. You have the rest of the night to hold him in your arms. This may be all you'll ever have of him.

"Wake up, Maggie."

Margaret tried to shrug off whatever was shaking her shoulder. She heard the voice again, louder this time, opened one eye, and was instantly awake. Chip was standing beside the bed.

"Are you going to sleep all day? I've been waiting for a couple of hours for you to wake up."

Margaret's eyes wandered over his smoothly shaved face and freshly washed hair. He was wearing a faded flannel shirt and a pair of the bleach-splotched jeans.

"I guess I was tired." She squinted her eyes to bring his face into focus.

"Arlene will be bringing Penny home this morning. You'd better get up unless you want them to catch you in my bed."

Naturally apprehensive, Margaret peered up at him, trying to discern his expression. Last night she had felt happy and young and cherished. They had made love all through the night. It was almost as much happiness as she could take at one time, and she wanted desperately to feel that the closeness of mind and body they'd shared had carried over into the light of day.

"Will I have time for a bath?" Everything was not as comfortable and easy as she had hoped it would be. The realization hit her like a dash of cold water.

"Sure. The house is warm. I found there was some fuel oil in the tank after all, so I started the furnace." He went to the door, and her heart settled with a sickening thud.

"Chip." She clutched the covers to her. "Will you get me a robe?"

He nodded and left the room. Margaret closed her eyes against an unwanted surge of hot tears. It had meant nothing to him! Nothing deep or lasting. She'd aroused him physically, and that was all. He'd used her body to relieve his needs. He came back with a blue robe in one hand and her glasses in the other. He tossed the robe onto the end of the bed and placed her glasses on the nightstand.

"You'll need these to find your way to the bathroom." There wasn't a trace of humor in his voice.

She held her breath through the seconds of silence that followed. The face that looked down at her was a blur, but it wasn't smiling—she could see clearly enough for that. Even his voice seemed different now. It was less friendly, though not really harsh. He turned abruptly and strode to the door, quietly closing it behind him.

Margaret slipped into the bathroom, her mind a buzzing hive of confusion. She sat in the tub of warm water and soaked her aching muscles. Chip had not let her sleep until near dawn. There had been an electric charge running between them that had generated new sparks with every touch, every murmured endearment. It was as if they'd been starving for each other. No caress was too rough or too soft. She swallowed the tightness in her throat. How could he be so indifferent after so many hours of sweet, hot, shared passion?

She uttered a small groan when she stepped out of the tub. Chip had made love to her as gently as her own passion would allow, but her body, unaccustomed to a man's rough hands and rock-hard intrusion, was rebelling now. She dusted herself with talc and smiled a secret, soft smile when she touched her sensitive nipples. The thought of his mouth on her breasts sent unexpected shivers through her body. Oh, God, I love him, she thought. But what do I do now?

She dressed in jeans and a flannel shirt and tied her hair at the nape of her neck with a shoestring ribbon. With the dark-rimmed glasses firmly on her nose she took a deep breath to steady her nerves and walked into the kitchen. Her new boots made squeaky sounds on the tile, but there was no one there to hear them. The electric coffee pot was perking, and a large slice of ham lay in the skillet on the stove. Voices were coming from outside the kitchen door, and she looked through the glass.

Tom MacMadden stood beside his dusty station wagon. He was wearing a dark suit and a small-brimmed felt hat. This was Sunday, Margaret thought, and he'd probably been to church. She opened the door to speak to him, but Chip's voice reached her before she could step out.

"She'll be ready to leave by the end of the week. Right now she's like a puppy let off the leash. Everything is new and exciting, but as soon as the novelty fades she'll be off to make fresh discoveries." His voice was brusque.

"She said somethin' about buyin' out your shares in the mill," Tom said slowly. "They could've sent her up here to feel you out."

"I don't think so. I doubt she knows any more about business than Penny does. I think Rachel knew we'd look out for her. Does it bother you having her around?"

"Nope. Guess I thought it would, but it don't."

"You think I should pack her out of here, don't you?"

"Makes no difference to me. Just don't go gettin' soft on her. She'll wind you 'round her finger."

Margaret stood fighting a strange tight feeling in her stomach. They were talking about her. The awkwardness of the situation made her clench her teeth.

"I'll take her to the mill and up to the logging camp on Flathead. That should satisfy her curiosity. She'll be ready to get back to the city after that."

Margaret was inwardly raging, her breath coming fast and hard. This was the same man who had held her in his arms last night and called her sweetheart. Today he was talking about getting rid of her! He was dismissing her as casually as he had dismissed Beth, the young girl who had a puppy-love crush on him. Margaret was flooded with resentment, and her heart pounded in response to her anger. The men had stopped talking. She waited a moment, took a deep breath, straightened her back stubbornly, and stepped out onto the porch.

"Good morning, Tom."

"Mornin'."

"Have you been to church already?"

"I usually go to early mass."

"Had I known, I would have asked to go with you. If you come by this way next Sunday, I'd appreciate a ride." She didn't look at Chip, but she could feel his eyes on her. Both men obviously knew she had overheard their conversation. What right did they have to discuss her as if she were an outsider nosing into company business. Damn them!

"I suppose I could give you a lift, if you're still here." Tom put emphasis on the last words.

"I'll be here." She glanced at Chip, then back to Tom.

Tom opened the door of the station wagon. "Guess I'd better be gettin' on. See ya, Chip. 'Bye, miss."

"Don't let me chase you away, Tom." Despite her determination to handle herself coolly, she felt defeated and humiliated. She had been so naïve! Chip was going to take her sightseeing, as if she were a tourist. Last night must have been an additional bonus in the package deal! Never had she had to fight so hard to keep her expression calm and pleasant.

"Nice seeing you again, Tom," she called before walking back into the kitchen.

Her knees felt weak, and she held tightly to the back of a chair. She was totally unnerved, and in order to have something to do she went to the counter and poured coffee from the percolator. She heard Chip come into the kitchen, but she didn't turn around. The silence lengthened. Why didn't he say something, for heaven's sake?

"Eavesdroppers seldom hear anything good about themselves." His voice was softer than she'd expected.

Damned if he was going to put her on the defensive! She whirled and faced him.

"What did you expect me to do? Say 'Hey, fellows, stop talking about me, I'm listening'?" She was engulfed in such hurt and rage she scarcely knew what she was saying. "If you don't want me here—and it's evident you don't—that's tough, because I'm staying if I have to use all my corporate clout. But I must warn you! I may be like a puppy let off the leash, but I certainly won't lick the hand that cuffs me." She was almost breathless when she finished, but she held her head proudly.

He continued to look at her, with unwavering eyes, eyes the color of a cloudless sky.

"I didn't mean that in a derogatory way." His lips barely seemed to move when he spoke.

"A dog's a dog!" she said lightly. More than anything in the world she wished to keep him from knowing how crushed she was, how miserable she felt, how his denial of her would tarnish forever the memories of the beautiful moments they had shared. Her glasses had slid down on her nose, and she jabbed them back into place.

"I didn't say I didn't want you here, Maggie. I said you'll be ready to leave once you've seen it all." His voice was patient, and it infuriated her that he was speaking to her as if she were a child.

"You showed me your particular kind of hospitality last night. Thanks for the show!" She flung the words in his face, and evidently they couldn't have been more cutting.

He reached her in two strides, and his hands came down on her shoulders like hundred-pound weights.

"Shut up! You mention that in a dirty way again and I swear I'll . . . slap you!"

"You do and I'll have you arrested!" she gasped. Forcibly calming herself, she said, "I came here to look things over and decide if I'm going to sell to you. I'm not leaving until I do." To herself she vowed: I'll never sell my shares to you, Duncan "Chip" Thorn. I'll give them to a charity first! He was staring down at her coldly. Why in the world was *he* acting this way? She was the one who had cause for anger.

He released her arms. "Eat some breakfast, and I'll take you upriver in the boat."

"Why? Is this one of the side trips of the tour?"

"You could call it that. You want to see the area, don't you? We'll just about have time before Penny and Arlene get here. I've got work to do this afternoon."

As she turned to take the cereal box from the cabinet she heard him leave the room. Then she was alone. It was simultaneously a relief and a sickening misery. She could cry now if she wanted, but she wasn't about to give him the satisfaction of seeing her red-rimmed eyes when he returned. She allowed herself the luxury of relaxing her tight features; they felt as if they'd been set in a plaster cast. Automatically she poured the cereal into the bowl and added the milk. She would eat if it killed her, although she wondered how she would get a single spoonful down her tight throat.

There were a million unanswered questions floating around in her mind. Why did Tom MacMadden care whether she stayed or not? Why did Chip speak about Rachel as if he knew her? And Chip never had fully explained why it was that Tom knew her identity and no one else did. She didn't allow her mind one thought of the night she'd spent in his arms. She couldn't think of that now—the hurt and humiliation were too raw.

Margaret doggedly finished the cereal, then went into the bathroom to put in her contact lenses. She tied a scarf about her head and picked up a pair of sunglasses, although the sun was obscured behind a gray cloud bank. With her mackinaw over her arm she waited in the kitchen for Chip. He came in wearing his coat, so she slipped on hers and followed him down the path to the wooden jetty where the outboard motorboat was moored.

Chip stepped into the boat and held out his hand to assist her. She put hers into it and looked into his face. He was looking at her in a way that shriveled her soul. It was a cold, angry, violent look. Even through the dark glasses his eyes trapped hers, and her heart beat so fast it seemed to fill her ears.

"Sit down over there and put on a life jacket," he instructed curtly.

"I can swim," she responded in a tone to match his.

"So can I. But you can get knocked cold if you're thrown from a boat. Put on the life jacket." He waited until she began fastening the buckles on the bulky orange vest, then turned his back and slipped into a vest hanging on the back of the seat.

The wind on the river was cold, and it stung her cheeks. Margaret was thankful for the scarf and the sunglasses that helped keep the wind out of her eyes. Chip lounged behind the wheel of the boat, seemingly immune to the cold. She was aware that the trees grew tall on each side of the river and that an occasional house nestled among them, but that was all.

Here I am, she thought, in a boat on a river that bends and twists through this beautiful wilderness, and all I can think of is the cold-blooded, calculating way he spoke about me. The power he had over her petrified her. He could engulf her, crush her, set a fire under her that would consume her. So why was she staying? Was she like a moth, compelled to flit ever closer to the flame?

Chip slowed the boat. Ahead a wooden dock jutted out into the river, and a large brown dog ran back and forth barking furiously. As they moved closer to the dock the trees gave way to a view of lawn sweeping down to the river. A log house was set back amid the pines. It was long and low with brown shakes and several cobblestone chimneys. The house seemed to be built around a huge patio with a large outdoor fireplace. It was a blend of old and new, and it looked settled, comfortable in its surroundings.

The nearer they came to the dock the more excited the dog became. As it dashed back and forth, still barking, it suddenly occurred to Margaret that the dog recognized both Chip and the boat and was barking a welcome. She barely had time for the thought to register before the boat picked up speed, shot ahead, and passed the wooden jetty. She looked back at the dog, which stood in surprised silence on the end of the dock. Of course the dog would know Chip, Margaret reasoned. Everyone from miles around would know him and the boat. Then why did she get the feeling that the dog had expected him to turn in and tie up to the dock?

She glanced at Chip, the question in her eyes hidden by the dark glasses, and studied his set profile. Slowly, as if feeling her appraisal, he turned his head and his narrowed eyes swept her face. A shiver unrelated to the cold wind shimmied down her spine, and she looked away quickly before his eyes could read the misery in hers. She felt the boat slow, and then he turned it in a wide arc and headed for home.

Back at the company house Chip silently helped her out of the rocking boat. She left him to moor it and walked up the path. Feeling lonely and miserable, she removed her coat, went into the living room, and stood with her back to the glowing coals in the fireplace. She was cold, chilled from the ride on the river, but her cheeks burned as she remembered how she had surrendered, willingly, eagerly, to his possession of her. She wanted to weep. What must he be thinking? There had been no challenge. She had simply been there for the taking. How could she face him here in this room? Her eyes wandered to the couch, and then she dashed for her own room, sighing with relief as she closed the door behind her. Tears flowed down her cheeks. What had made her declare that she was going to stay here? She had to go! To be with him and have him treat her so coldly tore at her heart. It couldn't be worse not to see him at all, she decided—although that thought was almost unbearable. She knew she had no choice, because if she stayed it wouldn't be long before those mocking sky-blue eyes would see that she was head-over-heels in love with him. She took her case from the floor of the closet and placed it on the bed. Methodically she began to pack. She had control of herself now. She'd had her moment of weakness.

She was pulling clothes from the closet when a sharp rap sounded on the door, which then swung open. Chip stood there, seemingly at ease, yet giving the impression he was as alert as a cat about to spring.

"I'm glad to see you're getting rid of the expensive duds. Be sure and lock the case—not that I think Penny or Dolly will snoop, but it's best to make sure." His cool glance went over her clothes and the toilet articles on the bed.

"Don't worry. Your troubles will soon be over," she answered in a softly controlled voice.

One brown brow arched. "Running away, princess?" Before she could say anything he continued, "I thought you'd at least last out the week. Can't take the primitive life, is that it? No servants to bring you breakfast in bed, no marble stairway to glide down, no one to stand at attention when you walk by?"

Margaret almost gasped at his attack. Then anger burned through her. Who did he think he was?

"I'm not leaving!" The words just popped out, and she stopped, shocked by her own statement. Only minutes before she had been determined to go back to Chicago. "I'm merely doing as you suggested. Now get out of my room and leave me to it."

"Funny, I'd have sworn you were packing to leave." He paused, then added slowly, "I'm sorry about last night. I had no way of knowing of your . . . innocence."

Margaret blanched as if he had struck her. She turned her back so he couldn't see her face. "So? You got a bonus for your troubles," she said coolly. "Isn't it every man's ambition to deflower as many maidens as possible?"

"Stop talking like that," he said sharply. "I didn't think any young woman today reached the age of twenty-five and remained innocent. I said I was sorry for your sake. I'm sure you'd rather have had the experience with a man you loved. I'm sorry if I've taken something from you. I mean that, though I'm glad I was first." He came into the room and stood behind her. She walked to the closet and took out the blue silk suit. He took it from her hand and flung it onto the bed. "Maggie! Leave the damn clothes and look at me!"

She whirled on him. "What more do you want me to say? I'm staying, I'm staying, I'm staying," she shouted. "Are you on a guilt trip, Mr. Thorn? Don't be. I knew exactly what I was doing. I used you as much as you used me! Get it? I started out later than most girls, but believe me, I intend to make up for lost time. You were the first, but you'll not be the last! You can count on that!" She sucked air into her lungs in jerky gasps. Distress was plain in her voice, and there was no way she could hide it.

He looked at her searchingly. "Do you feel better now?" His voice was lower than before. "Lashing out with rash statements is the act of a spoiled child."

In retaliation she said the first thing that came into her mind. "You didn't think I was a child last night!" Hating him, hating herself, she watched with fascination as light danced in his eyes and she realized he was actually trying to subdue his mirth. "Don't you dare laugh at me!" She balled her fist and prepared to swing.

He grabbed her wrist. Holding her eyes with the blue flame of his, he said softly, insinuatingly, "I certainly didn't think you were a child last night." The hand that curved around her waist drew her against him. He lowered his head, and his lips pressed tightly together.

"Okay. You're staying." His eyes were on her face; hers were on the hollow at the base of his throat. "We've still got to play our game so the others will believe you're my . . . ah . . . girlfriend. Do you think you can hide your resentment and pull it off?"

She looked up at him, her eyes wide, clear, and challenging. "Can you?"

"No doubt about it." His mouth widened in a slow smile that had more than a hint of satisfaction in it. One brow rose inquiringly. "And you?"

She nodded, words locked in her throat by a strong welling of emotion.

He left her, and she stood beside the bed staring at the closed door. She was emotionally shaken. Her only clear thought was that, if she'd had half the brains she was born with, she'd get the hell out of there.

Although she felt rather sick, nerves dancing like demons in her stomach, Margaret managed to walk calmly down the hall and stand quietly in the doorway, waiting for Chip to acknowledge her presence. He was listening attentively to a little girl with long blond braids and a pixie face.

"Grandma said she knew she was coming. Why didn't you tell me?"

"I thought your grandma would. How is she, anyway?"

"Fine. Beth said you won't be coming here anymore? Beth said you're going to marry her. Are you, Chip?"

"Marry who? Your grandma?"

"No, silly." The child giggled, revealing missing teeth.

"Her." She turned her head and focused wide brown eyes on Margaret.

Chip's head swiveled around. His smile was so charming, so full of welcome, that sharp shards of pleasure splintered along Margaret's veins. She reminded herself that he was pretending for the sake of the little girl—and the woman who stood nearby scrutinizing Margaret.

"Hi, sweetheart." Chip held out his hand. "Come meet Penny and Arlene."

Mindlessly Margaret walked to him and put her hand in his. She was watching his eyes, and she saw something there she couldn't quite interpret. It confused her already tired mind. Chip drew her against his side and slipped an arm around her waist.

"This is Maggie. Honey, this is Penny and one of her teachers, Arlene Rogers."

"Hello." Margaret smiled at the child, then lifted her gaze to the teacher. The woman was hurting—Margaret could see that at once. Her rather plump, makeup-free face was set, her hand was clenched at the back of the couch, and her dark eyes were shifting from Chip's face to Margaret's. She's in love with him, too, Margaret thought. How many more women have given their hearts to him?

"Hello, Miss Rogers." Margaret held out her hand. She tried to sound calm and collected, but she wasn't sure she was pulling it off. The woman touched her hand and then released it quickly. She was wearing a maroon velveteen blazer and a plaid skirt, paired with a frilly pink blouse and four-inch heels.

"Hello." Arlene's face was suffused with color, and Margaret hoped that Chip didn't notice. "I must be going.

I've a million things to do this afternoon. Dolly will be coming home tomorrow, Chip. She said to tell you she has a ride and she'll be here by the time Penny gets home from school."

"Don't rush away, Arlene. Maggie and I can scare up some lunch." Chip's arms tightened, and his hand spread out on the side of Margaret's waist, preventing her from moving away from him.

"I really don't have the time, but thanks just the same." Arlene paused at the door and looked down at Penny. "Don't forget your homework, Penny. There's a spelling test tomorrow."

"I won't, Miss Rogers," Penny said reluctantly, instantly conveying that spelling was almost as bad as having one's mouth washed out with soap. "Maybe Maggie will help me with it."

"Of course. I think Chip has some work to do this afternoon. You and I will concentrate on the spelling."

"Can we pop popcorn? Chip, can we?"

"I don't know about that." Chip grinned down at Margaret. "Maggie may not know how to pop it in a pan on the stove."

"I'll show her how." Penny slipped a small hand into Margaret's, and she squeezed it tightly.

"I think that between us we can get the job done, don't you, Penny?" Margaret spoke to the child, but her glance traveled upward. Chip was watching her with lazy indulgence. "One more new and exciting experience for the puppy." Her voice was a bare whisper, but he heard. His response was to gently pinch her waist.

CHAPTER NINE

THE AIR WAS crisp and cold. A light dusting of frost sparkled in the morning sun. Margaret stood on the porch and watched Penny skip down the lane toward the big yellow school bus. The little girl turned and waved before the door closed behind her. Margaret waved back and waited while the bus moved on down the dusty road.

Being the complete idiot that you are, she told herself wryly, you've not only let yourself fall in love with Chip, but you've also allowed yourself to go off the deep end about that child. Granted, she'd had little contact with children except for those of the people who worked on the estate. There had always been a summer picnic and a Christmas party for the staff and their families, but there had been no chance to really get to know the children. Was her fondness for this child another new and exciting experience for the puppy?

The day before, Chip had left the house shortly after lunch, and Margaret and Penny had spent the afternoon and evening together. Margaret had needed the time away from him to get her thoughts organized and her emotions under control once again. Penny had proved to be the perfect diversion. They'd made the popcorn, studied the spelling words, and then Penny had proudly exhibited her new Sunday school dress and shoes. They'd eaten warmed-up stew for dinner and spent the rest of the evening playing Candyland. Chip hadn't returned by the time they went to bed at nine o'clock.

This morning when she came into the kitchen Chip had been dishing scrambled eggs onto a plate for Penny. They both looked up and smiled; then Penny jumped out of her seat and ran to Margaret, wrapping her arms about her waist.

"I was afraid you wouldn't get up before I left for school."

"Of course I was going to get up. I've got to brush and rebraid your hair," she said, looking at Chip over Penny's head. She could feel the warmth rising under her skin.

Standing there in the kitchen, Margaret felt the curl of excitement, which had started the moment she'd heard Chip's voice, build inside her. She couldn't stop the feeling of happiness that washed over her, and she felt almost grateful to the unknown Dolly for allowing her this time alone with Chip and Penny. Oh, God, she thought. I can't believe that this is really me, Margaret Anthony, standing here in this kitchen feeling thankful for a small crumb of pleasure. Is this what it's like to have a man and a child of your very own? I almost feel as if this tall, blue-eyed man and this pixie child are mine! Her thoughts shifted into another direction. Had her arms really been about his neck, and had she boldly pressed her lips eagerly to his, and had he seen and touched her as no other person had ever seen and touched her? I must surely be going mad, she told herself, to feel so wildly happy, knowing I was only an evening's diversion for him.

When the school bus disappeared down the road, Margaret went back into the house, closed the door, and turned to see Chip watching her. He stood with his mackinaw looped over his shoulder, his legs slightly apart, and brushed a lock of hair back from his forehead. His eyes appraised her.

"You shouldn't go out without a jacket across your shoulders." His voice was softly chiding.

"I'm tougher than I appear to be. I seldom get sick."

"Glad to hear it."

"Oh?" seemed to be all Margaret could manage. She was held immobile by the compelling look in his eyes.

There was something different about him this morning. He seemed to be on edge, nervous, unsure of himself. For long seconds they were silent. Everything faded into insignificance for Margaret—everything but the still face and the quiet eyes looking at her. Then he turned and shrugged into his mackinaw.

"Will you be all right alone here for a short while? I've got a few things to do, and then I'll be back to take you to the mill."

"I'll be fine."

"There's absolutely nothing to be afraid of." He was lingering beside the door.

"I know. I wasn't afraid last night. I didn't give it a thought."

"Glad to hear it," he said for the second time. "I was over at Keith's." He jerked his head toward the other houses that made up the small complex. "I was keeping an eye on the place. I wouldn't have gone off and left you and Penny alone out here." He seemed to be waiting for her to say something, and when she didn't he continued, "Keith and I had to go over the prints for a building we're going to put up as soon as the mill shuts down. Ordinarily we would have done that on Saturday, but—"

"I'm sorry if I've interrupted your work schedule. I'm sure that by the first of the week I'll have seen enough to make up my mind about the shares, and you can get back to normal." She said it quickly and breathlessly and wondered at the strange look that sped across his face.

He looked at her silently, and the seconds ticked by. Something seemed to flow between them, and she was caught up in the blazing sensuality of promise in his eyes. She felt a melting sensation in her belly.

"I'll be back in about an hour. Wear something warm." He opened the door. "Wear your boots . . . and your glasses. There'll be a lot of sawdust flying around at the mill, and it's bound to get under those pesky contact lenses."

Margaret tried to make her mind go blank, shutting off memories of his sweet warm breath, firm lips, and fingers trailing lightly across her collarbone and down between her breasts. Drawing a deep, painful breath, she realized that he was still waiting beside the door.

"Okay."

She stood in the middle of the room after he left her. *Okay?* Did I really say that? she wondered. What's the matter with me? I know what's the matter. I'm so in love with him I can't even think, much less get out a complete sentence, when he looks at me like that.

Margaret could hear the mill long before they came into view of it. The scene of activity that met her eyes on rounding the last curve in the road was a total contrast to the peace of the last few miles from the house. They had turned off the main road and taken a track through the trees that was anything but smooth. Chip explained that the mill was situated on a stream that flowed down from the north and connected with Flathead River to the south. This stream winding through a curtain of trees was the principal carrier of the timber cut in the logging camps up north.

Chip left the car in a parking area strewn with wood-chips, and they walked toward the river. As far as the eye could see, the water was covered with logs sweeping majestically down into the broad basin of what appeared to be a man-made lake, to be caught by men wielding long, hooked poles. The logs were steered toward other men, who ran lightly over the floating logs and guided them into the calm waters of the lake.

They stood for a moment watching, and then Chip took her hand and led her to where men operated the machines that lifted the logs from the water as they came floating down and dropped them onto a conveyor belt that moved them up the slope to the mill. It was fascinating to watch the huge arm of the machine swing out and dip, the giant jaws closing about a log that measured several feet around, lift it dripping from the water, and lower it gently to the belt.

The mill itself was comprised of three large barnlike metal and wood buildings set well back and flanked by smaller structures. The screeching whine of the saws interspersed with a regular thud, like some heavy object being dropped, made talking impossible. They walked toward one of the smaller buildings. Actually, Chip walked and Margaret almost ran to keep up with him. The firm grasp he had on her hand allowed her to do nothing else. The smaller building must have been well insulated, because the second the door closed she was surrounded by blessed quiet.

The man seated with his feet propped up on the desk in front of him was perhaps in his late fifties or early sixties. His hair was thick and white, his skin tough and weathered, but he had a cheerful cast to his features and an easy grin. He unlocked his legs and allowed his tilting chair to crash back into an upright position when his gaze fell upon Margaret.

"Meet the boss, next to me, of course. Bill Wassal, Maggie Anderson." Chip smiled a little as he watched Bill's reaction.

"You don't say? Maggie, huh? Nice knowing you, Maggie." He got up and held out his hand. He wasn't much taller than Margaret, but his shoulders were wide and his chest deep.

"How do you do. I hope I'm not disturbing you."

"No bother at all. Chip showing you around, is he?" He had taken her hand in his hamlike paw as gently as if he were handling eggs. He let her hand go, stepped back, grinned, and scratched his head. His twinkling eyes went from Margaret to Chip and back again. "Mighty good-looking woman you got here, boy."

"Yeah. She looks pretty good when she's cleaned up a bit." Chip reached over and pushed Margaret's glasses up on her nose. "She'll do once I get her broken in to my way of doing things."

Margaret's face flushed, and she groped for words.

"Stop teasing, boy. We've got her blushing." Bill Wassal grinned unrepentantly.

"Speechless, love?" Amusement threaded through Chip's voice. "Never mind. You talk too much, sometimes anyway."

"And so do you! Like now!"

He stood looking at her for a moment, and she glared up at him. In a purely unnecessary, nervous gesture she jabbed at the crosspiece of her glasses, pushing them higher up on her nose.

"What are we going to do about those glasses, sweetheart? Don't you have a pair that fit?"

Margaret's teeth snapped together, frustration burning within at the easy way he goaded her, knowing perfectly well it was safe to do so in front of the other man.

"If you don't like my looks, don't look at me," she snapped.

"That's impossible, sweetheart. And stop fishing for compliments. You know I like the way you look."

Margaret turned her back on him and addressed herself to Bill. "How long have you worked here, Mr. Wassal?" She could hear Chip chuckling behind her. She searched for a cutting remark to pierce his armor, but then decided it would be better to ignore him.

"Must be close to thirty-two years."

Thirty-two years! Her head swiveled around, and she glanced at Chip. He smiled wryly.

"We both arrived about the same time."

"Yeah, we did. I got here just in time to get in on the celebration. The crew stayed drunk for a week." Bill leaned back against the desk and folded his arms across his chest. "I can remember the time when——"

"Whoa, Bill. Some of your remembered times are pretty long tales. Maggie would like to see what we do out here. Will you show her around while I catch up on a few things?" He flung an arm casually across Margaret's shoulders. "You'll be okay with Bill, honey." With one large hand encompassing her shoulder, he drew her to him and kissed her, hard and quick. "Don't stay away too long. Come back here and I'll treat you to lunch at the canteen." His smile was lazy, and there was a teasing glint in his blue eyes.

His soft chuckle set up vibrations in the pit of her stomach. Damn him! "I can hardly wait!" she sputtered.

"You're going to have to get over this habit of blushing when I kiss you, princess." His voice dropped to a murmur in her ear. "Think of me while you're gone."

Margaret moved away from him like someone in a fog, and she stood beside the door while Bill took his jacket from a hook on the wall behind his desk. *Think of me.* The deep purr of his voice echoed in her mind. She couldn't keep her eyes from glancing at him one more time. He was looking at her as intently as he had this morning when she'd felt that unspoken communication between them. She felt his warmth, his strength, winding around and through her as if there were a channel connecting them. Their eyes held, and for timeless seconds they were entirely alone in the world.

Chip pushed himself away from the desk where he'd

been leaning and came to her. She was hardly aware that she had taken a step to meet him. She closed her eyes and pressed her forehead to his shoulder when his hands gripped her upper arms.

"It's all right. There's nothing to be afraid of here," he whispered in her ear.

Unmoving, hardly breathing, Margaret realized that he thought she was frightened of going with Bill. The thought hadn't entered her mind! She took a deep shuddering breath and lifted her face. She watched his eyes, which were dark with concern as he bent his head to drop a warm, feathery kiss on her mouth.

"If you'd rather I leave, why don't you say so?" Bill's gravelly voice came from behind Chip.

"That won't be necessary. I don't mind kissing my girl in front of you, Bill," he declared with a teasing smile for Margaret. He opened the door. "Take care of my princess."

His voice floated to Margaret through the noise of the mill. He was smiling at her. She searched his face for a trace of mockery and found none.

Just inside the door to one of the large buildings, Bill picked up two yellow hard hats, shoving one down onto his head and handing the other to Margaret. When she put it on, it slid down over her eyes. Bill held out his hand in silent communication, and she handed the hat back to him. He adjusted the straps on the inside, gave it back to her, and waited to see if it fit snugly.

He leaned toward her and shouted, "Stay close!"

Margaret followed his instructions, and a few minutes later she understood why when his arm shot out to keep her a safe distance away from the huge discs of metal ripping into the giant logs. She also understood why Chip had told her to wear her glasses instead of the contact lenses. The air was full of flying sawdust, and she made a mental note to ask Bill about that when they were able to talk.

Some of the men wore guards over their ears to deaden the noise, and a few wore goggles to keep the sawdust out of their eyes. Talking was difficult if not impossible inside the building, and Margaret was glad when they passed through to the outside and she could breathe fresh air again.

"I'd think all that sawdust in the air would be harmful to the men," she said.

Bill looked surprised. "Chip keeps checking on that. It seems that sawdust is organic and not harmful. The real danger to the men is the lasting effect of the noise on their eardrums. We've issued ear guards, but few bother to wear them. Same with the goggles. We've spent thousands of dollars keeping those items available for the ones who'll use them."

At the rear of the long shed lay railway tracks with stacks of raw cut lumber waiting to be shipped out. Railway cars were being loaded while an ancient engine sat idly on the tracks beyond.

"There's one of the few wood-burners left," Bill said, indicating the engine.

"Why are you using such an old piece of outdated equipment?"

"Might be outdated for some, but it does the job for us." Bill looked at her with obvious interest. "We've got the fuel, and we only run between here and Kalispell. We leave the cars loaded in the freight yard down there, and they're picked up and shipped out. That's why this company is solvent and a lot of others have gone under—'cause Chip's used his head for something other than a place to put his hat."

"It's a larger operation than I thought," Margaret murmured, hesitant about asking more questions.

"You bet. But this is only a part of it. You don't get the full picture 'til you follow it down from the camps."

"How many camps do you have?"

"Four. But they move from year to year. Farthest one is about a hundred miles."

"And all the logs float down the river?"

"Nope. Some are trucked in. Seen enough?"

"I guess so."

Margaret walked beside him back to the small building. She would have liked to ask him if he'd known her father when he was young. If he had worked here for thirty-two years, he must have been here even before her father bought in. She wondered why her father had never talked about this part of his life.

Chip was sitting on the edge of the desk when they got back to the office. He was reading a report and glancing up at the large map that covered one wall. Like the one in the office in town, this map, too, was studded with pins, the heads of which were different colors. He glanced at Margaret and Bill and then back at the map.

"Seems like we've got some greenhorns roughing it out in section three. I hope to hell they've been instructed on fire prevention."

"If they haven't, we'll know damn quick," Bill said drily.

"Have camps one, two, or four reported in this morning?"

"Four called in. They'd spotted three backpackers. I've got a call in to the rangers to see if they have a permit to be in that wilderness area."

"That's all we can do for now. It's been an unusually dry month, but we should get some rain soon."

Margaret knew what he was saying. It was strange, she thought, how quickly one could gain a proprietary attitude. A couple of weeks ago the thought of a forest fire would have meant little to her. Now, they were *her* trees that were tinder-dry and needed the fall rains to wet them down.

"Can't you keep campers out of there when it's as dry as this?" she queried without thinking. She saw Chip's mouth pull into the familiar derisive line.

"We don't own the land, princess. We only have a contract to take out so many trees a year. The company has a plane that patrols the area regularly. That's about as much as we can do—except hope we finish the season without a serious fire." He was watching her with an enigmatic expression. "Feel like some lunch?" He looked at the watch strapped to his wrist. "If we get over to the canteen now we'll beat the rush."

"Why go over?" Bill asked. "They'll bring it here for you."

"How about it?" Chip said. "Do you think your sensibilities can stand being leered at? The men up here have healthy appetites—in more ways than one."

Margaret had the feeling he would have said more if Bill hadn't been listening. Her lips fluttered into a smile. "Why should I mind? I'll have the boss to protect me."

The canteen turned out to be a long timber building with the distinctive smell of new wood and paint. Formica-topped tables and metal chairs were laid out in orderly rows, and a stainless-steel serving counter stretched across one end. Hot meals were already being served by men in flannel shirts with rolled up sleeves exposing bulging muscles. White canvas aprons covered work jeans.

Chip took a tray and silverwear from the end of the bar and moved it along the counter. He was greeted with familiar ease by everyone. "Hi, Chip" . . . "What you doin' up here, boss?" . . . "We got that meat pie today, Chip," someone called from the kitchen.

"Why do ya think I'm here? I've been waiting all week for that!" he yelled to the unseen man in the kitchen.

"Give the kid an extra spoonful, Henry," the voice called back. Everyone laughed. "His woman, too."

Margaret had steeled herself to weather the frank stares and predictable comments without apparent discomfiture. She glanced at Chip's grin and then deliberately looked each man in the eye and smiled as they passed down the line.

The food had been prepared for hearty appetites: pans of the steaming meat pies, hot rolls, and fruit cobbler. Chip filled the tray without asking Margaret's preference and moved it down the bar to where large mugs sat beside a self-service coffee urn. She filled the mugs and followed him to a table at the end of the room.

"I'll never be able to eat all of this," she said when he set the plates on the table.

"I know that. I'll finish it off for you. That's the best damn meat pie in the state."

Margaret shook her head, watching him nod or wave at the men who were coming off their shift to eat. She was aware that she was the main topic of conversation and that every eye in the building was covertly watching her. She was also aware that Chip was awaiting her reaction, and she smiled at him after she swallowed her first forkful of the meat pie.

"Why do you have men cooks here and not women?"

"In the first place I try to give jobs to men who head families. Second, these men have years of experience cooking for crews. Any more questions?"

"Isn't that discrimination?"

"Against whom?"

"Women, of course."

"Are you a women's libber?"

"No." The denial came without hesitation, yet something inside her contracted as she said it. "I haven't really thought about it. Are you against women having equal rights?"

"If you mean am I against women working in the mill for pay equal to that of the men, yes. There's no way a woman could put in the kind of day a man puts in here. The work is too dangerous, the loads too heavy, and, what's more, they'd be too distracting."

"You're a chauvinist!" she said, pointing.

"Yeah," he agreed.

"What about the women whose men have left them? Like Beth's mother?"

"There's no way Anthony/Thorn can provide for every person who lives in this district. We do the best we can.

We have the best pension plan of any company our size in the northwest. I've had to battle old Ed and now your Justin to keep it that way." He was getting angry; she could tell by the way his voice lowered.

"He isn't *my* Justin anymore," she hissed.

"He thinks he is," he said with equal venom.

"What do you mean by that?" she responded through clamped teeth.

"He's called every day you've been here, and I'm getting damned sick of it." He looked at her as if she were guilty of some heinous crime.

She was stunned at this latest evidence of Justin's concern, and she didn't know whether to feel touched, guilty, or annoyed.

"That isn't my fault!" Her voice trembled with confused indignation. "He's paid to look after my interests," she defended.

"He's wanting to get you back behind that stone wall so he can keep his eye on you and protect his own interests." He waited a brief moment, his expression undergoing a change. She was about to protest his insults when he spoke again. "Why did you allow them to treat you like an adolescent?"

She was suddenly still. "I did it when my father was alive because it gave him peace of mind," she said bleakly. Chip reached across the table and moved her glasses farther up her nose. "I waited so long to break free that everyone thinks of me as someone without enough initiative to look after herself."

"And whose fault is that?" The strong mouth was taut.

"Mine," she admitted with a tilt to her head. "At least

I'm smart enough to know that I was weak. It doesn't mean, Mr. Thorn, that I'm weak now."

Their eyes did battle, and then he grinned. "Atta girl. Well, eat up. I'll drop you off at the house. Dolly should be there by now. I've got work to do at the office." He reached for her half-finished meat pie.

"Will I get to visit the logging camps?"

"You're still bent on going?"

"If it wouldn't be too much trouble for you to take me."

"And if it would be too much trouble?"

He was teasing, she could tell, so she gave him a wavering smile and admitted, "I'd still want to go."

He stood and loaded their empty plates onto a tray. "Push your glasses up, sweetheart."

It wasn't until they were outside that Margaret realized he'd called her sweetheart and there had been no one to hear it but her.

CHAPTER TEN

"WELCOME HOME, DOLLY."

Chip went forward to meet the short, full-bodied woman with the broad smile on her plain, lined face. He put an arm across her shoulders and hugged her affectionately. The woman had bustled in from the kitchen the moment they opened the front door.

"How are you feeling? You look as pert and sassy as ever."

"I feel like I could lick my weight in wildcats, Chip. I feel dandy. I'm glad to be back home."

"We're glad to have you. Did they get your insulin regulated so you won't have any more blackouts?"

"They think they did." She fairly beamed at him, then turned expectantly to Margaret.

"Dolly, this is Maggie Anderson—Maggie, Dolly Ashland."

Margaret put out her hand. "How do you do."

Dolly grasped Margaret's fingers in her broad, work-roughened hand. "I'm fine, just fine. You?"

"Fine," Margaret said, and they both laughed.

"I'm glad you two are fine," Chip said with a teasing grin. He leaned down to look into Margaret's face, then gently pulled off her glasses. "They're so coated with sawdust I'm surprised you can see at all." He whipped out a handkerchief, cleaned the lenses, and carefully settled the frames back onto her face. "Isn't that better?"

"Yes, thank you," she said softly.

"I'm leaving her here with you, Dolly. I've got a mountain of work to do at the office, and I want to take a few days off at the end of the week to show Maggie the logging camps. That means I'll have to burn the midnight oil for awhile. I may not be back tonight," he said to Margaret, "but you'll be okay here with Dolly and Penny."

"Of course I will. Isn't Penny due home soon? We worked on her spelling last night," she said to Dolly, "and I'm anxious to know how she did today."

A small smile tugged at the corner of Chip's mouth.

Dolly followed him to the door. "Now don't you be working through the night without any hot food in your stomach. You take time to go up to Donna's, or call and she'll send something down." Margaret laughed at the plump little woman talking to the tall, blue-eyed man as if he were a small boy. "And whatever did you do to those jeans? Chip Thorn, did you put them in with the whites?"

Chip's eyes caught Margaret's, and he laughed out loud. "Ask Maggie."

"He deserved it!" Margaret blurted. "I'm sorry there were only four pairs!"

Dolly's laughter bounced off the walls. "I just bet he did. You just might've met your match, Chip."

"I don't know about that. We've got a few rounds to go."

Margaret held her breath, watching his face to see if the remark held hidden sarcasm, but pure amusement was dancing in his eyes. Her own eyes must have given mute testimony of her anxiety, because suddenly he looked serious and he unfolded his arms and held them out to her.

"Come kiss me good-bye, sweetheart."

Letting her breath out in a shaky laugh, Margaret moved forward and into his arms, forcibly reminding herself that this was all for Dolly's benefit. It was her last coherent thought as he pressed his mouth to hers in a long, hard kiss. His arms held her, and she was suspended in a haze of longing. He lifted his head, and her eyes flew open to stare up into his. He lowered his head again, and his lips grazed her cheek and slipped to her ear.

"Do that again," he whispered.

"What?"

"Kiss me."

His mouth shaped itself to hers. She hesitated, then parted her lips against his and slowly traced the bottom curve of his inner lip with the tip of her tongue. This time there was a sense of familiarity in the feel of his mouth and in the flood of pleasure that washed over her.

Her eyes were cloudy and her mouth was half-parted, when he moved his head back so he could look into her face.

"Something tells me I should run like hell," he said for her ears alone. "But I'll be back tomorrow. You can count on it."

Margaret only half heard him. Still in a state of emotional confusion, she fixed unfocused eyes on his mouth and watched his lips form the words. His arms left her, and two big hands righted her glasses.

Dolly was chuckling behind them. "I thought you were going somewhere, Chip."

"Take care of my girl, Dolly. See you tomorrow." He went out the door, and Margaret moved toward it to watch as he got into the four-wheel drive, circled the yard, and sped away.

"Well, well, well." Dolly was smiling broadly when Margaret turned to look at her. "I think you've got old Chip horn-swoggled at last."

"Got him what?"

"Hog-tied. You know what I mean."

Margaret felt her face warm with telltale color. "Well, I don't know . . ."

Dolly laughed again. "Well, I do. You like him, don't you?"

Margaret turned away quickly and saw the yellow school bus at the end of the lane. "Here comes Penny." The cool air fanned her flushed face as she stepped out onto the porch to wait for the child. *Like him? I love him so desperately I may die from it.* Her thoughts raced and her heart pounded happily as she watched the little girl run toward her. *Could this ever be mine? Oh, God, I'd gladly give up every cent Daddy accumulated if there were just a chance I could live with Chip in a house like this and stand on the porch and watch our child run up the lane from the school bus.*

*   *   *

It became obvious as the evening progressed that Dolly and Penny adored Chip. Dolly's late husband had been one of the first men hired by Chip's father when he went into the lumber business. He had been killed in an accident, unrelated to the mill, several years ago, and Dolly had moved into the company house to act as housekeeper, bringing Penny with her. Penny's mother, Dolly's only child, lived in Denver. Although it was not voiced, Margaret was aware that Dolly disapproved of her daughter's lifestyle.

Margaret wanted desperately to reveal her identity to Dolly and ask her about Tom MacMadden, Edward Anthony, and August Thorn, but something held her back. Chip had gone to such lengths to keep her identity secret, and he must have had a very good reason for doing so.

It was after dinner and just before Penny's bedtime when the little girl dropped a piece of news that moved some of the puzzle pieces into place.

"I wish Chip wouldn't go back to his other house when Maggie goes home. I wish he'd stay here. Why doesn't he, Grandma? If Maggie stayed here, would he stay, too?"

Dolly's hands were still for a moment, and she let the needlework rest in her lap. "I don't know, honey."

Margaret's mind shifted into alertness and the picture of the barking dog on the dock flashed into it. "I'd think he'd have to go back and take care of his dog," she said, casually flipping the page of a magazine. Dolly's hands stilled once again, and she glanced at Margaret over the rims of her glasses.

"Hattie and Simon take care of Boozer," Penny said

quickly. "But Boozer likes me. Chip takes me up to his other house sometimes and lets me hit the balls on the pool table. I guess he wouldn't want to live here when he can live there." She sighed deeply. "It's got soft rugs and big bathrooms and a TV this big." Penny held her hands wide apart. "He's got one in his room, too. And you can punch on a little box by his bed and get whatever station you want. He let me do it once. Maybe he'll take you up there before you go home, Maggie."

"Maybe he will," Margaret murmured. She looked up to see Dolly's eyes fixed intently on hers, watching and judging her reaction. Refusing to allow her features to reflect her inner turmoil, she smiled at Penny and changed the subject. "We do good work, don't we? Was Miss Rogers surprised that you had a perfect spelling paper?"

"I want to get one next week, too. Will you be here to help me?" The child moved close and cuddled against her.

"I'll be here part of the week. Bring the list home tomorrow and we'll get a head start. Okay?"

After Penny went to bed, Dolly brought in mugs of hot chocolate, handed one to Margaret, and sat down again in the recliner.

"This is very good," Margaret said from her place at the end of the couch. This is where Chip and I made love, she suddenly thought. She moved her hand lovingly over the cushion beside her.

"You didn't know about Chip's house? You thought he lived here all the time?" Dolly asked, breaking into her thoughts.

"Ah, well, knowing he's a partner in Anthony/Thorn,

I was aware he could probably afford to live in his own house. But this is company property, so I assumed he had the right to live here."

"I don't know why he didn't tell you, Maggie. He must have his reasons. He's a fine man—and very young for all the responsibility he shoulders. This whole area depends on the jobs Chip provides." She paused as if groping for words to say something more in a tactful way. "I don't know whether you want to hear this or not, Maggie, but you're not the first girl to come out from the city to visit, and he's always brought them here."

Margaret and Dolly exchanged glances, and Margaret saw something like compassion in the older woman's eyes. "I like this house. It's cozy, and there's everything here a person could want. And you certainly don't have to hunt all over to find each other," Margaret said with a small laugh.

Dolly looked at her as if she couldn't believe her ears, and then her wrinkled face broke into a smile. "I like it, too. It's the nicest home Penny and I have ever had. I only hope we'll be able to live here until Penny is out of school and on her own."

"Is there any doubt of it?"

"There could be. Chip's partner died a few months ago, and his daughter inherited those shares. Chip said it could mean one of two things. She'll either want to expand the business and go for a foreign market—and he doesn't have the money for that—or she'll want to sell. And if he can't buy her out, she could sell to a big corporation that would close the mill down and use it for a tax deduction. I don't understand all that business stuff, but I know everyone is worried. Rich people from the city don't understand people like us."

"Has Chip met this woman?" she asked as casually as she could manage. As soon as the words were out of her mouth she wished she hadn't uttered them.

"Once, I guess. He said she was Ed's pampered little girl and we needn't expect her to see Anthony/Thorn as anything but small potatoes."

"You sound as if you knew her father."

"Oh, yes. We all liked him at first. Then he got into the big money and bought everything he wanted. After he got it, he didn't come around anymore." There was a bitter note in her voice. "You'll not find anyone 'round here who's got a good word for Ed Anthony."

"And why not? It was his money, too, that provided their jobs," Margaret defended, forgetting all thoughts of caution.

"His money, but it was August Thorn and his son who furnished the sweat and the know-how," Dolly said firmly. "Ed Anthony is a subject people 'round here don't talk much about. Tell me about yourself, Maggie. Chip said he met you on one of his trips to Chicago."

For the next half hour they chatted easily, and Margaret hoped her lies were convincing. The story she told was what she wished had happened, and that made the telling easier.

The next evening Chip phoned to say he wouldn't be coming out as he had planned. Several things had come up that needed his attention. Margaret swallowed her disappointment and listened as he told her that her friend had called from Chicago, and that he'd assured her that Maggie was having an enjoyable vacation.

"Maggie?" he said after a while when she didn't say anything.

"I'm here, Chip."

"This is a seven-party line, you know. Someone else may be wanting to use the phone."

"I understand." It was his way of reminding her to watch what she said, she realized.

"Be ready tomorrow morning and I'll come by and pick you up. We'll head on north."

Margaret thought she could hear someone breathing into the phone, and then she heard a muffled giggle.

"All right. How long will we be gone?"

"A couple of days. You don't need to take anything but a change of clothes. Tell Dolly to put a few things in a duffle bag for me. The Jeep is already packed with emergency supplies. Oh, yes. How about packing a food hamper? We should make it to the camp in time for dinner, but a snack on the way would be welcome."

"I'll do that."

"Have you missed me, sweetheart?"

You don't have to carry it that far, she thought angrily, and then she heard the giggle on the line again. She made a quick decision in favor of appropriate action.

"Of course I've missed you!" she breathed throatily. "Has it only been twenty-four hours, darling? It seems like years. Dolly and Penny are good company, but I want *you*," she purred. "And Chip, darling, you did say I could redo the house *upriver* after we're married, didn't you? I've been looking in the catalogs for ideas."

"Darling!" He cut her off abruptly. "Do you know you're announcing our engagement to everyone on the party line?" His voice had more than a hint of firmness in it.

"I told you he was going to marry her," said a muffled voice that sounded very much like Beth's. The hand held over the phone failed to keep the words from coming across the line.

"Oh! I'm sorry, darling," Margaret said in a soft, saccharine tone. "Didn't you want anyone to know?"

"Of course I did, sweetheart. But I wanted to wait until I had the ring on your finger. Would you like me to call the Chicago papers with the announcement?" There was an edge of a threat in his voice.

Margaret caught her breath. What would she do now? She hadn't intended for the joke to go this far. "That won't be necessary. I'll do it when I go home to make the arrangements." Her voice tightened; the fun had gone out of the game.

"Whatever you say, sweetheart." He paused, then said, "Beth, what were you doing in town today? I told you what would happen if you skipped school again."

"I didn't skip! Classes were canceled for a teachers' meeting. If you don't believe me, you can call the high school," the young voice rang out with no hesitation.

"I believe you."

"Then why'd you have to say it on the line? You know everybody listens."

"Not everybody. I don't think Tim Walker's on the line. Are you, Tim?"

"Oh, you make me so mad, Chip! I'm going to hang up. 'Bye!"

"Are you still there, Maggie?"

"Yes. You mean people listen to other people's conversations? How can you conduct private business?"

Chip laughed. "You can't—not on the phone, that's for sure."

"Who is Tim Walker?"

"A boy in Beth's class. I'll tell you about him sometime. Are you terribly bored?" he asked in a tone that seemed to assume that she was.

"Nooo," she drawled. "Keith's wife has been over, and I've been helping Dolly prepare apple pies for the freezer. We made six pies. Tomorrow we're going to make apple butter."

There was a pause on the other end of the line. "You like doing that?"

"Of course! I learned to do a lot of things in school. It's just that it's been so long since I've done any of them. Chip . . . ?"

"Yes."

"Guess what? Penny's class had a spelling bee today, and she won!"

He chuckled. "Great. I suppose you had a hand in it."

"Well, we did study together."

"I'll ring off, Maggie. Be ready at about ten, and I'll be by to pick you up. Dream of me," he whispered, and he rang off before she could reply.

Margaret was ready and waiting long before ten o'clock. A duffle bag containing a change of clothes for Chip, a backpack with Margaret's things, and a Styrofoam hamper of food rested beside the living room door. She was nervous and paced the floor restlessly.

Before leaving for school, Penny had put her arms around Margaret's neck and hugged her. "You're neat, Maggie. I wish you'd never go away."

Remembering now, Margaret stopped her pacing and looked at Dolly. "How can Penny's mother leave her here and not come see her? I'd give anything to have a child like Penny." She regretted the words instantly as a pained expression flashed across Dolly's face. "I'm sorry, Dolly. I—"

"It's all right. Marion is like a lot of other girls. She likes the things a city offers. She couldn't wait to leave here, and she took up with the first man who offered to take her away. Penny was the result. He left her, and she brought Penny to me. Penny will probably want to do the same. I've no hopes of holding on to her. I've seen it happen so many times. And . . . so has Chip." Dolly nervously wiped her hands on her apron. "Even his own mother—"

The scrunch of tires on gravel cut off Dolly's words, and she went to the door. Margaret stood in the middle of the room. Her jacket was on the back of the chair. Chip's eyes found hers the instant he came through the door, and a feeling of happiness swamped her.

"Ready to see what life in the backwater is all about?" Beneath his wool plaid jacket he wore a blue denim shirt tucked smoothly into his jeans. On his head was a visor cap with the Anthony/Thorn logo emblazoned in green on a white background.

"I'm ready if you are." Margaret reached for her jacket.

"It's a dusty drive. Sure you want to wear the contacts?"

"I have my glasses in my purse."

"Okay then. We'd better get started."

"Hi, Chip," Dolly finally said from her place beside the door.

"Oh, hello, Dolly. I didn't see you. I—"

"Don't make excuses," she chuckled. "I know why you didn't see me." She split a wickedly sparkling look between the two of them. "You'd better get started, unless you want a cup of coffee first."

"None for me, thanks. Is this it?" He glanced down at the bags beside the door.

"There're clean sleeping bags and blankets piled in the chair on the porch," Dolly said. "The ones up at the camp might be a little raunchy by now," she added with a note of derision in her voice.

Chip carried the bags and the hamper out onto the porch, and Margaret and Dolly followed.

"Hop in," Chip said without preamble. He opened the back of the Jeep and tossed in the bags.

"You'll have a good time, Maggie, if you can stand the rough ride," Dolly said.

Impulsively, Margaret hugged the older woman and kissed her cheek. "I can stand it all right. 'Bye, Dolly. Tell Penny I'll be looking for a star on her spelling paper."

As soon as Margaret was seated beside Chip he started the motor and turned to look at her. "It's no luxury hotel up there, you know." The sarcasm bit.

"I know," she said simply.

He shrugged and swung the car in a circle and headed down the lane.

They left the road before they reached the mill and

took a dusty track that almost immediately began to climb through the trees. The road was rough almost to the point of nonexistence, jolting the Jeep first to one side and then to the other. Chip didn't seem to mind the pitching, but Margaret found it distinctly uncomfortable. As she grasped the armrest on the door to minimize the turbulence, she wondered if Chip had chosen the worst route available solely for her benefit. If so, he would be disappointed, because she wasn't going to utter one word of complaint. Was he still angry because she'd made that remark about marriage on the telephone? As soon as I'm gone he can tell whatever story he wants to save face, if that's what's bothering him, she thought with a feeling almost like despair.

The track wound upward, and gradually the trees thinned out, bare rock taking over from earth. They drove along the edge of a deep wooded chasm. The air was cool and clean-smelling, and the sun shining through the windows was warm on her face. Margaret was sure she had never seen anything so achingly beautiful as the landscape stretched out before her.

Neither of them said much. Chip appeared to be preoccupied with his own thoughts. Margaret took a deep breath and half turned in her seat to look at his face. He was frowning, his lips set in a tight line. She couldn't see his eyes to read his expression, but she noticed that his knuckles were white as his tanned hands clenched the steering wheel. Not sure this was the right time to say anything to him, she was still compelled to murmur, "Oh, Chip! It's so beautiful up here."

"This was my father's favorite place," he said quietly after a moment or two.

"And yours?" she ventured. She saw the broad shoulders lift.

"There're hundreds of beautiful vistas like this all over the northwest."

"It seems impossible," she remarked softly.

The long magnificent sweep of landscape was green, yellow, and bronze. The colors glistened in the morning sun, providing a startling contrast to the snowcapped ridges of the mountains beyond. Margaret found it all breathtaking, overpowering, and beyond anything she could have imagined.

"It's magnificent!" Her voice was joyous. She turned her head sharply and looked at Chip. He had taken his eyes from the road for an instant, and they locked with hers.

"We'll be going down again soon, but first there's a place where we can turn off if you want to stop a bit."

"I'd like to, if we have time. Oh! Look, Chip!" A startled deer raced ahead of them and disappeared into the woods, its white tail standing straight out as it fled. She caught her breath and laughed with sheer delight.

At the top of the crest he pulled the car over and stopped. Margaret opened the door and got out. The ravine was only yards away. She moved a few feet and stood almost on the edge of it, gazing at the view of vast forest tracks falling away below.

"Careful." Chip had followed and was standing behind her. "The ground can give way in some of these places."

Margaret stepped back, and his hands came roughly about her waist, drawing her even farther from the edge. They stood quietly for a moment, and then Chip suddenly jerked away. He yanked open the Jeep door and reached for the fieldglasses in the glove compartment. He adjusted them and, holding them steady, focused on a distant spot.

It was several seconds before Margaret noticed the thin trail of vapor rising from the treetops below. Smoke—not a lot of it, but almost certainly too much for a small campfire.

Chip scanned the distance for several seconds before he brought the glasses down. "It can't be far off the road," he said tightly. "Hop in and hold on. It's going to be a rough ride." Inside the car he picked up the mike and flipped a button on the CB radio. "Break for Anthony/Thorn camp four. This is a ten-seventy. Repeat. This is a ten-seventy."

"Camp four. Go ahead."

"Chip Thorn. Smoke in the west section down a couple of miles from the ridge. I'm checking it out."

"Okay, Chip. Position noted. Will stand by for your report."

"Ten-four. I'm gone."

Margaret closed her eyes briefly as the rear wheels skidded on takeoff and the Jeep shot forward. She didn't speak, leaving Chip to concentrate on his driving. She kept her eyes on the spiral of smoke, and just as she thought they were about to pass it, Chip turned off into the trees. She registered how important it was for a vehicle to have four-wheel drive in this part of the country. The going was much slower as he angled the car downward between the trees, detouring around fallen logs and easing across gullies.

"Is it likely to be a serious fire?" Margaret queried

while clutching the dashboard to keep herself from being slammed into it.

"Any fire out here is serious. There's a lot of dry underbrush. We need the fall rains to dampen things down."

He didn't speak again. They were going downhill at a perilous angle. It didn't occur to Margaret to be frightened. It was exhilarating to be sharing this experience with Chip. They could smell the smoke long before they reached the bottom of the gully and turned to the right. Borne on a light breeze, the acrid scent stung her nostrils. The actual fire was in an open area and was so far confined to grass and the brush edging it. Chip slammed on the brakes, flipped off the ignition, and jumped out. Margaret saw little flames lick across another expanse of dry grass and into the brush, then run up a small tree like hungry red tongues.

"Come on. Grab those blankets. Use your feet on the small patches," he shouted. "Keep upwind from the flames." He jerked a fire extinguisher from the back of the truck and flung it over his shoulder. "Be careful. Stay out of heavy smoke."

Margaret beat at the larger flames with the blanket while stamping out the small ones with her feet. *No! No! You won't get to my trees!* Like red and gold dancers they raced toward a young fir tree, and with a swish of the blanket she beat them back. Tears were streaming down her face from the smoke in her eyes, her vision was blurred, and the heat seared her throat. When the flames engulfed a bush, she circled behind it, flailing the grass with the blanket to keep the fire from spreading. She worked purely on instinct while the sweat rolled down her face and her hands became locked onto the end of the blanket.

There was no time to think about her parched throat, her heat-flushed face, or her arms that felt as if they each weighed a hundred pounds. She worked as if her life depended on it, and gradually she began to win against the flames. It was an exhausting effort. As fast as one patch was stamped or beaten out, another seemed to flare into being. Chip had emptied the fire extinguisher and was now beside her, beating at the flames with another blanket.

When at last it was over, they stood smoke-grimed and red-eyed in the blackened section. Margaret walked back to the Jeep, dragging a scorched blanket. She leaned wearily against the car.

"Did we do it?" It was an asinine question uttered out of sheer exhaustion. She knew if they hadn't, they would both still be fighting the flames.

Chip grinned at her. His face was blackened by smoke and his head wet with sweat. "You bet we did," he said proudly, reaching into the Jeep for the CB to report the good news to the camp.

"It was caused by a campfire, Joe. Pass the word along. If they catch the bastards I'll file charges against them. This whole section would have gone up like a tinderbox in another hour."

"I never did see the smoke, Chip," the voice said. "Have you been fighting that fire all this time? It's been almost three hours."

"Is that all? It seemed more like three days to Maggie and me. If you see anything of those campers, let me know. Won't be moving from here for a while; we're too damned tired."

"Ten-four, Chip."

Chip hung up the mike, then stretched and rubbed his shoulders. "I couldn't have done it without you, Maggie."

"I never realized how fast a fire could travel. How terrifying it must be to get caught in a big one," she mused aloud.

"This was a little one that could have turned into a big one," he said after a few minutes of carefully studying the area. "Someone made a fire this morning and left it smoldering. A little puff of wind was all it took."

"Were they hunters?" she asked, remembering the graceful deer dashing into the trees.

"Hunters usually come in with a guide if they don't know the area. Anyone who lives around here would know better. More than likely it's a couple of backpackers out from the city." He looked and sounded grim. He took out a jug, poured water into a cup, and handed it to her. "Would you rather have a cola?"

"Oh, no. That was delicious," she said after draining the cup.

He refilled the cup for himself. "There's more water in the back of the truck if you want to wash up a bit." He pulled down the tailgate and held up another jug with a spigot. "An absolute necessity in this country. Never go anywhere without water and a fire extinguisher." He dug into his duffle bag and drew out a towel. After wetting the end of it, he held it out to her.

She took the towel and pressed it to her face. "Oh, that feels good!" Suddenly she started to laugh. "I've lost that contact again."

"Good. Take the other one out, throw it away, and put on your glasses."

"I think I will," she said, moving to do just that. She laughed up at him through squinted eyelids. "You'll just have to put up with my glasses sliding down my nose."

"I think I can handle that, but wash your face. You look like a kid who's been playing in the coal bin."

CHAPTER ELEVEN

MARGARET PULLED A scarf out of her bag and tied her hair back from her face. Her cheeks felt warm to the touch, as if they'd been sunburned. She smeared her face generously with cold cream and carefully removed it with a tissue before applying a skin lotion.

Chip had stripped off his shirt and hung it over the open car door to dry while he washed the soot from his neck and arms. She made a determined effort to keep her eyes away from his superbly built body, but they returned again and again. He was a strong man without an ounce of superfluous flesh on the whole of his muscular form. His back was wonderfully broad, the muscles across his shoulders and biceps well-developed and powerful.

Margaret felt a thrill of possession at the sight of him. The thought that she had really felt the full length of his naked body next to hers made the breath catch in her throat. She stayed where she was, breathing deeply to ease the ache in her chest.

"Are you hungry?" he asked, turning and putting on his shirt.

"More tired than hungry." She smiled apologetically.

"Hey, your cheeks are red. Did you burn your face?"

"A little. I've put some lotion on it." She pushed her glasses higher up on the bridge of her nose, a purely nervous gesture.

"How do you feel about staying out here tonight? We can make it to the lumber camp, but I'm not too crazy about driving that track at night."

"I've never camped out before."

"Afraid?"

"Nooo . . ."

"Well then, let's dig out the sleeping bags and take a rest before we eat. Okay?"

"Okay."

Chip backed the Jeep up to a level place beneath the pines. Margaret walked alongside, hardly believing this was happening. From the back of the truck he pulled out a canvas tarp and the sleeping bags and, after kicking pine needles into a thick layer, he spread them out atop it.

"If you lie on top you'd better use this. It'll start cooling down soon." He tossed her a clean blanket.

Margaret got stiffly to the ground, easing her limbs. "I'm not sleepy, just tired." She stretched out with her arms raised and her hands clasped beneath her head. Had anyone told her before she left Chicago that she would be sleeping in the woods with Duncan Thorn, she would have thought they were out of their minds. Yet here she was, and she had never felt so secure, so out of danger, in her life. She closed her eyes and slept, a small smile still on her lips.

*   *   *

It was almost dark when she awoke. Her limbs were stiff and aching. She rolled onto her back and stared up at the trees. For a few seconds she didn't know where she was, and she was startled. Then, as memory flooded back, she lay still again. Birds chattered to her from the treetops where they were preparing to roost for the night, but there was no other sound. Was she alone? Had Chip left her here? No. The Jeep was outlined against the darkness of the woods. She threw off the blanket and rolled onto her knees before she could get to her feet. It was cold, and she was tempted to crawl back under the blanket. Instead she went to the truck and reached for her jacket.

She could see now. Chip had built a small fire enclosed within a circle of stones. The smell of the wood smoke tingled her nostrils, but it was unlike the acrid smell of the burning grass and brush. Her eyes swept the area for Chip. Strangely, she was unafraid, and she stood with her hands held out to the small flames.

"Hello, sleeping beauty. I was beginning to think you'd sleep on through the night." Chip came out of the trees and into the clearing with an armful of small branches. He piled them a safe distance from the flames and knelt to place a stick of wood on the fire.

"Why didn't you wake me? I've wasted the whole afternoon sleeping."

"I figured you were tired. You did a terrific job helping me put out the fire, and you were exhausted." He stood and she squinted up at him. "I took your glasses off. They're on the dashboard in the car."

"So that's why I can't see. I thought I was still half asleep."

"Silly girl. Stay where you are and I'll get them for you." He returned with the glasses and set them in place. It was a gesture of tenderness, and she involuntarily began to tremble.

He took a flashlight from his jacket pocket and put it into her hands. "If you feel the need, you can go behind those bushes," he said, turning her with his hands on her shoulders and facing her in the opposite direction. "Hurry back. I'm starving."

"So am I. Don't start without me."

She felt the cold as soon as she stepped away from the fire, and she hastened to be out of sight so she could relieve herself. All her instincts urged her to hurry so she could get back to him. His mood toward her had changed since their battle against the fire. His fingers *had* lingered behind her ears when he set her glasses on her face, hadn't they? Oh, she chided herself, you're floating in a current of wishful thinking.

As she was pulling up her jeans, a crackling sound came from the underbrush. She froze. The sound came again, a shuffling, slithering, swishing. A prickle of fear ran up her spine. She felt on the ground for the flashlight. Her fingers curled around it, but she couldn't find the switch to turn it on. She heard the sound again, and this time a small squeak accompanied it.

"Chip!" she screamed.

Fear propelled her, and she bolted. She met him running to her, and she threw herself against him.

"There's something back there! I heard it under the brush." She clutched him in terror.

"Give me the flashlight and I'll see what it is. Go wait by the fire." His voice was the merest whisper in her ear.

She stood with her back to the fire and her eyes riveted on the beam of light flashing about the area. It seemed an eternity before the light was coming back toward the campfire.

"I didn't see anything. It was probably an owl catching a mouse." He turned off the light and put it into his pocket. "I can understand your fright. They can make a hell of a racket." His hands grasped her shoulders, and he shook her gently. "Okay? Hey, you haven't even zipped up your jeans," he chided softly. She stood, docile as a child, while he tucked her shirt down into her waistband, fastened the snap, and pulled up the zipper. "The moon will be up soon."

Margaret had the odd feeling that the world was standing still. "I'm sorry."

He smiled at her reassuringly. "I hope you put enough food in that hamper. My stomach thinks I've deserted it."

He brought the tarps and the sleeping bags over to the fire and spread them on the ground. They sat opposite each other with the hamper between them and pulled out thick meatloaf sandwiches, celery, cheese, deviled eggs, and a plastic sack of chocolate-chip cookies.

"Ahhhh," he sighed contentedly as he viewed the food. "Now if that coffee in the thermos is still hot, we've got it made." He smiled into her eyes, and at that moment she was sure she would never be frightened of anything as long as he was with her.

"Thank you," she murmured after taking a deep breath.

"You're welcome. But what did I do?"

"You're so calm, so unafraid. I feel perfectly safe with you."

"Why are you whispering? It's nice to know I inspire confidence, but I'm not all that sure it's such a compliment." He gave her an inquiring look. "Do you realize that you're alone with me, deep in the woods, miles from anyone?" He lowered his voice to a stage-villain's whisper. "I may ravish you!"

"Ravish?" Her laugh rang out. "Will you permit me to finish my sandwich first?"

Chip took a swallow of his coffee. "All that stands between you and that fate worse than death is the fact that I'm an Eagle Scout, dedicated to helping maidens in distress and old ladies crossing busy streets."

"Thank heaven for that!" Her eyes continued to smile into his, and her heart beat faster.

Chip built up the fire, moving methodically as he always did, while Margaret repacked the hamper. The moon had appeared from behind the treetops, rendering the flashlight unnecessary. The air was still and cold, and she missed the heat of the campfire when she rose stiffly to take the hamper back to the Jeep. By the time she returned, her body was shaking with a sudden chill not entirely due to the night air. Chip was feeding small sticks into the fire. She looked down on his bent head and broad back, and her legs suddenly went weak with a trembling awareness of him.

"We'll have to smother the fire when we go to bed," he said over his shoulder. "The woods are too dry to risk it. We really need a drenching rain."

"The fire doesn't give out much smoke," she observed.

He sat down beside her on the blanket. "I'm a Boy Scout. Remember?"

Margaret drew her legs up and wrapped her arms about them. "Do you do this often?"

"Camp out? Not as often as I'd like." One corner of his mouth tilted.

"You'd hate living in the city." It wasn't a question.

"I wouldn't do it," he said firmly. "Are you cold?"

"Only my back. The fire feels heavenly on the front."

"I can remedy that. Boy Scout Manual page two hundred and twelve." He moved until his back rested against a small sapling. "Come here." He held out his hand, and she walked on her knees toward him. She found herself sitting on the blanket with her back against his chest, his arms looped around her and his long legs stretched out on either side of hers.

"Now *your* back will be cold."

"I can fix that, too. Hand me that other blanket." He took it from her hand and draped it around his back. With his hands at her waist he pulled her to him and wrapped her in the folds of the blanket. "How's that? Ingenious, isn't it?" There was a thread of laughter in his voice. "Now sit still, wiggle-worm, and I'll get you warm."

"You have all sorts of hidden talents," she said, hoping he wouldn't notice that her heart was about to jump out of her breast.

"Surprised?" His hand came out from under the blanket and lifted her glasses off her nose. "You don't need these now. I'll lay them here by the tree so we can find them later. Okay?" He wrapped his arms tighter about her and rested his cheek against hers. "That's better," he sighed. "The night is young. What are you going to do to entertain me? Talk or sing?"

"Don't laugh. I sing quite well."

He did laugh. She could feel the movement of his chest against her back. His hand spread across her rib cage, his thumbs between her breasts.

"I talk much better than I sing," he admitted.

"It's a relief to know you're not perfect at everything."

His fingers tightened and raked her ribs. She wriggled, the movement bringing her against the pressure of his hard thighs. He lifted one hand to brush her hair from his face and to tuck a strand behind her right ear. His fingers stroked downward and wrapped about her neck while he rubbed his thumb along her jaw. She could feel his warmth and his strength engulfing her, and she closed her eyes, pressing her cheek to his.

"I thought you were going to sing. Instead you're going to sleep." His mustache tickled her ear.

"I was thinking of what I was going to sing."

"Liar. You were trying to get out of it."

"I was not! Just hush up and listen, Chip Thorn."

She began to sing, softly at first, then with gathering confidence. "Country roads, take me home . . . to the place I belong, West Virginia . . ." She finished the song without a trace of embarrassment.

"That was super. You *can* sing!" The low voice in her ear was obviously sincere. "How about an encore?"

"No, it's your turn."

"You won't like it," he warned.

"You're a coward!" she accused.

"Them's fighting words!" He nipped her ear. "On top of old Smokey, all covered with snow, I lost my true lover . . . for courting too slow. For courting . . ."

"You have a good voice," she cheered. "Let's sing one together. Anything. You start and I'll join in."

He began to sing an old ballad, and when she recognized it she joined in. "When I grow too old to dream, I'll have you to remember . . ." Happiness sang like a bird in her heart as their voices blended. She wasn't aware when the *I's* turned to *we's*. "And when we grow too old to dream, our love will live in our hearts . . ."

Margaret took a shuddering breath when they finished the song. Her hand had moved to cover his where it gripped her rib cage. She was conscious of his arms tightening. Her heart was pounding with the urge to turn and press her lips hotly to his. All her senses were filled with his overwhelming male presence. She could feel his lips and his mustache at the side of her neck and smell the wood smoke in his hair.

"Maggie, Maggie!" The words seemed torn out of him. "What am I going to do about you?" He placed small quick kisses along her jaw. "In one short week you've woven a beautiful silver web around me, drawing me to you as easily as if I had a ring in my nose!" He took a deep quivering breath. "I should have turned you over to Tom or Bill Wassal and gotten the hell up to the camps until you were gone. I knew it that first night. You've aroused something in me that makes my insides melt like honey when I look at you." Margaret heard a tinge of resentment in his last words.

He turned her sideways so that her cheek lay against his shoulder. One hand curved about her neck, tilting her face up to his; the other spread across her back, pressing her to him. It was too dark to see his eyes, but she knew they were looking into hers. Her hand reached up to his face. It was all there in her touch—the love, the warmth, the yearning.

"I love you. I feel I must tell you that." The words tumbled out of her parted lips even as the tears rolled out of her eyes.

He was as still as if he had turned to stone. A low moaning sound came from his throat, and he slowly lowered his lips to sip at her tears. "Oh, Maggie," he crooned, rocking her in his arms. "We're as different as daylight and dark. I'm a rough, coarse man who doesn't need or want a lot of physical comforts. I love my life here, my people, my work. I need a woman who loves this country as much as I do, one who wouldn't mind the isolation in the winter. I want a large family, sons to raise who will grow up to love this forest and these trees the way I do." His voice was a husky whisper against her face. "That's what I *need*, sweetheart." He kissed her eyes, her mouth, her cheeks. "But what I want . . . is you! My little princess, so utterly feminine that I want to put you in my pocket and keep you safe always."

Her hand tried to guide his lips to hers, but he resisted. She could feel his body tremble as his mind grappled with logic.

"You'd hate it here after a while. It's a pattern. I've seen it happen many times, and it leaves nothing but bitterness. My own mother thought it was the end of the earth. For her it was hell, but it was the only place my Dad and I wanted to be. Sweetheart, it would never work out for us. You have everything in the world back in Chicago."

"Oh, Chip! Darling . . ." It seemed that everything she

had ever dreamed of having was almost in reach, and yet it was slipping away from her. "Okay! I'll give it away! I'd give up every cent to live in that company house with you, ride in the Jeep, go shopping at Lemon's." She was almost sobbing.

"Sweetheart, don't cry. You're Ed Anthony's daughter, and you wouldn't be happy here for long." His cheeks were wet with tears.

"I would. I've never been so happy in my life. I could learn how to do things. Dolly would teach me. I love you," she said with quiet desperation, discarding all pride. "I love you."

"Stop it!" he said harshly against her mouth. His arms had tightened to the point that she could scarcely breathe. "You don't know what you're saying. One winter out here and you'd be screaming for the city lights."

"How do you know until you let me try?"

"I've seen it happen before. Most women feel as you do at first, but they don't care deeply enough—"

"I care, and I'm not *most* women! Don't you dare lump me into a group. I'm me, Margaret Anthony, and I know what I want. It's taken a long time for me to get to the time in my life when I can make a choice, and whether you want me or not, I'm staying!" She tried to push herself away from him, but he held her tightly.

"Oh, for heaven's sake! Be still!" He looked down into her flushed face. "Maggie, you've just begun to live. You've known no other man—"

"Don't talk to me as if I were Beth! I'm twenty-five years old, damn it! Maybe a naïve twenty-five, but a grown woman nevertheless!" She abruptly sat up, and the blanket and his arms fell away. "Don't cast me aside because of something your mother did. Perhaps your parents' feelings didn't go deep enough to surmount their problems. The trouble could have been with them and not with where they were living. If they had loved each other enough, they could have found a compromise." Her eyes were intent on his face, willing the hardness to relax. When it did, she snuggled back into his arms and pressed her face to his neck. "Hold me, darling. I love you. I know I can make you love me back if you let me stay."

He embraced her roughly, but there was nothing rough about the way he kissed her. There was a wild sweet singing in her heart, but tears of joy and hope would not stay back. He kissed her tenderly, holding her like some newfound treasure that he didn't want to break, and she held him as though he were a dream that would fade away if she let go. He kissed her throat, her cheeks wet with tears, her mouth, and when she laid her hand against his face he turned his lips to her palm.

"Chip . . ."

"Shhhh. Don't think about it anymore. I just want to love you, hold you, kiss you . . ." His exploring hands gripped her buttocks.

"Is that all?" she whispered, pulling her lips away. Her own wandering fingers brushed over tightly stretched denim, paused hesitantly, then slid down over hard, pulsing maleness. She felt his body jolt with the contact, and his breath came hot and uneven in her ear.

"No, you beautiful little wench, that's not all!" he gasped.

Margaret laughed joyously, lightly bit his neck, and held on for several seconds. When she let go she kissed the spot repeatedly and rubbed her tongue against it in a licking, healing movement.

"I'll ask you to get into the sleeping bag with me if I have to," she murmured giddily. "I lost my pride where you're concerned hours ago."

"Shameless little hussy!" She half lay at an angle across his lap. His free hand burrowed into the top of her jeans and caressed the indentation at the base of her spine. He nipped at her earlobe and growled, "Soft, beautiful little kitten. I may not let you out of that sleeping bag for days."

"Will you put that in writing?" She threw her arms about his neck and scattered kisses over his grinning face. "Just think of all you can teach me. Think of all the fantastic things I can do to keep you with me. I'm a fast learner, darling. I'll be your lover, your friend, your mistress—"

He abruptly lifted her off his lap and got to his feet, pulling her up and into his arms. He shook his head sadly, but he had a triumphant grin on his face. "Well, what do you know?" he mused aloud. "I've got a horny little sexpot on my hands."

"Complaining?" she challenged, gazing at him with a happy smile.

"Do you think I've got holes in my head? C'mon."

Chip quickly rearranged the bed of the truck so he could throw in several armloads of pine needles. He spread out the canvas and one of the opened sleeping bags while Margaret shoveled dirt onto the campfire. She was shaking with cold and anticipation when Chip lifted her into the truck.

"Oh, darling, I'm so cold." She had left on her shirt,

bra, and panties, and she quickly snuggled down under the blankets.

Chip crawled in beside her, pulled the covers over them, and wrapped his arms and legs around her. He had taken off everything except his undershorts, and she burrowed against the warm, hard length of his body.

"I thought we'd be sleeping on the ground," she said through chattering teeth. He began to rub her back and limbs with his hands.

"We could have if we'd left the fire going. Without it some nocturnal animal might wander too close, and I wouldn't care to wake up and startle a skunk." He nuzzled his lips against her face. "Not that I plan on doing much sleeping with you in my arms. Take this off, honey. You'll be warm soon." He helped her slide out of her shirt, then unhooked her bra. "Why do you wear this thing? You don't need it."

"I'm afraid I'll . . . sag," she stammered.

"Not for years. Maybe not even then . . . with proper handling." He fit his fingers about her soft flesh and squeezed gently.

"I like the feel of you." She raked her fingers over the soft fur on his chest.

"And I like the feel of you. I want to lose myself inside you," he whispered urgently, sliding out of his shorts while she removed the last thin barrier between them. His body tensed, and the hard muscles of his belly rippled under her exploring fingers. "Sweetheart, are you warm enough? . . . Are you ready?"

A powerful, sweeping tide of love flowed over her, making her feel stronger than the hard-muscled body entwined with hers. Her fingers touched him lightly and pulled him into her moist warmness. With a small throaty cry he cupped his hands over her hips and pushed himself more deeply into her. His mouth closed hungrily over hers in a moist, deep, endless kiss. It seemed to Margaret that they were no longer two separate people, but one blended together by magic.

"We're going to name our baby Duncan," she gasped, tearing her mouth free of his, "and we're going to make him tonight."

For a second he hesitated. "Oh, God! What a time to spring something like that on me!"

She laughed joyously, and her hand slapped at his taut hips. "Get on with what you're doing. We've got the rest of the night to talk."

"I can't believe you," he said hoarsely after he had shuddered with release and they lay so close together they could feel each other's heartbeats. "Where did you come from? What are you doing here?"

Her hand tickled down over his heart to the bottom of his rib cage. "They say I came from right here, close to your heart."

"Sweetheart, I believe you did!" Their noses were side by side and their mouths so close they touched when they spoke. "I never knew a woman like you existed, so small, so sweet . . ."

"If you'd wanted me bigger, you should have grown a bigger rib," she teased, nibbling playfully on his chin.

"I don't want you one bit different from what you are." He kissed her softly and held still as she ran her tongue over his lips. "Maybe a little different," he said hesitantly. "I'd rather you were as poor as a church-mouse."

A small spurt of fear knifed through her. "You said we wouldn't talk about it. Just love me, Chip. Pull the stars down from the heavens. Make me part of you again."

He kissed her deeply. She trembled with her need to have him fill the emptiness within her. His mouth stayed locked to hers as he pulled her over on top of him and molded her soft body to his. She stretched out atop him, feeling him throb against her belly once again.

His hands grasped her hips and settled her into position. "Oh, you feel so good," he groaned with fresh desperation. She buried her face in the hollow of his throat, whimpering at the glorious agony of sensation he was creating in her. Slowly he guided her to fulfillment. His hands on her hips pressed her downward, and she was consumed by rippling waves of exquisite convulsions that left her shaken and exhausted.

"Darling," she whispered when she returned to earth and found herself sprawled on top of him. "Now teach me how to please you."

He laughed into her ear and squeezed her languid frame tightly to his. "You're doing just fine." He rolled so that they lay side by side and tucked the covers more securely around them. They lay quietly contented for a long while.

"Don't go to sleep. Talk to me." Margaret's bare foot stroked his calves, and her hands explored his back.

"Talk? Why waste time talking?" His hand cradled her breast, his thumb stroking her nipple.

"They're not very big," she whispered apologetically against his shoulder. She instantly felt his silent laughter. She moved her face so she could look at him, although his features were a blur in the darkness. "Well? Don't men like big breasts? They're always making jokes about them, and that country singer who—"

The laughter broke free. "Maggie, sweetheart! Big isn't always best. Yours are just right. They fit into my hand as if made to order." He squeezed gently to emphasize his point.

"That's a relief," she sighed. "Chip, will you still want to do this when I'm pregnant?"

"You crazy girl! Talk, talk, talk! Keep talking and I'll keep you awake all night long," he threatened. His hand roamed over her hip and thigh, his mouth journeyed across her face.

"Tell me about your mother."

"Oh, for Pete's sake!" He rolled onto his back and spoke to the top of the truck. "I've got an armful of warm, naked woman, and she wants to talk about my *mother?*"

"Please, Chip." Margaret pressed close to his side, hugging him with her arms and legs.

He talked hurriedly in tense, short sentences. His father had met his mother in Seattle during the war, married her, and brought her to Montana. She'd hated it from the very first day. When Chip was ten years old she took him back to Seattle, and he didn't spend much time with his father until he turned fourteen. After that as long as he was in school, he spent summer vacations in Montana. He loved the country, and his father taught him the lumber business. August Thorn lived to see his son take over the management of the company he had sacrificed his marriage to build.

"He was lonely," Chip said quietly. "He should have found another woman, but I guess he loved my mother too much."

"Did she remarry?"

"Oh, yes. She married a rich doctor, and they spend part of every year in Hawaii. I see her about once a year because it's the thing to do. She doesn't approve of me any more than she did of my dad."

"Why not?" Margaret was indignant. She flopped over so she could peer down into his face. "You're wonderful! Everyone loves you—the men who work for you, Dolly, Penny, me. I don't like your mother," she concluded with a tremor in her voice.

"She'll like you," he said drily. "When she finds out about you, she'll think she's died and gone to heaven."

"Don't tell her!" She sprawled on top of him and hid her face in his neck. "Dolly and Penny liked me without knowing, and you like me in spite of who I am. Oh, why do things have to be so complicated?"

"C'mon, princess. It isn't that bad." He chuckled softly. "I'd rather play than talk anyway. How about you? Hmmmm?" His experienced hands moved over her, stroking, fondling, arousing.

She lay quietly against him. Her arms around his waist were firm in their possession, still trying to protect him from the hurt of a disapproving mother. His touch became more intimate, and she felt movement against her thigh as his passion mounted.

"Darling, I read somewhere it wasn't good for a man to do it so many times." Her hand wandered down across his flat belly.

He laughed and hugged her hard. "Oh, princess! You're priceless! If you weren't so damn sweet, I'd think you were dangerous!"

CHAPTER TWELVE

THE MOTOR STRAINED, and the back tires skidded on the wet grass as Chip brought the Jeep up out of the woods and onto the road at the top of the ridge. It was almost noon.

Margaret had opened her eyes to see him leaning on one elbow looking down at her, his other hand playing with her, touching, stroking, caressing. His eyes were clear. He had been awake for some time. She closed her eyes and then opened them again, floating, drifting, lost in feeling. She lifted her arms and encircled his neck. She saw love and passion in his eyes, and infinite tenderness.

"It's magic. I feel like a princess in fairyland."

"Hi, princess," he murmured before lowering his mouth, his lips brushing hers, kissing her with teasing slowness. A restless urgency surfaced, and she clung to him in response, overwhelmed by a primitive hungry yearning.

"I love you, love you."

A quiver ran through his body, and he began to make slow, tender love to her. Passion came sweeping in like a tide, carrying them on its tumultuous journey until all need, all sensation erupted in physical release.

Now, sitting beside him in the Jeep, Margaret inched closer and slid her hand over his thigh and pinched him. The foot on the gas pedal lifted, and the truck slowed.

"What was that for?" he demanded.

"For not telling me about your house upriver, or about Boozer. And for taking me on that long, cold boat ride. And for not turning the heat on in the house, thinking if I was uncomfortable I'd leave. You're a real . . . nerd, Chip Thorn!"

He grinned down at her unrepentantly. "You figured that out, did you?"

"About your being a nerd?"

"That and other things. You turned the tables on me, princess."

Margaret pressed her cheek against his shoulder. He called her princess now as if he were saying, *darling*, or *sweetheart*. She wished they could be alone together for a little while longer. What would all those people out there do to them?

They came upon the camp from above, emerging out of the forest to look down on several prefabricated buildings and a water tower raised on stilts. Some machinery stood about, but there were no signs of people.

"The boys, except for Virgil, will be out," Chip said as they came down into the flattened dust patch in front of one of the buildings. "Virgil is cook, camp boss, and radio operator. I hope he's got something left to eat. Are you hungry?"

"I'd rather have a bath."

"Then our timing is just right. Come in and meet Virgil, and then I'll take you to the shower house. The facilities are primitive, but they serve the purpose."

After a bath and a meal of hotcakes and eggs, Margaret wandered about the camp while Chip talked with Virgil.

"Howdy, gal," he'd said when Chip introduced her. "Ain't you taking a risk strayin' 'round with the boss here?" He grinned and screwed his baseball cap farther down on his head. "Ain't many bears out there meaner'n him when he's riled."

Margaret laughed warmly at the small Chinese man who spoke like a northwestern logger. "Thanks for the warning. I'll try not to get him riled."

There had been another fire reported across the river in forest leased by Anthony/Thorn. Messages had been going back and forth all day from headquarters in Aaronville. Virgil wanted to hear all the details of the first fire, so Margaret explored the camp while Chip did the telling.

The men returned at sunset. All were wearing the white hard hats Margaret had always associated with miners. To say that they were surprised to see her would have been an understatement, she decided. Some looked at her and then quickly looked away, while others blatantly stared. Several young men let out whoops and dashed for the bathhouse.

The evening meal was a huge communal affair relished with great gusto by the hungry lumberjacks. Margaret sat at a table with Chip and four others, the constraint caused by her presence quickly subsiding once it became apparent that she enjoyed the talk—which was chiefly about lumber. The men lived and breathed for lumber: it was their way of life.

Margaret knew the men were curious as to why she was here in the camp with Chip. He had introduced her simply as Maggie, and she wondered if they would be as friendly if they knew who she really was. Her curiosity was soon to be satisfied.

"You didn't bring this pretty thing all the way up here to talk lumber, did you, Chip?" The question was from Jim Logan, the camp foreman.

"I sure did," Chip said, the familiar grin tilting his mouth. "This pretty little thing happens to own half the company you're working for."

Margaret swallowed the bitter taste of fear that rose in her throat. There it was, all out in the open. She felt every eye in the cookshack focused on her, and she bit down hard on her lower lip. Darn you, Chip Thorn, she fumed silently. Why didn't you give me some time to prepare myself before springing this? She shot an inquisitive look about the room and worked at keeping her composure. Nerves were jumping inside her stomach and refused to settle down.

Then the unexpected happened. Jim Logan laughed loud and long. "Well, glory be!" he exclaimed. "Why, she ain't no bigger than a minute, Chip. We could stuff 'er down a hollow tree and the bear'd think she was honey." His weathered face was creased with a grin, and he ran work-roughened fingers through graying hair. "I guess we're all dumbfounded, Maggie. Guess we thought you'd be one of them glittery, spruced-up gals, since you come from the city and all."

Margaret's alarm was transformed to happy relief.

"I'm sorry to disappoint you, Jim. I'll try and spruce up all glittery before my next visit."

"Don't go to no bother, Maggie. We like ya just like ya are." And that's all there was to it.

The cookshack was also the recreation area. After the tables were cleared, the men played cards or gathered in groups to talk. Margaret sat quietly beside Chip while he talked "shop" with Jim. When she put her hand over her mouth to suppress a yawn, Chip's eyes caught hers.

"Are you tired, sweetheart?"

Margaret allowed all the love she felt for him to show in her gaze. The endearment was his announcement to the men that she was more than a business partner, more than a friend.

"A little," she admitted.

"She can use my place, Chip. I'll bed down in the bunkhouse."

Chip took her sleeping bag and backpack and walked with her to the door of an old trailer parked under the trees at the edge of the camp. He reached inside and turned on the lights.

"Where will you be?" she asked.

"In the bunkhouse. Are you afraid?"

"Nooooo . . . but if I said yes, would you stay?" She moved close to him and rested her forehead against his chest. "I wish you could stay here with me."

"I wish I could, too. But you know I can't." He ran his hands down over her hair and rested them on her shoulders. "They're all waiting to see if I sleep with you." His voice was rough as he tightened his hands to bring her closer.

"I suppose. Do you think they liked me?"

"Sure. Are you surprised?"

"Yes. Are you?" she tossed back.

"Not really. I was prepared to fire every one of them if they didn't," he murmured against her mouth before his tongue and teeth set fire to her senses.

"I love you," she cried softly, fitting her body to his. She slipped her arms inside his jacket and around his middle and waited expectantly. *Say it, darling! Oh, please say it!* her heart cried out.

"I love you, too." His lips were against her ear.

In an instant he was kissing her and she was clinging to him, surrendering her mouth, giving more and more until she was limp in his arms.

"Was that so hard to say?" she murmured as the blood drummed in her head.

"It'll take some getting used to. I've never said it before. I'll have to practice. I love you. I love you." He kissed her quick and hard. "I'd better go while I still can. I'm already going to have to walk around awhile before I go in," he said accusingly.

"Oh, poor Chip!" she teased, and she slipped inside the door.

They came out of the forest and onto the main road late the next afternoon. Margaret was sorry it was over. She had looked longingly when they passed the place where they had turned off to fight the fire and wondered if they would ever go back so she could see the trees they had saved from the flames. That small burned-out spot in the woods would forever be her special place.

"Maggie, Maggie, guess what?" Penny came bouncing

off the porch the instant the Jeep stopped beside the company house. "I did it again. I got a star on my spelling paper."

"Super!" Margaret caught her in her arms and whirled her around. "You'd better get back into the house, young lady. You're not wearing a sweater," she chided.

"Go on in," Chip urged. "I'll unload." The look in his eyes made her feel suddenly lightheaded and treacherously weak with happiness. It had really happened, everything she had ever longed for.

"Hurry on in here. Supper's ready," Dolly called from the doorway.

"Hi, Dolly," Margaret called back. "I hope you've got a lot. We're starving."

"Somebody else is coming, too!" Penny shouted.

Margaret glanced up and saw a big black car approaching the drive. The instant the car stopped, the door on the passenger side was flung open.

"Margaret!" Rachel, in a teal-blue suit and short mink cape, got out of the car. "Margaret! Are you all right? I've never been so frightened in my whole life!"

A deadly silence followed her words. Margaret glanced at Chip and was stunned by the expression on his face. He was clearly holding his anger on a very tight leash. Tension gripped her.

"Of course I'm all right. Why wouldn't I be?" By this time the older woman had stumbled toward her and was hugging her desperately.

"The fire! I called the office yesterday and was told you and Chip were out fighting a fire. I called back and they said another had broken out." She turned on Chip, angry sparks lighting her usually calm eyes. "What do you mean by taking her into a dangerous area? I thought you more dependable than to let her take unnecessary risks!"

Though soft, the oath Chip uttered was so violent that Margaret shuddered. His temper was about to be unleashed on Rachel, and she didn't know what to do about it.

"It wasn't Chip's fault, Rachel. I was never in any danger." Margaret's eyes pleaded with her to say no more about it.

"If it wasn't his fault, then whose was it?" a harsh male voice demanded.

Margaret's eyes flew to the man who had come up beside Rachel. Justin had a proprietary look on his face as he stared at Margaret, and it suddenly infuriated her. She drew in a quick, deep breath and flicked her eyes at Chip. He stood with arms folded across his chest, his back against the Jeep, watching her, waiting to see how she handled the situation. His stance was loose, but she knew his temper was boiling just below the surface. His eyes were narrowed, and his mouth twisted in disgust. Was it for them or for her?

Anger and panic vied for supremacy in her mind.

"Margaret!" When Justin spoke the second time it seemed to her that her father was speaking from the grave. Justin's voice had the same tone, the same dictatorial character. "If you're quite finished with your little fling, we have a plane waiting."

For the first time in her life, Margaret knew pure rage. Triggered by his words and by the domineering tone of Justin's voice chipping at her self-esteem, the adrenaline surged through her body. She wrenched herself away from Rachel and backed up a few steps.

"Don't you dare talk to me like that!" she snarled. "Who do you think you are? You work for me, Justin Whittier, and that's all. If you want to keep your job, you'll get back into that car and keep your damned mouth shut and your nose out of my private life!" She flung her arm toward the car. "If Rachel was worried about me it was more than likely your prodding that brought it on."

Justin looked stunned, and then his face turned white with anger. He spun on his heel and started back toward the car. Rachel made a move to follow, but Margaret caught her arm.

"Don't go, Rachel. I want to talk to you, but first I have a few more things to say to Justin." She left Rachel standing beside the porch and followed Justin to the car. "Did Rachel bring a bag? If she did, set it out." She was still almost blind with fury. Her words were short and clipped. "Rachel will stay here with me for a few days. You can get back on that plane and return to Chicago. You'll make no more unauthorized trips on my behalf. Furthermore, I want you to set the wheels in motion to turn over twenty-five percent of my stock in Anthony/Thorn to Duncan Thorn." Justin opened his mouth in shocked disbelief, but closed it when Margaret said softly but firmly, "If you don't care to follow my orders, you may hand in your resignation. The rest of my shares are to be divided among the employees according to seniority. Is that understood?"

"You can't mean to do that! Your father—"

"Is dead," she interrupted bluntly.

"He'll have control!" he protested, glancing at Chip.

"And what business of yours is that?" Margaret retorted haughtily. She turned and picked up Rachel's bag. "I'll expect a report in a few days, and if any of this is leaked to the papers, you're fired!" She walked a few steps toward the house and turned to look back at the man in the tailor-made suit and the shiny black shoes standing beside the rented limousine. She looked at her ex-fiancé as if seeing him for the first time. The skin on his face was sallow, and there were pouches beneath his eyes. But it was his hands that caused a chill of revulsion to travel the length of her spine. How could she have even considered allowing his puffy white hands to touch her body?

"I mean what I say, Justin. If one word about me or my business reaches the papers, you can look for another job. And from what I hear, two-hundred-thousand-a-year jobs are hard to find."

"I'll go with Justin." Rachel came to take the case from Margaret's hand.

"Please stay, Rachel."

"But—"

"I'll explain later." She put an arm around the older woman. "Good-bye, Justin. I'll call in a few days with further instructions."

The gravel crunched when the car pulled away and shot off down the drive. Margaret smiled at Rachel for the first time. "I'm glad you're here. I've missed you."

"I'll take that." Chip took the case from her hand, and Margaret saw something like frustration flicker over his face. Her eyes were dark and grave. She wasn't feeling strong and capable now, but tired, vulnerable, and afraid. She needed him desperately to take her hand, but instead he simply said, "C'mon in."

Inside the house another shock awaited her. Dolly and Penny stood waiting beside the door. Dolly's usually cheerful face was solemn, and her bright eyes zeroed in on Rachel, who stood hesitantly after entering.

"Hello, Rachel."

"Hello, Dolly."

At first Margaret's brain rejected what her ears were hearing, but then realization dawned. Rachel and Dolly knew each other! How could they? She looked from one to the other disbelievingly. If Dolly knew who Rachel was, then she must also know that Maggie Anderson was really Margaret Anthony. But Dolly was looking as baffled as Margaret felt.

"Dolly . . ." Margaret felt as if she had betrayed a friend, and her eyes flashed help signals to Chip.

"It was my idea for Maggie to come here incognito, Dolly," he explained. "So don't blame her for not telling you who she was." Chip had shrugged out of his jacket and was hanging it on a peg beside the door.

"Well," seemed to be all Dolly could say. She wrapped her hands in the apron tied about her ample middle. "Well . . . we'll set another plate on the table. Supper's ready."

"Rachel, Dolly . . ." Margaret's eyes went from one to the other. "I'm so confused!" She looked again to Chip for help, but he raised his shoulders in a noncommittal gesture.

"I knew Dolly a long time ago, Margaret," Rachel said tiredly. "I lived here many years ago. I should have told you before." She took off her fur cape and draped it over the back of the couch. "It's a relief to have it all out in the open."

"My pot roast won't hold through the tellin' of life stories," Dolly said with a trace of irritation. "Let's eat. I know Chip is hungry."

"Can I sit by Maggie, Grandma?" Penny hung back, her large eyes on Margaret's face.

Margaret held out her arms, and the child ran to her. "Maybe if we both say *please* we can sit together," she said in a loud whisper.

Both Margaret and Rachel offered to help Dolly clean up after the meal, but Dolly wouldn't hear of it.

"Penny will help me," she announced, much to Penny's obvious disappointment.

In the living room Margaret stood silently looking at the two people she cared most about in the world. She went to Chip and put her arms around his waist.

"I'm staying here with Chip, Rachel. I love him. I think I've always loved him." She laughed, but it was not a nervous laugh: it was a joyous, happy laugh. "Maybe not always, but for a long, long time."

"I thought so. I'm very happy for you." Her words were a direct contradiction to the expression on her face. She looked as if she were about to burst into tears.

"If you ladies will excuse me, I have things to do, and you two have a lot to discuss, I'm sure." Chip gave Margaret a brief kiss.

"Don't leave," she whispered.

"I wouldn't think of it," he whispered back.

It seemed strange to Margaret to see Rachel in this comfortable but less than elegant room. Her white hair was carefully styled, her nails well-tended, and her clothes perfectly coordinated. She was dear and familiar, and Margaret loved her.

"I'm so glad you're here, Rachel. I've missed you." Margaret sat close to her on the couch and took both her hands in hers. They were cold and trembly. "I never thought I'd be this happy. Something just seemed to happen between Chip and me, something rare and beautiful. Somehow I know that I was born to live here with him, be his wife, raise his children, grow old with him. But oh, Rachel . . . there are so many unanswered questions floating around in my mind. Not that the answers will make the slightest difference in the way I feel about this place or about Chip. But I've got to know, so I'll be able to cope with things later on."

"Darling, you've changed in the weeks since Edward died. You're lovelier than ever. I could hardly believe it was you out there sending Justin on his way. The change in you has been a long time coming, but you've found yourself at last."

"Why didn't you tell me that you'd lived here at one time? Why do people here dislike my father so much?" Margaret asked with unmasked concern.

Rachel took a shaky breath. "Your father and I met when he came out here to see about his interest in the company he'd bought into, sight unseen, after his old friend August Thorn came to Chicago looking for a partner to save the business." Rachel glanced nervously at the doorway leading to the other part of the house. "We fell in love, Margaret. I want you to believe that." She took her hands from Margaret's and held them tightly together in her lap. "I was married to a good man, but there was no excitement in our relationship. I have no excuse," she admitted. "I married young, but I understood it was a lifetime commitment. Then I met Edward, and he set me on fire with wanting him. Although he wasn't terribly handsome and he was considerably older, I believe I would have followed him to the edge of the earth even if he'd been ragged and barefoot."

She paused to catch her breath, but not long enough for Margaret to speak. "My husband was a hardworking, decent man, well-liked in the community. When I left him to go away with a rich man, naturally he had everyone's sympathy. Edward was the villain and I the . . . harlot. Edward didn't care in the least what people thought, but he did care and was very angry when I refused to marry him. Although I resumed using my maiden name—Riley—I never did divorce MacMadden."

"Tom?" Margaret said in a voice that trembled with her surprise. "Tom MacMadden?"

"Yes. Tom is my husband." Rachel's hands reached out to grasp Margaret's with sudden desperation.

"Why wasn't I told any of this?"

"You were Edward's life, an extension of himself, and were to be protected from all unpleasantness at any cost." The first tiny hint of resentment whispered through her words.

"That wouldn't have made me love you or Daddy any less."

"Tell her the rest, Rachel," Chip commanded from the doorway, having silently returned.

With a quick glance Margaret took in his cool expression. He walked into the room and stood with his back to the fire. She took several quick deep breaths to control the shimmer of fear that flashed through her.

"You knew Rachel when she lived here, didn't you?"

"I was just a kid when she left. Tom's been like a second father to me. Naturally I knew about Rachel and Ed Anthony and . . . you."

"Please, Chip!" Rachel's voice raised to a nervous pitch.

"Tell her, or I will! She's not a child. She's a grown woman, in spite of the fact that you and Ed tried to keep her a child." The hardness of his tone and the straight, steady look in his eyes as he watched Rachel caused Margaret's fear to escalate into near panic.

"Well . . ." Against her sudden pallor, Rachel's eyes looked dark with despair. "Tom wasn't able to have children, and when I discovered I was pregnant, I knew it was Edward's." Her head was bowed so low her chin almost touched her chest, and the hands in her lap twisted and clung. She looked up suddenly, her eyes swimming with tears. "I wanted to tell you so badly. I begged Edward to let me tell you, but he didn't want a breath of scandal to touch you. So he put out the story that your mother had died in childbirth." Her voice was unsteady, anguished.

Margaret's shocked gasp was trapped by the large constriction in her throat. She sat absolutely still, feeling the color drain from her face. Dazed, she stared at Rachel's crumbling features during the deadly silence that followed her words. Her breath came back, and she gave a hysterical little laugh.

"Rachel? Are you saying that you're my mother?" She heard the words as if they came from someone else's mouth.

Rachel had squeezed her eyes tightly shut while the tears rolled down her cheeks. Impatiently, Margaret's hands grasped her arms and shook her.

"Are you my mother? . . . You're my mother!" she said incredulously. Relief fluttered through her, and she felt as if a ton of bricks had been removed from her chest. "But, that's wonderful! I've always loved you. You're my mother!" She threw her arms about the sobbing woman, and her glasses fell away unnoticed. "Don't cry, darling. You can't know how happy I am. I used to dream that you were my mother, and I longed to call you Mom. Now I can! I just don't understand why this wonderful news was kept from me."

Chip placed a clean handkerchief in Margaret's hand, and she used it to wipe Rachel's tears.

"You were legally Tom's daughter," Chip said quietly. "Tom had to sign papers allowing Ed to adopt you, even though you were Ed's biological daughter. That's how I knew Rachel was your mother."

"But . . ." Margaret tried unsuccessfully to keep her lips from trembling. "I should have been allowed to know my mother while I was growing up. I always thought she was some stranger in a picture. It would have meant so much to me to know I had two parents who loved me. Not that I didn't feel close to you, Rachel . . . Mother . . . but there was always that fear in the back of my mind, that you worked for Daddy, and that you might move on like some of the other employees. It wasn't fair," she protested.

"No. It wasn't fair to either of us. I realized it then just as I realize it now." Rachel made a helpless gesture with her hands. "It was all my doing." Tearing her gaze away from her daughter, she twisted her hands in her lap. "Adultery is a sin. I didn't want to compound it by divorcing my husband and marrying my lover. I think now that Edward was punishing me for not divorcing Tom and marrying him by refusing to let me acknowledge you as my child. And Tom, who could have petitioned for a divorce on grounds of desertion, was probably punishing me for leaving him." Tears spilled and slid slowly down her face, and she continued in a strangled voice. "My daughter was caught in the middle."

"Not anymore, Mother. I love saying it! Mother, Mother!" Margaret's eyes were moist. She reached up to grasp Chip's hand. "So many good things have happened to me, I don't know if I can handle them all."

"Sure you can, princess. You're doing just fine."

Rachel's eyes moved from Margaret's face to Chip's. When she slowly extended her hand, he reached out and enclosed it in his.

"She hasn't experienced life as we know it, Chip."

"I know that, Rachel. But she's learning . . . fast." His voice was gentle, and their eyes met and held. "Don't worry about her. She's made of pretty strong stuff."

Rachel's eyes filled up again as she gazed back at Margaret. "I worried so about you, darling." She brought Margaret's hand to her face and held it to her cheek. "I didn't want you to spend your life in that cold stone house married to a man you didn't love. I wanted you to be young—and free to love." She placed Margaret's hand in Chip's. "Don't hurt her, Chip. Keep her happy."

She stood. "If you'll excuse me, I think I should go to bed. I can't remember ever being this tired." She smiled, and age lines fell from her face. "It's tiring for a woman my age to find a daughter and lose her all in the course of a few hours."

"You haven't lost me. You'll never lose me," Margaret

said sincerely. "Come. You can use Chip's room, and he'll sleep out here on the couch. Tomorrow he'll take us upriver and show us where he really lives—when he's not trying to discourage city girls from moving to Montana." Margaret turned her face up to Chip's and took her time studying the loving expression she saw there. Rising on her toes, she kissed his mouth and felt the evening's tension melt away. "Isn't that right, darling?"

"I guess so, sweetheart," he said with a deep chuckle. His eyes smiled into hers.

EPILOGUE

THE SILENCE WAS utter and complete except for the rustle of the birds roosting in the treetops for the night and the gentle crackling of the burning branches in the campfire inside the circle of stones. Margaret sat on the sleeping bag with her legs drawn up, her arms about them, her chin resting on her knees.

For the past three Octobers she and Chip had made a pilgrimage to this place where they had first declared their love. It was their special place, and they always approached it with reverence. The sapling Chip had rested his back against had grown so that Margaret could no longer circle it with her two hands, and there wasn't a trace left of the fire that had brought them here in the first place.

A smile played around the corner of her mouth as Chip came out of the woods with an armful of small dead branches for the fire. He was her everything: husband, lover, advisor, friend. She loved him with such fierce intensity that it sometimes puzzled her.

"Cold, princess?" His voice drifted to her on the crisp breeze.

She loved it when he called her his princess.

Later, he wrapped her in his arms, stretching his long legs out on either side of hers, and resting his back against the tree. His hands found their way beneath her sweater and cupped her breasts.

"The baby filled them out some. I wonder what another will do." He slid his lips along her cheek and up to her temple, where they paused, and the tip of his tongue made a foray into her ear.

"You've been watching that country singer again," she accused, turning in his arms so she could wrap hers about him. "Are we going to tell Duncan he was conceived here that night?"

"Maybe when he's older. Right now all he's interested in is conning Grandma Rachel into letting him stay up past his bedtime. Each time she comes, so I can have you all to myself for a while, she spoils him more."

"Chip, darling, so much has happened in the last few years. Just think: we have Duncan, Beth is in college, and Dolly married a company man and lives in the company house. Penny's mother gave up her rights to Penny, so we don't have to worry about losing her. She spends almost as much time with us as she does with Dolly. How come things have worked out so wonderfully for me?" She placed a string of little kisses along his jaw, and her hands burrowed beneath his sweater. "Even the men like me. If you ever tell them it wasn't in Daddy's will that they became partners in the mill, I'll . . . sock you in the nose!"

He chuckled. "I sure don't want that to happen. You've built up muscles carrying that big boy around."

"Now if only Mother and Tom could forgive each other and at least be friends." She sighed.

"Don't count on it, honey. There's too much bitterness on both sides. Let it rest. We're not responsible for their lives any more than they are for ours."

His mouth sought hers and kissed it with gentle reassurance and then with rising passion. His hands moved over her body, touching her with sensual, intimate caresses. Her senses reeled as they always did when he made love to her. The magic had never faded. This was real. This was forever. She lifted her face and looked at him. It was all there in his eyes, and the wonder of it filled her with joy.

"Are you going to dally around here all night, Mr. Thorn, or do I have to ask you to get into that sleeping bag with me?" Her hand moved across tightly stretched denim and fumbled with a zipper. "There's another baby there just begging to be started," she murmured in a seductive tone, and she felt his body jolt as it always did when she first touched him.

"Princess!" he groaned huskily. "You're wreaking havoc with my self-control!" When she continued to caress him he dumped her off his lap and stood up. "Little devil! I just may keep you on your back all weekend," he threatened, and he hurried to shovel dirt onto the campfire.

Margaret jumped up, her green eyes sparkling. "Will you put that in writing?" she challenged saucily.

He reached to swat her behind. She evaded him, and with squeals of joyous laughter she dashed for the truck.

BOOK TWO

SHE WANTED
RED VELVET

To special people—
my cousins,
Norma and Ken Slane—
with special love.

CHAPTER ONE

IT WAS LATE afternoon. The sun made patterns of speckled brightness on the leaf-strewn ground where it filtered through the trees surrounding the clearing beside the highway. The slim blond woman closed the door to the primitive outhouse, grabbed the hand of the four-year-old boy, and urged him along the path to the parking area.

"Why are we hurryin', Mom?"

"Come on, Peter. I'll tell you later." The woman took short running steps so the boy could keep up with her. When they reached the compact car, she quickly unlocked the door.

"Mom—"

"Get in the car," she commanded sharply with a glance back over her shoulder. She crowded into the bucket seat beside her son, locked the door, and reached over to make sure the door on the driver's side was locked.

"What are you scared of, Mom? You're scared, aren't ya? Is it them? What'd they say?" Peter pressed his nose against the window and stared at the two men coming down the graveled path from the building set back in the woods.

"I'm not scared, Peter," she said with far more confidence than she felt. *Dammit!* she thought. *If the car hadn't overheated, we wouldn't be sitting in this deserted rest area; we would practically be at Aunt Ethel's by now.*

"I'm hot. Can I roll down the window?"

"No," she said sharply, then moaned silently to herself. *Why didn't I think to put the hood down before we got in the car?* Aloud she said, "As soon as they leave, we'll go."

"They've got big motorcycles, and pictures on their arms. They're funny."

"Crawl into the backseat, honey. Come on, I'll help you."

She boosted the child into a small space next to pillows, toys, blankets, a small overnight case, and a cardboard box containing a whining puppy. She looked out the window and wondered if she'd be able to back out of the circular drive with the U-Haul trailer attached to the car. All the way out from Cincinnati she had been careful to keep out of a situation that would require backing the car for any distance.

The men were standing in front of the car, now, out of sight behind the raised hood.

"Cisco's crying. He's got to pee-pee."

"He'll have to wait."

"Mom—he don't want to wait. He's got to go—bad."

"Shhh . . ." She scarcely heard what Peter said. The uneasiness that had flooded her the moment she came out of the rest room with her small son and saw the two huge motorcycles parked in front of her car, and the men who then stepped from around the end of the men's building, now escalated into full-fledged fear.

They had passed her fifty miles back down the highway, slowed down to twenty miles an hour, and weaved back and forth in front of her for several miles. She had honked the horn and tried to get away from them, to no avail; then, suddenly, they had let her go, when they spotted a highway patrol car parked on an overpass ahead. She had increased her speed to get as far ahead of them as possible, and had put them out of her mind when she could no longer see them in the rearview mirror.

This part of Montana was sparsely populated, and the small towns were far apart; at times she and Peter would go for miles and miles without meeting a car. In Lewistown she had pulled into a service station and filled her gas tank to be sure she would have enough fuel to get to her Aunt Ethel's motel and trailer park.

Soon after Lewistown the state highway had begun winding around the foothills and climbing into the rugged mountainous region. The small car that had brought them so far without so much as a cough from the engine had started to send distress signals in the form of a flashing red light on the dashboard. She had been so relieved to see the rest area, because by this time Peter was complaining he had to "go."

Now Gloria wished fervently she had taken a chance on the car's making the top of the hill; she could have coasted on the way down the other side and cooled the motor. In the middle of checking the engine she had stopped to take Peter to the bathroom. As a result the stupid hood was up. She couldn't drive away, and she couldn't see what the men were doing in front of her.

Suddenly the hood came down, and a whiskered face grinned at her. The hood was lifted, then lowered, in rapid succession.

"Peekaboo, pretty woman."

Oh, dear God! What will they do? The words never came out of her mouth; she didn't want to frighten Peter. She turned the key in the ignition, started the motor, and put the car in reverse, praying she would be able to back the car and trailer around the curve and onto the highway. The motor stopped. Damn! She turned the switch and pumped the accelerator. Nothing!

"What's the matter, Mom?"

"Be still, Peter . . . please—" Panic began to take hold, and she turned the key again and again. Grrrr . . . Grrrr . . . "Please start! Oh, start, damn you!"

The hood was slammed down so hard the car shook. "Doggy! Looky here what we found." The man with a sleeveless shirt and brass armbands yelled triumphantly and waved several long wires in front of the windshield.

"Go away and leave us alone!" Gloria yelled. The fear that rose in her throat almost choked her. They had taken some wires out of her engine; now she and Peter were really trapped.

"C'mon out an' play, pretty thin'. Ain't ya hot in there with them windows rolled up?"

One of the men sprang up onto the hood of the car and jumped up and down. He had long, frizzy hair and a leather thong tied about his forehead. The thin metal crackled and protested, and finally gave way under the weight of the heavy man.

Peter began to cry. "Mom! What're they doin'? I'm scared!"

"They can't get in the car, honey. Someone will be along soon and they'll go away. Then we'll go on to Aunt Ethel's." She made a great effort to speak calmly. *If anyone does come along,* she thought, *it's doubtful they'll turn in while those two despicable creatures are in sight.* "We'll just sit here and not look at them—Hey, stop that!" Gloria yelled. They were rocking the car, now, so violently that her head banged against the window.

"Who-eee! Ain't she a hot mama chick? Here, chicky, chick, chick—"

"Make 'em stop, Mom!"

The roar of a motor coming into the rest area caused her to turn hopefully, but hope turned to panic when she saw another large, black motorcycle come past the trailer and pull up ahead of the car. The rider wore boots, jeans, a sleeveless shirt, and a bright-blue helmet with a visor. He sat for a moment watching the two men rock the car before he leisurely got off the cycle and stood beside it.

"Whatta you got here?"

"What's it to ya?"

"Not friendly, huh?"

"If'n ya mean are we sharin', we ain't." The man on the hood jumped onto the top of the car, and the roof crackled and groaned beneath his weight.

"I know most of the cycle boys around here. Where're you from?" The newcomer stood leaning against his machine with his arms folded over his chest.

"We're from Chicago, man. From the Big Windy. What's your play? You figurin' to move in?"

"Maybe."

The man on the top of the car jumped to the ground.

The two hoodlums moved to the front and stood shoulder to shoulder against the man in the blue helmet.

"Ya gonna do it all by yourself?" The frizzy-haired man took a step away from his friend.

The big shoulders lifted in a careless shrug. "Do you see anyone else?"

"Back off while ya can, big man."

"I'll say the same to you."

"You got no brains a-tall," the frizzy-haired man said, then glanced toward his more heavily built companion.

"Maybe," the newcomer said again. "Ride out. Leave her alone. You've got no business hasslin' a woman with a kid."

"Ha! Ya hear that, Boomy? The country boy's tellin' us to ride out. He's got cow manure for brains if he thinks we'll ride out and leave the split for him. Didn't ya hear us say we're from the Big Windy, hayseed?"

"Yeah, I heard you. That makes you pretty tough, huh?" The man moved away from his motorcycle, his legs spread apart, his fists resting on his hipbones.

Gloria rolled down the window a few inches so she could hear what was being said.

"Tough enough," Boomy said boastfully. He spit in the dirt, and it landed dangerously close to the other man's feet. "I think I'll take me a little spin on that machine of his." He grinned at his friend.

"Don't try it," the man said quietly.

"Haw, haw, haw—we're goin' to have to teach him some manners."

Boomy took only two steps toward the cycle before the man in the helmet exploded into action. His hands and his feet seemed to lash out simultaneously, knocking

Boomy off his feet and sending him into the dirt. The other man got a foot in the groin; he screamed and doubled up on the ground. Boomy rolled to his feet like a cat, started forward, then stopped. Holding his arms out to his side menacingly, he spread his feet and edged forward, waiting for his chance to attack.

"Don't do it, punk. I'm warning you, I can break your neck." The voice from behind the visored helmet cautioned, "Get on your machine and clear out while you're in one piece."

"Who in the hell's going to help you, country boy? I'll bust head, man. We was here first."

"Okay. If you want to ride out of here with some broken bones, c'mon and get it."

The hoodlum sprang; the other man grabbed his arm, twisted it, and threw him over his shoulder. Boomy fell out of sight in front of the car. Gloria heard a screech of pain and held her breath; Peter's arms were wound so tight about her neck she could scarcely breathe anyway. The man in the helmet stood calmly looking down at the man on the ground. Boomy got slowly to his feet, holding his elbow.

"Ya broke my arm!" he accused, his voice quivering. His face was deathly white.

"I told you what you'd get, but you wouldn't listen. You're lucky I didn't break your neck. Now, get the hell outta here and take this jerk with you before I break your leg too."

"I can't ride," he whined, holding his arm close to his chest.

"Ride or walk. It makes no difference to me. Go on back to Chicago and crawl into your hole. You're not fit to be among decent people." The man's broad back was to Gloria. He stood by while the men mounted their cycles and rode slowly out of the rest area. He followed a short distance and watched them go down the highway.

It was stifling hot inside the car. Gloria rolled the window down a few more inches and held Peter's face to the breeze. The child sniffled, the puppy yelped. Gloria watched the man cautiously. He unfastened the chin strap on his helmet, lifted it from his head, and placed it on the seat of his motorcycle before he turned toward the car.

Gloria sucked in her breath and quickly rolled up the window. The man had thick, curly black hair and a full black beard; the only part of his face she could see were his eyes, beneath heavy black brows. His shirt was open to the waist, and his chest was covered with dark hair. He was big, broad shouldered, and had heavily muscled arms and a thick neck. She looked into light greenish-gray eyes. *Oh, Lord! At least there's only one of him,* she thought fearfully.

"Aren't you about to burn up in there?"

Gloria shook her head.

"You must be." Peter began to cry again. "Look, lady, I'm not going to hurt you. Open the window before the kid has heatstroke."

"Go away."

"Okay." He went to his cycle and leaned against it with his arms crossed over his chest.

Gloria waited, hoping he would ride away. When he continued to stand there, she rolled down the window, watching him carefully to see if he might make a sudden move toward the car. Peter lifted his face to the cool breeze.

"Is he goin' to hurt our car, Mom?"

"I don't know, honey. We've got to wait—"

"Can't we go? You said we was almost to Aunt Ethel's."

"We are, but the other men pulled some wires out of our car and it won't start."

"Why'd they do that?"

"I don't know. They were bad men."

"Is he bad too?"

"I . . . don't know—"

"I'm no saint, boy. But I don't hurt women and kids." The man flashed a smile that was almost lost behind the beard. The only way Gloria knew it was there was by the crinkles at the corners of his eyes.

She rolled the glass down partway. Peter stuck his head out the window, but she tried to pull him back.

"I'd a beat 'em up, if I was big."

"Yeah? Well, I did it for you, this time. You can pay me back someday."

"My dog's got to potty."

"Peter! Hush up!"

"Let him out and I'll watch him."

"No! Peter—"

"Lady, I can understand your being nervous and scared. Those jerks were for real. But I sent 'em packin', didn't I? Look, I've not attacked a woman with a kid for a whole week now."

She ignored his attempt to be funny. "How do I know you won't harm us?"

"'Cause I'm tellin' you. Are you going to sit there on your butt all night?"

"My car won't start."

"I know that. I can see the wires hanging out."

"Why did you stop?"

"I saw you at the station back in Lewistown and knew you and the kid were alone."

"You were following me!"

"I was going home. Where are you going, anyway? And what in hell are you doing out on the highway dressed like that?"

Gloria's mouth dropped open and a tingling warmth flooded her face that had nothing to do with the heat in the car. She glanced quickly down at the brief tan shorts and the backless halter she was wearing.

"There's no air conditioning in this car, not that it's any business of yours."

"You're asking for trouble going around half naked," he insisted. "Half of Lewistown was gawking at you."

"Cisco wants out." Peter was holding the squirming puppy.

The man came to the car. "Hand me the pup, boy."

"Will ya hurt him, mister?"

"Naw. I like dogs."

Without hesitation Peter passed the puppy through the opening and watched anxiously as the big hands took him. "His name's Cisco," he called. "What's yours?"

"Jack. Here, now, little fellow . . ." He held the small brown body close to his chest and rubbed between the furry ears with long, strong fingers before he gently set him on the ground. The puppy scurried about in the grass and Peter craned his neck to watch him. The man looked directly at Gloria. "Have you decided what you're going to do?"

"Not . . . yet."

"We're goin' to Aunt Ethel's and we're almost there," Peter said, no longer shy and afraid.

"Where's that?"

"My aunt has a motel west of here."

"The Rusty Cove? I pass it on my way home. It's about ten miles from here."

"Will you stop there and tell my aunt where we are and ask her to send someone for us?"

"I could do that, but it'll be night long before they come back for you. Do you want to sit here in the dark?"

"I don't *want* to," Gloria said crossly. "I don't have much choice."

"Yes, you do. Lock up the car. I'll take you and the boy to the motel on my cycle. They've got a pickup and I'll bring it back and tow your car in."

"We can't ride on . . . that *thing!*" The idea was out of the question. Ride with him? For all she knew he was cut from the same cloth as the men who had wrecked her car. He certainly looked just like them.

"Cisco! Come back—" Peter opened the door on the passenger side and darted after the puppy, who was running toward the highway.

"Peter!" Gloria yelled frantically.

Jack ran after the puppy and scooped him up before he reached the road. He came back and knelt down beside Peter.

"How long have you had him?"

"We got him in Des Moines. He was in a store window by the motel. He was cryin' and wantin' out. Mom said I could have him if I learned how to take care of him. She said Aunt Ethel lived in the country and she wouldn't mind. Mom said I could name him what I wanted to, so I named him Cisco like the man on TV. He's the good guy."

"Is the Cisco Kid still on? I used to watch him when I was a kid."

"Peter," Gloria called sharply. "Get back in the car." She stood beside the open door, her heart hammering with fear, her shapely bare legs trembling. Sweat plastered her short blond hair to her forehead and pale cheeks.

Peter and the man came back to the car. His height topped Gloria's five-foot-seven-inch frame by more than a half a foot. He was broad in the shoulders and chest, yet solid and lean through the waist and hips. His clothes were clean, but his hair was too long and his boots were old and scuffed. She wished he didn't have that damned beard so she could see his face.

Gloria stood still, her head tilted back and a big flashlight clinched in her fist like a weapon. She reached out and grabbed Peter's arm and pulled him close to her. The green eyes glinted as the man assessed her stance. Suddenly he laughed. It was a pleasant laugh, full of amusement.

"You've got more guts than brains, sister. Didn't you see me break that punk's arm? I could have just as easily broken his leg or his stupid neck. You wouldn't stand a chance against me with that flashlight, but I admire your courage. A mother protecting her cub—"

"What . . . are you going to do?"

"Nothin', dammit! If I didn't have this beard and wasn't riding a motorcycle you'd be glad to accept my help. Isn't that true? You're a redneck, sister! You don't like what you see. Well, that's too damn bad. I don't like what I see either." He paused, and when she didn't say anything, he continued, slowly and patiently, "I don't hassle women with kids and I don't really like being on my cycle in these mountains at night, so if you're coming with me, let's get going."

"You can't take both of us . . . and the puppy. We can't leave him here."

"Of course not. The boy can sit in front of me, you can sit behind."

"I've never ridden—"

"There's nothing to it."

"Let's go, Mom. I'll hold Cisco. I want to ride on the motorcycle. *Var . . . oom! Var . . . oom!*"

"Hush up, Peter," Gloria said impatiently. "I . . . want to see some identification."

"Oh, for God's sake! What difference would that make? I could show you anything, and you'd know no more about me than you do now. Believe me, I don't have designs on your *body*, lady. It's nice enough, but kinda skinny for my taste. Besides I'd have to be a pervert to take you with the hotshot looking on."

"Watch your mouth," she warned, glancing at her son.

"Mom's name's Gloria. Mine's Peter. Yours is Jack. I know a girl in Cincinnati named Jackie. I don't like 'er."

"Get your purse and lock the car."

"But—"

"Lady!"

"Her name's Gloria."

"Okay, okay. C'mon, Glory." He chuckled, reached for his helmet, and put it down over Peter's head. "You'll have to wear this, big shot. It's too big, but it's better than nothin'."

Peter was delighted. "Look at me, Mom."

The man's thoughtful gesture finally convinced her to go with him. She reached inside the car for her bag and swung it over her shoulder.

"Does the boy have a jacket he can zip or button up? That way he can carry the pup." The man's voice was close to her ear, and she froze. Sensing her tension he backed away and laughed softly. "You're about to go up with the shades, Glory. Have a little faith. Jesus had a beard too."

"Don't be sacrilegious," she snapped.

Gloria rummaged among the blankets and found the jacket, then locked the car. Peter asked if he looked like a spaceman in the helmet.

"Just like an astronaut," she said lightly, helping him into the jacket.

"Cisco'll have to ride in here, sport. Do you think you can keep him still?" The man knelt beside Peter, slipped Cisco inside the jacket, and zipped it up to make a deep pocket.

"Sure. He likes me better'n anybody."

"Okay. Let's go." He straddled the machine and balanced it with a foot planted on each side. He lifted Peter up and set him in front of him. "Hop on." He looked at Gloria over his shoulder, and his eyes traveled from hers to the V of the halter and on down to the bare midriff.

"I . . . where do I sit?" Now she was painfully aware of her abbreviated costume. She hadn't given it a thought until he'd mentioned it.

"Straddle the seat. You didn't expect to ride side-saddle, did you?" At the hint of amusement in his voice her wide, generous mouth tightened, and her chin lifted defiantly. She looked back at him with cold dislike in her amber eyes, swung her leg over, and sat down.

"Put your feet here." He reached back and grasped the calf of her bare leg and guided her foot to the place behind his. "Hold on to my belt. I doubt if you're too anxious to put your arms around me," he said with a chuckle, and pushed down on the lever that started the machine.

"Hold on, Peter," she yelled over the roar. *Oh, Christ and all that's holy! What in the world are we doing on this thing?*

"Don't worry about him." The words came from the bearded face.

Don't worry! How can I help it, for goodness' sake? The machine bumped over the uneven ground and up onto the smooth highway. There was not a car in sight, and as the cycle picked up speed, Gloria's arms inched around the man's waist, and her hands grabbed hold of her son's jacket. *Oh, baby! What have I gotten you into?*

The breeze was cool on her damp skin, and soon she was shivering and hovering close to the broad back in front of her. Her short blond hair, with its simple, stylish cut, was swept back by the wind. After the first few minutes she had to admit that he *wasn't* going terribly fast and that he *was* being careful. They reached the top of a long incline and started down.

Gloria relaxed a little. *Oh, Marvin, if you could see me now!* A small giggle escaped her lips. He would be horrified at the thought of his wife, his ex-wife, on a motorcycle with a bearded giant who looked as if he were a member of the Hell's Angels. Unbending, fastidious, status-conscious Marvin, who was humiliated when his wife stooped to help a servant clean up a spilled drink, but who thought nothing of maneuvering a small businessman out of his holdings in order to add them to his conglomerate, would see nothing at all amusing about her and Peter on the motorcycle. As a matter of fact he was more than likely going through Cincinnati with a fine-tooth comb looking for them.

There were times when Gloria was completely mystified by Marvin's attitude toward her. They had been divorced for a year, yet he still thought he could control her life. He detested Peter and had told her, time and again, that he fervently regretted the day they had adopted him.

How foolish she had been to think she wanted red velvet. She gave herself a few minutes to remember how it had been in those days. She had lived all her life in a small town in southern Ohio. Her mother and father, and her older brothers and sisters, had always worked in the local bakery, and they were determined she would seek employment there too. But, equally determined not to be trapped in a dead-end situation, she went to Cincinnati to work for a company who collected rating statistics for everything from television programs to politics. Every day, eight hours a day, five days a week, she had sat at a machine and punched in numbers for a salary that barely covered car payments, rent, and food. The work was boring, but the city offered many cultural activities lacking in the small town.

It was at Christmastime, just a few days before the company dance, when she saw the red velvet dress in the store window. The rich red material symbolized everything she had ever dreamed of having, and she wanted that dress more than she had ever wanted anything in her life. It had been totally out of character for her to withdraw all her savings and buy the dress, but she did. When she wore it to the dance she felt like a princess. And in it she attracted one of Cincinnati's wealthiest men, Marvin Eugene Masterson, the owner of the company she worked for, and her life was drastically changed forever.

I wanted red velvet, she mused. *But I soon discovered that red velvet doesn't wear well day after day. After a while it looks tawdry and cheap, just as Marvin's values were tawdry and cheap, false and insincere, when the glamorous facing was torn away.*

Thank God, she murmured against the stranger's back, *Peter and I have finally gotten away from Cincinnati. This is a new beginning for us. I'll work hard and teach my son respect for himself and for others and that the world doesn't begin and end with a bank account or prestigious friends.*

Now, if only we get to Aunt Ethel's—if only I haven't made another serious mistake in judging a man's character. . . .

The arms encircled her tighter as if to reassure her. She maintained, the injured cold silence as long as she could bear, good humor stood out on her arms and neck, and she clenched her jaw to keep her teeth from chattering. She was too numb to notice that the chilly air had made her whiplike rock-hard, and that only two thin layers of material lay between them and the heat of the man's back.

Peter knew she was more than aware of the man stupidly cuddled woman who clung to his back, the out-line that pressed against him, and the arms about his waist. He grew colder, deep inside, for the soft warmth and companionship. The sweetness, of a woman, and the love and trust of well that are annoyes him, the wind had dredged from his mind all the thoughts he supposedly

CHAPTER TWO

GLORIA WAS TOO cold to notice that the mountain road wound through a densely wooded area, and that they had not passed a single dwelling since leaving the rest area. Her arms circled the man in front of her and her hands clutched her son's jacket. The minute the sun finished its daily journey across the sky and was out of sight behind the mountains, the air turned cold. Shivering, she hugged the man's back; goose bumps stood out on her arms and legs, and she clenched her jaws to keep her teeth from chattering. She was too numb to realize that the chilly air had made her nipples rock hard, and that only two thin layers of material lay between them and the skin on the man's back.

Jack Evans was more than aware of the small, skimpily dressed woman who clung to his back, the nipples that pressed against him, and the arms about his waist. He felt a sudden, deep hunger for the soft warmth and companionship, the sweetness, of a woman, and the love and trust of a child. He squinted into the wind and dredged from his mind all the reasons for suppressing that longing. *Hell, Evans,* he said to himself, *get her and the kid on down to Ethel's and flag your butt on home. You're free as the breeze. If you let yourself get involved with this kind of woman, the first thing you know she'll be wanting you to get a nine-to-five job, a briefcase, a house, a station wagon, a three-piece suit . . .*

They rounded a deep bend in the road and turned onto a graveled drive, bumped over a span of metal that covered the deep drainage ditch that ran alongside the highway, and passed beneath the orange-lettered sign: RUSTIC COVE. They stopped in front of the long, narrow brown building surrounded by a thick stand of trees. The doors along the length of the motel were bright orange.

Gloria was too stiff and cold to move. Jack loosened her hold on Peter's jacket so he could lift the boy off the machine. She stirred when the warmth of his body left hers and looked at him dully. Her short hair was a tangled mess, her nose red as a cherry, and her lips blue. He placed two large hands around her waist and lifted her up and off the cycle as he had done with Peter. He held her for the space of a couple of breaths until her legs could hold her.

"Are you all right?"

"Noooo—I'll ne-ver be all ri-ght again." Was the clicking sound she heard her teeth chattering? It was no wonder she couldn't talk.

"If you'd have dressed decently you wouldn't be so cold," he said unfeelingly. "How about you, hotshot? Are you cold too?" He lifted the helmet off Peter's head and placed it on the seat of the cycle.

"Naw . . . that was *fun!* I'm goin' to get me a motor-cycle when I grow up."

"Heaven forbid," Gloria muttered.

"Gloria! Is that you?" A short, plump woman in a royal-blue jogging suit flung open the screen door. The metal sign, OFFICE, clanged when it slammed shut.

"What's left of me, Aunt Ethel."

"Land-a-Goshen'! What happened? What are you doin' with Jack? Oh, never mind, you're here, that's what matters. I thought you'd be bigger, but you ain't no bigger than when I saw you last. I figured you was about thirteen then." She talked in a steady stream as she wrapped her arms around Gloria. Her twinkling eyes looked down. "This is Peter? *Eeekkk . . . ,*" she squealed. "I thought you were a baby, but you're almost as big as your ma. Come give Aunt Ethel a kiss."

"I got a puppy," he announced as soon as he had kissed the smooth cheek. "See!" He pulled the squirming ball of brown fur out of the front of his jacket. "I think he's got to pee-pee. Do you like dogs? Can I put him down?"

"Oh, Peter," Gloria groaned.

"Course I like dogs. Land sakes! Put him down. You can't expect such a little fellow to hold it forever." She took the puppy and sat him down on a grassy patch beside the drive. "Watch that he don't go to the woods," she cautioned. Then, "Hi, Jack."

"Hello, Ethel. Is this the new help you were expecting?"

"Aunt Ethel, I'm freezing."

"Well, I should think so. What in the world were you doin' on that cycle? Where's your clothes? Where's your car? C'mon in. I'll swear, I wasn't lookin' for you to come ridin' in with Jack."

"Her car's down at the rest area, Ethel. Give me the keys to your pickup and I'll go pull it in."

"Way down there? Heavens! What's it doin' there? No wonder you're cold, if'n you rode that cycle all the way up here."

"I . . . had car trouble. It's got a U-Haul hooked on behind it. Aunt Ethel, I don't think he can—"

"Is there anyone here who can go with me?" Jack asked, ignoring Gloria's protest and looking at Ethel.

"Gary's out back working on his rig; he'll go with you. C'mon in, Gloria. Ain't no sense you standing out here freezing. Jack'll take care of your car." Ethel opened the door and motioned her inside. Jack followed Ethel, looming over her five-foot figure; *He looks more than ever like a caveman,* Gloria thought.

"The keys are on the desk, Jack. When you and Gary get back, c'mon in for supper."

Gloria stood hugging herself, trying not to shiver. Her eyes went from her aunt to the black-bearded man and back again; her little gray-haired aunt seemed to be perfectly at ease with him. He walked across the room and then went outside without a word or a glance at her. She heard him say something to Peter, and she started for the door just as her son came in holding the puppy.

"We'll have to find a box and make him a bed, and teach him what he can do and what he can't," Ethel said. "We'll lay out some papers too. We don't want him to get in the habit of piddlin' on the floor."

"Oh, Aunt Ethel! I didn't realize how much trouble the dog would be," Gloria said apologetically.

"Ain't no trouble." Ethel's eyes sparkled vividly. "All

boys ought'a have a dog to take care of. Why, Peter an' that pup'll liven this ol' place up considerably."

"No doubt," Gloria said with a worried frown. She and Peter followed her into the living quarters behind the office. Ethel went through a door and was back almost instantly.

"Here. Put on this old bathrobe. Land sakes, didn't you know that just as soon as the sun goes down it gets colder than the bottom of a well out here?"

"I didn't, but I certainly do now." Gloria slipped into the worn flannel robe that was too short for her, and belted it tightly around her waist.

The room was small, but warm and cozy. An oval braided rug covered most of the floor. A couch with a freshly washed slipcover and pillows stood on one side of a cobblestone fireplace, and a rocking chair on the other. The walls were lined with paintings of Western scenes. Gloria moved over to peer at the one over the fireplace.

"Don't look too close," Ethel said with a merry laugh. "I'm one of those paint-by-number artists. I love doin' it, and it passes the time during the winter when things slow up around here."

"You're kidding," Gloria exclaimed. "They're beautiful."

"My, my." Ethel shook her head. "I just can't get over that you're here. And of all the times we've talked on the phone I pictured you as bigger than what you are; why, a good wind from the north would blow you clear to Mexico." She turned on a lamp beside the rocker. "Here, sit down and tell me about the trip. I swear, it was a shock to see you come ridin' in on that cycle with Jack. It's a good thing he come along, though. Traffic slows to almost nothin' in the late evenin'."

Gloria sat down and Peter came to lean against her knee. "We had a good time driving out, didn't we, Peter? Our only problem was when we stopped at the rest area down the road. The car had started to heat up; I guess it was from pulling the trailer." She told her aunt about the two hoodlums, downplaying the seriousness of the encounter because Peter was listening with rapt attention.

"They stomped on our car, but Jack come and beat 'em up. He hit 'em." Peter put the dog in Gloria's lap and demonstrated as he talked. "He hit 'em to the ground and he said, 'Get the hell out—'"

"Peter! Watch what you're saying. Little boys don't use words like that."

"That's what Jack said. He said—"

"Never mind." The dog began to whine. Gloria lifted her eyes to the ceiling in a gesture of silent suffering.

Ethel laughed and pointed toward the swinging doors. "Honey, there's a clothes basket in that room behind the kitchen and a stack of old towels on the washer. Fix that pup a bed. He's tired and wants to sleep."

After Peter left, Ethel sank down on the couch. "He took to Jack, seems like."

"He's had so little male companionship that he takes to anyone who gives him a little attention. As I told you on the phone, Marvin's name is on his adoption papers, but he's never been a father figure. Peter doesn't even think of him as his father. He seldom speaks of him, and when he does he refers to him as 'he.'"

Ethel clicked her tongue against the roof of her mouth and shook her head sadly. "If that ain't the limit! What's the world comin' to? Oh, well . . . you and Peter are here now. I never had a chick of my own. George and I just rammed around in the Oklahoma oil fields most all our married life. He loved workin' on the oil rigs; he did it until his hands were so crippled up with arthritis that he couldn't do it anymore. Then we sunk our nest egg in this here motel and campground. Two, three years after we come here he had his heart attack and was gone." She paused. "My, my, I miss him. Sometimes I get so low my tail's draggin' in the mud. Then I think of what George said a few days before he died: 'Ethel,' he said, 'if anythin' happens to me, you take the bit in yore teeth and stay right here. This here's a good place for you. The folks like you, and them truckers think yore a jim-dandy.' You know, George was right. Oh, I don't mean about the truckers likin' me, I mean that this is a good place for me. I've got a lot of friends that come and go and keep tabs on me, and I like doin' for 'em." Ethel's bright-blue eyes glinted and her round face broke into a smile. "Now, after all these years, I got me a family too."

"How come you and Dad never kept in touch with each other, Aunt Ethel?"

"George and I used to go back East once in a while. The last time we was back, you was just a young sprout. I think your mother kind of resented the affection me and Ernest had for each other, so . . ." Her voice trailed away. "How is Ernest?"

"He's fine. He retired from the bakery two years ago. Now he's working part time at a self-service gas station. He had so much time on his hands that he didn't know what to do with himself."

"I can understand it. If you got any gumption a-tall

you'll keep on a doin' somethin', anythin', till you drop dead, else you'll wither on the vine. Well . . . did you burn your bridges behind you when you pulled up to come out here?"

"Yes, I did, Aunt Ethel. Maybe it was foolish. I should have come out and stayed awhile before we moved in on you lock, stock, and barrel. Peter and I may be too much for you."

"You and Peter won't be too much for me," Ethel said staunchly. "My worry is that being a city girl, you'll get tired of being stuck out here in the boonies. We're more than twenty miles from town. Sometimes, after a heavy snowfall, it's days before the highway gets plowed out."

"I won't mind that. I like to read and to sew, but I've told you that before." Gloria smiled warmly at her aunt. "During the last few years our talks on the phone helped me to keep my sanity. You always said things that made perfectly good sense. Aunt Ethel, I feel closer to you than I do to my mother, father, or any of my brothers and sisters." She frowned. "I never told them about any of my problems with Marvin. They thought I had made a good 'catch' and that I was crazy when I left him."

"Dear child, you only get one time around in this life, and it ain't all downhill in the shade. Just because you've made a mistake, God doesn't expect you to live with it and be miserable for the rest of your life. George always said, 'Do what you want to do as long as it don't hurt anybody else. It won't make any difference a hundred years from now, anyway.'" She bounded off the couch. "I'd better look at the casserole. And I might ought to add more lettuce to the salad. I hadn't planned on feeding Jack. He's a lot of man to fill up."

Gloria followed her to the kitchen. "Who is he, Aunt Ethel? I didn't want to tell you in front of Peter, but he flew into those two hoodlums like a whirlwind and sent one of them off with a broken arm."

Ethel chuckled. "He's Jack Evans. He lives up north of us four or five miles in an old ghost town. He's fixed himself up a little place up there. It takes a lot to get Jack riled, but when he is—watch out. He's all right, and he's no dummy."

"Maybe not," Gloria said dryly. "But he sure looks like one. I was just as scared of him as I was of the other two. Why would a man want to look like that?"

"Oh, you mean the beard?" she asked with a twinkle in her eye. "Maybe it keeps him warm in the winter."

"This isn't winter. And I didn't mean only the beard. I mean the long hair, the sleeveless shirt, the tattoo on his arm, and that stupid motorcycle. Right away I thought he was a member of the Hell's Angels gang."

Ethel shot her niece a look of amusement. "Jack's all right." She put on two oven mitts and lifted the large pan out of the oven. "While we were working the oil fields, I learned not to judge a man by what was on the outside. Some of those greasy, shaggy-headed ol' boys were just as sweet as could be, honest as the day is long, and would give you the shirt off their backs. Then, sometimes we'd run into a dressed-up dandy who was all pretty and smelled nice, and find out that he was so crooked he'd have to be screwed into the ground when he died." She lifted the foil off the pan and put it back in the oven. "I hope you like lasagna."

"Peter and I love it. Aunt Ethel—how many people do you usually cook dinner for?"

"All the way from four to eight. I got started giving them supper when George and I discovered that's why people didn't stop here. People's got to stop where they can eat. The truckers will give me a call on the CB and let me know that they'll be here. I have regulars that stop on their way out and on their way back. I get a few salesmen, and some tourists in the summer. A few backpackers and tenters come in once in a while."

"I'm so glad you asked us to come out. This is the perfect time, before we have to move on to find a place for Peter to go to school."

"There's a good community school only ten miles up the road. Ain't no reason to cut your stay short for that. The school bus will pick him up."

"*Only* ten miles! Oh, Aunt Ethel, he'll be five years old! I couldn't possibly put him on a bus to travel ten miles to school every day."

"Don't worry about it now." Ethel took a stack of plates from the cabinet and carried them to the long table at the end of the kitchen. "You've got a whole year before your chick has to go out to meet the world."

"Come look, Mom. Come look at the bed I made for Cisco." Peter came into the kitchen, rubbing his eyes with the back of his hand.

Gloria went to him. "You're tired, honey. I bet Aunt Ethel could find you a little something to eat so you can go to bed."

"I wanna wait till Jack comes back. I'm not tired, Mom. Honest."

"I want to show you your room before Jack gets back with your things." Ethel came and took his hand. "C'mon. We'll go back to the front office. I had a connecting door put in. You and your mom will be in unit one."

"Aunt Ethel! Are we taking up one of your paying units? I thought you had two bedrooms in your living quarters. We'll be using a unit you can rent out."

"Land sakes! Quit your frettin'. You need a place where you can spread your things out and make yourself at home. I've nine other units, and they're hardly ever full. If one of my regulars comes and we're full up, he can sleep on the couch."

She opened the door into a spacious room. There was a large double bed at one end with a rose-colored satin spread, and a twin bed at the other with a spread splashed with bright comic-book characters. Along one wall was a double chest, and in the corner a single. A warm beige carpet covered the floor. Ethel pranced in, turned on the light, and opened the door to the dressing room that also served as closet. Off this room was the bathroom.

Peter began to open the empty drawers and to play with the three-way lamp beside his bed.

"It isn't fancy," Ethel said lamely, as if she were seeing it through Gloria's eyes.

"It's perfect! I didn't expect to have so much room or a private bath. Oh, thank you, Aunt Ethel." She put her arms around the little woman and hugged her. "You've gone to so much trouble for us. I hope I'll be worth it to you."

Gloria was glad her aunt wasn't aware of the grandiose style she had lived in while married to Marvin. Even the high-rise she and Peter had moved into after the divorce was plush; Marvin owned the building, and in the settlement had insisted she was to live there with their son. In her desperation to leave him she had agreed. Marvin couldn't bear to lose control of anything, even a woman who didn't measure up to what he expected his wife to be. He had to have her under his thumb. Well . . . that was over now.

"Just having you and Peter here is all the thanks I want," Ethel was saying. "Now, let's shake a leg. I ring the supper gong at six-thirty. If Jack and Gary aren't here by then, we'll keep the food warm for them."

That proved to be unnecessary.

Gloria came to the table in an Indian-print caftan with a high neck and three-quarter-length sleeves. She and Peter took their places after Ethel had introduced them to an insurance adjuster, a bulk-paper salesman, an independent trucker, and to Gary, the man who had gone with Jack to get her car. He was a short, husky man who made no attempt to mask his curiosity. Bright, friendly eyes swept over her in frank appraisal, and she found herself returning his smile.

The meal was served family style; dishes were passed from left to right. Ethel kept up a merry line of chatter while she refilled the bread plate and poured coffee. The men teased her.

"Is this all we get?" Gary asked.

"You say that every time," Ethel shot back. "But I see you're not losing any weight."

Gloria was grateful that she wasn't expected to add much to the conversation. She placed tiny servings of food on Peter's plate and urged him to eat. He was so tired and sleepy he could barely keep his eyes open.

One time she lifted her head to find Jack's green eyes staring at her from across the table. Her large, tawny-gold eyes widened perceptibly and her lips suddenly felt dry. She was the first to look away. When she glanced back at him later, she was surprised to catch him studying her again. He really was a monolith of a man, she thought. His size alone was enough to intimidate without the hair and the beard. He seemed to be perfectly at ease, and ate enormous portions of food.

Gloria had caught the paper salesman eying him apprehensively and had to suppress a smile. She wondered what Jack would look like without all that hair on his face. The one thing she was sure of was that he was not young, for all his wild look. He was somewhere between thirty and forty, and she could detect a certain amount of polish beneath the rough exterior, when he chose to let it shine through.

Peter was half asleep by the time the meal was finished. His eyelids drooped and his legs were rubbery. Gloria stood, excused herself, and struggled to get him on his feet. For some time now he had been too heavy for her to carry.

"Come on, honey. Let's get you to bed." She shook him gently. He sagged against her. She took a few steps and he wrapped his arms about her legs. "Oh, honey, I know you're tired, but—"

"C'mon, hotshot. You're dead on your feet." Jack knelt down beside Peter and touched his shoulder. The child turned immediately, and his hands went up and about the man's neck. He was scooped up with one powerful arm.

"Where's . . . Cisco?" Peter mumbled.

"The pup's gone to bed. Don't you think that's where you should be?"

"Can I feel your whiskers, Jack?"

"Sure."

"They tickle."

"Yeah?" Gray-green eyes looked down into Gloria's. Surprised by the amusement that shone so blatantly, she flickered her eyelids in an instant of confusion. "Where to, ma'am?"

"Ah . . . this way." She went ahead of him to the office and through the door to their room. She flicked on the soft light beside Peter's bed and turned down the spread.

Jack laid the boy gently on the bed, lifted his small feet, slipped off his canvas shoes without untying them, and dropped them on the floor. He reached for the blanket and covered him.

"Are you goin' now, Jack?" Peter's eyes were only half open.

"Yeah, hotshot. I'm goin'."

"Will . . . you come back?"

"I don't know about that, kid. I've got things to do. You'd better get to sleep now."

"I want ya to come back—" Peter tried to sit up, but Jack held him down gently.

"We'll see, kid."

"That means no. *He* always said that. You're not ever comin' back." Peter's eyes filled with tears and his mouth trembled as if he was going to cry.

"Who said so? Well . . . okay, hotshot. I come by here once in a while. I'll stop in. How's that?"

"You're not just sayin' it?"

"Hey . . . I don't talk to hear my head rattle." Jack pretended to frown.

"Are you . . . sure? You're not just sayin' it?"

"Course, I'm not just sayin' it. If I say I'll be back, you can make book on it."

"What's that mean?"

"It means I'll see you the next time I come by. Good night, hotshot."

"Night, Jack. Night, Mom," Peter sang out happily. He snuggled contentedly under the blanket and was almost instantly asleep.

Gloria batted her lashes furiously to keep the tears at bay. She had had no idea of the depth of the child's disappointment concerning the man who was his legal father. Marvin's stock answer for everything Peter asked him had been "We'll see." Peter was right in saying it was the same as no.

"I should put on his pajamas," Gloria said, opening the suitcase.

"Why?"

"Well . . . because he always sleeps in pajamas."

"Why? Is there a law that says the kid's got to be roused up out of a good sleep to undress him so he can sleep? Doesn't make sense to me."

"I doubt if many of the things I do would make sense to you, Mr. Evans," she said carefully.

"Is that right?" He looked around the room. "Are you going to stay here?"

"I'm planning on it."

"You won't like it. You'll be bored," he said flatly.

"How do you know?" She felt a shiver of anticipation

each time she looked at him. Anticipation of what? It was absurd that he was even here in her room.

"I know, You've run out here to escape from something. Is it being divorced?"

"What makes you so sure I'm divorced?"

He shrugged. "One out of every three women your age has been married at least once. There's no reason to believe you're any different."

"Thank you for the information, Mr. Gallup."

He ignored her sarcasm and glanced over to where Peter was sleeping, then down at her. His eyes narrowed. "Did your old man take his frustrations out on the kid?"

Gloria felt a tremor in her heart. "What makes you say that?"

"I'm not blind or deaf, Glory. The kid's hurtin' for masculine company. He's been disappointed a lot, hasn't he? Why didn't he say 'my dad'? Before I left with the pickup he told me that *he* didn't like puppies." He waited. "Well?" he insisted when she didn't say anything.

"It's none of your business."

"Yeah." He shrugged again and bent forward, and she imagined she felt his breath on her face. "You're right. It seems stupid to me that people get married in the first place. Stupider yet, when they have kids they don't want."

"For your information, Peter is wanted and loved. But I can understand why *you* would think the way you do about marriage. I'm sure it's too conventional for the likes of you."

He chuckled at her sarcasm, then he looked at her for so long a time that her self-confidence began to crumble.

Critical eyes traveled over her trim body. She searched her mind for something cutting and clever to say that would put him firmly in his place. Why didn't he leave? Why was he still standing there? Her eyes held a definite shimmer of defiance when she met his glance. His eyes traveled over her face, taking in the wide amber eyes beneath arched brows, the straight nose, wide mouth, and the proud way her head lifted above her slender neck. Then he nodded his head, as if he had come to a decision about her.

There was something in his eyes, in the way they were assessing her, that made her breath quicken. She wasn't *afraid* of him, yet all her defenses were raised. She didn't fully understand this inner need to protect herself from him, it was just there and seemed to be purely instinctive. The chaos existed only in her mind, she was sure of that.

"Poor, scared little girl," he murmured, raising his hand to cup the back of her head. "You're almost as helpless as that kid over there." Then as if talking to himself, he said on a breath of a whisper, "Two little lambs being chased by the big, bad wolf."

"I'm neither poor, scared, nor chased, Mr. Evans." Gloria stepped back away from his hand, hoping her lie was convincing. She inhaled deeply, forcing herself to be calm; she desperately hoped that he didn't know how nervous she was. She moistened her dry lips. "Thank you for your help today. I'd like to pay you for going after my car."

"Okay. What are you offering?"

"Whatever you think it's worth," she said coolly. "I

won't quibble about the bill." It irritated and disappointed her that he was so willing to accept payment.

"Is that a promise?" he asked softly. His tone, more than his words, jarred her nerves. "On the surface you appear to be a typical example of a liberated woman, but underneath you're vulnerable, and scared to death. What in hell did that man do to you?"

She wanted to say something flip to let him know, in no uncertain terms, that the conversation was too personal and that she didn't appreciate his humor. But all she could manage was a look of disapproval, which did nothing but intensify the devilish look in his eyes.

"I'll write you a check, Mr. Evans," she stated curtly.

"I don't want your check, Mrs. Masterson."

"I'll pay you in cash."

"You said you wouldn't quibble about the price."

"I won't—"

"I want the boy for a day. I'll take him up to my place—"

"No!"

He was watching her, trying to read her face; her features were clouded by anger and confused emotions.

"I can see the wheels turning in her mind." He looked over her shoulder, as if he were talking to someone else. "She's thinking that I'm a pervert, a child molester, a ruthless criminal—"

"You could be . . . all those things," she said in a tight, breathless whisper.

"Instant analysis based on . . ."

"Based on . . . appearance!" Gloria's temper flared.

"Okay. Based on appearance. Your opinion of me would have been quite different if I had come into that rest area in a Buick station wagon, a Bill Blass suit, with a short haircut and a clean-shaven face. But remember the old saying, You can't tell a book by its cover."

"You said it, I didn't. I still appreciate what you did for us," she said with a proud lift of her head.

"Yeah, sure. Brawn comes in handy once in a while."

"Well . . . thank you, Mr. Evans, and . . . good night."

"You're quite welcome, Mrs. Masterson, and good night to you too." He placed one bent arm behind him and one in front and bowed deeply. "I really must be going. There's an orgy going on up at my place and a whole harem of naked women are waitin' to be pleasured by their favorite stud."

Gloria didn't allow a muscle in her face to move, although she felt his twinkling green eyes mocking her all the way down to her toes. Her heart began to race, and the awakening of some emotion she didn't quite understand coursed through her.

"Don't let me keep you," she said, keeping her features carefully composed. As if being alerted by his close scrutiny her heartbeat picked up speed.

"Oh, I won't, ma'am. I won't." He gave her a playful salute, and left.

Gloria resisted the temptation to slam the door behind him. Instead she closed it softly and leaned against it; she could hear him laughing, lingering on the other side. *Go away,* she commanded silently. When she put her ear to the door to listen more closely, he began singing in a hushed, low, surprisingly good imitation of Elvis Presley's voice: "Glo-ree-a, Glo-ree-a . . ."

Gloria stood there for a long while after Jack walked away chuckling to himself. *What a strange, infuriating man,* she thought. *I could almost like him if . . . he didn't have that beard,* she admitted begrudgingly. Well, they wouldn't be seeing much of him, thank goodness, and Peter would soon forget him. They'd come West to start a new life and, damn it, she wasn't going to allow it to be complicated by an . . . aging hippie!

CHAPTER THREE

GLORIA STAYED IN her room until she heard the sound of the motorcycle going down the highway. She was angry at herself for allowing Jack Evans to irritate her. What right did he have to voice her innermost feelings? Yes, she was scared. Dammit! She'd been scared, poor, and alone most of her life—that was one reason she'd grabbed at the carrot of security Marvin had dangled in front of her eyes. But she'd discovered there are things worse than not having financial security: being in a love-less relationship that was eroding her self-worth and crushing her spirit, for one. She was proud of herself for being able to break it off, then later finding the courage to leave Cincinnati and the rent-free apartment and the al-lowance paid into her account every month. She was on her own now, with a four-year-old son to support. If she was ever going to break free of Marvin's domination and stand on her own two feet, it was now.

She went out to the kitchen. The men had all left, and Ethel was cleaning up. Gloria carried the dishes from the table to the sink. Ethel rinsed them and stacked them in the dishwasher.

"That didn't take long," Ethel exclaimed when they had finished. "Let's sit down, put our feet up, and have a good visit. I leave the vacancy sign on until about ten o'clock in the summer, then turn it off and go to bed."

Gloria followed her to the living room and watched as she knelt down to start a fire in the fireplace. "My, **my**. Here it is the first of September, and already the fire feels good in the evenings. We'll more than likely have snow flurries six weeks from now. It took me a while to get used to the winters here, but now I like the coziness of being snowed in, having a good fire going and a pot of chili on the stove." She tilted her head to one side and smiled at Gloria. "Do you think your old aunt has lost her mind?"

"Of course not." Gloria sat down on the couch and pulled her feet up under her caftan. "Fall is my favorite time of year. I love to watch the seasons change; I don't think I'd like to live where it's hot all year round."

Ethel sat down in the rocker and picked up a ball of yarn and a crochet hook, and pulled a half-finished afghan from the wooden bucket beside the chair. "There's somethin' about crochetin' that's relaxin'. I've made so many of these over the years, I can almost do it with my eyes closed."

"I'll always treasure the one you made for me, Aunt Ethel."

"Now that we've got some time to ourselves, tell me what finally pushed you into breaking away and coming out here. You said you wanted Peter to know that there was more to life than apartments and pavements and tall buildings. Is that all there was to it?"

"Yes, I wanted that, but I did it for myself too." Gloria gazed into the fire, letting her memories wash over her. "When I look back on my life, Aunt Ethel, I find that the only constructive thing I've done has been to get Peter. Like I told you before, it was wanting a better life for him that gave me the courage to break away from Marvin in the first place." Gloria turned large, luminous amber eyes toward her aunt. "I knew immediately that I'd made a mistake marrying him. I didn't tell anyone. I just resigned myself to make the best of it."

"You stuck it out for five years. I'd give you an A for trying."

"I was a coward, and I still am to a certain degree. Marvin is powerful and ruthless. He provided me with all the material things as long as I was willing to be an invisible person in the house, a nonentity, and let his mother run things and not interfere in his life. I was merely one of the props of a production he created to show the world what a wonderful man he was. He went about his daily existence as if I wasn't there, until the occasion called for him to appear at some social function with a young, devoted wife on his arm. Then I was dressed up and put on display."

There was no bitterness in her voice, only a strange kind of sadness. She talked on as if compelled to tell it all.

"He was shocked and outraged when I announced I wanted to adopt an abandoned child. I found Peter while I was doing volunteer work at the center for abused children."

"I'm surprised he changed his mind."

"Marvin is a very strange man. To him appearance is everything. That was why he needed a wife and I guess he decided that adopting an abused child wouldn't hurt his image either." Gloria paused, and a picture of a man with thinning black hair, piercing blue eyes behind black-rimmed glasses, dark suit, white shirt, and conservative tie flashed across the screen of her mind. Suddenly there was another image superimposed over Marvin's—curly black hair, bushy beard, and laughing green eyes. Startled, Gloria shook her head to bring her thoughts back to what she was saying. "It's almost a requirement for a Masterson to do a certain amount of volunteer work among the less fortunate." The words were heavily laced with sarcasm.

Ethel clicked her tongue sympathetically.

"Marvin is the product of what he was raised to be. He was forty-five years old and had never been married when he married me. I was twenty-one. Aunt Ethel, I was so stupidly young and naive. Now I understand that was why he chose me. As the old saying goes—he swept me off my feet. If I had stopped to think for two minutes I would have realized we were from two different worlds and that I had mistaken security for love."

"Sometimes you have to flunk the course to learn the lesson," Ethel said dryly. "What did Ernest think about you marrying a man so much older than you?"

"He didn't meet him until the day of the wedding, and then we were off to Mexico City for our honeymoon. I don't think Daddy liked him much, but Mother was walking on clouds."

"Humph! That figures," Ethel said under her breath.

Aloud she said, "Sometimes people are blinded by glitter."

"I wanted Peter so much," Gloria said. She bit her lower lip as she remembered. "He was so sweet and so helpless. I began to spend all day, every day, at the center. At first Marvin refused to even discuss the idea of adoption. He doesn't like children and has never wanted any of his own."

"What did he think when you left him?"

"By this time he was getting nervous that I might refuse to continue playacting as his wife. Besides, he was seeing a woman a few years older than himself. The fact that this woman had been married to someone on the fringe of European royalty was important to him. Marvin has a vast number of interests, the least of them being a physical relationship with a wife."

Ethel gave her a sideways glance, but Gloria had turned her face away. When next she looked at her aunt her eyes sparkled with devilish amusement.

"I heard that his new lady friend and Mother Masterson locked horns, and he had to end the relationship."

"Well, hallelujah!" Ethel chortled.

"I'm so glad I'm out of the whole mess. Aunt Ethel, I appreciate your letting me come here and giving me time to get on my feet and decide where to take my life from here on."

"This could be a new beginning for both of us. In a few years we could have a string of Rusty Cove motels all across the state."

Gloria giggled happily. "You'd better teach me how to clean the rooms first."

"We'll start on that in the morning, just as soon as the

guests leave. The truckers are up and gone early, the salesman a little later. I keep a pot of coffee, rolls, and cookies in the office, and they come in and help themselves before they go. Everyone who isn't staying over is usually out by ten o'clock. Gary rents number ten by the week and I make the bed when he's used it and change his bedding and clean the room on Friday, if it needs it."

"Do you wash everything here, or do you send it out?"

"We have a big washer and dryer in the room behind the kitchen. George got disgusted with the laundry service and went to town one day and ordered them. It took a hunk out of our savings, but now I'm glad we have them; they've already paid for themselves. Of course, when something goes wrong it costs an arm and a leg to have it fixed. But Gary's pretty good at fixin' things."

"Who stays here when you go to town? You must have a lot of grocery shopping to do."

"Gary is usually here on Saturday. He looks after things while I'm gone. He was here when George died; I don't know what I'd have done without him."

"Then he's the one you were telling me about on the phone? His wife died, and his little girl lives with his mother-in-law in Great Falls, right?"

"Yes. He lives in his truck when he's on the road. He dotes on that child, but knows she's better off with her grandma."

Gloria looked thoughtful.

"Aunt Ethel, do you know what I notice the most about this place? It's the quiet and the darkness. I stood on the porch for a few minutes before I came in, and there isn't a light anywhere except here at the motel. It's the strangest feeling to look out into all that black void."

"I guess I don't even notice it anymore . . ." Ethel's head was resting against the back of the rocker, and her eyes were closed.

"Aunt Ethel, it's past ten o'clock. Do you want me to turn off the vacancy sign?"

Ethel didn't answer. Gloria got up from the couch just as her aunt opened her eyes, looked up at her, and shook her head as if to clear it.

"I must of dozed off." She put the half-finished afghan back in the bucket and got slowly to her feet, holding onto the chair.

"Are you all right?" Gloria asked anxiously. Her aunt didn't say anything. "Aunt Ethel, are you all right?"

"Just a little dizzy. Nothin' that hasn't happened a hundred times before. Too much excitement for an old lady, I guess." She straightened up. "See . . . it passed. I'm as good as new. You run along to bed and I'll turn off the vacancy light. Good heavens! It's later than I thought it was."

"I can turn off the lights, Aunt Ethel. What time do you get up?"

"Anywhere from 5:30 to 6:30, but you don't have to get up that early."

"I'll set my alarm for 5:30." Gloria put her arms around the small woman and hugged her. "Good night, Aunt Ethel. I . . . love you."

"Ah . . . go on with ya!" Ethel smiled embarrassedly. "Check the door and turn out the lights as you go through the office."

On her way out, Gloria looked back over her shoulder at her aunt, who was still standing beside the chair. A little, nagging fear possessed Gloria's heart. Had she imagined the white spots on each side of her aunt's mouth and the almost vacant look in her eyes when she first opened them? Had her words been slurred the slightest bit? She thought about it as she washed her face and pulled a nightgown over her head. Tomorrow, she decided firmly, I'm going to insist that she make an appointment with her doctor for a checkup.

Jack Evans sipped at the soft drink he had taken out of the refrigerator, and then wondered why he had taken it. He didn't want it; it was simply something to do. He considered building a fire in the potbellied stove in the center of the room, decided against it, and put on a jacket instead. He was restless tonight. It had been damned cold coming up that mountain road on the motorcycle; there'd been only a few times he'd let night catch him away from home unless he was in the Jeep. The town seemed more forlorn than ever tonight. There had been no light in the saloon at the end of the dusty street when he came into town; old Cliff Rice, his sole neighbor, had either gone to bed, or had been too drunk to light the lamp.

Hangtown, Montana, population two: one old drunk and one worthless hippie, Jack mused. He sat down in a chair, tilted it back against the wall, and propped his feet on the table. Critical green eyes swept the neat but primitive home, surveying it as if through other eyes than his own. The bed on a headboardless frame, a three-burner stove for summer, a cookstove for winter, a table, a bookcase, a reading chair, and a gas-powered refrigerator-freezer made up the furnishings, along with a couple of standing TV trays. Every month he made a trip to Lewistown to get bottled gas to keep the lamp and refrigerator running.

Jack had a strong suspicion that the building he lived in had been a funeral parlor back in the 1870s. He had found a chest of moldy ribbons upstairs and a half-finished coffin in the shed out back. He had chosen the building because it had survived the ravages of time better than any of the other eleven buildings that made up the town, regardless of what it had been used for during the town's heyday.

Eight years ago he had founded the town, completely abandoned by all businesses and permanent residents, and bought it, not dreaming that, four years later, he would come back to the ghost town and call it home. Almost everyone thought he was a squatter, a hippie, or whatever they called bums these days. It didn't matter to him what anyone thought of him . . . that is, not until today. *Hell, it still doesn't matter,* he told himself, and the front legs of the chair he had tilted back against the wall came crashing down with a bang.

Dammit! What the hell is the matter with you, Evans? You acted like a love-sick kid today; you couldn't keep your eyes off the woman. The questions that had nagged at him all the way up the mountain continued to nag at him now. *Why in the hell did it irritate me when she looked at me as if I was something that had just crawled out of the sewer? I even enjoyed breaking that punk's arm when I found him harassing her and the kid, and God knows, I hate violence. And why did I have the urge to smash someone when the kid started to cry because I said I wasn't coming back to see him? Dammit, Evans. Stay*

*away from that woman and that kid or you're letting
yourself in for some sleepless nights.*

He placed his folded arms on the table and rested his
forehead on them. He sat that way for a long time thinking, and trying not to think. Being with the boy had
brought forth a flood of memories that he had managed to
keep at bay for a long while. There had been a time when
he was sure he would lose his sanity; now, he was more
able to cope with his feelings. And yet he was hearing,
once again, the voice of his small, green-eyed, golden-
haired daughter: *I love you, Daddy. . . . I want to stay
with you. . . . You'll come get me? Promise me, Daddy*—

"If only I'd've done things differently," he groaned
aloud. "If only I'd fought harder, dirtier, instead of trying
to be Mr. Nice Guy. Why in hell didn't I go against the
damn courts and just take her? I'd be in prison now, but
she'd be alive!"

The Chicago traffic was heavy the morning his attorney
had called for him to come to his office. He had filed a
lawsuit against the FBI months ago, trying to force them
to tell him where they had secreted his daughter, his ex-
wife, and her new husband after the man had testified and
caused the conviction of the head of a gigantic drug operation. He contended it was a violation of his visitation
rights that he was no longer able to have Wendy with him
every other weekend.

He resisted every attempt of the FBI to force him to
drop the litigation. Naively he thought the courts would
give him custody of Wendy, at least for part of each year.
But he had underestimated the power of the FBI. It had

been almost a year since he filed the suit, and he had yet to have his day in court.

On the way to George's office he firmly believed the case was coming to trial, that George had good news. The moment he stepped into the office he knew that he was wrong. George Fisher, his attorney and friend, stood with his back to the door gazing out the window. A bald, over-weight man with a cigar between his fingers pushed him-self up out of one of the chairs and held out his hand.

"Mr. Evans, I'm Paul Blake of the FBI."

George turned from the window and came to stand be-fore his desk. His face was gray and still.

"What's happened, George?" A feeling of dread began to overtake him; he felt the queer tension that hovered over the room. His first thought was: *Oh, my God! The judge has refused to hear the case.*

"Mr. Blake has something to tell you, Jack." There was anger in George's trembling voice.

The rotund man took a drag from his cigar, walked a few paces, and turned. "They found them. In spite of all we could do to ensure their safety, they found them."

"What do you mean?" Jack whispered hoarsely.

"I'm sorry, Evans. They planted a bomb in the car."

"Wendy?" Her name came out in a spasm of agony.

"All of them." The words were spoken quietly and with a finality that rocked his very soul.

A desolate silence followed while the enormity of the words sank into Jack's mind. Grief, then anger so black and great that it seemed to explode in his head, brought a roar of rage from his throat. He leapt to his feet and grabbed the fat man about the neck.

"You bastard! You goddamned bastard! You protected

a goddamn criminal and let him kill my little girl! I'll kill you . . . I'll kill you—"

He came to much later on the floor. George was bending over him, holding a wet cloth to the large lump on the side of his head; he had been hit by the man's partner, who had burst into the room thinking that Jack was about to kill the man. Jack looked at George with dazed eyes, then rolled over, hid his face in his arms, and cried endless tears of despair.

A week later, after he had buried his daughter, he locked his house, mailed the key to George, and drove out of the city.

Even after four years there were still times when grief and frustration almost tore him apart. This was one of those times.

"Goddamn the law! Goddamn the courts, the FBI, and the whole stinkin', rotten system!" He lifted his head, shouted into the emptiness, and banged his fist down hard on the table, scattering papers and pencils.

Jack lowered his head miserably. His eyes flooded with tears as the memories came rushing back: silky blond hair in braids, sad green eyes, small arms about his neck, wet, sticky kisses on his face. After a while he turned out the light and felt his way in the dark to the bed, threw himself down on it, and prayed for the sleep that he knew wouldn't come.

He lay staring into the black night, the room silent except for the groaning of the floorboards when he shifted his weight on the bed. Out of the blackness came a woman's face, a perfect oval with a small fine nose and full soft lips, honey-gold hair, clear, tawny-gold eyes filled with fear and uncertainty. He felt a deep hunger for the companionship and sweetness of a woman to share his life. The lonely years stretched ahead—

"Get out of my mind," he whispered, almost savagely. "I don't *need* anyone and I don't *want* anyone."

By nine A.M. the motel and campgrounds were empty except for Gloria, Peter, and Ethel. Gary left on a run that would take at least five days. Before he left he promised that on his return he would fix Gloria's car, and he attached the U-Haul to the pickup so she could take it to Lewistown and turn it in.

Gary was a cheerful, easygoing man in his mid-thirties. There was almost a mother-son affection between himself and Ethel; he teased her, and she scolded him. He appeared to be genuinely glad Gloria and Peter had come to live with Ethel.

"The old girl needs someone with her," he confided to Gloria just before he climbed up into the cab of his big eighteen-wheeler. He handed her a card with the address and phone number of a freight center in Kansas City. "I'll be there most of the time. If you should need me, and I'm on the road, send word out on the CB; the truckers will pass it along."

Gloria felt a tingle of apprehension and looked over her shoulder to be sure they were alone before she spoke. "Do you think Aunt Ethel is . . . unwell?"

"She's slowed down a lot the last few weeks." He glanced over at where Ethel and Peter were putting a rope on the clothesline for the puppy. "She put on a good show last night for your benefit, but she's not up to running this place alone. I've tried to get her to see a doctor, but the old girl's got a mind of her own."

"Thank you for telling me. It confirms my suspicions. Do you know if she's had a checkup lately?"

"Not that I know of. She used to take the pickup to town on Saturday. But lately she's been giving me a list to fill when I go to Great Falls to see my little girl. I don't think she trusts herself to drive the pickup anymore." He climbed up into the cab and grinned at her. "I'm glad you're here. See ya on Friday."

Gloria went to stand beside Ethel and Peter, and waved to Gary as he pulled the big rig out onto the highway. The two long, powerful blasts of the horn delighted Peter, scared the puppy, and jarred Gloria's eardrums. She slipped the card he had given her into the pocket of her jeans and turned to look at her aunt. She was still looking at the truck, and she continued watching it until it went over the hill and out of sight.

The morning passed quickly. By lunchtime the rooms had been cleaned and the soiled linen piled in the laundry room. Gloria had done the majority of the work, over the protest of her aunt.

"I'll learn faster by doing than by watching, Aunt Ethel. Sit down and tell me what to do."

It wasn't until the middle of the afternoon, while Peter was napping and they were sitting at the kitchen table planning the evening meal, that Gloria had the opportunity to bring up the subject that had been on her mind all morning.

"Is your doctor in Lewistown or Great Falls, Aunt Ethel? I brought along Peter's medical records, and I should get a doctor lined up for him. He'll need booster shots soon."

"I don't doctor much. But there's one in Lewistown, and it's closer. Is there something wrong with Peter?"

"No. But in case there is, I want a doctor who is acquainted with his medical history."

"Pshaw! What good'll that do? One's as good as 'nother when you're sick. They mostly guess, anyway." Ethel avoided Gloria's eyes and shuffled through a notebook of handwritten recipes.

"Aunt Ethel." Gloria uttered her aunt's name in a way that compelled the older woman to look at her. "When did you last see a doctor?"

"About a year after me'n George came here," Ethel answered staunchly. "We both went. George made me go."

"You haven't been back since?"

"I haven't been sick. Doctors don't know everything, by a long shot! Sometimes I think all they're good for is to set broken bones and sew up holes. They said George was fit as a fiddle, and a few months later he was dead. What'll happen'll happen, and there ain't no sense in worryin' about it."

"Will you go with me when I go to take Peter's records? I want to be sure you're all right, Aunt Ethel. You're . . . very dear to me."

"We'll see. Anyway, we have to wait until Gary's here before we both can leave," Ethel said with a perky smile, and Gloria knew her aunt's "we'll see" meant no, she wouldn't go.

Ethel continued to chatter. "Now, what do you think about having Swiss steak for dinner? I'm looking for

Harry and Neil tonight; they're truckers who make a run up to Kalispell every week. Bill Woler is due too; he's an auto supply salesman out of Bozeman. They'll call me on the CB when they get within calling distance, which in these mountains is about twenty miles out. And, you can't tell, we may have a tourist or two stop for the night. The weather is still nice. Although after school starts the bottom falls out of the tourist season."

Gloria knew her aunt was talking because the subject of going to the doctor had made her nervous. She said nothing more, deciding to wait until Gary was back to help in persuading her aunt to have the checkup.

Several days went by, and the pickup with the U-Haul attached still sat in the parking area. Gloria and Peter adjusted to life at the motel far more easily than she had imagined they would. She had no desire to go to town, and kept putting off the trip to return the trailer. In a couple of days the work pattern was established. Gloria insisted on doing all the cleaning, and Ethel filled the big washing machine and folded the clean laundry. Together they planned the evening meal and cooked it, Gloria maneuvering her aunt into the "sit-down" portion of the work. The time always passed very quickly.

Gloria had set boundaries for Peter, and he played happily with the puppy or rode his Big Wheel up and down the walk in front of the motel. The first few evenings found her exhausted, but it was a tiredness she welcomed. At night they watched a few hours of television, and then went to bed as soon as the VACANCY light was turned off.

Most of the people who stopped for the night had been guests of the motel before. The occasional new tourists who came by were usually those caught between towns late in the evening. Most of them were delighted with the home-cooked evening meal; it saved them from having to rely on snacks from the machines. Of course, there were exceptions.

The first night Gloria had charge of the desk, an older couple in a new Cadillac drove in and wanted to inspect the room before they signed the register. She understood their concern and cheerfully led them to the room, waiting patiently while they lifted the covers to see the condition of the mattress. They rejected two of the towels because of some small rust spots, and wanted paper to cover the toilet seat although Gloria assured them it had been washed that morning with disinfectant. They haughtily refused the offer of the evening meal, and when they turned in their key the next morning they just as haughtily refused the offer of coffee and fresh rolls. Gloria was glad to see the last of them, and secretly hoped they would get a flat tire before they reached Great Falls.

"Don't let 'em bother you," Ethel said. "For every one like them there are dozens of really nice people."

Peter asked Gloria several times when Jack was coming back. Whenever he heard the sound of a motorcycle coming down the highway, which wasn't often, he ran out to watch it pass, then turned away with a disappointed look. Gloria had to admit to a quickening of her own pulse when she heard the sound, and was sure that what she felt was relief when the cycle kept going instead of turning in to the drive.

On the fourth day, the day before Gary was due back, Gloria heard the roar of a motorcycle coming from the west. Somehow she knew it would be *him*. She was right. She glanced out the window of the room she was cleaning and saw him turn in to the drive and stop in front of the office.

"Jack! Jack!" Peter jumped off his Big Wheel and ran to him as fast as his stubby little legs could carry him. They talked for a moment, and then Jack took off his helmet and set it down on the boy's head. He picked him up and carefully placed him on the seat in front of him, then rode around the circular drive several times before stopping in front of the office again and lifting the boy off. Gloria thought he would drive away, but he turned off the machine and put down the kickstand.

"Mom! Mom! Jack's here," Peter screeched as he ran down the walk.

"Don't shout, Peter." Gloria wheeled the vacuum cleaner out the door, down the walk, and into the next room.

"C'mon, Mom. Come see Jack."

"I've got to finish this room first. You run along." She unlooped the cord and plugged it into the outlet.

"Hurry, Mom. Jack! Jack!" he yelled. "Come see Cisco. Aunt Ethel says he needs a pen. She says he might get with a skunk if he goes to the woods. Can you stay for lunch, Jack?"

Gloria watched her son grab Jack's hand and drag him toward the door. She turned on the vacuum cleaner and moved it across the carpet vigorously while her mind churned. Damn that man! He wasn't the type of man she wanted as a role model for her son. *It's the motorcycle that fascinates Peter,* she told herself. Well, she'd put a stop to that! *It's disgusting for a grown man to be so oblivious to conventions that he'd let himself look like something that escaped from the zoo. No job, no respon-*

sibilities. What contribution would he ever make to society? How does he live? He's probably collecting a pension on some imaginary injury, letting the taxpayers support him. She swept every inch of the carpet, several times, before she turned off the sweeper and leaned on the handle.

"*Va . . . room! Va . . . room!*" Peter's version of a roaring motor accompanied the rattle of the plastic toy he loved.

Gloria's eyes were drawn to the window. Peter, with the blue helmet on his head, was riding his Big Wheel down the walk, his small legs pumping energetically, pretending to be riding the black Harley-Davidson parked in the drive. *Being here* has *opened a whole new world for him,* she thought as she watched him. Having a puppy, being able to play in the dirt and shout without being chastised, and exploring among the trees were experiences he had not had before.

"Glory hallelujah! I thought you'd never turn that thing off."

Gloria spun around. Jack stood in the doorway. She had forgotten how big he was and how much hair he had. Today he wore a black jacket and a red bandana around his head. He stood looking at her, absently cleaning his nails with a long, thin-bladed knife. He tilted his head at an angle, his green eyes, full of amusement, holding hers.

Gloria pressed her lips tightly together, noting with disgust a gold earring dangling from his right ear, shining brightly against his black hair.

CHAPTER FOUR

"HELLO, GLORY. AREN'T you about ready to hightail it back to the city?"

"Good morning, Mr. Evans." Gloria spoke lightly without looking at him and pulled the plug from the outlet, looped the cord over the sweeper handle, and pushed it determinedly toward the door.

"Peter said this was your last room." He stood there, his big frame blocking the doorway.

"It is, but I have other things to do. Excuse me. Please—"

"You didn't answer my question."

"No, I didn't. It's none of your business." She hated the nervous quiver in her voice.

"You're right." He chuckled. "I'm only curious." His eyes toured her figure in the faded jeans and the T-shirt, proclaiming in bright-red letters, YOU'VE COME A LONG WAY, BABY, that accentuated her small, firm breasts.

Gloria felt the heat that flushed her cheeks. She hated it when she blushed. It was his fault, and she wanted to slap him. He didn't budge from the doorway, so she backed off and smoothed the spread over the pillows on the bed in a purely superfluous gesture. She gave the room a sweeping, critical glance to make sure everything was in place and moved toward the doorway again in a businesslike way, determined to not let this bear of a man intimidate her.

"You may not have anything to do, Mr. Evans, but I do. Please move out of the doorway." The nervous quiver was gone from her voice. It made her proud of herself and gave her the courage to lift her brows along with her small, pointed chin and look squarely into deep-set green eyes.

Jack looked down into twin pools of flashing amber lights. He could see a tiny mole on the lower lid of her right eye and a small puckered scar above her lip. It was faint, but showed plainly on the makeup-free skin of her face. That, and the fact that she couldn't weigh much more than a hundred pounds, gave her a childlike, vulnerable look.

Glory, Glory—sweet, sweet child. *Good grief,* he thought. *Did I say it aloud?* No, thank God, he hadn't. The tension-charged atmosphere had silenced him. *The way I feel right this minute,* he thought, *scares the hell out of me.*

Gloria shifted in acute discomfort. *I'm crazy, purely crazy.* The thought popped into her head and she wanted to laugh. *Why do I always want to laugh when I'm with this man?* A gray hair glinted here and there in the shiny black hair that curled about his ears and drooped down over the red band on his forehead. His beard was as glossy black as the brush of lashes that framed his green eyes, but with a sprinkling of silver. She could smell the faint odor of some spicy soap.

Gloria pressed her lips together and retreated a step so she didn't have to tilt her head so far back to look at him. Faded jeans were molded to his taut buttocks and long thighs. Their snug fit declared his sex in no uncertain terms; he was masculinity epitomized. She was brought out of her trance by an amused chuckle and made aware that she had looked at him too long and too hard.

"Do you like what you see?"

"Not . . . especially," she said lightly, feeling irritation at the fluttery sensation dancing in her stomach.

The twist of her lips produced a dimple, and Jack's gaze was drawn to it. There was something about this small, golden-eyed little redneck that compelled him to needle her, and he didn't understand it at all. Her body was dainty, compact, and utterly feminine. He fought down the urge to hold it against him, nuzzle her ear with his nose, taste the sweetness of her full lips.

She had persistently dogged his thoughts for the last few days. He had tried to clear his mind with hard, physical work by downing several dead trees he had saved to use for firewood. But even as he worked, thoughts of her danced in his head. After coming to within inches of his leg with the chain saw and barely missing his foot with the ax, he'd decided to purge himself of thoughts of her and ride over to the motel. After all, he reasoned, he'd promised the kid he'd come back to see him.

Now, as he watched her, he instinctively sensed the fawnlike unease she felt in his presence. *You stupid jackass!* he chided himself. *Why did you spend an hour making an old cuff link into an earring and why did you stop a mile up the road to put it on?* He chuckled as much at his own foolishness as he did at the look she had given him when she saw it.

"Hummmm . . ." He stroked his beard thoughtfully. "I take it you're not impressed with my good looks. I'm very impressed with yours. I like what I see very much."

"That just thrills me to death," she shot back curtly. "Are you hiding something under all that brush? Wrinkles? Sagging jowls? Ah . . . I bet it's a receding chin." A tiny amused curl of her lips accompanied the words.

"I've been told I'm very handsome," he retorted quickly, with brazen arrogance. He watched in fascination as the amber eyes changed from frosty stones to sparkling sunshine that penetrated his very soul, grabbed him, and shook him. "You're . . . very pretty when you smile." The words came out slowly, and he hadn't meant to say them. There was warmth in her eyes, and he suddenly wanted that warmth, needed it.

"I know it," she replied with a small shake of her tilted chin. Her lashes fanned down, then lifted over mischievous, laughing eyes.

Gloria's mental machinery, intent on maintaining an icy chill toward this . . . nonconformist, switched to lightness and laughter, and there wasn't a thing she could do about it. Her sense of humor took over, and before she realized it, she was completely out of control.

Watching as the laughter burst from her lips, Jack laughed too—a deep, rumbling, uncontrollable sound that he hadn't heard for so long it almost startled him. *Christ! You're like nothing I've ever seen before.* Again he wondered if he'd spoken aloud and made an effort to gather in the threads of his scattered thoughts. There was an electric aura about her that threw his mind completely out of sync. *I've got to be careful of you,* he warned himself. *You could take more of a man's heart than he's willing to give.*

"Mom! Jack! Mom! Jack!" Peter squealed and squeezed through the door, grabbing Jack's jacket. "Cisco got away. He's lost in the woods."

"Oh, Peter. Aunt Ethel said to keep him tied up."

"I was bringin' him to see . . . Jack," he said with a downward turn of his quivering lips.

"No sweat, hotshot," Jack said calmly, and took Peter's hand. "He won't go far. What he needs is a pen. I wouldn't want to be tied to that clothesline all day, would you?" He glanced at Gloria's troubled face. "C'mon. We'll see what he's up to."

Gloria watched Peter skip happily alongside the big man. A thoughtful frown covered her features. It occurred to her that prejudices didn't come naturally. They were taught. Peter didn't care that Jack looked tough as rawhide, or that he lacked the ambition to hold a steady job, or that, provoked enough, he would deliberately break a man's arm. *Children are like animals when it comes to love,* she thought sadly. *They don't care if a person is old or young, slim or fat, smart or stupid, or if he has long hair and a beard. It's the way in which that person treats them that sets the tone of the relationship.* A bit of guilt laid itself on Gloria's conscience, and she didn't like the feeling at all.

Jack stayed for lunch, and afterward he and Peter left the kitchen to finish building a pen for Cisco that they had started with a roll of chicken wire they'd found in the shed. When they returned, Gloria and Ethel had finished the cleanup and were having a second cup of coffee. Gloria reminded Peter that it was time for his nap.

"But . . . Mom! Jack's here."

Jack sat down in a chair, and Peter wiggled his way between his knees and leaned against them.

"He'll be leaving soon. You know what will happen if you don't have your afternoon nap. You'll be too tired and too sleepy to eat your supper."

"Are ya goin', Jack? Are ya?"

"I wasn't planning on it, hotshot." Jack looked into Gloria's flashing eyes and smiled innocently.

"See, Mom! See! He's not going." Peter climbed onto Jack's lap.

"Well, that's just . . . dandy. Perhaps Mr. Evans will *still* be here when you wake up." Gloria got to her feet and held out her hand. "C'mon. You'll have to be washed. I think you've got most of Montana on your face and hands."

"Washed too?" Peter said dejectedly.

"Run along, sport. Moms get these crazy ideas about naps and baths, and there's not much a guy can do but go along with 'em." Jack nudged Peter's chin with his fist and lifted him off his lap.

"Don't go, Jack. You'll stay till I wake up?" Peter asked hopefully.

"Sure. I might even stay for supper if it's okay with Ethel." His eyes met Gloria's. She was looking at him as if she'd like to run him through with a saber. *She's mad as a hornet,* he thought gleefully. *She thinks I'm a bad influence on her son.* Absurdly he wished he hadn't lost his earring when he and Peter were building the pen. He'd have to pick up a supply at the dime store the next time he was in town. On second thought it might improve his image if he hung a few gold chains around his neck too.

"You're welcome anytime, Jack," Ethel declared. "I'll just throw in another potato or two. Anyhow, I want you to get on the roof before you go and tear that old bird's nest out of the dryer vent." She tried to keep from breaking into a smile. Something was going on between these two; a person would have to be deaf, dumb, and blind to not see the sparks they struck off in each other.

"Let's go, Peter," Gloria said sharply.

When Gloria returned to the kitchen she had showered and changed into a pair of forest-green slacks and a soft striped shirt with a small white, round collar. She had put on makeup for the first time since she and Peter arrived, and was carrying a jacket and a purse.

Jack was talking on the CB radio to his neighbor back in Hangtown, and Ethel was still sitting at the table.

"Break for that base station in Hangtown. Break. Break. Hey, Boozer, are you on the channel?"

"Yeah, I'm here, Bigfoot. Whatta ya want?" The slurred voice came in very faintly.

"Wiggle the squelch, Boozer. You're not coming in very clear."

"Ten-four. How's that?"

"Better. I'll not be back for a while. Ethel's new helper invited me to supper here at the Rustic Cove and you know I can't resist an invitation from a pretty woman." His amused green eyes watched Gloria's mouth tighten and her nostrils flare angrily. "Will you check to see if my hound has plenty of water and feed him along about sun-down?"

"Ten-four, Bigfoot."

"And, Boozer, keep an eye on the road. You know what to do if you see the . . . feds," he murmured, his eyes full of mischievous laughter.

"The . . . what?"

"Feds, Boozer. The feds. Over and out," he said quickly, and put the microphone back on the hook. "And please don't burn down my town," he said silently to the dead mike.

"Break for that Bigfoot." Another voice came in on the set and Jack picked up the microphone again.

"You got the Bigfoot."

Gloria lifted her eyes to the ceiling in a gesture of impatience. *For crying out loud—the games grown men play! Bigfoot? I can think of a handle more suitable for him than that,* she thought. *Hummmm . . . How about Bushman, Hairy Harry, Blackbeard, Billy Whiskers, Montana DingBat?* As her mind churned, the impulse to giggle almost overwhelmed her. She turned her back to him, keeping it stiffly straight, until she could control her rebellious, smiling mouth.

"Red Baron, back atcha." The voice came over the speaker. "Tell Ma Brown I'll be there for chow and I'm hungry as a starved coyote."

"Ten-four, Red Baron. I'll pass the word to Ma Brown and that Barbie doll. There's roast beef in the oven and pie on the table. Keep 'er between the ditches, the rubber side down, and roll 'er on home."

"Obliged, Bigfoot. I'm gone."

"Dwight's always starved. I'll swear, I don't think that

man eats a bite all day when he knows he'll be here for supper." Ethel bounced up from the table to peer into the oven. The truckers were her family, and her boys were coming home for supper. Dwight Anderson, known as Red Baron on the CB, had been stopping every week for several years. She loved every one of her boys and worried about them when the weather was bad. Something Jack had said flashed through her mind, and she turned to smile happily at Gloria.

"You've got a CB handle," she exclaimed brightly. "Barbie doll fits you too. I got to hand it to you, Jack. When they were passin' out brains, you were right up front."

"And when they were passing out humility, he was at the end of the line," Gloria said heatedly. She ignored her aunt's What's-got-into-you look and whipped her jacket about her shoulders. "I'm going to take the U-Haul to town while Peter is napping, Aunt Ethel. Sit down and rest while I'm gone. I'll be back in plenty of time to help with dinner." She spun around and walked determinedly out the door.

"Hey, Glory. Wait a minute." She heard the screen door bang shut as she was going down the walk toward the pickup. "I think I'll come along."

She whirled around to face Jack. "And I think you won't." She opened the door of the truck, tossed her purse inside, and climbed up onto the seat.

"Oh, yes, I will." Jack grabbed the door and stopped her from closing it. "This old truck flops out of gear once in a while if you don't shift it just right. I'm not anxious to come rescue you *again*, Glory, Glory."

Gloria forced herself to count to ten before speaking,

knowing that by using her name like that he was hoping she would lose her composure.

"I suppose you intend to hold that over my head for the rest of my life," she said calmly, but with an unmistakable edge in her voice. "It won't work. I don't feel the least bit obligated to you. I thanked you for your help. I offered to pay you. It's over and done with. Good-bye."

"At least we agree on one thing. Move over." He got into the truck and crowded her out from under the wheel.

"Just a doggone minute!" Gloria sputtered. "I don't want you to go with me."

"That's obvious. You'd rather swallow a toad than be seen in town with me, wouldn't you?" His eyes were twinkling merrily. "Glory, Glory . . . I'm the one taking the chance going off alone with you. How do I know you won't drag me off into the woods and have your way with me? You might come at me with a knife or an ax. You could be a psychopathic killer, a female Jack the Ripper who's killed hundreds of men in Ohio! Who knows what evil lurks behind that innocent face and beautiful wildcat eyes—"

"Funny! You should be a comedian. But I suppose even *that* would be too much work for you." His teasing had fanned her temper, and her voice rose with heated anger.

"Could be," he said agreeably, and shrugged. "Give me the keys and we'll talk about it on the way to town."

Gloria's mouth opened, then snapped shut. Damned if she'd give him the satisfaction of an argument. She slapped the keys into his hand and slid over to the passenger side.

Jack put the truck in motion and they moved out onto

the highway. She looked with pretended interest out the window, knowing that he was studying her, wondering why this bothered her so much.

"Glo-ry, glo-ry, hallelujah. Glo-ry, glo-ry, hallelujah . . . ," he sang softly.

She refused to rise to the bait and continued to gaze stoically out the window.

The highway cut through a thick stand of spruce and pine. The sky overhead was a clear blue with a few puffy white clouds rolling lazily along on a slight breeze, and the air was clean and fresh. The long, magnificent sweep of landscape was green, yellow, and bronze; the colors glistened in the afternoon sun, providing a startling contrast to the blue sky above. It was all so breathtakingly beautiful. Gloria realized she could easily fall in love with this country, and now understood why her aunt had not wanted to leave it.

A tired sigh escaped her lips. Being constantly on guard with this man was energy consuming.

She turned to see Jack darting glances at her. He had rolled down the window, and the wind was whipping his hair back from his face. She studied the big man driving her aunt's truck and wondered why in the world the elderly woman trusted this unconventional screwball. She swung around and forced from her mind the thought that he really might be a handsome man beneath all that . . . brush.

"Does Peter look like his father? He certainly doesn't resemble you."

"No."

"She's a woman of few words," he said, as if talking to someone else. "But that's not all bad. A woman with her mouth flapping all the time would soon get on a man's nerves." He shot her a devilish look that fueled her temper again.

"If you think I'm going to tell you my life history, forget it," she snapped.

"I know part of it."

"You've been pumping my aunt for information!"

He laughed. "What I know about you, I heard before you got here."

"Then . . . you knew who I was when you stopped at the rest area," she said accusingly.

"I had a pretty good idea."

"Then why didn't you say so? And why ask about Peter's father? You must know that he's my adopted son and that he was left in the rest room of a sleazy tavern—an abused, frightened child who was picked up by the police and brought to the center for abandoned children. He had never been loved or wanted, held or cuddled . . ." Her voice rose with an anger that had nothing to do with him. She looked into his eyes and was startled by the tenderness she saw there.

"I didn't know that," he said slowly.

They lapsed into silence. During this time they passed the rest area where he had beaten up the two hoodlums who had harassed her. She glanced at him. The flip manner was gone. His brows were drawn together as if in deep concentration. She looked away from him and allowed her eyes to feast on the panorama stretched out before her: forest-covered slopes that after a while gave way to the cluster of buildings that made up the town of Lewistown.

There was a soft quality to the afternoon light as it filtered through the windshield of the truck, evidence of the autumn sun's waning strength. To Gloria this peaceful scene seemed a million miles away from the crowded and sometimes smoggy streets of Cincinnati.

The pickup bounced over the railroad tracks and down the long main street of the town. Other streets branched off at intervals, dividing groups of stores, some of which were faced in brick. A new modern bank sprawled on a corner, reminding Gloria of Marvin. Banks always have the newest and the most modern-looking buildings in town, she mused.

A white church, its cupola stark against a background of trees whose leaves were faded green, muted rust, and brilliant gold, was set back on a side street looking stately and serene.

Jack turned the truck into the drive of a service station. Along one side was a row of rental trailers and trucks. He pulled into that area and stopped.

"Give me your papers."

It wasn't *Do you want me to take care of it for you?* It was simply *Give me your papers.* She fought down the resentment that bubbled up and gave him a searing glance. With her chin set at a stubborn angle she opened the door, got out, and went into the office. She had rented the trailer and she would turn it in without any help from "Bushman," she thought with an impulse to giggle in spite of her irritation.

When Gloria returned to the pickup, the trailer had been unhitched and moved away. Jack was not in sight, and her first impulse was to slide beneath the wheel and drive away. But when she reached to start the motor, she realized that the keys were not in the ignition. Damn! He was taking no chances on being left in town.

Frustrated, knowing that he had anticipated what she would do if she had the chance, she sat in the truck and watched the cars come in, fill with gas, and leave. Five minutes went by and then ten. She fidgeted on the seat, looked at her watch, and tapped her foot against the floorboard of the truck. *Damn him! I should have expected this,* she mumbled to herself. *Isn't this typical of a loafer, a good-for-nothing?* He *has all the time in the world,* she fumed. *Time means nothing to* him. He *isn't doing anything.*

Her temper was on the verge of skyrocketing when she saw him saunter out of the service station where the mechanics were working on cars and walk in leisurely fashion toward the truck. He opened the door, hopped in, and grinned at her. At least she thought it was a grin, judging by the creases at the corners of his eyes.

"Did you get things squared away?" The amusement in his eyes was undeniable, and his smug attitude made her all the more determined not to allow him to goad her to anger.

"Of course," she answered with a haughty lift of her brows.

"Hungry?"

"No. We just ate lunch."

"That was a couple of hours ago, Glory. Let's grab a hamburger and a beer."

"No. I want to go home."

His green eyes roamed over her face, taking in the shining nose, windblown hair, and tight-lipped mouth.

He reached out and covered with one of his the hands she had clasped in her lap.

"Don't worry. You look just fine," he said in a reassuring tone. "I'd not be ashamed to take you into any restaurant in town."

"Well . . . that's big of you," she sputtered, and yanked her hand from beneath his. "You're going to drive me out of my mind! Do you know that? I'm not hungry. I want to go home. Spelled h-o-m-e. Can't you get that through your thick head?"

"Ah, ah, ah . . . temper, temper," he chided gently, as if she were a child. "You need to eat, Glory. You're as skinny as a starved alley cat and as cross as a junkyard dog." He boldly stared at the length of her figure and he shook his head sadly.

"Oh, my God!"

"It's not ladylike to swear, darlin'." He started the motor and they moved out onto the street. "We'll go to a hangout of mine. It's down by the tracks. It's usually pretty tame during the day, but at night—*wow!* It's every fantasy a guy dreams about. They serve everything from a little Coke, ah . . . er . . . Coca Cola, to rustled steak not a day off the range. And the girls upstairs . . . Ooops, sorry, you'd not be interested in them." He glanced at her, but all he could see was the back of her head. She was staring out the side window. "If you're worryin' about how you look, Glory—don't." His voice rambled on with exaggerated patience. "The people down there are pretty tolerant of 'straights.' But you could unbutton that shirt a little and show a little bosom. That way you'd not be quite so conspicuous."

This man was crazy! No longer able to control her

anger she spun around to face him. The smug look on his face caused her to clench her fist and do something she'd not dreamed she was capable of doing. She hit him a resounding blow on the upper arm.

"If I were a man, I'd beat you up!" Her poise completely abandoned her, and she heard herself shouting. It felt so good to yell, she did it again. "Ohhhh . . . you smart-ass! You make me so mad. You're the most aggravating creature I've ever met. You're a sixties hippie living in the eighties. You're impossible, rude, and . . . a lazy, no-good deadbeat." She stopped, then took a deep breath. Her pulses were thudding like a jackhammer in her head. This oversized teddy bear was driving her out of her mind and she desperately needed to be delivered from his presence.

"Atta girl. Let it all out. It feels good to yell, doesn't it? I do it sometimes when I feel uptight," he murmured, his eyes bouncing from her to the street and back again. "I walk out into the middle of Hangtown, face the empty buildings that once made up a town of over a thousand hardy souls, and I yell as loud and as long as I want to. It's good for the heart, the lungs, and the digestive system. If a person lets off steam once in a while it'll keep 'im from getting an ulcer. It also helps if you've got something to kick," he added with green eyes dancing and his mouth curving into a grin.

Gloria stared back at him and desperately tried to hold on to her anger. Unwelcome thoughts trampled through her mind. She had never seen such eyes on a man. Between the spread of black lashes they were as green as a new leaf in the spring. There was strength and stubbornness there, just as there was in his hard, muscled body.

Yet they were so soft and so deep, seeming to contain a knowledge about her that was strangely disconcerting. It was as if he knew everything about her—everything, from her childhood to her sheltered life as Marvin's wife. He even knew that she was repelled by, yet attracted to him. She swallowed, feeling a sudden aching tightness in her throat.

"Jack Evans," she said quietly. "You're . . . giving me a headache."

CHAPTER FIVE

JACK TURNED ONTO a street that ran parallel with the railroad tracks.

"What's the matter with you? You didn't pay one bit of attention to me when I said I wanted to go home," Gloria said, her voice hard with irritation.

"Yes, I did. I heard you loud and clear." They bounced onto a graveled drive and he parked the truck beside a frame building with beer signs nailed to the siding on each side of the door and a weathered swinging sign above. "You said you weren't hungry. You said you wanted to go home. You said I was giving you a headache. See there? I'm no dummy."

"That's your opinion."

"I'm starved," he said, ignoring her sarcasm. "That bacon-and-tomato sandwich you gave me for lunch didn't amount to anything. It'll only take a few minutes to have a hamburger and a beer." He made it sound quite sensible.

"I'll wait out here."

"Stubborn little mule," he murmured, and the intensity

of his gaze caused her to blush, but she returned his look steadily. He opened his shirt pocket and dropped the truck keys inside. "Suit yourself. But it'll take much longer for me to eat if you're not with me."

"Are you blackmailing me?"

"Uh-huh."

Gloria jerked at the door handle. "That figures. C'mon, let's get it over with."

"Wow! Such enthusiasm." Jack met her at the front of the truck and attempted to take her arm, but she jerked it away. He was chuckling as they entered the café.

Gloria headed straight for the first booth and dropped down on the red vinyl padded seat. Jack eased his bulk into the seat opposite her. His knees touched hers and she moved over next to the wall and placed her purse on the seat beside her. She looked around the room to keep from looking at him.

Three men—ranchers, by the look of the wide-brimmed hats pushed to the back of their heads and the boot heels hooked over the braces of the stools—sat at the counter. The other five booths and the four tables between the booths and the counter were empty, but all were laid with heavy white china, the cups turned upside down on the saucers, and the silver for each place setting folded neatly in a paper napkin. The men at the bar glanced at them and then continued eating. The woman behind the counter drew two glasses of water and, carrying both in one hand and a menu under her arm, came to the booth.

"Hi, Jack. How're ya doin'?"

"Fine, Helen. You?"

"Fine."

The woman looked down at Gloria and smiled. She was tall, blond, and large boned, with every hair stiffly in place. She was past middle age, but her lined face was carefully made up, her white uniform and low-wedge shoes spotlessly clean.

Gloria noticed her hands as she placed the menu on the table in front of her. They were large, capable, work-worn hands that told her life hadn't been easy for this woman. She returned her friendly smile, accepted the menu, and murmured, "Thank you."

"This is Gloria, Helen. She came to give Ethel a hand at the motel . . . for a while." Jack added the last words with a measured, narrow-eyed glance at Gloria before he opened the menu.

"That's nice. I'm glad Ethel will have some help. She looked peaked and tired the last time she was here." Helen spoke with such sincere concern that Gloria looked up in surprise.

"Do you know my aunt?"

"Know Ethel? Mercy! I've known that woman since the day she and George bought that motel. My land! So you're the niece from Cincinnati she's talked about so much. Welcome to Montana. I hope you like cold weather; it can be a bear here at times."

"I'm used to cold weather. It won't bother me at all."

"We'll see about that," Jack murmured with his eyes on the menu. Gloria pursed her lips stubbornly.

"What'll you have, Jack?" Helen's gaze bounced between Gloria and Jack, and her brows drew together in a puzzled frown. She added, "You know what we've got without looking at the menu. Heavens! You've been eating here for several years."

"Give us a couple of hamburgers and a piece of pie. Glory needs to be fattened up if she's going to stand up to the work out at the motel." He looked into Gloria's resentful amber eyes steadily. "Make mine apple. What kind do you want? Helen makes the best pie in the state."

"I told you I didn't want anything. I'm not hungry." She gave Jack a searing glance before she looked up at Helen. "I'll have a cup of coffee, please."

"Two hamburgers, two pieces of apple pie, and a pot of coffee." Jack handed the menu back to Helen. "Glory's being contrary again. She hardly ate anything for lunch. I think she's one of those women who're afraid they'll get drumstick thighs," he added in a loud whisper and with a conspiratorial wink.

Helen hesitated. "Now, Jack, quit your funning. If she—"

"If she doesn't eat it, I will," he said pleasantly.

"Suit yourself." Helen lifted her shoulders and walked away. Jack's eyes wandered around the room before coming back to Gloria's frozen features.

"Do you practice being rude, or does it just come naturally to you?" Gloria was so angry her voice trembled, but she made herself look him directly in the eyes. "I don't have a weight problem. I've *never* had a weight problem. And if I did, anyone with any manners at all wouldn't comment on it."

"That got to you, didn't it?" He raised his eyebrows.

"And . . . you led me to believe this was a . . . hangout for thugs and . . . and . . . drug users!" She felt the color rise in her cheeks as she spoke, so she looked out the window, afraid that if she continued to look at him, the gleam in his eyes would goad her to hit him again.

"I told you what you expected to hear," he said, and there was laughter in his voice. "You've come from a nice, orderly, sheltered little world where you were taught to be wary and look down your pretty little nose at an uncouth character like me. Just because I don't fit into the mold of what you think is 'respectable,' you shoved me into the 'undesirable' category." He chuckled. "Glory, Glory, this is the eighties. People are more tolerant now of us . . . hippies."

She turned to look at him. Her anger was replaced with quiet dignity. "Don't laugh at me and don't analyze my life. You know nothing about it! You may think me naive for a woman my age, and that may be true to a certain extent. But I have my principles just the same. I'm just learning to stand on my own two feet after five years of being told, do this, do that—eat this, eat that—wear this, wear that. I was brainwashed into thinking I had to be subservient to a man's wishes. That's over—done with—finished! I'm a person in my own right, with my own opinions, and I'm perfectly capable of making my own decisions without help from you or . . . anyone." At the end she was striving to keep her tone level and her lips from trembling, but her traitorous voice betrayed her on the last word. She felt the tears rising and looked away from him.

"I'm sorry. It wasn't my intention to make fun of you." The softness of his voice was like a caress, and brought her eyes back to him. A faint frown pleated his brow, and his eyes, full of concern, were fastened on her face. She stared into their depths, and her mind went blank. She found herself tongue-tied and couldn't remember the rest of what she had wanted to say.

She looked away from him to some distant spot behind his head and willed her eyes to stay dry. Heartache parted her lips and she gulped small gasps of air into her lungs. She wished desperately that she were back at the motel. This bearded man disturbed her in more ways than she cared to acknowledge. He could make her reveal more about herself than she wanted him to know. She'd never met anyone quite so vibrant, so aggressively masculine, in her life. At times he was like a gentle giant. He attracted her, confused her, angered her, and made her feel achingly alive and feminine, something no other man had ever done. His smile and warm, caressing voice caused an unwelcome glow of happiness to start in her knees and work its way up to her chest.

They sat silently while Jack mentally kicked himself for having caused the pain reflected in her wide amber eyes. More than anything he wanted to cradle her face in his hands, bring her head to his shoulder, and comfort her. For a few moments he was completely honest with himself. She was a lovely woman, very desirable. He wanted to hold her and to kiss her. He wanted her to look at him with bright laughter in her eyes instead of the pain he saw there now. For the first time in years he wanted more from a woman than the quick satisfaction of a primitive desire. He wanted her mind, her body, her . . . love. The knowledge hit him with the force of a hurricane. *Christ! You stupid bastard! The last thing you need is a woman to complicate your life.*

Helen brought their food, and without conscious thought of what she was doing, Gloria picked up the hamburger and began to eat. It was half consumed before she realized how hungry she was. She glanced at Jack, fully expecting to find him watching her with a taunting gleam in his eyes, but he was concentrating on his food. She glanced at the hands that held the sandwich. His fingers were long and slim and tipped with blunt, clean nails. A thin gold watch was nestled in the fine black hair on his wrist.

Jack looked up and met her gaze. "What are you thinking while those amber eyes are boring holes through me?" His voice was soft, without the slightest hint of sarcasm.

"What are *you* thinking?" she replied, unwilling to answer his question.

"I'm thinking you have the most beautiful eyes I've ever seen." His voice was lower than before and his eyes had darkened to a clear jade.

"Thank you." She was flustered at this unexpected turn in the conversation, but absurdly pleased by his compliment.

They didn't speak again until they had finished their meal, then Jack said, "Ready?"

Gloria nodded. He went to the register and waited for Helen to finish pouring coffee for the cowboys. One of them spoke to him.

"How're ya doin', Jack?"

"Pretty good, Roy. You got them mangy old steer of yours ready for shipping?"

"Just about."

The man cast admiring glances at Gloria, who was now standing beside the door. His look invited an introduction; Jack ignored it and turned his attention to digging bills out of his jeans pocket. The cowboy had a dark, weathered face, light-brown hair, and a long, slim body.

His eyes were frankly admiring as they toured Gloria's trim figure. When she met his gaze, he smiled, and his face lit up with charm. He nodded to her and narrowed his eyes in a way that said he would like to know her, but she turned away.

Gloria climbed into the dusty pickup and wondered idly if comfortable cars were banned in this part of the country. Almost everyone drove either a pickup truck or some other type of four-wheel-drive equipment. After five years of riding in Lincolns and Cadillacs, it had taken her a while to get used to her small compact car, which was a luxury compared to this jolting truck.

They were headed down the highway toward the motel before Jack spoke.

"Roy considers himself God's gift to the ladies. You'd be smart to not encourage him." He spoke softly, but his words were accompanied by a cool look.

"Is he married?"

"No. But he's on his fourth or fifth 'live-in,' as far as I know."

"Does he own a big ranch?" Sensing his irritation, some little devil in Gloria prodded her to ask the question.

Jack's head swiveled around and he eyed her unsmilingly. "His pa owns the ranch. Roy'll have to share it with a raft of brothers and sisters. That is, if there's anything left to inherit."

"Does he live on the ranch?"

"In a trailer house. He needs his privacy." There wasn't a trace of humor in his voice.

"Does his family approve of his 'live-ins'?"

"I don't know, I haven't asked them. Why all the questions? Are you thinking of making a play for Roy?"

The bitterness in his voice caused her to look at him sharply. His brows were drawn together in a deep frown of disapproval; suddenly the fun had gone out of the game. Without answering his question she turned to stare out the window.

There were a million questions floating around in her mind. Who was Jack Evans? What had happened to cause him to drop out of the mainstream and live this unconventional lifestyle? Why was he so hostile all of a sudden? Why wasn't she feeling elated because she had, at last, managed to get under his thick skin and irritate him? Was he angry because the cowboy had flirted with her? Did he think she was so shallow that she'd be flattered by the man's rakish attention?

The highway from the rest area to the motel seemed infinitely shorter than it had the day she'd ridden over it with Jack on the motorcycle. Still, it was full of hills and curves, and Gloria was relieved when she could see the familiar orange doors of the motel.

The truck rattled over the metal bridge that covered the drainage ditch and proceeded through the empty parking area. Dusk had settled, and Gloria vaguely wondered why Aunt Ethel hadn't turned on the office lights. Jack braked to a stop just short of the yawning doors of the shed where Ethel parked the truck. Gloria got out without a word or a backward glance. The back door of the motel slammed shut, and Peter ran to meet her.

"Mom! Mom! I c-couldn't f-find you!" Ragged, desperate sobs accompanied his frantic words. Tears streaked his face. He grabbed her around the legs and held on.

"Oh, honey! Didn't Aunt Ethel tell you I went to Lewistown to take the U-Haul back?" She dropped her purse, knelt down beside him, and hugged him to her. "There, there, don't cry. I should have told you I was going."

"I was s-scared," he stammered.

"There was nothing to be scared about. You knew I'd be back. Aunt Ethel was with you."

"Aunt Ethel is sleepin'. I made noise, but she didn't wake up. People called on the radio and she didn't wake up."

"Aunt Ethel is . . . sleeping? At five o'clock?"

Gloria blanched, remembering that her aunt never napped, and a cold hand of fear began to squeeze the breath out of her.

"Oh, my God!" She loosened herself from Peter's clinging arms and ran to the door. "Aunt Ethel! Aunt Ethel!"

The kitchen was dark and she fumbled with the light switch. She went quickly through the swinging doors to the living area, switched on another light, then stopped short, the back of her hand going to her mouth.

Her aunt lay on the couch with an arm hanging down, palm out. Her mouth was open and twisted to the side. Gloria leaned over her. She was so pale and still. Fear shattered her heart. *No! No! Oh, dear God! Don't let her be . . . dead!* Her mind raced, imagining the worst.

"Jack!" Her scream was like a lost wail. In blind panic

she ran to the back door. "Jack!" She sucked air into her lungs in jerky gasps. "Come quick! Aunt Ethel—"

Jack shot past her with Peter clinging to his neck. When he reached the couch he set Peter on his feet, and the distraught child flung himself against his mother's legs, sobbing helplessly. Gloria fell on her knees and gathered him to her.

"Hush, darling, hush. Please hush," she begged.

Jack searched Ethel's wrist for a pulse and lifted her eyelid. Then he got to his feet.

"She's alive," Jack murmured gently, and a feeling of relief and gratitude flooded Gloria's numbed senses. "I think she's had a stroke."

"We've got to get her to the hospital. I'll call an ambulance."

"It'll take an hour for an ambulance to get here and back." Jack put a reassuring hand on Gloria's shoulder. "Gary's car is in the shed. I'll get the master key from the office and unlock his room—the car keys are bound to be there. Lock up the front and leave a note on the table for him; he and Dwight should be here soon. Then gather up a bunch of blankets and a couple of pillows." He was gone before Gloria could get to her feet.

"Aunt Ethel is sick, Peter. You're going to have to help us get her to the hospital. Go put on your jacket and bring the pillow from my bed." The child stood there sniffling. "You're a big boy, and . . . Jack and I need you. Hurry now." Her words seemed to calm him, and he ran toward their room.

Gloria scribbled a brief note to Gary, put it on the kitchen table, and went to her aunt's bedroom. She took several blankets from the closet shelf. She thanked God

Jack was with her; her mind was so fettered with fear that she was only half aware of what she was doing. Peter returned, and with trembling hands she helped him into his jacket.

"Take the pillow to the back door and wait for Jack, honey. Oh, I'm so glad I have you to help me."

"I love Aunt Ethel."

"I love her, too, honey," Gloria said, zipping up his jacket and hugging him briefly.

"Will she get a shot?" he asked gravely.

"I don't know, love. We'll have to wait and see."

Jack parked the big sedan just a few steps from the back door. Gloria spread pillows on the backseat, and Jack carried Ethel out to the car. He gently laid her down on the seat and covered her with blankets. Gloria climbed in and sat beside her aunt. Jack lifted Peter into the front and fastened the seat belt around him.

"You sit up here with me, hotshot, and hold Aunt Ethel's pocketbook. There may be things in there the hospital will want to know." He put the car in gear and drove out onto the highway.

Less than five miles down the road they met Gary headed for the motel. Jack pressed on the horn, blinked the car lights, and sped on past. Gloria glanced out the rear window to see the brake lights come on the big eighteen-wheeler, then go off as Gary speeded up again. She wondered what he thought at seeing his own car go racing toward town.

Gloria teetered on the edge of the seat, holding her aunt's hand. She had no idea of how she would have reacted to this emergency if she had been there alone. She wanted to talk, wanted to tell Jack how grateful she was that he was with her, but she remained silent, and the big car ate up the miles.

They reached the railroad tracks at the edge of town and Jack slowed the car to ease over them, then turned onto a wide, tree-lined side street; at the end of it was a large gray building. At one side was a circular drive that passed under an enclosure with a large bold sign that said EMERGENCY ONLY. Jack drove the car in, stopped, and pressed on the horn before he got out. A white-coated orderly met him at the door and, after a few words from Jack, turned back to call for a stretcher.

Although she felt nervous and sick, Gloria managed to walk calmly down the corridor to the admittance desk and answer the questions they asked about her aunt. She was terribly glad Jack had thought to bring Aunt Ethel's purse; from it she extracted her insurance card, social security card, and driver's license. She fidgeted while the woman took what seemed like an eternity to note down the information. Her fear grew with each passing second. When the woman was finally done she hurried back to the room where Jack and Peter waited—wanting, *needing*, the security of Jack's calm presence.

She stood in the doorway and watched Jack cuddle Peter in his arms. The child was asleep, and Jack was shifting him so his head lay comfortably in the crook of his arm.

"He didn't have any dinner," Gloria said absently.

"I got him a sandwich from the vending machine, but

he was asleep before he could eat the whole thing. Did you get Ethel checked in?"

"Yes. Has the doctor said anything?"

"He said they had put her on life support systems, and that another doctor had been called in. Sit down, Gloria. We can't do anything but wait."

She sat down with a deep sigh, and when he reached for her hand she curled her fingers tightly around his and gripped hard. The warmth and closeness were comforting. She suddenly longed to cuddle against him, as Peter was doing, and absorb his strength.

Time flew past as they sat on the couch, hands clasped, Gloria's shoulder against his.

"Jack," she whispered softly, unaware of the intimacy of her tone. "I don't know what I'll do if anything happens to Aunt Ethel. She means a lot to me."

"You'll just have to do the best you can, Glory. We all have an inner strength we don't even know we possess; that's how we endure times of terrible grief."

"I'm glad you're with me." She looked up at him, her eyes flooding with tears.

"I'm glad I am too. Are you hungry? I ate what was left of Peter's sandwich, but I can get another one from the dispenser. And there's coffee too."

"I don't know if I could eat or not, but I could use the coffee. But don't you think you should call Gary?"

"I thought I'd wait until I had something definite to tell him. I'll lay Peter on the other couch and get some coffee."

After Jack had left the waiting room, Gloria reached for a magazine and began flipping through the pages, hardly reading a word. She was filled with apprehension, her heart fluttering and her fingers trembling as she turned the pages, her ears attuned to the sound of footsteps. The waiting seemed to be more agonizing without Jack; it was easier when he was there to share it with her. She threw the magazine down onto the table and went to the door. At the end of the long hall a white-coated orderly was pushing a cart. She was surprised at the lack of activity, then remembered the time of day and the fact that this was a small hospital, unlike the busy hospitals in Cincinnati where she had occasionally taken children from the center where she worked.

She was very glad when Jack's big frame filled the doorway. His eyes searched her eyes, asking the question: "Any news?"

She shook her head despairingly. "No one has come at all."

He looked down at her tired, pale face, her dark-circled eyes dulled with fatigue. He had never longed to hold, or kiss, or comfort a woman so badly. She was so small, and looked so forlorn sitting there. He desperately wanted to see her eyes bright with laughter, her chin tilted proudly, her cheeks dimpling merrily.

Jack felt suspended as he stood looking down at her. He was unable to understand or accept the overpowering protective feeling that swept over him. A corner of his heart that had never been filled was suddenly overflowing. Almost in a daze he held out the foam cup.

Gloria accepted the coffee with a bleak smile of thanks.

"It seems like we've been waiting forever," she said in a choked, tired voice.

"It hasn't been an hour, Glory. We'll know something soon."

They sat close together on the couch, and when Jack felt a shiver run through her slight body, he took off his jacket and draped it about her shoulders.

His arm stayed about her to hug her to his side.

CHAPTER SIX

IT WAS PAST midnight. Jack wrapped his jacket around the sleeping child and carried him out to the car. Gloria walked beside him. The air was crisp and cool, the moon clear and bright. He placed the child on the backseat and covered him with the blankets. And then he turned to Gloria and put his jacket about her shoulders.

"No. You'll need it."

"Get in. I'll get the heater going."

He opened the door and she slid under the wheel to the other side. She watched him in the flashing lights of a passing car; his face was turned toward her as he inserted the key to start the motor. It was incredible that in just a few hours' time her feelings for him had changed so drastically.

"Move over close to me and we'll keep each other warm until the heater gets going." His voice came softly out of the darkness over the purr of the engine.

"You can have your jacket." She was suddenly flustered and at a loss for words. Her gaze was drawn to the shadowed outline of his face and his eyes gleaming at her through the darkness.

"C'mon. Move over." His hand was on her knee. "Closer," he commanded softly after she had moved a few inches toward him. "You're shivering." She moved again, and he adjusted his own position until her shoulder was tucked behind his and her hip, leg, and thigh fit snugly along his muscular length. "That's better. You'll be warm soon." He shifted the gears and put the car into motion. "We'll be home before you know it, and I'll make us a cup of hot chocolate."

After they had driven a few blocks, the lights of the town were left behind. Gloria looked straight ahead at the road; she thought about her aunt's condition and willed herself to not panic. Jack placed his hand in her lap; without hesitation she pressed her palm against his, and his fingers entwined with hers.

"I like holding your hand, Glory."

"Thank you for being with me tonight." It was pleasant, comforting, to be with him. She was weary in mind and weary in body, and hovered against his masculine strength in a dreamlike state. She felt . . . sheltered, cherished. His hand was like a lifeline in a storm.

He briefly released her hand to adjust the heater, then blindly sought it again. She clasped it and laced her fingers through his.

"You do realize that Ethel may never be completely well again even if she does come through this crisis?"

"Yes, I know that," she answered in a small voice. "Oh, Jack, she'll never speak again."

"The doctor said there was the *possibility* of that. It's not a certainty. She had a massive stroke, and they'll not be sure of the damage for several days. She knew that you were there and that she wasn't alone. I'm sure that meant a lot to her."

"I'll try to keep the motel going until she can decide what she wants to do with it," she whispered huskily.

Jack was quiet. The car sped along the highway with only the sound of the motor filling the moonlit silence of the night. He needed time to sort out his emotions, untangle his confused thoughts, and decide what he *really* wanted out of life. The feelings he had for this woman scared the hell out of him. It was a shock to him to realize that he'd never felt so complete as he had sitting beside her at the hospital, his arm holding her close, sharing her anxiety as they waited for the doctor. All he'd wanted to do, then, was to be with her, comfort her, take care of her. *Now* he wanted to kiss her with her arms about his neck. He wanted to hold her hips in his hands and feel her breasts against his naked chest, have her to *want* him. *Dammit, Evans, don't think about it! She doesn't feel that way about you.*

"You can't run the motel by yourself," he said, struggling to get his mind back to reality.

"I'll have to."

"I'm not sure it's a good idea for you and Peter to be out there alone. Gary's gone five nights a week, and there's all kinds of riffraff traveling the highway."

"I know. I've met some of them. Remember?" She glanced at him and saw the frown creasing his brow. "But if Aunt Ethel could handle them, I can."

"Ethel is not young and beautiful."

"Should I thank you for a compliment?"

He searched her features for a trace of sarcasm and

found none. Rather, she was trying to suppress a grin. He glanced at the road ahead, then back to her soft mouth and glowing eyes. A lovely, leaping flame of desire flickered through him.

"No," he said slowly while his mind ached to say something else. "I wouldn't want you to slip out of character."

That brought an unexpected trill of laughter. "Have I been that bad?"

"You've been a regular shrew," he murmured teasingly.

"Well, what about you? You irritated me something awful!" Her smile jarred his senses.

"I did bug you a bit, didn't I?" He chuckled softly.

"Yes, you did."

He glanced down at her. Her image stayed with him when he turned back to watch the road. She looked so damned fragile. Her face was pale in the moonlight, her lips quivering, her eyes dancing with more enjoyment than he'd ever seen, yet still full of vulnerability. When she laughed, the musical sound struck a chord deep in a part of him that he had thought was closed off forever.

"Jack . . ." Her voice was low, her face close to his shoulder. He knew she was looking at his profile. "I really do appreciate having you with me tonight. And . . . I'm sorry for the nasty things I said about . . . your appearance and your lifestyle. I guess I'm what you'd consider . . . super-straight."

"It's all right, Glory. A lot of people agree with you. You don't like my hair and my beard. You think I'm a tough character who goes around bullying people, and that I'm shiftless, too lazy to keep a regular job. You don't approve of me or my lifestyle. Well, it's your pre-rogative." There was no censure in his tone. It was deep and serious.

"Oh, my! Did I say all that? I had no right—it was presumptuous of me."

He glanced down at her. "You didn't have to *say* it. I could tell by the way you looked at me. But don't worry about it. You were honest enough to let your feelings show."

"I've never met anyone like you. Most of the people I've known live in a more conventional way—they're employed, or do something . . . useful."

"We're not all made in the same mold, Gloria. I don't feel the need to achieve a status in the community in order to be comfortable with myself. I depend on no one, and no one depends on me. It's as simple as that."

She waited, hoping he would keep talking and tell her something about himself, but he remained silent. It occurred to her that not once since they had taken Aunt Ethel to the hospital had she thought about his appearance. He still had the red bandana about his forehead, the long, unruly hair, and the bushy beard; but she hadn't noticed anyone at the hospital giving him so much as a second look. Why had she judged him so harshly because he didn't conform? Why was appearance so important to her? Had more of Marvin's values rubbed off on her than she realized?

Gloria loosened her hand from his, pulled his jacket more tightly about her shoulders, and moved a little away from him. The tangled lines of her thoughts emerged at one junction: She was attracted to him! The revelation both fascinated and confused her.

"I've never met anyone like you," she said again, breaking the silence.

To her relief he chuckled. "Oh, yes, you have. Have you forgotten the tough guys from the Big Windy?"

"You're not like them!"

"How do you know?"

"I just know, that's all. Now, hush up about them. Every time I think about that terrible encounter I get a nervous stomach."

"Speaking of stomachs, I hope Gary left some food," he said as he turned the car into the motel drive. "I'm starved. How about you?"

"I guess I am hungry, now that you mention it. Gary must have forgotten to turn the vacancy sign on, which means we only have one guest tonight other than him and Dwight."

Jack drove past the lone car in front of unit three and pulled around to the back of the motel, where two large semitrailer trucks were parked.

"When I talked to Gary, he said he'd leave a key under the brick beside the back step, in case you didn't have one."

"I don't, unless there's one in Aunt Ethel's purse."

"Don't bother looking for it. Stay put. I'll turn on a light and come back for you and Peter." He was out of the car before Gloria thought about giving him his jacket.

The lights in the kitchen sprang on. Jack came back to lift Peter from the backseat, blankets and all, and carry him to the house. Gloria held open the door and they went inside, much like a family returning home, she thought briefly. She led the way, turning on lights as she went through the office to her room. Jack laid Peter down, removed his shoes, took off his jacket, and covered him. He looked up at Gloria standing on the other side of the bed watching him.

"No argument about undressing him tonight?" he said, lifting his brows.

Her gaze met his, and she blinked. *Oh, my God, I've lost my mind. I'm really beginning to like him . . . very much.*

"Why wake him just so he can go back to sleep again?" She murmured lightly, tossing back the same words he'd used that night a week ago.

His eyes were laughing as they stared into hers. It should be a sin for a man to have such large, beautiful, expressive eyes, she thought, and turned her back to dim the light beside her son's bed. A flood of pleasure washed over her, sending excitement coursing through her veins. She was frightened by the odd fluttering in her stomach. It's hunger pangs, she told herself, just hunger pangs.

"How old is he?"

"He'll be four in a couple of weeks." She glanced over her shoulder and saw that his fingertips were combing the dark hair back from Peter's forehead. A wave of tenderness for this big, gentle man flooded her heart.

"He's a fine boy," he said softly.

Gloria went to the foot of the bed and turned to look at him. "He's had to endure more than his share of difficulties for one so young."

"He seems well adjusted and . . . happy."

"He is now. It's not always been that way."

"And you?" He was looking at her with those great, knowing eyes while his fingertips continued to caress the child's head.

"Me too. I like it here." She said it almost defensively.

"You've had a few bad breaks, too, huh?"

"A few. But I like to think they've made me a stronger person." Her voice was shaky, and she felt a tingly sensation travel up her spine.

He nodded solemnly. "Peter's lucky he's got you."

Gloria stood glued to the floor, incapable of replying. There was a tightness across her chest, a fullness in her throat, and she couldn't utter a word. She stood there until he came toward her, then she moved ahead of him to the door.

The expression on her face hurt him deep inside. She had lowered her lashes and bitten her bottom lip, a sure sign of distress. Had her ex-husband rejected her for another woman? Was she still in love with him? It was amazing how disturbing the thought was; he didn't want her upset by anything or anyone.

Jack followed her out the door and through the office to the kitchen. There was evidence that Gary and Dwight had eaten at the kitchen table, although they had put the dirty dishes in the dishwasher.

"There's roast and potatoes." Gloria stood before the open refrigerator. "Sit down and I'll warm them up for you."

"No. You sit down and I'll fix something for you."

He was standing behind her, his hands lightly grazing her arms. A shiver of pure physical awareness ran down her spine. She was blatantly aware that this was the first time in her life she had ever experienced such primitive sexual feelings for a man. She resisted the urge to lean back, rest against him, and take comfort in his strength.

"You've done so much. The least I can do is feed—"

His hand slid beneath her arms and he casually lifted her out of the way. "Sit, Glory, before I put you in that chair and tie you there with a dish towel," he commanded gently.

She sat down, propped her elbows on the table, and rested her chin in her palms. Fatigue washed over her. The thoughts in her mind tumbled over each other in riotous confusion.

"Nothing is for sure, is it?" she said wearily. "I thought I had the tangles in my life sorted out. Now I feel like I've been run over with a steamroller." She hadn't realized she had spoken aloud until Jack answered her.

"You've just had an especially bad day. Had Ethel said anything to you about not feeling well?"

"No. But I knew she didn't, so I mentioned that she should go to the doctor for a checkup; but she was reluctant to go. I was going to try to get her there when I took Peter in for shots. What are you doing?"

"I'm making a cup of chocolate for you to drink while I fix you the best hot beef sandwich you ever ate. Just wait until—" He stopped when he saw the tears rolling down her cheeks. She was crying soundlessly. "Glory, Glory . . ."

Great sobs welled up from her throat and shuddered through her. His thoughtful concern had been the final blow to the protective shield she had wrapped around herself.

Jack came to the table, set the steaming cup in front of her, and knelt down. With a soft groan he slid his fingers into her hair and pulled her head against him. He caressed the nape of her neck with gentle fingertips.

"Let it out, honey. Let it all out. Cry, my sweet, and

then we'll talk about it." He held her close, waiting for the storm of tears to run itself dry.

"It's just hit. me, Jack. Aunt Ethel will never come back to this kitchen."

"You're thinking the worst, Glory, Glory." Her cheek was pressed to his denim shirt and she pressed her face against him.

"All I can give her is my love, my support. She has no one but me." Her voice was muffled.

"She has you and Gary, and I'll . . . be around."

"I don't know if I can do it, Jack. I just don't know," she blurted.

"You don't know what, Glory?"

"I don't know if I can keep this place running. She'll need money if she goes to a nursing home."

"Don't borrow trouble, pretty girl. She may have insurance and a nice little nest egg laid away."

"She doesn't," she said stubbornly.

"Don't worry about it now. Drink the chocolate while 1 fix a sandwich. Then you're off to bed. I'll sleep on Ethel's couch tonight."

"You can't. You're too . . . big. Take one of the rooms."

"We'll see. C'mon. Drink up."

Gloria drank from the cup, waging a constant battle with tears that threatened to spill down her cheeks. She was suddenly aware of how she had let herself go in front of this man and how comfortable she felt leaning against him and confessing her fears. In all the five years she had been married to Marvin she had never allowed him to see her shed one tear.

Jack talked while he prepared the meal. "I'll get Gary

to help me drag some dead trees down out of the hills, and I'll tackle that woodpile. You'll need fireplace wood and—"

"Aunt Ethel said the chain saw was broken."

"I'll bring mine down. I saw some downed oak out back. Oak makes the best firewood. Burns longer." He took toast from the toaster and put it on a plate. "I'll check the water pipes and be sure the heat tapes are working. We don't want a freeze-up."

"Heat tapes? What's that? There's so much I don't know about running this place that it scares me."

"Don't worry about it. What I don't know, Gary will." He set a plate in front of her and picked up her empty cup. "How about more chocolate?"

"No, thank you."

He fixed a plate for himself and they ate in silence. When they had finished, Jack put the dishes in the dishwasher and started the machine.

"Go to bed, Glory. I'll bunk down here on the couch, and in the morning we'll go back to the hospital."

"You don't have to go. I can take the pickup."

"We'll talk about it in the morning," he said, and gave her a gentle push toward her room. "Go to bed."

During the week that followed, Jack spent every day at the motel and every night that Gary was not there. He fixed Gloria's car so she didn't have to drive the truck, and stayed with Peter while she went to the hospital to visit her aunt. He took care of winterizing the motel, things Gloria didn't even know about, cut up a supply of wood, put on the storm windows, and cleaned out the eave troughs. If she was late getting back to the motel, he started the evening meal.

Gloria was grateful for his help, but scolded herself when she realized how much she had come to depend upon him. She shouldn't allow herself to rely on this man, or any man, she told herself crossly; he would come to expect something in return. *But,* she reasoned, *he hasn't as much as touched my hand since the night we came back from the hospital.*

The doctors assured Gloria that Ethel's condition was not life threatening at the moment, although she was paralyzed on the right side and could not speak.

"We're not getting many tourists," she told her aunt one day. "Jack says people are afraid to venture off the beaten track in case the weather turns bad. He said for me to tell you he drained the water pipes going to the campground and to the end units at the motel; he turned off the heat and the electricity to those units. Jack's been a big help; I don't know what I'd have done without him. Peter thinks he gets up every morning and hangs out the sun," she said with a small laugh.

"Gary would like for his girlfriend Janet to come out and stay with me for a while," she contrived. "He says she's between jobs. I said I'd have to ask you. Is it okay?" Ethel squeezed her hand. "You've met her? And liked her? I'm glad. Gary seems to think a lot of her. He said she's a teacher, but she lost her contract when the school system had to cut back due to less federal aid."

At the end of the second week Gloria was told by the doctors that her aunt could be moved to a nursing home. She returned to the motel with a long face.

"Oh, Jack. I wish I could take care of her here. She cried when the doctor told her she couldn't come home."

"She needs therapy you can't give her, pretty girl. Maybe in a few months she'll be well enough to come home." Jack was sitting in the rocking chair in front of the fireplace with Peter on his lap. The weather had turned surprisingly cold, and Gloria stood with her hands behind her and her back to the fire.

"I know, but I wish I could take care of her. I promised her I'd come to see her as often as I can."

"You can't make the trip alone when the weather gets bad. Your car is too light; you could slide off the road. Peter and I will take you in my four-wheel drive, won't we, Pete?"

"Gary said Janet will move out here tomorrow. She'll be here to stay with Peter."

They stared at each other for a long moment, and Gloria wondered what he was thinking. At times he pulled a mask over his emotions, and she had the feeling he was about to walk out and never come back. The thought ravaged her, sending a shiver of dread down her spine. A feeling of misery and loneliness washed over her. She stared into his eyes and asked herself how things could have developed to such a point that she would care if she ever saw him again or not. Where was her painfully acquired resolve to not get emotionally involved with any man, much less a man like Jack Evans?

Peter moved up in Jack's arms and combed his short, stubby fingers through his beard. "I'm gonna stay with Jack. I love Jack."

Small arms wrapped themselves around Jack's neck and he looked up at Gloria, his eyes not veiled anymore.

She saw such pain, anxiety, love, tenderness, and compassion in those deep, beautiful green eyes that she had an almost uncontrollable impulse to hold his shaggy head to her breast and comfort him. He held her with his eyes. She stood clenching her hands behind her while her cheeks reddened under his steady gaze. A bewildering complex of thoughts, each fleeting, merging into one another, filled her mind until one managed to stick. *Peter was becoming too attached to him.* Peter? Oh, God! What about herself? Her heart shook with apprehension. She was dangerously tempting fate. She knew it, but she couldn't do a thing about it.

"We'll have two truckers for dinner tonight. I put a meat loaf in the oven," Jack said, breaking her train of thought. "I found a recipe in Ethel's cookbook."

"I could smell it the minute I came in. I'll put some potatoes in the microwave." Anxious to break the connection that pulsed so powerfully between them, Gloria escaped to the kitchen.

CHAPTER SEVEN

"YOU THINK THE boy is getting too attached to me."

Gloria glanced over her shoulder as she placed the plates in the dishwasher. Jack was standing beside the kitchen table, his hands on the knobs of the high-backed chair.

After the meal Peter had insisted that Jack put him to bed. Gloria, with a small frown creasing her brows, had watched him sweep the small boy up into his arms. The frown hadn't escaped Jack's watchful eyes.

"I . . . don't want him disappointed."

"Do you think I'd do that?"

"Not intentionally." Gloria rinsed the silverware in the sink and arranged it in the basket in the dishwasher. "He doesn't understand—"

"That I'm not a permanent fixture in his life."

"Something like that."

"Do you want me to stay away from the boy?"

"No!" The cry of protest came straight from her heart. She was on the verge of tears and blinked rapidly. "It . . .

would break his heart. He looks forward to each day because of you."

"I don't want you to worry about me ever doing anything to upset you . . . or Peter. He's a smart little fellow, a fine boy—a boy any man would be proud of," he said softly.

Not *any* man. The words were a silent scream filling her mind. Gloria swallowed hard, fighting back the tears. Marvin wasn't proud of Peter. Marvin couldn't stand to look at him; he thought of him as a stray to be fed and patted on the head occasionally, not a real person with feelings. But that was in the past. She didn't want to think about it and hurried to rally her thoughts.

"He's been happy here. It's mostly because of you."

"What about you, Glory? Have you been happy here?"

She made herself look him directly in the eyes. Hers were wet, her vision blurred. "Yes. It's such a relief to be able to be . . . myself."

They stared at each other for a moment that was so still, it was as though time had stopped moving. Then, slowly and haltingly, Jack came to her and stood towering over her. He held out his hand. The gesture caught her off guard, and she looked at him searchingly before putting her hand in his.

"I know the feeling." The words came out as if it was a relief to say them. Still holding her hand, he reached for the light switch and shut it off, plunging the room into semidarkness. "Come sit with me for a while," he invited softly. He steered her to the couch; she would have preferred the rocking chair. "Shall we see what's on?" He knelt down in front of the television and turned it on. The movie that came on was an old John Wayne Western she'd seen several times before.

"Is this okay?"

"Fine."

He sat down beside her, reached for her hand, and engulfed it in his. He stretched his long legs out in front of him, his head resting on the back of the couch.

"This is nice." He let out a half sigh, half yawn. "I like the peace and quiet, the companionship, the . . . just being here with you. I didn't realize how lonely my life had become until I met you and Peter."

She glanced at him. His head was turned toward her and his green eyes held hers like a magnet. There was a sense of unreality in having him here, sharing in the preparation of the meal, taking Peter to bed together, sitting with him during the quiet of the evening. The careful way he had pushed her down onto the couch, his soft, sincere words, the touch of his hand holding hers, called out to something deep inside of her, brought her emotions to the brink of exploding. Ten seconds passed while Gloria drew a shallow breath, followed by a deeper one. She shook her head as if in answer to a question.

"You think I want to make love to you. Is that it?" The question was delivered suddenly.

"No, I just think . . ." She continued to shake her head. Her heart began to beat heavily.

"You're wrong. I want to . . . very much. I've wanted to since the first time I saw you. Since the very first," he whispered once more, his face near hers, his hands drawing her to him. "I doubt if there's a man alive who wouldn't want to make love to you if he were here with you like this."

Oh, yes, there is, she thought. *But a man like you wouldn't understand that. He looks tired,* she thought; *he has shadows beneath his eyes. Has he been working too hard, not sleeping well?* She felt warmth sweeping over her. *Oh, God! What if he can read my mind?* Her breath caught in the back of her throat, but when she spoke, she chose her tone carefully.

"You'd never force me."

He lifted her hand, gently disengaged her fingers from around his, and held it tightly between his two palms. He looked at it intently, then brought her fingers to his mouth and gently brushed his lips across her knuckles.

"No. I'd never do that." He placed her hand, palm up, in his. "Such a little hand." He spoke as if he were talking to himself. "I like it." He turned his head toward her. "I like everything about you, Glory."

She didn't move. She felt her insides warm with pleasure as she looked into the quiet face and soft green eyes now anxiously waiting to see if she would take his admission lightly and throw back a sassy retort. Love and tenderness welled within her. She lifted her free hand and held it to his cheek. Still holding her eyes with his, he turned his lips into her palm. She felt them move, felt the warmth of his breath. There had been no games between them, no sassy retorts, no pretense, since the night they had taken her aunt to the hospital. He had offered her his help, his friendship, openly and honestly, with no strings attached. Suddenly all the emotional bruising she'd had to endure from Marvin flowed and melted away under the serious but tender look in his eyes.

"There's a lot I like about you, too, Jack." She was so absorbed in her own thoughts that it was seconds, or minutes, before she realized that his eyes were no longer serious. They were twinkling.

"In spite of the beard?"

"And the hair . . . and the earring. . . ."

His hand went to his ear and he tugged. "I don't know how you women wear such things. It hurt like hell!"

"It serves you right for trying to aggravate me."

He gazed at her for a long moment before he reached out a hand to stroke a finger down her cheek with a feather-light touch. Her thoughts shifted to how absolutely masculine he was, how capable he was of doing anything he wanted to do. He would have made a wonderful pioneer, a man who would have blazed a trail into the wilderness, built a cabin with his own hands, taken care of his woman—

"Have you ever kissed a man with a beard?"

"Thousands."

He growled fiercely, and his long arms reached out to envelop her and lock her to him. "How about making it a thousand and one?"

Gloria heard herself, amazingly, laughing. She turned her head from side to side, until his fingers cupped her chin. The eyes that smiled into his were glittering pools of molten gold.

"Aha!" she cried. "Now your caveman character comes out!"

"I don't think you realize what a sweet invitation you are, sitting there with your eyes shining and your soft mouth smiling. I've wanted to kiss you from the first minute I saw you," he said huskily, and lowered his mouth to hers. His lips were soft and gentle. The brush of his beard caressed her face and was surprisingly pleasant.

"Everything about you turns me on, in spite of all I can do to resist you. This little upper lip of yours—this little crease beside your mouth that's caused by pressing your lips together to keep from smiling." He licked it with his tongue. "You're going to have smile lines here." His lips touched the corners of her eyes. "And when you're older, and your hair is twisted in a knot on the top of your head, you'll be even more beautiful than you are now." Her lids fluttered down. "Open your eyes, Glory, Glory, and look at me."

"Jack, I don't sleep around." She raised gold-tipped lashes and immediately became lost in the clear-green pools of his eyes.

"I know that. Put your arms around me, Glory," he whispered. Warm fingers smoothed her hair away from her face and then cupped the back of her head.

Mindless, unconscious of time or place, she lifted her arms and encircled his neck in complete disregard of the common sense that told her she was acting wantonly, unrestrainedly, and foolishly. She leaned back to look into his eyes.

"You have beautiful eyes, Jack."

"Yours are like those I've seen on a beautiful little mountain lion—wide, questioning, soft, but fierce too." His arms tightened and his lips nuzzled her ear. They felt so good, she pressed against them.

"I scratch too."

"Nooo." He drew the word out. "You purr. You're a delicious armful, Glory, Glory. I've wanted to kiss you with your arms around my neck, your breasts pressed against me, and your hips in my hands for . . . oh, so long.

But I won't do it, if you tell me to stop. Are you going to?"

"I should. . . ."

A wild, sweet enchantment rippled through her veins as his mouth moved over hers with warm urgency. The desire to push her fingers through his hair was an impulse she couldn't resist. It was so thick and so soft, like the mustache and beard that swept across her face. His kiss deepened and her head began to spin helplessly from the torrent of churning desires racking her body. The intensity of these feelings was strange to her, but she was not frightened by them. The sensations were heightened when his tongue caressed her lips, sought entrance, and found welcome. When she felt his mouth leaving hers, she held the back of his head with her hand more tightly. Finally, reluctantly, they broke the kiss so they could breathe.

"Glory, sweet one . . . I shouldn't have started this! You're so soft to touch, so sweet to taste, and you smell so womanly." He gently pulled her over onto him, and his hand moved down her back to her hips. He cupped them and pressed her to his male hardness; arousing her, taking her over, making her want the physical gratification of uniting with him in the most intimate way. "Tell me to stop . . . to go home—or it'll be too late." The words seemed to be wrenched from him. "I . . . ache for you. . . ."

Caught in a spinning whirlwind of desire Gloria was aware that his pulse was racing as wildly as hers. She was causing this! His virile, vitally strong body was reacting to hers! It was something she'd never experienced with Marvin. Stirred by this incredible discovery, she met his passion with intimate sensuousness and parted her lips to run the tip of her tongue across his mouth.

"God! Sweetheart . . . help me to stop this . . . while I still can!"

"No!" Her chin tilted almost fearlessly, as joyous thoughts whirled and flitted through her mind. *I'm doing what I want, for once. This is dangerous, but it could very well be the most precious moment of my life!*

She moved her hips against him in an instinctive invitation as old as time. Finding what her body had craved for so long, Gloria ignored the warning signals flashing in her brain and allowed the warmth of his desire and tenderness to wash over her. The world could be ending the next minute and her only concern would be to stay with him, relieve them both of the trembling hunger bedeviling them.

"Don't tease me, Glory!" he whispered hoarsely. His lips ravaged her face from cheek to chin. "Night after lonely night I've thought about being with you like this."

"I'm not teasing. . . ." She moaned desperately, her face flaming with shame.

"It's everything or nothing! Say it, now, while I can still leave you!" he said raggedly.

She burrowed her face into the softness of his beard. "Don't leave me," she whispered, her voice anxious. "Love me, Jack."

"You're sure?"

"Please!"

Her plea seemed to act as a potent aphrodisiac. His body responded with violent trembling. He pulled her roughly against his hard arousal, as if to leave her no doubt that he was desperate for her. "Oh, sweet one . . ."

Jack stood and lifted her in his arms. A half-dozen strides brought him to Ethel's bedroom. The only light in the room was what came through the open doorway from the living room. He stood her on her feet and put his arms around her. They stood for a long moment, arms wrapped around each other, close, savoring the feel of standing for the first time in each other's arms. His face was against the top of her head, hers in the curve of his neck.

"I'm afraid to leave you," he muttered thickly. "I'm afraid you'll not be here when I come back. Sweetheart . . . sweet, sweet girl . . . I must go lock the door, turn off the TV, and the vacancy light—"

"I'll be here. Hurry."

He left her, and she turned her back to the door. Her eyes were wide open, staring at nothing. Her mind grappled, not with what she was doing, but with her lack of sexual experience and the violence of her own need for him to make love to her. She had experienced nothing but humiliation at the hands of her husband, and her female heart cried out to know if that was all there was. *Please, God, show me that what happens between a man and a woman can be beautiful.*

It seemed to her she had stood there for an eternity before arms encircled her from behind, and warm lips and a soft beard nuzzled the sensitive spot below her ear. His hands moved to cup her breasts, squeezing them gently.

"You're the most utterly feminine woman I've ever met." Gloria closed her eyes and let the soft purr of his voice and the feel of his hands consume her. "You've bewitched me. I seem to have lost control where you're concerned."

"Oh, Jack . . ." His persuasive whisper, the touch of

his hands, called out to a deep need inside her, and the explosion of sensation choked off her voice.

"My head says stay away from you, but my hands want to know every soft curve of your body." He moved his hand down to pull her tightly back against him. "Glory, Glory, come quench this thirst I have for you!"

When she didn't answer, or move, he backed up a step with her in his arms, sat down on Ethel's bed, and pulled her onto his lap. She clung to his shoulders, which were wide and powerful and sheltering. The feel of his body, the stroking of his hands, the warm moistness of his breath, and the love spilling from her heart erased the last shred of her inhibitions, and with a soft cry she gave herself up to the sweet abandonment he was urging upon her, telling herself that no matter what happened in the morning, she could face it if she had this night to remember always.

Their mouths met and were no longer gentle. They kissed deeply, hungrily. His hand found her breast, cupped and lifted it. Her own fingers curled feverishly into the solid muscle of his back, and her lips ravaged his neck. When his fingers moved to the front zipper of her jeans her hand went automatically to his and he stopped immediately.

"Do you have doubts?" he moaned hoarsely against her cheek.

"No . . . no. . . ." Her hand caressed his silky beard. "It's just . . . I'm afraid you'll think I'm . . . easy."

A low protest came from his throat. "Easy? Oh, God, no! You're anything but that. I'm thinking you're so small, so perfect, so beautiful—I get the feeling you've not done this before . . . yet I know you have. But I don't want to think of it, or for you to think of it. I want you to think I'm your first, that you're mine alone," he murmured.

She felt a sweetness, a rightness, when he lowered her to the bed and stretched out beside her. She gave a shiver of pure pleasure when he unbuttoned her shirt and slipped it off her shoulders. Slowly he tugged her jeans down over her hips, but left her panties in place. When he left her to take off his clothes, she lifted the covers and moved between the sheets.

She wasn't prepared for the warmth or the strength of his hard, muscular body, the long, hairy legs against her, the enormous arms under and around her. Her trembling body was gathered tenderly to a warm, naked chest thickly matted with soft hair.

"Sweetheart . . ." He smoothed her hair back from her face. Even now his concern was for her, and she cherished it.

"I can't believe I'm here with you, like this." Even as she spoke, her hands clutched him closer, her stomach muscles tightened, her breathing and heartbeat were all mixed up. *I love him,* she thought wildly. *I wouldn't be here in bed with him if I didn't love him. Oh, dear heaven! It's happened so fast. It's unreal that I'm doing this, feeling this.*

"Glory, Glory. You're every sweet dream I've ever dreamed, every fantasy." His hungry mouth searched, found hers, and held it with fierce but tender possession. His hands moved urgently over her, and she felt as if her heart would gallop right out of her breast.

She wanted to speak, to tell him she was still a girl in a woman's body, that she was afraid of the hurt that would follow this giving of herself. She opened her mouth to voice her fears, but it was too late. He covered her parted lips, his tongue darting hotly in and out of her mouth, exploring every curve of the sweetness that trembled beneath his demanding kiss. She moaned gently and panted for breath.

"Are you shy with me?" he whispered between kisses. "Don't be. I'll not do anything you don't want me to do. You're beautiful. Your little body is tight and neat. Your skin is soft—like velvet. . . ." His fingers fumbled with the hooks on her bra, then swept it from her breasts. He nuzzled them gently, kissed them reverently, and then for the first time she experienced having her nipples pressed to a man's lips. His hand pushed at her panties and she lifted her hips to help him.

So this is what it's like to really make love with a man, she thought dreamily, and threaded her legs between his. His sex was large and firm and throbbed against her stomach. She gloried in the feel of him, knowing that soon he could fill that aching emptiness. Her hands moved over his ribs and sides, down over his back to his hips.

He kissed her breast; his tongue flicked the bud, then he grasped it gently with his teeth. The softness of his beard was a silky caress on her stomach. Tremors shot through her with earth-shaking waves as his exploring fingers moved over her body, prowling ever closer to the ultimate goal. Suddenly they were *there,* sliding into the mysterious moistness. She welcomed the gentle probing with parted thighs and an urgency that incited him to lift his mouth to hers in a kiss that stripped away everything but the need to assuage the ache building to unbearable heights within her. He slid smoothly over her body and she welcomed the weight that pressed onto her.

"Now? Little sweet one . . . now?" he murmured, and sought entrance while she waited in rapt and aching anguish. She pressed herself to him, her arms winding tightly around his neck. She was caught up in overpowering desire and the need for physical release. "Oh, Lord! You're so small, so tight. Will I hurt you?" His chest heaved as he attempted to control his breathing.

"You won't hurt me, darling. Don't stop!" she pleaded, her need for him overcoming her shyness. Her hands feverishly clung to him, holding him tightly while she rained fervent kisses on his mouth.

He raised his head, his eyes searching her passion-clouded ones, and then with a muttered whisper he closed his arms about her in fierce demand. He moved into her, reverently guiding her to accept the gently rhythmic sliding. This joining would be forever imprinted in her memory. She was part of this man. He was the universe, vibrating with all the love in the world, and he was lifting her to undreamed of sensual heights, reaching, reaching. . . .

He supported himself on his forearms, tangled his hands in her hair. "I wanted our first time to be long and sweet . . . but, darling . . . I can't wait much longer!"

"You . . . don't have to wait. . . ." She arched to impale herself more completely on his throbbing warmth.

"Oh, God! Oh, love—" He probed urgently, turning this way and that, and moaned with pleasure.

Gloria desperately wanted what they were reaching for, dreaded missing it, and quivered with expectation beneath the pressure of his body. She clung to him, aware only of that thrusting, pulsing rhythm increasing unbearably to a tempo that brought her higher . . . higher—

She came languidly back to reality and found her hands clasping Jack's tight buttocks, his bearded face pressed to her neck. He was still huge and deep inside her, but the waves of frenzied pleasure that had ripped through her were subsiding. In their place swelled a burning desire to comfort and pleasure him. Her hands moved lovingly over him, smoothed his hair back from his face, stroked it, hugged his head to her breast. With utmost tenderness she pressed her lips to his forehead. She had learned the mysteries about which she had read and imagined, but which she'd never truly believed were accompanied by such overwhelmingly forceful feelings. It was almost as if they were totally and completely in love!

He was a stranger to her, his background as different from hers as night from day, she thought frantically. And yet she felt as though she'd known him all her life, wanted him, needed him, loved him.

His heart was still thundering against hers when he wrapped his legs around her and turned on his side, taking her with him. They lay quietly facing each other, her soft belly tight against his hard one. They kissed for a long time, as if it were the first time and there never could be anything beyond a kiss. His tongue was inside her mouth and moving softly and slowly while his fingers teased the nipple on her breast and then drifted lightly down to her belly and fluttered their way to the place where they were joined. The varieties of stroking thrilled her in a thousand different ways, creating a hunger deep, deep inside her. She knew she should be shocked, but she wasn't. The feeling was so acutely pleasurable that she tightened her arms and legs about him and murmured unintelligible words in his ear. He laughed deep in his throat. It was a tender, loving, knowing laugh.

"I wish I could see your eyes. You're so incredibly sweet, Glory, Glory. I want you to feel everything—"

"I'll explode—" She arched against him when he flexed his hips. "Jack . . ."

"Talk to me, darling. Tell me what you want, what you feel. I've never known anything more wonderful than the feel of you tight against me, surrounding me. You're like a warm, living china doll—sweet, fragile, yet strong, passionate. Oh, be still, darling!" He breathed in gasps when she moved urgently. Then, "Yes! Oh, yes!" With a long breath he thrust at her full force, and incredibly her body responded to his. They merged into a long, long, unbelievably beautiful release and lay shuddering in each other's arms.

Gloria held him tenderly. She felt an odd sense of power. This big, rough man had quivered in her arms as she had in his. He had made her feel as if she were wonderful, precious, worthwhile—they had come together, as equals, in dignity and need. Slowly his breathing steadied, and he rolled onto his back. His arms pulled her to him and his hand sought her thigh to bring it up to rest on his. They were quiet for a long while, her head on his shoulder, his hand stroking her thigh.

"This brings a new dimension to our relationship," he said softly.

Gloria held her breath through the seconds of silence that followed. She looked up. The face that was so close to hers was not smiling—she could see clearly enough for that.

"Oh, there's no need for you to feel obligated," she said, trying to keep the quiver out of her voice.

"Obligated? What the hell are you talking about?"

"I don't want you to think . . . that I expect—"

"Hush!" The word was sharp, and there wasn't a trace of humor in his voice.

Gloria peered at him apprehensively, trying to read his expression. A few seconds ago she had felt young and happy and cherished, and she wanted desperately to feel again that closeness of mind and body they'd shared.

Jack turned his head toward her. "You're not just a one-night stand. There's much more between us than that. We've got to get it all sorted out."

She shut her eyes tightly to hold back the tears. *Don't spoil it,* she cautioned. *Don't let him know how afraid you are of being alone, or how much his tenderness means to you.* Their union had been everything she had dreamed a union between a man and a woman in love would be. But he had not said anything to her about love. . . .

"I can't leave Peter in there by himself. He might wake up and be frightened." She threw back the sheet covering them. Jack's arms tightened around her, refusing to let her go.

"I thought about that. I'll bring him in to sleep on the couch where we can hear him if he wakes up."

"No. I'll go."

"Don't go. Stay here with me, Glory. Let me sleep with you in my arms. You keep all my ghosts at bay, my sweet one." His voice was husky and pleading, and tore at her heart. "Say you'll stay."

"All right," she said mindlessly.

"I'll get Peter."

When he was gone, her hands sought the warm spot where his body had lain. *Oh, dear Lord! I've gotten myself in deep trouble this time. I've fallen in love with an aging hippie!* she thought miserably. *He's sweet and kind, but there's nothing else about him that I admire. He has no ambition. He's content with his hand-to-mouth existence in an old shack in the mountains, and he's ruthless when crossed. I could never live the way he lives, especially with Peter—I need security. Besides, I know absolutely nothing about his background. He could have a criminal record, or be married, for all I know. And what would my family think if I came riding up to the house on a motorcycle with a man with long hair and a beard? They'd be sure, then, that I'd lost my mind.*

Something he'd muttered in her ear while in the throes of passion came filtering into her mind. *I want our first time to be long and sweet.* Did he plan for this to be a regular arrangement—that they would perform a service for each other? Dear God! Did he think she was the type of woman who would enter into such a relationship?

Such thoughts ran wildly through her mind as she stared into the darkness, but when Jack returned, slipped into bed beside her, and gathered her tenderly to him, she went to him eagerly and nestled against his strength. In spite of all the reasons she'd cited against continuing a relationship with this big, rugged, sometimes fierce man— he made her feel wanted and . . . safe.

Long after Jack had fallen into a deep sleep, Gloria lay cozily against his very male body. No one could doubt *his* fundamental virility—it radiated from every pore in his aggressively masculine body. She pushed the thought of the *other* sexual experience she'd had out of her mind.

Jack's lovemaking had been tumultuous, and she had responded vigorously to his instruction in the elementary pleasures of loving.

As far as she was concerned, he was her first and only *real* lover.

CHAPTER EIGHT

MORNING CAME, AND with it the realization that she was alone in Ethel's bed. The bedroom door was closed, but she could hear the sound of voices coming from the living room—Gary's, Jack's, and Peter's. The clock on the bedside table was turned face down. She turned it up and was astonished to see that it was nine o'clock. Heavens! She hadn't slept that late in ages.

She threw back the covers, and the cold air hit her naked body, giving her goose bumps. There was a soreness and a stickiness between her legs. She grabbed her clothes and went into the bathroom, carefully locking the door behind her. The face that looked back at her from the mirror was the same face she'd seen yesterday morning. How could that be, when she felt so different inside? A man had made love to her all through the night—a tender, caring, considerate man, a man as different from her former husband as day from night. Marvin had cruelly, and hurtfully, taken her virginity, leaving no doubt that it was distasteful to him to do so, but that duty was duty and *legally* he was required to consummate the marriage; then he had left their bed on their wedding night, never to return. Jack had made sure that she shared in the enjoyment of their union, kissed away her tears when heightened emotion caused them to spill from her eyes, held her in his arms while she slept.

Gloria stepped into the shower and let the warm water splash over her. She wondered with increasing anxiety what Jack's attitude toward her would be this morning. Would he be flippant about what happened between them? Would he simply ignore it? Had it meant anything to him, beyond physical relief? Would he take it for granted that he was welcome in her bed for as long as he wanted her?

She washed herself quickly, dressed, then combed her short blond hair into place. No use in prolonging the agony, she told herself. Face him and get it over with.

She found Gary alone in the kitchen; he was getting ready to go out the back door.

"Morning. I heard Peter. Did he go back to our room?"

"Jack took him up to his place. He said to let you sleep. He thinks you've about wore yourself out."

"I . . . was tired." She turned to pour a cup of coffee, because she could feel her cheeks tingle.

"I'm on my way to get Janet. She'll be a big help to you."

"She can have Aunt Ethel's room. I'll get it ready."

"No way," Gary said with an earthy laugh. "That woman's stayin' with me!"

"Oh! Of course. Um . . . Gary, did Jack say when he'd be back?"

"No. He just said tell you he had Peter with him. Don't worry about the kid. Jack'll take care of him."

"I know that. I was just wondering—"

"I'll stop and see Ethel. I should be back by noon, and then you can go."

Gloria stood at the sink and watched Gary back his station wagon out of the garage. She gulped down the coffee, then gathered up her cleaning supplies and started her rounds. Work was the only thing that would keep her thoughts at bay this morning.

Gary returned with Janet shortly after noon. She was a short, full-figured woman with shoulder-length dark hair and soft, dark eyes. Gloria liked her immediately; she was warm and friendly, and obviously very much in love with Gary. She made fresh coffee while Gloria made sandwiches. The three of them sat at the kitchen table and talked about Ethel and the motel until the clock struck two.

"I thought Peter would be back by now," Gloria remarked anxiously.

"Are you going to see Ethel today? I told her you'd probably come this afternoon," Gary said.

"I was, but I hate to go not knowing about Peter."

"Janet and I will be here. We'll look after him if Jack comes back and wants to leave again—which I doubt." Gary grinned and winked at Janet.

The realization hit Gloria like a dash of cold water that Gary knew she and Jack had spent the night in Ethel's room. *Well, so what?* she thought stubbornly. *I'm an adult, and I don't feel one bit guilty.* Yet, despite her determination to handle herself coolly in this new situation she found herself in, she was frightened, anxious, and apprehensive about seeing Jack again.

"If you're sure you don't mind looking after Peter, I'll go on to town. I want to get back before dark."

"Don't worry about a thing." Janet got up to clear the table. "I'm here to help."

Jack had brought Peter back to the motel while she was in town, and left again before she returned. Peter chattered endlessly about the day: about his dog, watching a jackrabbit run, seeing kittens, a covey of quail, a pocket gopher, a badger. The small boy was so full of all he'd seen and heard, the words tumbled over each other as they spilled out of his small mouth.

"Jack's dog's name's Ringo. It's big and black and has a short tail. Jack makes him mind. He yells and Ringo walks beside him. Guess what, Mom? Jack's town is old . . . the streets are all dirt . . . Jack let me dig in the street—"

Jack, Jack, Jack. Peter had said his name a hundred times since coming home. It was hours after his usual bedtime that he calmed down enough to go to sleep. Gloria sat beside him for a long while before she got into her own bed.

"Oh, Jack," she whispered into the silent room. "Thank you for giving my son such a wonderful day." Almost without knowing it she added, "And me such a wonderful night."

Gloria thought about her visit earlier that day with her Aunt Ethel. She had been pleased to see how well her aunt was adjusting to the home. She was in a wheelchair now, and there was always someone willing to take her out into the main room where there were a television and a pool table, and where numerous card games were going on almost all day. Gradually she was getting her speech back and no longer cried when Gloria had to leave. Her eyes sparkled when Gloria told her Janet and Gary were going to be married, and that they planned to stay at the motel until they found a house so they could have Gary's little girl with them.

"Good . . . good . . . but you?" Ethel had asked her with an anxious look in her eyes.

"Don't worry about me. Peter and I will keep the motel going until you can come home. I have an income from Marvin." Gloria knew the white lie was necessary. It wouldn't do at all for her aunt to know she'd cut herself off from Marvin's money when she left Ohio, and that all she had was her small personal savings and a little money from the sale of a few pieces of jewelry he'd given her.

The days passed slowly until a week had gone by, with no sign of Jack. Gloria became increasingly sure that he was deliberately staying away to convey the message that he wanted no deep or lasting relationship with her. She was angry at herself for thinking about him, and angry at him for presuming she wanted a relationship with him.

She had promised herself she could handle whatever came up as the result of this impulsive trip west, and so far she had, even Aunt Ethel's illness. Now it was time to take another step, and she had done so. She'd sent out queries about job opportunities in Great Falls. She had decided that if Ethel sold the motel she would move on.

After a morning visit to the nursing home she stopped at the grocery store for a few things, and at the ten-cent store she got a new coloring book for Peter. The air was cold and damp, and dark clouds rolled out of the north-west. The smell of woodsmoke, hanging low, greeted her when she turned into the drive. She parked the car and hurried into the living quarters of the motel.

Janet was putting a load of sheets and towels in the washer when Gloria came in the back door with her arms filled with sacks.

"Wow! You must've bought out the town."

"Not quite. But I did get the makings for a yummy cake, a couple boxes of cereal for Peter, and a new coloring book."

"Yummy cake? Sounds good . . . and fattening."

"It is good, and loaded with calories, but what the heck. You melt caramels and add chocolate chips and co-conut for the filling of a chocolate cake. I'll copy the recipe for you."

"I'd like that. Gary loves desserts." Janet added soap to the machine and turned the dial to start it. "Jack was here while you were gone. He took Peter back home with him. I didn't think you'd mind."

Gloria turned quickly and started taking the groceries from the sack. "Did he say when they'd be back? It's get-ting terribly cold, and it could snow."

"He wasn't on the cycle. He had the Ranger, and he put Peter in his snowsuit. He'll be all right."

"Yes, of course," Gloria said absently. She put the gro-ceries away automatically. It was clear now that he was avoiding her. But how had he known she wouldn't be here? He must have called on the CB, she reasoned, and Janet must have told him she'd gone to town. She wished she had the nerve to ask Janet.

The day moved slowly. Janet went to the room she

shared with Gary. Gloria made the yummy cake and left it on the kitchen counter to cool. The stillness of the house bore down on her. She missed Peter's chatter, his endless questions. She thought of using the CB radio to call the Hangtown station. If Jack answered, she didn't know what she'd say to him besides, "What the hell do you mean coming here and taking my son?" No, she wouldn't say that. Peter had talked of nothing but Jack, and how he was going to come get him and show him the antelope that came down to the salt blocks he'd put just outside of his town.

She wouldn't chastise him for taking Peter; it would be mean to deprive Peter of his company just because she and Jack were having their problems. When she saw him again, she'd treat him the same as she had *before:* friendly, but strictly impersonal. There was no way she would let him know how crushed she was, how miserable she felt, how used. His denial of her, now, would tarnish forever the memories of the beautiful moments they'd shared.

She sat on a stool behind the counter in the office and watched the cars go by. She was deep in thought when the long, shiny black car with the tinted glass turned into the drive and stopped in front of the office door. Gloria gaped in surprise; she knew immediately who it was, and was gripped with apprehension. She got slowly to her feet and was standing when the back door of the car opened and Marvin, holding his hat with one gloved hand, stepped out.

He stood beside the car and looked the building up and down; Gloria was sure he was mentally assessing its worth, for money was forever on his mind. The wind blew open his long black overcoat, and it flapped out behind him like wings. When he reached the office door, the driver opened it for him, then went back to the car.

Marvin looked around the office haughtily, ignoring Gloria until he'd finished his survey of the premises. Then he looked at her.

"Well, Gloria, I must say you've certainly buried yourself in the sticks. Back to your roots, huh?" He removed his hat, placed it on the counter, removed his gloves, and carefully smoothed with his fingertips the silver hair at his temples. Almost colorless gray eyes looked into hers, and he lifted his arched brows disdainfully. His every word, his every gesture, was meant to intimidate.

"What do you want?" Gloria demanded angrily. She was surprised at what little effect he had on her. Where was the old fear, the feeling of inferiority, she used to experience when she was with him?

Marvin sensed her detachment and gave her the silent treatment, looking at her with narrowed eyes, mouth turned down slightly at the corners as if he smelled something unpleasant, hand poised in front of him as if ready to flick away dust or lint from his coat. The look had been cultivated and refined over the years, and usually managed to reduce even the most self-assured person into quivering servitude.

Suddenly laughter bubbled up in Gloria's throat. How could she ever have been frightened by this . . . phony? Something goaded her to say, "Stop playacting, Marvin. I've seen this act a hundred times. What do you want?"

"Be careful what you say, Gloria. I still have the means of taking from you what you treasure the most. Why you value this cheap, tawdry lifestyle or the company of truckers and barroom scum is beyond me, but as long as you do, I'll not hesitate to use it to my advantage."

"You'll never get your hands on Peter—not as long as I live!"

"That's up to you, entirely up to you."

"I'm not coming back to you, Marvin. I've got the right to live my own life without interference from you. Understand that right now."

"My dear girl, if it were at all possible I'd just as soon never see you or that . . . child again. But unfortunately, you made an impression on some of my friends and business associates and they have inquired about you. I simply cannot let you and my . . . *son* disappear. People will think I've cast you off. So I've come to take you back to Cincinnati."

"I'm not going!"

"Very well, stay. I'll take the boy."

"He's not *your* boy, dammit!" Her poise completely abandoned her, and she heard herself shouting.

"Control yourself. Your lack of breeding is showing."

Gloria drew in a deep, pained breath. "Don't tell me about breeding, you fatheaded stuffed shirt! I've got more breeding in my little finger than you've got in your whole body."

"Gloria, you really are a stupid girl; beautiful, but stupid." Marvin raised his brows, and his mocking eyes surveyed her face.

"You're not taking Peter! You don't even like him!"

"No, I don't. But that's beside the point. You and Peter are coming back with me. We are going to remarry and you will conduct yourself in such a manner as to not cast a blemish on the Masterson name."

"I will not marry you again!" she hissed, glaring into his cold gray eyes.

Marvin reached into the inside pocket of his overcoat and drew out a long white envelope. He opened it and unfolded a legal document.

"The court has given me custody of the boy for six months out of the year." There was a triumphant gleam in his eyes as he watched her face turn ashen. "Come back with me, take your place as Mrs. Marvin Masterson, or I take him now."

"When we got the divorce you didn't want custody. Why are you doing this?"

"If you had not run off like a silly girl, it wouldn't have been necessary."

"I don't understand you. I don't understand you at all. Why do you want us there?"

"My dear girl, I plan to run for governor, and the image I wish to project is of a devoted family man who carefully guards the welfare of his young wife and child."

"Peter and I despise you!"

His eyes narrowed with anger. "Do you think that matters to me? You carry the Masterson name."

Something in his eyes caused a feeling of panic to sweep over her. Her heart pounded, and she felt a compelling urgency to turn and run. She felt as if she were floating through space, and tried to get her scattered thoughts together. There had to be something she could do—if only she had time to think! She breathed deeply and tried to stem the tears of rage that were stinging her eyelids. Vaguely she heard the back door slam.

"Mom! Mom! Look what I got. Look what Jack—" Peter's happy shout stopped abruptly when he saw Marvin.

A fierce pain pierced Gloria's heart when she saw the look of terror on the face of her small son. She knelt down beside him. "What do you have here? A kitten! Oh, Peter—it's beautiful!"

Peter moved close to her and peered over her shoulder at the man who stared at him so coldly.

"Where are your manners, boy? Get rid of that animal and step up here and shake hands as you've been taught to do. I've come to take you home. What you need is a good school where you'll not be coddled and allowed to run wild."

Peter's stricken eyes sought Gloria's. "I'm afraid we have no choice," she said softly, and hugged him.

Peter looked up at Marvin, then back to Gloria. His face crumbled and he burst into tears. The kitten became frightened and jumped out of his arms. Peter struggled to leave Gloria's embrace and she let him go.

"Jack! Jack!" he cried between sobs, and ran out of the office.

Gloria felt sick. Poor little fellow, poor little boy; he'd been so happy here. She could hear the low murmur of Jack's voice as he talked to the boy.

"Well—are you coming or not? The sooner I get out of this backwater and back to civilization, the better." Marvin folded the paper and put it back into the envelope.

"Now?"

"Now. I'll wait in the car. Be out in ten minutes."

"What's going on here, Gloria?" Jack came into the

room and stood at the end of the counter. Peter's arms were locked tightly about his neck, and his small legs were around his waist.

Gloria's eyes flew to Marvin, and the contempt she saw on his face as he looked at Jack only ignited her anger into full-fledged rage.

"Marvin Masterson, my ex-husband, has come to take me and Peter back to Cincinnati. His image as the devoted patriarch of the Masterson dynasty, which, by the way, includes servants, ex-wives, and adopted children, slipped when Peter and I left. He can't afford to have his friends think he's anything but a loving family man." She shouted the last few words, and tears rolled down her cheeks.

"You're divorced, aren't you? He can't make you do anything you don't want to do," Jack said calmly.

"Oh, but he can! He's got a court order that gives him custody of Peter for six months out of the year. I can't let Peter go alone with him," she wailed.

"I'll wait in the car." Marvin carefully placed his hat on his head and pulled on his gloves.

"Stay here!" Jack spoke so sharply that Marvin turned to stare at him as if he couldn't quite believe this bearded, long-haired, leather-coated yokel would have the nerve to speak to him. "Take the boy," Jack said gently, and handed Peter over to Gloria. "I want to take a look at that court order."

Peter wrapped his arms about Gloria and buried his face in her neck. The agony that pierced her heart was unbearable; she longed to be out from under the sneering gaze of the man she had married when she was so young and so naive.

"I want to see the court order," Jack repeated, and held out his hand.

Marvin's cold gray eyes flicked from Jack to Gloria and back again. Disapproval etched lines between his carefully arched brows. The grim line of his jaw and his tightly pressed lips told her that he was burning with anger.

"My advice to you is—stay out of things that don't concern you." With the faintest suggestion of a sardonic sneer he turned to go out the door.

"You're beginning to annoy me. Give me the court order!" Jack put a hand on Marvin's shoulder and spun him around. He slammed him against the wall and held him there with his forearm jammed against his Adam's apple. "Give it to me or I'll break both of your goddamn legs!"

"Get your hands off me, you ruffian. I'll call my driver."

"Do that, you bastard! I'll mop up the floor with both of you."

Gloria's heart was thudding like a jackhammer in her breast. She had no doubt that Jack would do exactly what he said he'd do. Oh, God! If he beat up Marvin, it would only make matters worse.

"Jack, don't!" The words left her mouth in a whisper.

"Now, listen, you arrogant son of a bitch, I don't intend to mess around with you. I mean to see that court order before you leave here. Give it to me, or I'll take it." Jack punctuated his words by slamming Marvin's head back against the wall.

"Ah . . . ah . . . all right." Marvin reached into his pocket for the envelope.

Jack snatched it out of his hand. "Stay right there," he snarled when Marvin started to move away from him.

Marvin straightened his hat and threw Gloria a furious glance. "You'll hear from my attorney," he threatened.

Jack ignored the warning and thumbed through the papers, scanning each sheet. When he came to the last page he studied it thoroughly. A moment of dead silence passed slowly. He looked Marvin in the eye as he folded the papers. Suddenly he slapped him across the face with them.

"You stupid bastard!" His voice boomed angrily. "What kind of a bluff are you trying to pull on this woman? These papers are not even notarized. All you've got here is a legal form with a signature. Now, if you don't want me to beat the holy hell out of you, get out of here and don't come back."

"A mere technicality that I will remedy immediately. I'm not without influence in this state, as you'll soon discover." Marvin stuffed the papers in his pocket. "I'll be back with my attorney and the sheriff."

"Fine. If it's a fight for the boy you're wanting, I think we can give it to you."

Marvin opened his mouth as if to say something, but he changed his mind, and slowly pulled on his gloves instead. His face was unreadable as he turned and went out the door.

Jack stood at the door and watched him leave. Not a word was spoken until the long black car moved out of the drive and onto the highway. He turned to look at Gloria. Peter's arms were still locked about her neck.

"The papers are probably phony. Don't worry about it," he said lightly.

She shook her head. "No one has ever talked to him like that. He'll be back."

"Good. I hope he will, and I'll finish what I started."

"Oh, Jack! You shouldn't have interfered. He's very powerful. He won't rest until he's put you in jail!"

"Is . . . he gone?" Peter looked fearfully over his shoulder.

"Yup, he's gone. Come here, Bronco Billy. You're getting too big for your mother to hold."

"Do we have to go with . . . him?"

"Naw—who'd take care of Cisco and the cat?" Jack lifted him from Gloria's arms and set him on the floor. "You'd better find that cat before Cisco does. It'll take a while for them to get acquainted."

"You sent him away, didn't you, Jack? You didn't let him take us, did you?" Peter's eyes shone brightly through his tears. "Mom! Jack woulda hit him. I'll hit him, too, when I grow up."

"Hold on, Bronco. We'll have to talk about this hittin' business sometime."

"It's goin' to be all right, isn't it, Mom?" Peter looked up at her hopefully.

Gloria clamped her lips together and willed the tears to stay behind her eyelids. She nodded and tried to smile, silently saying, *I hope so, but don't count on it.*

"Sure it's goin' to be all right, Bronco. Now scoot and find that cat before he and Cisco tangle." Jack gave him a little push toward the door.

CHAPTER NINE

THE CLOCK ON the shelf struck the quarter hour. The sound wafted into the small eternity of silence that followed Peter's happy shout at finding the kitten. Gloria had turned her back to Jack, not wanting him to see the tear-filled eyes she was dabbing with the balled tissue. When she felt his hands on her shoulders, she stiffened. She was deep in the pit of despair.

"Don't!"

"Look at me, Glory."

"You've really done it, now, Mr. Smart Guy. He'll come back with the sheriff and take Peter. Why couldn't you just stay out of it?" she added bitterly.

"It didn't occur to me that you'd give up without a fight."

She whirled. Her eyes blazed into his. "Fight? You don't fight a man as powerful as Marvin Masterson, especially if you're a *peon* like me! You run. If he catches up with you, you wait your chance and run again!" Rage, and a blinding headache, were making her sick to her stomach. "That's exactly what I'm going to do, and you'd better do the same or you'll find yourself in jail!" She brushed past him and headed for the room she shared with Peter.

Safely behind the closed door the tight reins she had held on her emotions broke, her face crumbled, and she burst into tears. Still crying, she jerked open the dresser drawers and stuffed her clothes and Peter's into suitcases. When they were filled, she piled some things in the middle of a bedsheet and tied the corners together. She flung on her coat and pulled a stocking cap down over her ears. She didn't care that her face was tear streaked, or that her hair was hanging in strings about her face. All that mattered was to get away as fast as possible, and maybe, just maybe, Marvin wouldn't find her, and would give up and go back to Ohio.

Gloria threw open the door and ran straight into Jack. He put out his hands to steady her. "Ready? I was just coming to get you."

"Get your hands off me, you . . . bushman!" she snapped. "I don't need any help from you."

"Yes, you do. I'm all that's standing between you and that cold fish that's using Peter to get you back." His grip on her arms tightened.

She pushed at his chest. "Let me go! I don't want you to touch me ever again. I hate it!"

"You didn't hate it the other night."

Shame and anger seared through her. How could he be so vile as to remind her? Desperately and recklessly she tried to defend herself, but the words that fell from her lips came out in a torrent of lies and accusations that were uncharacteristic of her, words that she didn't really mean at all.

"You must admit there's quite a difference between you and Marvin. After *him*, I wanted to see what it was like to have a real man! Can you blame me for taking advantage of your offer?"

"Shut up!" he snarled. His eyes darkened as his fingers hardened like steel bands about her arms. His face was like a stone statue, hard and bitter. Gloria was sure he was going to shake her. But instead his hands slipped around her throat and his mouth came down on hers savagely, relentlessly, prying her lips apart. His hands beneath her chin held her head immobile, and his mouth burned, delved, bruised.

He lifted his head, and she gasped for breath. Her heart was hammering so hard that her ears were ringing. She couldn't think. She couldn't speak. He stared down at her, and she shook her head in silent protest.

"Be my Glory of the other night," he whispered. She heard the words as if they were coming from a distance. She stood stock still, waiting for the dizziness to pass.

"No. . . ."

"You know there's something wonderful between us," he murmured. "I stayed away from you for a whole week to find out if what I felt for you was real and lasting. It is!" His mouth closed over hers as he kissed her gently. Her mouth trembled. "You see how it is with us?"

"No. I don't see that at all." She tried to twist away from him.

"Yes, you do. You're fighting it. You've totally disrupted my life and you're not going to scamper out of it like a pup with your tail between your legs until I'm sure it's what we both want."

"You have nothing to say about what I do! Now, bug

off! You're nothing to me, and . . . I despise everything about you . . . especially that beard!"

His bright-green eyes mocked her. "You're a liar, Glory, Glory," he drawled softly. "Not a word of what you've said is true, and you know it. You're hurt and miserable and frightened. I can understand that. But pretending that you hate me is juvenile."

She wanted so badly to hit him that her fists curled into tight balls. Only the fact that Peter was coming into the room stopped her.

"Mom! Mom! Are you coming? I got Cisco and the kitty in the car." Gloria felt the blast of cool air from the open door. "Jack said I could name the kitty, Mom. Jack said I ought to call her Lucy."

Jack's hands fell from her arms. "We're coming, Bronco Billy. Get back in the car." He stepped around Gloria and picked up the suitcases. "Is this all you're taking?"

"Yes. But I can manage by myself."

"I don't doubt that for a minute, but this time you're not going to. Leave it, I'll get it," he said when she attempted to intercept him. She could tell that he was angry, but his voice remained calm. He nudged her in the back to force her out the door ahead of him.

Janet was in the office. She looked anxiously at Gloria, and then followed her to the back door.

"Jack explained why you're leaving. That bastard! That no-good bum! Don't worry about the motel. Gary and I will be here."

"Tell Aunt Ethel I'll get in touch with her as soon as I can. Hey!" she yelled at Jack. "Don't put my things in that car."

"It's not a car, Mom. Jack said it's a Jeep. He said it can go through snow." Peter's eyes danced with excitement as he climbed into the back of the vehicle.

Gloria fumed. *Jack said! Jack said!*

Jack lowered the back door of the Jeep and set the suitcases inside. He passed her without a glance and went back to the motel for the bundle. Gloria had the suitcases on the ground and was trying to get Peter out of the truck when Jack returned. Silently, and calmly, he put the suitcases back in, wedged the bundle between them, and slammed the door.

"Get in."

"No. I'm taking my own car. Peter, get out of—" Jack swung her up in his arms and sat her on the seat. "Now, wait just a doggone minute," she sputtered. "Who do you think—"

Peter shrieked with laughter. "Mom! Jack picked you up like he does me. Jack's stronger than anybody, Mom."

Jack grinned at her, slid in beside her, crowding her over to the passenger's side, and slammed the door. Before Gloria could find the door handle, the engine roared to life. He shifted the gears and backed the Jeep up so fast that Peter toppled over on the bundle, Cisco barked, and the frightened cat jumped over the seat and into Gloria's lap. They careened out onto the highway, Gloria grabbing the dash to keep from falling against Jack. She glanced at his face. His thick black hair was going in all directions, his eyes were mere slits, and his dark brows were drawn together. *He looks as fierce as a medieval warrior; all he needs is a suit of armor and a lance,* she thought.

"Where are you taking us?" she demanded. When he

ignored her she shouted the question, angrily, forgetting about Peter. "I said, where are you taking us?"

"To Hangtown."

If Jack had suddenly sprouted horns Gloria couldn't have been more shocked. For seconds she couldn't speak. Her heart fell right down through her stomach to her toes. It hadn't occurred to her that he would take them *there!*

"No way! We're going to Great Falls. I'll get a job—"

"Do you *want* him to find you?"

"You know I don't!"

"Can you think of a better place? The sheriff won't come out there; Hangtown is in another county. By the time he goes to Great Falls and gets a warrant, I'll have my lawyer in Chicago breathing down his neck."

"Your what?"

"Even bums like me have the right to legal counsel." He grinned at her.

Gloria snapped her teeth together in frustration, gave him a freezing look, and turned to gaze unseeingly out the window at the landscape that was flying by.

They turned off the highway and took a dirt road that wound among the foothills. Grass and weeds grew between the wheel tracks, and occasionally Jack had to slow the Jeep to a mere crawl. It was rugged, lonely country where stately cedars were scattered along the hillsides and gnarled oak clung to the ridges of an occasional arroyo. The Jeep rattled over a cattle guard and picked up speed, stirring the dry dirt into a cloud of red dust that floated along behind them like the tail of a giant kite.

The day was as dark and dreary as Gloria's mood. Gray clouds banked the northern sky, and the wind was damp and cold. Warm air from the heater blew on her legs and wafted up, making the inside of the car toasty warm. Gloria sat huddled in the corner, listening to the merry sound of her son playing with the puppy and the kitten. The dog barked, the kitten jumped up on Jack's shoulder, and Peter shrieked. Gloria couldn't even imagine Marvin in a situation such as this. She glanced at Jack. He didn't seem to even notice the confusion; in fact he seemed to be enjoying it.

When they reached Hangtown, Gloria understood what her aunt had meant when she said it was a ghost town. The main street wound steeply up a slope and ended abruptly at the bottom of a huge tailing dump below a gaping hole in the mountain and the relic of a mill that clung precariously to the side of it. Beyond that rose the shoulder of the mountain, its slopes covered with blue spruce, pine, and aspen. On each side of the street was a straggled line of old and weathered buildings; the roofs of some were caved in, their windows were mostly without glass, and their doors were missing or hanging by one hinge, making them look gaunt and cadaverous. An imposing false-fronted "saloon" sat on the corner and lorded it over the stores, which were all fronted by a sagging boardwalk. Some of the structures leaned one way, some another, some seemed in imminent danger of collapsing, and indeed several of those without stone foundations had.

"Welcome to Hangtown. The population is now four people, two dogs, six cats, and an ever-fluctuating number of wild animals."

"Who lives there?" she asked, pointing to the smoke

curling upward from a cobblestone chimney at the end of the town.

"Another, slightly older hippie by the name of Cliff Rice. He's a part-time prospector."

Jack had stopped the Jeep in front of a building that had a new door and shiny new windows. The porch and steps had been replaced, but left unpainted. A CB antenna was attached to the side of the building and seemed to Gloria to be grossly out of place. She felt as if she had stepped back into time and that at any moment the saloon door would swing open and she would hear the tinkling sound of a piano. She looked down the dusty street, almost expecting to see a group of horsemen ride into town with blazing six-shooters.

Forgetting her earlier hostility she turned shining eyes to Jack. "It's right out of a John Wayne movie!"

"You like it?"

"Of course. I'm a Western fan. I read every Western novel I get my hands on."

He chuckled. "The ones, I suppose, where the hero and heroine ride off into the sunset and live happily ever after?"

"So? What's wrong with living happily ever after? When I finish a book I want to leave it with the feeling that all is right with the people I've met in the story. A bad ending leaves me depressed."

"You've got something there. If you want to feel depressed, you can read the newspaper."

"At least we agree about something."

"We agree about a lot of things, Glory, Glory. You just don't realize it yet." His hand reached out and gripped her shoulder. "You and Peter will stay here in Hangtown until I find out which way the wind is blowing, okay?"

"Okay," she said reluctantly. "But it'll only delay the inevitable."

"Have a little faith in me, honey."

Peter jumped out of the car and the puppy followed. "I want to see your dog. I want to see Ringo."

"Hold it! Ringo's down with Cliff. We'd better leave him there until he gets acquainted with Cisco."

"Peter! Come back!" Gloria called anxiously.

"He'll be all right. He knows not to go into any of the buildings and to stay in sight. He's a smart boy."

She looked into his eyes and thought for the hundredth time that it should be a crime for a man to have such beautiful, expressive eyes. They were soft and moved lovingly over her face as his fingertips caressed her neck. *He fully intends to take advantage of the situation and seduce me into his bed again!* The bitter, shocking thought rocked her. Blood drained from her face, and her heartbeat slowed to a dull thud.

"I won't!"

"You won't what?"

"Sleep with you again!"

He laughed. "Want to bet on it?"

"You're conceited and crude!"

"Yeah, I am. Come to think about it, we didn't do much *sleeping* that night, did we?"

"You may think I'm old-fashioned and super-straight, but as I told you before, I don't sleep around."

"Thank God!"

"What does that mean?"

"It means that I'm glad you don't sleep around." His eyes were sparkling with laughter.

"Don't you dare laugh at me, you . . . you hairy ape!"

"If you're worried about your reputation, we can get married."

"That's very kind of you." She murmured softly, suddenly self-conscious. "Thank you very much, but I must decline your most generous offer to *save* my reputation."

"Good. I don't want you to marry me out of gratitude. I don't want you to marry me for any reason except the right one."

"And that is?" Her throat was tight, and the words were difficult to get out.

"Love, little sweet one. Love, spelled L-O-V-E. The only way I'll marry you is if you love me madly and want to live with me for the rest of your life, and because you want to share my dreams, my problems, raise my children, and be my companion as we grow old." His eyes raced over her and then rested on her trembling lips. She thought he was going to kiss her, and she moved back quickly.

"Is that all, Mr. Evans?"

"No, Glory, Glory. That isn't all. I want you to want me every night of my life as you did the other night. I want you to give yourself to me, laugh, play, break out of that shell you've built around yourself. I want to take care of you and Peter. I want to be the most important person in your lives."

"You think that covers all the bases, don't you? What about what *I* want?" The question was meant to sound menacing, as she tried to hide her confused thoughts behind anger. She felt as if she were floating away, losing control of her senses.

"What do you want, pretty girl?" He tugged at a strand of her hair and leaned close so he could look into her face.

Pride kept her rigid. "I *don't* want to raise my son in a hippie commune. I want more security for him than that! I want us to live a more structured life: steady income, a roof over our heads, a chance to make friends, plant roots somewhere. I want permanence."

"That's important to you, huh? You had all of that with the stuffed shirt." He yanked her to him, lowered his head, and kissed her softly, then more urgently. It took her breath from her. She struggled without success, and then finally surrendered to his superior strength. At last he lifted his head. His arms held her so tightly, she thought she would faint, and the blood pounded in her temples.

"You don't know what you want, Glory, Glory," he muttered. "I *know* that I want you in my life, in my bed, and . . . hell! I want you, period!" He grabbed her hand and held it against the aching hardness that throbbed between his legs. When she gasped and tried to pull her hand away, he tightened his grip on her wrist and held it there. "You've done that to me. You do it almost every time I'm with you. Dammit! Do you think I *want* to think of you every waking moment? I haven't had a peaceful moment since I met you. Sometimes I get so frustrated I could beat you!" She winced at the anger in his voice and tried to return his gaze coolly.

"Don't you threaten me, you . . . sex maniac!"

His scorching eyes ran over each feature of her face;

then he laughed, a deep, rumbling, masculine laugh that boomed in her ears. He moved his face close to hers and tickled the end of her nose with his mustache. His eyes were sparkling green pools of amusement.

"Oh, Glory, you're a lot of things, but boring isn't one of them. You'd make a wonderful wife for a . . . sex maniac. It's almost as much fun to tease you as it is to make love to you. C'mon, honey. Melt a little and kiss me back."

Gloria squeezed her eyelids tightly together and tried desperately not to think about how warm and comforting it was to be in his arms. She fought the temptation to yield to the persuasive voice and gentle, coaxing lips. She was concentrating so hard that his hand moved under her jacket, and his long fingers delved beneath the waistband of her jeans and thin panties, and cupped the fullness of her rounded naked bottom before she came out of her trance.

"Stop that! Get your sneaky hand out of there!" she demanded. She pushed on his chest with all her strength. The arm across her shoulders tightened, the fingers in her jeans pinched her bottom. She let out a shriek. "Stop that!"

"Not until you kiss me." Laughter lines crinkled the corners of his eyes.

Gloria considered kicking him, but decided to capitulate due to his superior strength. She despised herself for doing it, but she forced herself to kiss him lightly on the lips, then moved her face as far back as his hold on her would allow.

"That won't do a-tall—not a-tall," he drawled. "Put your arms around my neck and kiss me like I know you can." His voice was a husky whisper, stirring little waves of response inside of her.

"What about Peter?"

"Happily playing on the porch," he murmured. His fingers caressed her flesh and traveled gently down the valley between her buttocks.

Gloria's arms moved up and around his neck, and she closed her eyes as she placed her mouth on his. A low triumphant sound came from his throat, crowing his power over her, but she didn't care anymore. When he lifted his lips to demand that she open her mouth, she unhesitantly obeyed. His tongue stroked her smooth, even lips, and the hand in her jeans caressed her bottom. Gloria felt a sudden rip in the fabric of her resentment that she had so tenuously wrapped around herself as protection from him. Swamped as she was by mounting desire, it became impossible for her to remain passive. Every cell in her body surged to life, blocking out everything except the touch of his mouth, the warm strength of his arms, and the gentle fingers inside her jeans.

A banging on the car door brought Gloria out of the haze and into the present. Her mind was foggy. Jack raised his mouth from hers and she looked over her shoulder to see Peter peering at them through the window. Jack reached across her lap and cranked down the window.

"How ya doin', Bronco?"

"What was you doing to Mom?"

"I was kissing her."

"Did she want you to?"

"Yeah—I think so."

Peter frowned. "Did you, Mom? Did you want Jack to kiss you?"

Gloria saw the worry on his small face. "Yes, I did. Grown-ups . . . ah . . . like to kiss . . . sometimes."

"You never kissed *him!* You like Jack, don't you, Mom?" Peter said hopefully. "You like him a lot?"

"Sure she does," Jack said, and the fingers in her jeans pinched gently.

"Okay . . . you can kiss her."

"Thanks, ol' man. We'll talk about this sometime, but now we'd better get inside and get you settled in before it gets dark. Get a hold on Cisco," Jack called, and reluctantly withdrew his hand from Gloria's naked flesh. He reached behind the seat for a leash and tossed it out to Peter. "Tie him up, Bronco. He doesn't know enough yet to stay away from a skunk." The arm around Gloria shook her gently in an attempt to make her look at him. She gazed out the window, and he spoke to her profile. "The sacrifices a man must make sometimes are enough to tear him up."

"Bull—"

"Don't be crude, sweetheart! Come on, shake a leg. If you're nice, I'll give you the fifty-cent tour of my home."

When Gloria stepped inside Jack's house, her first thought was that he had obviously put a lot of work into fixing it up. The long narrow main room was insulated and paneled. A big iron cookstove sat along side a white refrigerator-freezer. The room was sparsely furnished, but comfortable. A queen-size bed and bookshelves dominated the far end of the room. The living space, kitchen, and sleeping area all flowed together and were amazingly neat.

"No electricity, so there's no TV," Jack said on his way to the back of the room with a suitcase under each arm. "Also, the bathroom is out back. There's hot water in the cookstove reservoir, if you can bathe in a washtub."

"If there's no electricity, how does the refrigerator work?"

"Bottled gas, sweetheart. We've also got a gaslight. By the way, back in the town's heyday, this building was the funeral parlor," he said gleefully as he went out the door.

"Wonderful," Gloria snapped over her shoulder. A small hand tugged at hers, and she looked down at her son.

"You like it here, don't you, Mom? Can we stay with Jack? You like him, don't you?"

The tight, worried, anxious little face pulled at her heartstrings. She knelt down beside him and folded him in her arms.

"Is that what you want to do, Peter?"

"I love Jack. He won't let *him* take us back."

"And I love you. We can't stay here forever, honey, but we'll stay a little while. Later on we must find us a place where I can get a job. Next year you'll be going to school." She tried to keep the anxiety out of her voice.

"Are we having a family conference?" Jack asked when he came in carrying the rest of the luggage. "If so, I want in on it."

"Mom says we'll stay here a little while, Jack. Then she's got to get a job in a town where I can go to school. When I grow up I'll get a job and take care of Mom."

Tears welled up in Gloria's eyes and she hugged her

small son to her so he wouldn't see them, but she couldn't hide them from Jack.

"Ya just might have ta fight me fer the job, Bronco," Jack murmured in a staged voice. "C'mon, put up yer dukes!" He crouched and doubled up his fists. Shrieking with laughter, Peter broke out of his mother's embrace. He knotted his small fists and began to pound Jack on the thigh. Jack groaned and doubled over as if in pain.

Gloria hastily wiped her tear-drenched eyes. Obviously Jack had played this game with her son before. With Jack, Peter was not at all quiet and withdrawn as he had been back in Ohio, where he had experienced Marvin's dislike. Now he was a personable, outgoing little boy, and Jack was responsible for the change. *Jack's enjoying himself, too,* Gloria thought. *He really and truly likes Peter!*

Jack lit the gas lamp and added more fuel to the cookstove. "When it gets really cold, I fire up the potbellied stove, too, and the two stoves keep this place surprisingly warm. But most of the time the cookstove is enough. How about ham and eggs for supper?"

"Fine. I'll fix it." Gloria dipped water from the reservoir and washed her hands in the granite washbowl. She could see Jack watching her. She'd show him that she wasn't helpless in these primitive surroundings. Her grandmother, on the farm in Ohio, had a wood-burning cookstove. She'd spent summers with her while she was growing up. She'd learned how to build up the fire, shake down the ashes, and bank it for the night. "Move out of the way, I'll have supper ready in no time," she said, lifting the stove lid and setting an iron skillet directly over the flame.

"Hummm . . . hidden talents. This woman is keeping secrets from me." He watched her as she placed the slices of ham in the skillet. "Cook plenty, honey. I'm hungry as a bear." She raised her brows and looked pointedly at his beard. He laughed and scratched his chin. "You'd better get used to it, Glory. I'd sure hate to shave off these *glorious* whiskers. It's taken two years to grow them." When she didn't answer, he said, "No comment?"

"No comment."

"Okay. I'll leave it to you. I've got a bedroll and a camp cot in the back room. I'll make up a bed . . . for Peter," he added softly as he passed her.

Gloria's back stiffened, but she refused to rise to the bait.

CHAPTER TEN

IN SPITE OF the nagging feeling that she and Peter should not be here, that everything she'd ever believed in revolted at the thought of living in this primitive outback with a man like Jack Evans, Glory felt safe and peacefully content. She realized that if anyone could help her out of the predicament she was in, it was Jack.

After dinner she gave Peter a sponge bath, put him in his flannel pajamas, and tucked him in the big bed. He called for Jack to come and say good-night, then was almost instantly asleep.

Gloria was standing with her hands on her hips wondering how she was going to change her clothes, much less bathe herself, when she felt his hands on her shoulders. She jumped, and her frightened heart began to pound.

"Did I scare you?" Jack murmured.

"Don't sneak up on me like that."

He grinned. "I wasn't sneaking. You didn't hear me because your mind was far away. Peter is asleep."

"You must have worn him out today."

"Come sit down."

"I'm trying to figure out how I can hang a sheet in the corner so I'll have some privacy to bathe."

"Why? I've already seen all of you. Remember?"

"Yes!" she snapped. "And you're no gentleman to remind me!"

"I guess I'm no gentleman to ask you this either—but do you have to use the bathroom?" When she didn't answer, he laughed softly. "Embarrassed, sweetheart? Don't be. It's a natural function. I noticed you let Peter go outside the back door. Do you want me to get a chamber pot for him when I go to town?"

"No need. We'll only be here a day or two."

He took his jacket from the peg on the wall and draped it around her shoulders. He put a flashlight in her hand. "Come on. I'll point you in the right direction and wait in case you're attacked by a band of marauding Indians." The tone of his voice was light and teasing and intimate.

This is absolutely unreal, Gloria thought as he guided her to the door with an arm about her waist. Unreal as it was, she had never been as physically aware of a man as she was this big, gruff, hairy, sometimes aggravating man, who was so thoughtful of her and her son. Equally unreal was the overwhelming feeling of security she had when she was with him.

The new privy stood like a sentinel in the light from the sliver of moon coming up over the crest of the mountain. Gloria was not a stranger to outdoor toilets and realized this one had been constructed for comfort as well as for privacy and sanitation. She chuckled when she saw the reading material stacked neatly on the bench—*Sports Illustrated, Field and Stream, Playboy.* She'd have to bring out *Women's World,* she thought with a suppressed giggle. But on second thought it was too cold to linger longer than was absolutely necessary.

Jack was waiting for her on the path. "I'll go down and see old Cliff while you get ready for bed."

"It's awfully dark, isn't it?"

"Are you afraid?"

"No."

"Good girl. Will fifteen minutes give you enough time?"

"I suppose so. What about Peeping Toms? You don't have shades." He stood close to her and she had to tilt her head to look into his eyes.

"We usually have only four-legged Peeping Toms, but tonight there might be a two-legged one." He stuck out his tongue and began to pant and breathe heavily.

"Stop teasing, you . . . fathead!" Laughing, she turned the beam of the flashlight on his face in retaliation.

"Gimme that, you squirrely little screwball!" He put his arms around her and snatched the flashlight from her hand. Her low, soft laugh pleased every part of him. "I like to hear you laugh, Glory."

"Do you, now?" she murmured flippantly. "Here's your jacket. Get lost and don't come back for at least fifteen minutes."

She thrust the fleece-lined coat into his hands and stepped into the building. She closed the door, leaned her back against it, and wondered if she had lost her mind. Just being with him brought her pure, happy enjoyment. She *was* in love with this man; she was deeply, desperately, head over heels in love with this unconventional social outcast. She felt her heart leap, then settle into a pounding that left her breathless. Nothing good could come from loving such a man, her practical mind told her. But, oh, God, the gentle way he had kissed her! It couldn't have been a lie; he did care for her. She stood there for a long while trying to accept this totally impossible situation.

Gloria was in her long granny gown and woolly robe when Jack knocked on the back door. When he came in, he had a stack of firewood in his arms.

"It's going to get cold tonight." He knelt down in front of the cookstove and shoved in a few sticks of wood.

Gloria stared at his broad back, his shaggy dark hair. He was a sweet and gentle man, but he could be angry and violent too. What made him this way? she wondered. She searched her memory for a scrap of information about his past and realized that although she had been intimate with him, he had told her absolutely nothing about himself.

He stood up and closed the firebox door with his foot. "In the morning I'll start a fire in the heater and bring in enough wood to keep you warm all day. I told Cliff I'd be gone for a while tomorrow and for him to stick around."

"You're leaving us here alone?"

"Do you mind?"

"No. I'm surprised. I didn't think you'd bring us out here and leave us." Gloria turned to hide the disappointment on her face.

Jack walked over and stood beside her. "I'm not abandoning you and Peter. You're safe here. I'm going into town to make a few phone calls; I know a lawyer in Chicago who can tell us what we're up against. Trust me, sweetheart. Masterson won't find you here, but if by some miracle he does, I'll not let him take you and Peter back to Ohio."

"He might find you."

"I hope so. It'll save me the trouble of looking for him."

"Oh, Jack—"

"Don't worry. Everything is going to be all right. I promise."

"I don't see how," she said grimly. "He *buys* everything! He'll file charges against you and have you put in jail!" Her face creased in worry lines, and she gripped his upper arms. "I don't want you to get in trouble on our account."

"Would it bother you if I was in trouble?" His voice was soft and his beautiful green eyes were achingly anxious. Gloria yearned to tell him it would devastate her if he was in trouble, but of course she couldn't do *that*.

"You know it would! You've been a good . . . friend."

"Friend?" The word came out slowly. "I want to be your friend, but I want to be your husband and your lover too." Her head was lowered, but the raw pain in his voice made her raise her eyes and look deeply into his. They stood for a long, silent moment, gazing at each other as if mesmerized, and then he said softly, "It's strange, Glory, I didn't think I was ready for a woman in my life. But I stayed away from you, and discovered I'm only half alive when I'm not with you."

Gloria's hands dropped from his arms and she moved away from him. She stood with her back to him, her head bowed. *Oh, Lord,* she thought. *I don't want to hurt him! If I only had myself to consider, I'd live with him and take what happiness I could get. But I've got Peter. I want my son to know the security of belonging to a family, not to be attached to someone who would be here today and gone tomorrow. I can't tie myself to a man who is content to live a hand-to-mouth existence.*

"Please understand. I've got to think of Peter."

"It's a short life we live, Glory. How people feel about each other is much more important than money."

"I know that. Oh, how I know that. It's other things, Jack. Please don't talk about it."

He pulled her back against him. "When I'm near you, I can't keep my hands off you," he whispered in her ear. "It's more than wanting to take you to bed, it's wanting to hold you gently, take care of you, have you there when I wake in the morning, and all the rest of the day."

She turned and put her arms around his neck. "Oh, Jack, I don't want to hurt you. I don't know what I would have done without you these last few weeks. You've been so good to me and to Peter." She began to cry, silently, with tears streaming down her face.

"Sweetheart, don't cry. I know what's bothering you. You think I'm a lazy, shiftless bum, squatting on another man's property. You think I'm a social dropout living on welfare, and you'd be ashamed to take me home to your folks." She buried her face against him and refused to look at him. He held her for a long while, stroking her back. "It's all right, my honey, my love." The words were torn from him in an agonized whisper.

"I owe you so much."

His hands on her back stopped for a minute. He took a deep breath. "Mention that again, dear heart, and I'll have to do one of two things—spank you, or kiss you. You *owe* me absolutely nothing." His voice was shaky and his breathing ragged in her ear. "Come sit with me and let me hold you."

Jack took the Indian blanket from the back of the big armchair, sat down, and drew her carefully down on his lap. He held her tightly to him and tucked the blanket around her. It was like holding a skinny little kitten, he thought, cuddling her close against his chest. His face was engulfed in the fragrance of her hair, and her body felt warm against his. He drew a very unsteady breath, his mind racing, thoughts of the past and the future tumbling over each other.

Glory, Glory, I was so sure that after I lost Wendy, I'd never love anything or anyone again. And here I am, desperately, hopelessly in love with you. I want you for my wife. I want to raise Peter as my son, I want us to be a family. I want! I want! His mind skidded in another direction and he thought with a sudden realization—*Evans, you bastard! You want it all without giving up a thing!*

An hour passed while his mind grappled with endless questions. He tilted his head so he could look into the face of the woman in his arms. She was asleep, and she was softly, sweetly, sublimely beautiful! He looked at her as if seeing her for the first time. He had never noticed the unbelievable delicacy of her face, her bones, her shell-pink ear, so perfectly formed. Her pink lips were slightly parted and the breath that came from them was warm and moist; he fought the urge to kiss them lest he awaken her. She was a curious combination of innocence and sensuality, which had become an obsession with him. He felt lightheaded with all the swelling and churning going on inside him.

Long past midnight Jack rose from the chair with Gloria in his arms and carried her to the big bed. He stood holding her for a long moment, reluctant to put her down. Then he gently placed her beside Peter and covered them. He turned off the light and went back to the chair. He had some heavy thinking to do before morning.

As soon as Gloria was awake, she knew that she and Peter were alone in the building. The room was filled with light. She sat up in bed and looked toward the front windows. There was snow on the roof of the building across the street. She slipped her bare feet into her slippers and picked up the robe that lay on the foot of the bed. While putting it on she crossed the room and peered out the window. A foot of snow covered the ground. The entire town looked fresh and clean.

She stared at the empty space in front of the building where Jack had left the Jeep last night. The fact that there were no tracks in the snow told her he must have left hours ago. Snow was still coming down in huge fluffy flakes. It seemed to her the whole world was white, silent, and eerie, and she and Peter were alone in the center of it.

A tight little core of misery, Gloria stood beside the window looking out on the vastness, her body erect, her eyes wide and unseeing, her heart beating in painful bursts. Confused and terribly lonely, she wondered how she would get through the day.

When Peter awakened he was disappointed to find that Jack had gone. He sulked through breakfast, but brightened with the promise that he could go out and play in the snow. It took ten minutes to get him into his snowsuit and boots and out the door; in another ten minutes, however, he was back inside. It wasn't much fun playing alone; Gloria understood. She let him sit at the table with a pencil and paper, but that didn't last long either.

"When's Jack coming back?" He asked for what seemed like the hundredth time.

"I don't know, honey. He'll be back sometime today. Why don't you play with the kitten?"

"Mom . . ."

"Sshhh! I hear something." Gloria went to the window and looked down the snow-covered street. The empty buildings stood gaunt and lonely, like silent sentinels, on either side of it. The sound that had alerted her was louder now; it reminded her of the buzz saw her grandfather had used on the farm in Ohio.

But it wasn't a buzz saw. Two squat, dark objects came skimming over the snow. Snowmobiles. They came into town from the far end, stirring up a fine flurry of snow in their wake. The dark-clad, helmeted figures looked as if they were from outer space. The machines came through town and stopped in front of the building where Jack lived as if they knew exactly where they were going.

Gloria darted back from the window. Fright set her heart pounding like a drum.

"Come here, Peter," she whispered. Frightened by the urgency in his mother's voice, Peter ran to her. Gloria wrapped her arms around him and the two of them crouched in the corner beside the door.

"Be quiet, honey!"

"Who is it?"

"I don't know, but—" The sharp rap on the door cut off her words. She glanced quickly to assure herself that the bar was in place. The loud banging came again. Gloria's fear was slowly turning to panic. Marvin had sent someone to get her and Peter!

"He ain't here," the man on the porch yelled to his companion.

"There's a fire inside."

"Yeah, he probably built it up before he left. He'll be back. We might meet him on the road."

"How about the old man down at the other end?"

"He don't know nothin'. Let's go."

When the roar of the motors had faded in the distance, Gloria drew a deep breath and released Peter so he could go look out the window.

"They're gone, Mom. Why didn't we talk to them?"

Gloria didn't answer her son. She was more aware than ever that the drama with Marvin was still unfinished. She tried not to think about it, because to think about it made her feel hopelessly panicked.

Irrationally Gloria felt outraged at Jack. Jack had deserted her when she most needed him. Her anger soon threatened to give way to tears; she now realized how much she had grown to depend on him. She pulled herself together and took a roast from the freezer; if she didn't keep busy she'd lose her mind, she thought as she worked with quick, jerky motions. A voice in her head berated her: *See what happens, you jerk, when you count on a man like Jack Evans? He takes you to the middle of nowhere and goes off and leaves you.*

Instantly she was ashamed, and she made herself breathe deeply to calm herself. "What if those men were thugs Marvin had sent to beat him up! Please, God, don't let them find him, don't let anything happen to him!" The thought haunted her mind.

It was the longest, most miserable day of Gloria's life. From the moment the men on the snowmobiles left town she had a sick, uneasy feeling in the pit of her stomach. At first she was angry because Jack had left her without saying where he was going or what he was going to do. Then, after thinking about it, she decided that Jack was a man who explained himself to no one. Life with him would be one crisis after another.

"But, oh, dear God," she muttered to herself. "I love him and I'd be far more unhappy without him than with him."

Jack looked out the window of the phone booth and watched the snowplow scraping the street while he listened to George Fisher, his lawyer and friend.

"If he's got a court order there isn't much you can do, Jack. I know the arrogant, puffed-up son of a bitch; he wants to be governor of Ohio so bad he can taste it. I'd run a bluff on him if I were you. You could tell him you'll take him to court for mentally abusing the child. The newspapers would love it."

"That's a good idea, George."

"Are you in love with the woman, Jack?"

"Absolutely."

"I'm glad for you. You've needed something stable in your life for a long time."

"By the way, I'm not coming back to Chicago. If you get a chance to sell the apartment houses, go ahead."

"It's been a good income. Are you sure you want out of the real estate business completely?"

"I'll keep Hangtown. Let the rest go, George. I want to try my hand at running a motel. A few years down the line I might even consider making Hangtown a tourist attraction."

"I don't doubt that you'd do it, if you set your mind to it. Okay, I'll put the apartments up for sale."

"I might have to get back to you about Masterson. He's not getting his hands on Gloria and Peter. If I can't run a bluff on him, I'll take him to court; then you might end up with the apartment houses."

"Just don't lose your temper and get arrested for assault and battery."

Jack laughed. "I'll give it a good try. Bye."

He turned up the collar of his coat, left the booth, and walked quickly down the street to the hotel. The black limousine in the parking lot could only belong to Masterson.

"What room is Masterson in?" he asked the desk clerk.

"Two oh three." The clerk looked up and stared at the big man in a fur-lined jacket with snowflakes on his thick, dark hair and beard. "But . . ."

"But what?" Jack's green eyes bored into the man's face.

"Nothing."

Jack didn't wait for the elevator. He took the stairs two at a time. He rapped on the door of room 203.

"Who is it?"

"Room service."

The door swung wide open and Jack was inside before

Marvin could stop him. He sputtered and drew several deep breaths before he could regain his composure.

"Get out of here!"

"In a minute," Jack said evenly. "I want to make a few things clear to you."

"Get out, or I'll call the police."

"You try it, and I'll break your arm." Jack spoke softly, but he stared fixedly at Marvin.

"I've put in a call for the sheriff. He'll be here any moment."

"Then you'd better listen to what I have to say before he gets here. I just talked to my lawyer in Chicago, who, by the way, is a good friend of the chairman of the Republican party in your district."

"So what?" Marvin sneered. "I'm one of the largest contributors to the party."

"So this, you bastard!" Jack took a step forward and grabbed the front of Marvin's shirt. "If you make another move to force Gloria to come back to you, you'll find yourself in court on child abuse charges. Then the Republican party will dissociate themselves from you so fast it'll make your head swim, with or without your large donations."

"Why—why, I've never laid a hand on that kid!"

"There is such a thing as *mental* abuse, you know. That kid is scared to death of you! I wonder how the voters in your district would feel about a candidate who abused his wife *and* his child?"

Marvin's cheeks turned red. "I never abused her. I never even touched her after our wedding night."

Jack stood back and scratched his beard. "There's not a red-blooded man in your district who'd understand a man having a wife like Gloria and sleeping with her *one* time in five years. That would make mighty good copy for the tabloids."

"Damn you! I gave her everything."

"Everything but love and companionship."

"What can *you* give her? Look at you," Marvin sneered. "She wouldn't have been seen on the streets of Cincinnati talking to you."

"Maybe. Maybe not. But I've got a heart full of love for that woman, and, by God, you'd better leave her alone and flag your ass out of town while you've got one to flag. Gloria is through with you. Do I make myself clear? So get on the phone and call that judge, or I'm setting the wheels in motion that will ruin your political career whether a jury finds you guilty or not."

"It's blackmail!"

"Yeah."

Ten minutes later Jack left the room with the court order in his pocket and a smile on his face. He met the sheriff on the stairs and nodded a greeting as they passed.

CHAPTER ELEVEN

AFTERNOON TURNED INTO evening. Gloria fixed dinner for herself and Peter and made a pretense of eating with him. He was unusually quiet, and when she suggested he get ready for bed, he went willingly. She put him in the sleeping bag on the cot, and before she'd finished reading him a bedtime story, he was asleep. It was only seven o'clock, but to Gloria it seemed like the middle of the night.

She washed the dishes and put the roast in the warming oven of the cookstove. After that she filled the firebox and that of the potbellied stove with fuel Jack had left in the woodbox. She suddenly understood how the pioneer woman, alone with her children in an isolated cabin, must have felt as she waited for her man to come home from a dangerous mission. Almost without realizing it she went to Jack's old leather jacket hanging on a peg beside the door and buried her face in the soft lining. The familiar smell of his maleness brought a flood of tears to her eyes. She turned out the gas light, plunging the room into darkness, and took up vigil beside the window.

Minutes turned into hours. She became chilled, and

reached for the jacket to drape about her shoulders. She found herself obsessed with the memory of Jack's face, especially his beautiful green eyes. She had seen those eyes in so many different moods; they had laughed, teased, smiled, grown fierce with anger. She found she could not bear to think of them looking into hers with icy coolness in their depths, or into another woman's with warmth and love. She wondered if she would be able to bear the loneliness if she went away from him for good. *It's lonely now, knowing he'll be back,* she told herself, *but how would it be if I knew he'd never . . .* She shook her head, not wanting to think about it. She strained her eyes toward the horizon, watching and waiting for a moving speck, anything that would mean Jack was on his way home.

When she finally saw headlights in the darkness, she didn't know if she was sorry or glad; they could mean the two men were coming back, or they could mean Jack had returned. But soon she could see that it was one vehicle and not two separate ones. The lights came steadily forward, at times bright, at other times blurred, as the wheels stirred the light, fluffy snow.

When at last she could see the outline of the Jeep, such an overwhelming gush of relief swept over her that at first she felt weak and sagged against the window. By the time the Jeep had stopped in front of the building, new life had surged through her and she flung open the door and vaulted out onto the snow-covered porch.

"Jack!"

The lights and the motor were turned off and the door opened almost at the same time. Gloria jumped off the porch into knee-deep snow and struggled to reach the man getting out of the car.

"Jack! Oh, Jack—"

"Gloria, baby! What's wrong?" He came to meet her. She threw herself into his embrace. He clasped her to him, trying to hold her up out of the snow. Her arms were around him and her face pressed against his chest.

"I love you! Oh, I love you, Jack!" She sobbed. "I was so afraid they'd find you and hurt you. Don't leave me again!" Her arms tightened fiercely.

"It's all okay, baby. Everything's taken care of. Oh, my God! You'll freeze! You don't even have on a coat." He lifted her up in his arms and walked carefully, searching with his booted foot for the steps in the snow, then carried her into the building and kicked the door shut. "It's pitch-black in here."

"Did you hear what I said? I said, I love you." Gloria's voice was loud and insistent. "I want to live with you. I don't care if it's here . . . or in a shack . . . or on the road. . . . I'll get Peter to school somehow. Did you hear me, Jack?" she went on anxiously. "I love you . . . you idiot! Say something! Have you changed your mind about me?"

"Yes, I heard you, sweet and pretty girl. And I'll never hear words more beautiful," Jack said softly, and stood her on her feet. "And, no, I've not changed my mind about you. The day was a year long while I was trying to do what I had to do so I could get back to you." He wrapped her in his arms and strained her to him. "Say it again, sweetheart."

"I love you . . . Peter loves you. We need you," she whispered hoarsely, breathlessly.

"And I love you." He felt as if he would weep. "Oh, sweetheart, we've got to get a light on and get you out of those wet jeans. Stay right here."

Jack found his way to the gaslight and lit it. Gloria blinked against the brightness, then her mouth dropped open as she gazed in stunned silence at the stranger looking back at her.

Handsome? No, beautiful. The curly dark hair was cut and styled to cover just the tops of his ears, and was lightly dusted with snow. His cheeks were flat, clean plains that sloped to a strong, square chin beneath his wide mouth. But for the moment his quizzical green eyes commanded all her attention; they were all that was familiar to her.

"Jack!" she moaned. "Say something so I'll know it's you."

"Glory, Glory, sweetheart—"

"You're a . . . stranger!"

"No. I'm the same. I'm the same on the inside."

"But . . . you loved the beard."

"I love you more."

"I don't know if . . . I like it."

He laughed, and the sound bounced into every corner of the room. "It'll take two years to grow another that long."

Gloria couldn't take her eyes off him. "It'll take some getting used to. Why did you do it?"

"I decided I couldn't face the next fifty years without you, and if you wanted a conventional husband, complete with clean-shaven face, three-piece suits and a briefcase, that's what you'd have—if I was lucky enough for you to accept me." The words fell from his lips softly and sincerely.

"I don't know what to say!" She ran to him and threw herself in his arms. "I'm sorry, darling. I don't want you to change. I want you like you are." Slim arms wrapped themselves around his neck. He saw her lips trembling into the shape of syllables that were surely endearments, but her tears made them unintelligible, so that what reached his ears was the strangled rasping of a sob.

"Silly girl. I've not changed. What's on the outside of me doesn't change what's on the inside. I love you. I'll make a home for you and Peter wherever you want it to be."

He held her so tight she could scarcely breathe. She turned her face and nuzzled the warm flesh of his neck. The crackle of the fire was the only sound she heard above the beating of his heart. Her arms slid from his neck to wrap around his waist. She pressed her full length against him.

"Darling," he groaned huskily. "You're wreaking havoc with my self-control. If I start kissing you the way I want to kiss you, I'll not be able to stop. We've got to get you out of these wet clothes or you'll be sick."

She raised her head to look at him. He was so close, she could see every little detail of his face: the smoldering green eyes, the strong nose, the sensual curve of his mouth. She could smell the masculine smell of his body, and an aching stirred inside her. Then his lips were against hers, rough and demanding with an insistence that sent her blood thundering through her ears. His hands moved down her back, touching her hungrily, urgently. Naked desire left her trembling in his arms.

Jack was breathing heavily. He moved his lips from hers and they traveled over her face and then, as if compelled, back to her mouth. He kissed her deeply.

"Glory, Glory . . ." He clasped her shoulders and pushed her from him. "Go get out of those wet clothes," he said almost crossly while his eyes lovingly devoured her.

She sat on his lap in the armchair beside the potbellied stove. The lamp was turned low, so that most of the room was in shadows. Gloria had put on her gown and robe, and Jack an old jogging suit and sheepskin slippers; the Indian blanket covered them. Her fingers moved gently over his face, tracing his lips, his brows. They were peacefully content to be together.

"I've got a lot to tell you," Jack murmured.

"I've something to tell you too. Two men were here today. I didn't go to the door."

"Good girl. In this case it would have been all right. I saw them down by Ethel's. They said they'd been here and there was a good plume of smoke coming out the chimney, so they knew someone was here. They're neighboring ranchers looking for a cat that's been bringing down their calves."

Gloria raised herself up so she could look at him. "I thought Marvin had sent them out here to hurt you."

"No, pretty girl. You can forget Marvin. I scared the pants off him. He'll not give you any more trouble."

"You what? Marvin isn't scared of anything. He'll hire thugs—"

"I scared him with the power of the press." Jack

laughed at the puzzled look on her face and pressed her head to his shoulder. "I talked to a friend of mine in Chicago and he suggested I run a bluff. But it really wasn't a bluff; I was prepared to drag him through the courts for mentally abusing that child. He's so set on a political career, he backed off and called the judge in Ohio and told him he was relinquishing custody rights and would allow me to adopt Peter. For the child's good, of course."

"Of course! Oh, Jack. Do you mean we don't have to worry about Marvin?"

"That's just what I mean, pretty girl." He kissed her lingeringly. "Glory, it's time I bared all the secrets of my sordid past, if you're going to share my future."

"I don't care about your past," Gloria said, suddenly frightened that what he would tell her would snatch away her happiness.

"I want to tell you . . . before I start making love to you. I may never stop." He punctuated the words with soft, loving kisses.

He proceeded to tell her about his marriage to his high-school sweetheart and how, because of their immaturity, the marriage had been doomed from the start. He told her about the divorce, and his wife's subsequent remarriage to a man with underworld connections that eventually led to her and his daughter's death.

"I felt I had failed Wendy. My spirits were at the lowest ebb of my life when I came here to Hangtown. My little girl had died in a faraway place. . . ." He paused and buried his face in her hair, then continued in a husky whisper. "I didn't care for anything or anybody. I was living in a kind of limbo until I met you and Peter. I kept thinking that if I could break out and reach you, I'd find peace."

"Oh, Jack! Oh, darling . . ." Gloria stroked his head. "And I was so nasty to you, so narrow minded!" Her face was against his, and she felt his wet lashes against her skin.

"She was just a little girl and she's gone." There was anguish in his voice.

Gloria cradled his head in her arms and kissed him on his brow. "No, darling. She isn't gone. She'll always be in your heart—as you'll be in mine."

"I fought back the only way I knew how—in the courts. I had a small real estate business and spent everything I made trying to get custody of Wendy. When it was over, I just drove out of town. I'd bought Hangtown several years before while I was out here on a hunting trip. So I came here and holed up, licking my wounds."

Gloria looked at him, her amber eyes filled with love. "I don't know that I would have done differently, under the same circumstances."

"I really am kind of a hippie, sweetheart. I own two apartment buildings in Chicago, and the rent money goes to pay the mortgages. There's a little left over, but not a lot. We can live here, and I'll get a job, or we can run Ethel's motel, and someday maybe turn this town into a tourist attraction. It's your choice."

"Are your intentions honorable, Mr. Evans?"

"Right at the moment? No way! Later, like tomorrow, we're jumping the broomstick together."

"Like the pioneers?"

"Like the pioneers."

"I've decided." She giggled happily. "We can run Aunt

Ethel's motel for now—then, later, I want to live right here in Hangtown. After all, how many women have a town all to themselves?"

"You're sure?"

"I was never more sure of anything in my life. Oh, darling, I'm so glad Peter and I came out here." Gloria's eyes became misty. "Jack, my sweet, wonderful bear of a man! Thank you! Peter and I were so afraid we'd have to go back to Ohio."

"The only man you'll ever have to obey again is me," he growled, and began to kiss her. "Hummm . . . you taste so good." His hand moved up under her gown and stroked the naked flesh of her thigh and hips. "Can we go to bed now?"

"Jack, be good. It's almost like kissing a stranger. I miss your beard!"

"You miss my beard?" His head came up and laughing green eyes caught laughing amber ones. "Good God, woman! For weeks you've been telling me I looked like a hairy ape. It cost me thirty bucks to get my hair cut and styled and my beard shaved off. I did it to please you, and almost froze my face on the way home."

She let out a girlish little gurgle of laughter.

"Poor baby," she crooned tenderly. "You can grow it back." She pulled his head down to hers and kissed him firmly on the lips. "But forget the earring!"

"Is there no pleasing you, little squirrely worry-wart?" he demanded, pinching her bottom gently.

"Yes. Did you notice that Peter is sleeping on the cot?"

"You bet! It's the first thing I noticed when I turned on the light."

"Well . . . ?"

Jack laughed joyously and hugged her close. "There's more I want to tell you, and I'd better do it now. Once I get you in that bed, there'll be no more talking." He began to kiss her and nuzzle her cheek with his nose. "Someday when we've made our fortune, we'll build a house right here in Hangtown."

"You're going to open up the town?"

"We'll have to wait and see about that. This is our town. We'll populate it ourselves."

"Ahhh . . . nice. . . ." She breathed against his cheek. "Can we get started now?"

"You wouldn't mind living out here?"

"Not as long as you're here and we're working on our . . . project of . . . populating the town." She stroked the dark curls back from his forehead, loving the freedom to caress him. This precious intimacy was making her light-headed with happiness.

"Our house will have two stories and plenty of bedrooms for Peter and his brothers and sisters. One for Aunt Ethel, too, if she is able to come." His voice grew husky as his lips moved over her face, but he continued determinedly. "It'll have a high-pitched roof, gables, a big porch with gingerbread, and a chandelier from Austria—all straight out of the 1870s. How does that sound?"

"Fine, but we've got to make our fortune first," she whispered, her lips taking up the kissing. "You can tell me about it tomorrow. Right now I'd rather find out what it's like to have a . . . sex maniac make love to me."

"You're not going to forget that, are you?" He laughed joyously and got to his feet with her in his arms.

"No. And I'm not going to let you forget it either. I

hope we're snowed in for a week," she said saucily, her amber eyes sparkling. She placed a little string of kisses along his jaw, and her fingers burrowed beneath his shirt and pulled at a tuft of hair on his chest. "Ya think you're pretty tough, don'tcha, big man?"

"I'm tough enough to handle you, mama chick. I'm from the Big Windy."

"Yeah . . . yeah . . . play it again, Sam."

"You're cruisin' for a bruisin', babe."

He dropped her on the bed and stood over her. She looked up at him with adoration in her eyes, but her voice was mockingly stern.

"Well, get on with it, tough guy, or I'll . . . break your arm!"

FOR MY READERS:

GLORIA'S YUMMY CAKE

    1 package chocolate cake mix
    ¾ cup butter or margarine
    ½ cup evaporated milk
    1 16-oz. package caramels
    1 cup chocolate chips
    1 cup nut meats
    Optional: 1 cup coconut
             Whipped cream

1. Preheat oven to 350° F.
2. Prepare chocolate cake batter according to directions on package. Bake ⅔ of the batter in a 9 x 13 pan and let cool.
3. In a double boiler melt together butter or margarine, milk, and caramels. Allow to cool and spread on cake.
4. Sprinkle chocolate chips and nut meats on top of cake. Coconut may be used instead of chocolate chips and nuts.
5. Dribble the remainder of the batter on top and bake for 15 minutes.
6. Allow to cool and serve with whipped cream.

More
Dorothy Garlock!

Please turn this page
for a preview of

On Tall Pine Lake

available in January 2007.

Prologue

NONA LOOKED DOWN at the package Mr. Dryden had given her.

"I wasn't expecting a package."

"It was delivered by a postman in a truck about an hour ago. I heard someone pounding on your door and went out into the hallway. The postman asked me if Nona Conrad lived there and when I said yes he asked me to give you this package."

"Thank you, Mr. Dryden." Nona tried to make out a return address, but the writing was smeared. "Mabel is doing some shopping this afternoon. Maggie won't be home until late. She wanted to see her friends one last time before we leave. I'm sorry you were bothered with this."

Nona went back into the apartment clutching the package. *What in the world could it be? I haven't ordered anything.* She opened the heavily taped package only to discover another package inside with a letter addressed to her on top. Pulling off the letter, she opened it and to her amazement discovered it was from her half-brother, Harold. She quickly scanned the contents of the letter and then slowly read it again with a puzzled look on her face.

> *Dear Nona,*
> *I know we have not been close in the past and I am sorry for it. Please keep this package until you hear from me. DO NOT OPEN IT UNLESS SOMETHING SHOULD HAPPEN TO ME! Regardless of how you feel about me, I do have feelings for you and Maggie and want to make up for the wrongs that I have done you. You are the only person in the world that I feel I can trust. I will explain everything when I see you. For the sake of our father, I'm asking you to do this one thing for me. I promise that I will have your money and Maggie's from our father's estate soon.*
>
> > *Your brother,*
> > *Harold*

Now he's my brother. Other times he's called himself our half-brother.

Nona's curiosity tempted her to open the package, but she resisted and buried it deep in the bottom of the suitcase she planned to take with her to Tall Pine Camp.

Mabel came into the apartment and shut the door behind her. "I've got a few things for us to take on the trip and to eat on the way."

"Are you ready to go?" Nona closed and locked her suitcase.

"Yes, the janitor helped me carry the things we're leaving behind in the storage shed. He said the owner told him to assure us they would be here when we wanted them."

"That was nice of him."

"Are we leaving tonight or waiting until morning?"

"We're leaving as soon as Maggie gets back."

The next afternoon, Mr. Dryden opened the door to two well-dressed men. The bald one did all the talking.

"Good afternoon, sir. We're from the U.S. Postal Department and are checking on a package that was delivered to this address, but we lack confirmation. You know how strict the government is about little things." He laughed. "Do you know who the package was delivered to?"

"A package came yesterday for Miss Conrad. She wasn't at home. The postman left it with me. He didn't ask me to sign for it. I gave it to Miss Conrad as soon as she got home."

"Thank you. I guess that takes care of it."

"It's a good thing it came yesterday because she has left for Tall Pine Lake. She accepted a job managing a camp there."

"You don't say? I've never heard of Tall Pine Lake."

"It's a beautiful place up in the Ozarks. You should visit sometime. There's fishing and hunting."

"How far is it from here?"

"I don't rightly know."

"Thank you, sir. You've been a big help. The United States government appreciates it."

As soon as the two men got into their car, the bald-headed man slapped the steering wheel with his palm.

"What do you think? Pretty slick, huh? I told you that blood was thicker than water and that she would be the one he would confide in."

"Yeah, it worked out better than I thought it would. All we've got to do now is find a map and locate Tall Pine Lake and then the camp where she is working."

chapter one

Home, Arkansas, 1980

Excuse me." Nona had come out of the small grocery store carrying two heavy sacks of groceries. She ran head-on into a man coming into the business. She hadn't hit him hard, but she felt the red sting of embarrassment just the same. Glancing up quickly, she saw that he was definitely a city man. He didn't look like a person who belonged in Home, Arkansas.

His clothes were expensive, certainly too new to have been worn long, unlike most of the men in town who wore faded work clothes that had seen many washings. His head was bald, but the black mustache on his upper lip was thick. Nona wondered why bald men were compelled to have hair on their faces. It was hard to tell if he was young or old. The coldness of his dark eyes surprised her. Her mind absorbed these impressions in a few seconds. She hadn't realized that she'd been staring until he reached out and grabbed her arm.

"Apology accepted," he mumbled through uneven teeth. Even from those two words, Nona could hear an accent but one that she couldn't place. With an expanding smile, the man added, "You're Mrs. Conrad, aren't you?"

"No," she answered, "I'm *Miss* Conrad."

"I was told you managed the camp at Tall Pine Lake. My friend and I are looking for a place to fish. Do you have a vacancy?"

"Not for a couple of weeks." The words came out of Nona's mouth before she'd given them any thought. Even though most of the cabins were currently empty, something about the man prompted her to lie.

"That's too bad," he said. "Are you sure?"

"Of course, I'm sure!" she snapped.

"It might be worth waiting for." His eyes began to roam across her body before settling on her breasts. The thumb on the hand that held her arm began to move across her skin in a caressing motion. Suddenly angry, Nona tried to jerk her arm away, but his grip tightened.

"Let go." Her voice was loud and strong. She felt a quiver of fear and looked around to see if anyone was near. Her hopes leapt as she saw a deliveryman carrying a large box toward the store.

But before she could say anything, the man abruptly released her arm, stepped back, and opened the door for the deliveryman, who quickly disappeared inside the store. Nona feared that the stranger would grab her again, but instead he said gruffly, "I'll be seeing you, Miss Conrad." With that, he turned and walked away.

For a moment, she stood frozen in front of the store. *He knew my name!*

Shaking the thought loose, Nona hurried to her car.

Ripe sunlight bathed the small town and the first hint of June's heat was in the air. The leaves of the maple and oak trees fluttered in the light breeze.

As she moved down the boardwalk, Nona caught sight of her reflection in the large window of the hardware store. Mr. Finnegan's window was full of saws, hammers, nails, and even an antique cast-iron stove, looking out of season in the warm weather. Amid the clutter, there was still enough space for her to clearly see a slim woman with a mop of curly, fiery red hair. It floated around her face like a halo. It was what drew people's eyes to her. She wore slacks and a tucked-in shirt. Nona thought she was only passably pretty. Although a small woman, she appeared taller because she carried herself proudly. She considered her large sky-blue eyes her best feature. They sparkled when she was angry or when she was extremely happy. She had a light sprinkling of freckles across her nose. When she was younger, she had hated her red hair, but now, she must accept it or dye it and she didn't want the bother of that. Although she preferred to be referred to by her name, she had grown used to being called "that red-haired girl."

Finally, she reached her car, a ten-year-old Ford, dust-covered from its travels down the dirt roads. When Nona moved to open the driver's door, she was startled to find another hand there before hers. In that split second, her heart sank at the thought that the strange man had followed her. But when she looked up, she found the bright eyes of a tall cowboy in a battered Stetson and a faded plaid shirt.

"Ma'am." A smile split the man's handsome, sun-browned face. "A pretty woman shouldn't be carrying such a load."

"My husband will be here shortly," Nona said defensively.

"He's a lucky man." The friendly cowboy opened the car door. "But until he gets here, let me help." Nona placed her bags on the seat and pushed them across to the other side. After she got into the car and slid under the wheel, the man shut the door behind her and stood at the open window.

"Thank you," she said softly.

"My pleasure. Good day, ma'am." He smiled warmly as he put his fingers to his hat brim. "Till we meet again." His grin was contagious; Nona couldn't help but return the smile.

She started the car, put it in reverse, and began to back out. The loud blast of a horn caused her to slam her foot down on the brakes. Glancing quickly over her shoulder, Nona saw the deliveryman frown at her before driving his truck past her and down the street. *Damn that bald-headed man! He's got me rattled.* When the road was clear behind her, she eased out and drove out of town.

Home, Arkansas, was a small town at the foot of the Ozark Mountains in the southwestern part of the state. It was the main supply hub for a twenty-square-mile area. Home got its unlikely name more than a hundred years ago when a travel-weary family from Ohio paused to spend the night along a clear stream. The man looked around, liked what he saw, and declared, "We're home."

The town was little more than two rows of business buildings that lined the main street. The businesses that remained in the Ozark Mountain town were the grocery store, hardware store, barbershop, pool hall, gun shop, and two cafes, Alice's Diner and the Grizzly Tavern, where a man could get nearly anything that he wanted to drink. Most evenings, the tavern was crowded to overflowing. Nona had learned all of this when she and Maggie came to town to attend the Baptist church, a small clapboard building that sat on the edge of town. Church was the ideal place to catch up on the local gossip.

The Ozark Mountains loomed over a wild and unsettled terrain. The merchants in Home depended on hunters, fishermen, and campers for their livelihoods and the region drew them in droves. This was not only a haven for hunters, but also hippies for the last ten years. The town was usually peaceful until sunset, when the roughnecks came to town. Nona was becoming fond of the rough little town and its wooded surroundings.

She drove east along a road that snaked through a heavily wooded area. The sound of the car's tires crunching over loose stone echoed off of the looming pines that lined both sides of her route. She had traveled this road at least once a week since she and Maggie, her sister, had come to manage the camp and had never been nervous about traveling it, but now for some reason she was uneasy as she drove away from town. Was it that the bald-headed man had held onto her arm so tightly? The encounter bothered her more than she was willing to admit.

After a couple of miles, Nona became aware of a black car coming up behind her. Furtively, she glanced in her rearview mirror. In the mirror, she could see a truck behind the car. It was probably old Mr. Wilson who lived on the other side of the lake. He was almost eighty years old.

Fearfully, Nona gripped the wheel. There was nothing along this lonely stretch of road until she came to the camp. She kept her eyes on the road and waited.

She would feel more comfortable when she made it to the turnoff to the camp! A little afraid but determined, Nona concentrated on her driving.

Glancing in the mirror, she was stunned to see the car pull out to pass her! Tapping on the brakes lightly to keep from spinning out of control, Nona saw that the driver was the bald-headed man who had grabbed her arm at the store. The black car passed her, and barreled on down the road. The man in the passenger seat didn't even glance at her. The car rounded a bend and was soon out of sight. For the next several miles, Nona kept expecting to see the car blocking the road, the man out, a gun in his hand.

Nona rounded an easy curve in the road and came within sight of Tall Pine Camp. She could not remember it looking so inviting. The manager's house itself wasn't much; it was the largest of the buildings but was otherwise identical to the seven other cabins set back from Tall Pine Lake. All of the cabins were roomy and painted a crisp shade of green. As she turned onto the lane leading to the cabins, Nona was proud of what she saw. With her sister Maggie's help she had cleaned the grounds around the cabins.

As she approached the three-room house she shared with her sister and Mabel Rogers, a longtime friend, her eyes roamed the campgrounds. A battered old house trailer sat near the lake. Russell Story, the old man who lived in the trailer, took care of the boats and the bait for the camp. He also cleaned, filleted, and packed the fish in ice for the camp guests. Aunt Mabel had won him over with her apple pie and in return he kept them well supplied with fresh fish.

"Oh, for crying out loud!"

Nona spat the words out as she came up the dirt road and turned her Ford into the drive in front of her cabin. For the second time in the last three days, the man who was staying in cabin number two had parked his pickup in her drive and she couldn't squeeze past it.

"Some people have a lot of nerve," she muttered angrily. She pressed her hand down on the horn and held it there. The horn's blaring bounced off the buildings and over the lake. Nona hoped it sounded as belligerent as she felt.

"Nona! Chill out!" Maggie shouted as she came down the steps of their cabin and knocked on the window of the passenger's side.

Nona let up on the horn, leaned over the seat, and rolled down the window.

"He isn't here," Maggie yelled over the knocks and ticks of the idling engine. "He took his dog and went off into the woods."

"Not here?" Stress lines formed between Nona's eyes and the corners of her mouth turned down in a frown. "I'll just park behind him and see how he likes it."

Maggie stood by the car with her hands on her bony hips. At fourteen, she was a pencil-straight girl with light brown hair who had just begun to emerge from her childish awkwardness. While she and her sister were both slim, Maggie was already taller than Nona, who was twelve years her senior. Maggie's legs seemed endless and her blue eyes looked too large for her perky, freckled face. She wore blue jeans and a faded T-shirt. Not at all shy, she had an openness that was a large part of her charm. She made a frown of her own as she watched her sister park directly behind the truck, then get out of the Ford with a mischievous grin on her face.

"Take a chill pill, Nona. Why are you so mad? You'd think this is the only parking place in the whole world."

"I'm not mad . . . just exasperated." She was still shaken from her encounter with the man at the store and on the road. "Our cabin is number one," she explained impatiently. "This is our drive. He has his own drive. It's simple. Why does he insist on parking on this side of his cabin in our drive?"

"Seems like you're making a mountain out of a molehill to me," Maggie retorted with a shrug. She gathered up one of the bags of groceries and leapt up the steps like a young colt.

Nona edged through the front door that Maggie held open, dumped her large sack on the table, and sighed. A thin woman in slacks and a sleeveless shirt stood in front of the sink peeling potatoes. She turned and smiled at the two girls, her high cheekbones rosy with rouge and a cigarette hanging from her bright red lips.

"Hi, Mabel," Nona said.

"Is something wrong, dear?" Mabel asked with concern. "Why were you honking the horn?"

"She's having a cow, Aunt Mabel."

When Nona and Maggie moved into an apartment after the death of their parents, Mabel Rogers, a widow, had been their neighbor. A woman who had no family of her own, she had taken the two girls to her heart. Mabel had volunteered to care for Maggie while Nona was at work, a blessing to both of the sisters. They loved her dearly. She had been "Aunt Mabel" to Maggie since she was four years old. When Nona had taken the job of managing the camp, it seemed only natural that Mabel would come with them.

"A what?" Mabel asked, wrinkling her brow.

"You know. Losing her cool."

"I am not!" Nona caught herself before she said anything about what had happened in town and on the road to the camp. She didn't see the need to worry them unnecessarily. "There's the whole out-of-doors for him to park in, yet he insists on putting that pickup in our drive!"

"He's really very nice," Mabel said. "Handsome, too," she added with a wink at Maggie. Pushing a strand of henna-colored hair behind her ears, she began unloading the sacks of groceries.

"This sack is Mrs. Leasure's. I'll have Maggie take it down to her."

Once everything had been placed on the table, Maggie wailed, "Nona! You didn't get my *Seventeen* magazine!"

"I had to choose between a magazine and Raisin Bran. The bran won. Our grocery dollars will only stretch so far, you know. When I think of how fast our money is going, I get panicky."

"Did you call Little Rock, again?" Mabel asked.

Nona was reluctant to place a long distance call on the camp telephone. "I tried to call while I was in town, but they said he was out to lunch."

"That's a heck of a note," Mabel mused as she carefully folded the empty sacks.

"I think it was a lie. He just didn't want to talk to me."

"Did you try to call the man who hired you?"

"No."

"We've been here for four weeks and haven't heard a word from the owner of the camp."

"I send everything we take in, plus the bills, to the accountant. Unless we get more bookings in a hurry, there'll be only the bills to send. To make matters worse, the pump on the well is acting up again. It'll cost a mint to have someone out here to fix it."

As she took a load of groceries over to the cupboard, Nona stumbled over a big dog stretched out on the kitchen floor. The large mutt with the yellow coat looked up from where it lay, and then plopped its head back down onto the wooden floor. "Maggie! What's Sam Houston doing in here? I've told you time after time to leave him outside. He gets hair all over the place."

"Sam Houston doesn't like the dog next door."

"That's because he's a coward! It's time he decided if he's a dog or a pussycat," Nona declared.

"He's no coward."

Nona knew that Maggie regarded her complaints with the usual teenage tolerance for adults' irritations, but she couldn't help insisting on what was right. The mass of red hair curled around Nona's face and little tendrils of it clung to her cheeks and forehead. She blew the bangs away from her forehead and decided that rather than argue with Maggie, she would take Sam Houston and go outside.

"Come on, you mangy hound."

"You're going to hurt Sam Houston's feelings, calling him that."

"I should call him a hairy, worthless, mangy hound."

Following Nona through the kitchen and out the back door, Sam Houston lumbered down the steps and eased himself into a cool spot of shade at the base of the porch. Nona sat down on the steps, rested her chin in her hand, and let her mind drift. She found herself back in Home, the strange man's hand on her arm. Inwardly, she shivered. Most of the men she had encountered since coming to the camp had been polite and rather bashful. This man had been different.

The loud blast from a car horn startled her, but then a secretive smile curled on her lips. The man in the next cabin was back and wanted to move his truck. *Not much fun, is it, buster,* she thought. She went back into the kitchen and peeked out the window. A tall, well-muscled man in faded jeans and an old plaid work shirt had his hand firmly on the truck's horn.

"Nona! Do something!" Maggie wailed.

"Not yet," Nona replied with a grin. "Let him stew for a while."

At a loud knock on the door her smile widened. She stayed in the kitchen while Maggie opened the door.

If you or someone you know
wants to improve their reading skills,
call the Literacy Help Line.

WORDS ARE YOUR WHEELS
1-800-929-4458